Su... *...n*

Baby

50p

Shocking secrets are in store for these confirmed bachelors…

Barbara McCauley and Kathie DeNosky have produced two stories with life-changing surprises for two successful, sexy men who wanted to be bachelors for the rest of their lives…

Dear Reader,

Welcome to Desire!

Kicking off this month we have **Taming Her Man**—two stories of irresistible, stubborn men, *The Taming of Jackson Cade*, a MEN OF BELLE TERRE book by BJ James, and Kristi Gold's *Cowboy for Keeps*.

There are two surprise 'packages' in store for the unsuspecting bachelors in Barbara McCauley's *Sinclair's Surprise Baby* and Kathie DeNosky's *His Baby Surprise*, coming to you in **Surprise Baby**. (Well, we couldn't call it anything else…)

Finally, in **His Bride at Last** Cindy Gerard's *The Bridal Arrangement* and *A Cowboy, a Bride & a Wedding Vow* by Shirley Rogers take us through the pitfalls and benefits of marriage to two handsome but proud hunks.

We hope you love them all!

The Editors

Surprise Baby

BARBARA McCAULEY
KATHIE DeNOSKY

SILHOUETTE®
DESIRE™

*Silhouette, Silhouette Desire and Colophon
are registered trademarks of Harlequin Books S.A.,
used under licence.*

*First published in Great Britain 2002
Silhouette Books, Eton House, 18-24 Paradise Road,
Richmond, Surrey TW9 1SR*

SURPRISE BABY © Harlequin Books S.A. 2002

The publisher acknowledges the copyright holders of the
individual works as follows:

Sinclair's Surprise Baby © Barbara Joel 2001
His Baby Surprise © Kathie DeNosky 2001

ISBN 0 373 04761 4

51-0902

*Printed and bound in Spain
by Litografia Rosés S.A., Barcelona*

SINCLAIR'S SURPRISE BABY

by
Barbara McCauley

BARBARA McCAULEY

lives in Southern California with her own handsome hero husband, Frank, who makes it easy to believe in and write about the magic of romance. With over twenty books written for Silhouette, Barbara has won and been nominated for numerous awards, including the prestigious RITA Award from the Romance Writers of America, Best Desire of the Year from *Romantic Times Magazine* and Best Short Contemporary from the National Readers' Choice Awards.

To Jo Leigh and Debbi Rawlins—
you guys are the best!

a plane to catch in less than four hours and, since she'd had so little sleep last night, he thought it best not to wake her.

But then, he thought with a smile, he hadn't had much sleep last night, either.

Raina Sarbanes—he stood by the bed and looked down at her—had to be the most beautiful woman he'd ever seen.

Last night at Gabe and Melanie's wedding reception, he'd heard his new sister-in-law mention that her maid of honor had graced the cover of several fashion magazines before she'd started her own business three years ago as a clothing designer. He'd also heard she'd been married briefly to a Greek shipping tycoon six years ago, when she was twenty-two, that she'd studied design in New York and she was leaving tomorrow morning to work with a top designer in Italy.

But most of that he'd heard secondhand, from Melanie. Raina hadn't seemed to want to talk about herself, so over the course of the night they'd discussed a variety of safe subjects: Gabe and Melanie, Kevin, Melanie's son from a previous marriage, Lucian's construction business, the design school Raina had gone to in Italy. The fact that neither one of them was interested in a relationship at the moment.

Though brief, that discussion had been an important one. They'd both agreed that, while they were obviously extremely attracted to each other, they weren't looking for commitment or marriage.

But no conversation between them had been long or detailed. A kiss or a touch would quickly end whatever discussion they had been having. And then they would be in each other's arms once again, breathless, eager. *Hungry.*

He glanced down at her, fascinated by the way the early-morning light streamed softly through the lacy bedroom window and lit her stunning face. Unable to resist, he reached out and touched a strand of hair the color of dark, rich chocolate. Long, thick, glossy hair that flowed over a man's skin like a river of liquid silk—a river a man could easily dive into, then let himself be swept away.

The face that glorious hair framed was heart shaped, her smooth skin porcelain pale over high cheekbones and a straight nose. Her mouth was wide, her lips curved and full. Seductive. Enticing. And though her eyes were closed peacefully now, he knew they were blue. Startling blue, fringed by thick, dark lashes and delicately arched brows. It had been those eyes that had made his breath catch in his throat when he'd first met her at his brother's rehearsal dinner only two days ago.

He'd wanted her that quickly, with a desperation that had knocked the wind out of him. And to be honest, scared the hell out of him, as well. Never had a woman so completely disarmed him.

For that reason he'd kept his distance from her the past two days. Not that she'd given him any encouragement. If anything, he'd thought Raina had been indifferent to him, if not downright cold. Even his brothers had teased him that Melanie's best friend obviously had brains as well as looks, since she'd appeared to be immune to Lucian's dark, dangerous looks, which most women seemed so drawn to.

Then he'd offered to drive Raina back to Melanie

and Gabe's house after the wedding. In the blink of an eye everything had changed.

He was still a little confused as to who exactly had made the first move. All he knew was that once they'd stepped into the house, out of the softly falling snow, once they were alone, she was suddenly in his arms, her mouth hot and urgent under his. They barely made it to the bed before he was inside her, both of them gasping at the intensity of the need that consumed them. And when they managed to finally shed their clothes, the need had still been as strong, as powerful.

Was still there, he realized as he stared down at her.

He'd experienced lust before. Hell, at thirty-three, he'd certainly been no monk. But last night had been something different. Something indefinable. Something that went way beyond your average run-of-the-mill mutual attraction.

He wondered if maybe, just maybe, she might consider staying a few more days. With Gabe and Melanie gone on their honeymoon, he and Raina could have the house to themselves. Not that he was looking for anything beyond that, he told himself. Of course he wasn't.

But a few days, he thought. There was nothing permanent about that. He'd love to show her some of the Pennsylvania countryside, maybe take her to the five-acre lot he'd bought outside of town where he was framing the house he planned to live in one day.

He just wasn't quite ready to let her go.

He'd ask her with flowers, he decided. He wasn't sure where he'd find a bouquet at six-thirty in the morning, but he knew that Sydney Taylor, the woman his brother was head over heels in love with, always kept roses in her restaurant. He hated to wake Sydney up so early, but he was desperate.

He dressed quietly, found a piece of paper in the bedside table and left Raina a note on the pillow beside hers. "Be back in fifteen. Please don't leave. Lucian."

He grabbed his jacket and crept quietly from the bedroom. Outside, he drew the crisp winter air into his lungs, noted the icicles that had formed on the eaves overnight and the white mounds of fresh snow on the ground.

A perfect morning, he thought, then headed for his truck. He couldn't wait to get back.

Several minutes later, with a smile on her lips, the sleeping woman stirred. Her arm moved restlessly over the now-empty pillow beside hers.

Lucian's note slipped soundlessly between the antique headboard and the mattress.

At the exact same time, with his mind on Raina and anxious to get back, Lucian missed the patch of ice at Jordan's Junction. His truck fishtailed, then skidded off the road, and his world went black.

One

The town of Bloomfield County came alive in spring. Winter-naked trees sprouted new leaves. Brown, barren pastures turned lush green. Cherry blossoms scented the still-crisp air. It was a time for the earth to stir, to stretch and awaken to the warm sun. A time for beginnings.

A time for babies.

Just this afternoon, on the drive over to his brother Gabe's house, Lucian had spotted a dozen or so new calves at the Johnson farm and at least five new colts at the Bainbridge ranch. And yesterday, nestled under the front porch of the house he was building a few miles outside of town, he had discovered a litter of kittens. Six little balls of fur that hadn't even opened their eyes yet, mewing for their mama, a pretty orange tabby who watched anxiously from the edge of the nearby woods. Lucian had sweet-talked, but Mama Kitty would have no part of him. He knew that sooner or later he'd have to catch her and find a safer place for her and her family, but he hoped he'd be able to win her over first. She might be a cat, Lucian thought with a smile, but she was still female, after all. He'd have her purring in his lap in no time.

And speaking of females—Lucian stood in Gabe and Melanie's dining-room doorway and watched the four women busily making decorations for Melanie's baby shower tomorrow. His sister, Cara, with her fourteen-month-old son, Matthew, and his sisters-in-law Abby, Sydney and Melanie were all currently elbow deep in pink and blue tissue paper and string. A pretty sight, he thought, enjoying the sound of their laughter. No reason not to stick around for a while.

And besides, he was certain he smelled cookies.

"Lucian, you're a sweetheart to bring those folding chairs over." Smiling, Abby looked up from the pink tissue flower she was making and tucked a loose strand of blond hair behind her ear. "Callan would have done it but he flew out this morning to meet with the architect on the Thorndale job."

"And Gabe's taken Kevin to the father-son ball game in Pine Flats." Melanie, who'd insisted on helping with the decorations, even though the other women had said no, was making a blue flower. "They won't be home for a couple of hours yet."

"Reese has a waitress on maternity leave and is short-handed." Sydney was busy assembling a centerpiece that said, It's a Baby.

"No sweat." Lucian wandered closer. There were pink and blue balloons, streamers and little baby decorations everywhere. No wonder all the Sinclair men and Cara's husband, Ian, had disappeared. "The Ridgeway project is shut down until Callan gets those changes approved on the blueprints, anyway. I've got all the time in the world right now."

Bingo. Lucian caught sight of a plate of cookies on the table. Unless he missed his mark—and when it came to women and food, he rarely missed—those were Sydney's famous chocolate cookies.

Sydney saw him staring at the plate and held it up. "Cookie?"

"Thought you'd never ask." Lucian moaned as he took a bite of sweet chocolate. "Damn, why did my brother have to marry you first?"

"That's the same line he gave *me* last week when Callan and I had him over for dinner," Abby told Sydney.

"Me, too," Melanie said. "When I baked an apple pie for him three days ago."

"It's the truth, I swear." Lucian held up a hand. "My brothers got the last three women in the entire world that I would have married myself. I'm destined to be alone forever."

All the women rolled their eyes and groaned.

"My entire life I've had to live with this blarney from all four of my brothers." Cara shifted Matthew from one side of her lap to the other. "And from what I hear, dear brother, you aren't exactly wanting for female companionship."

"There've been a lot of devastated women in this town since all my brothers went and got married." Lucian handed a cookie to his nephew, and the baby gurgled with delight. "It's been my duty as the last single Sinclair man to comfort them."

"A job he takes very seriously, from what I'm hearing at the beauty salon." Melanie laid her hands on her rounded belly, then leaned close and whispered, "Sally Lyn Wetters told Annie Edmonds that she was certain Lucian was about to pop the question."

Lucian choked on the cookie he'd just swallowed.

Abby's blue eyes opened wide. "Lucian pop the question to Sally Lyn?"

"She'd make a nice sister-in-law. A little flighty, but sweet," Sydney said. "But Marsha Brenner told me that Laura Greenley and Lucian were an item. Just last week—"

"Hey!" Lucian slammed a fist to his chest and dislodged the stuck cookie. "I'm standing here, you know. And I'm not an item with, or popping any questions to, anybody. Unless, of course—" Lucian grinned at Sydney, Abby and Melanie "—one of you gorgeous ladies decide to dump one of my brothers and run away with me."

"Watch out, ladies, here comes the Sinclair male charm," Abby warned. "There's not a woman alive who can resist it."

"Don't we know it." Sydney arched a brow and smiled. "Not that I'm complaining, you understand."

"Well, there was Raina, Melanie's maid of honor." Cara wiped chocolate from Matthew's cheek. "If I remember correctly, she was quite immune to Lucian's animal magnetism. Melanie had to practically beg Raina to even dance with Lucian at the reception."

Lucian winced at the verbal blow to his pride. "Hey, now, wait just a darned minute. That's not fair. How can I defend myself when I can't even remember that night?"

And not just that night, either. When he'd hit his head in the accident he'd been in the next morning, he'd wiped out nearly two days of his life. He had no memory of even meeting Melanie's friend, let alone dancing with her.

It was the oddest thing, to wake up in the hospital and have absolutely no recollection of the previous forty-eight hours. It was weird and…unsettling. Even now, after all these months, he still couldn't remember anything more than the wedding toast he'd given to Gabe and Melanie that night.

"She was probably playing hard to get." Lucian plucked his nephew from Cara's arms and tossed him up in the air. Matthew shrieked with delight and said, "Mo!" As much as Lucian enjoyed babies, it was especially nice to hand them back over when it was time to go. "I'm sure if she had a little more time to get to know me, I'd dazzle her."

"I'm glad you feel that way." Melanie glanced at her wristwatch. "She's flying in from New York for my baby shower. If you're not too busy, how 'bout you get started dazzling her by picking her up at the airport for me in one hour?"

"Never too busy for you, Mel." He winked at his sister-in-law, then bounced Matthew again, eliciting more giggles. "But I thought you said she was living in Italy."

"She moved her design company to New York two months ago. I'm hoping I can convince her to stay there for good.'' Melanie smiled at the laughing child in Lucian's arms. ''You sure you don't mind picking her up?''

''You did say she was single, right?'' Lucian wiggled his eyebrows.

Sydney, Cara and Abby all shook their heads. Chuckling, Melanie wrote her friend's arrival time and flight number on a piece of paper.

''I know you don't remember meeting her, so here's a snapshot from one of the wedding-table cameras.'' Melanie shuffled through a stack of photographs sitting on the table, then handed Lucian the picture. ''It should fill in the blank spot in your brain.''

Cara stood and removed her son from Lucian's arms. ''You'd need more than a photograph to do that, Mel.''

Lucian raised a brow at his sister's comment, then took the photo from Melanie and looked at it. He'd seen pictures of Raina in Gabe and Melanie's wedding album, but that was over a year ago and it was a group picture. This picture, taken candidly by one of the wedding guests, captured her laughing with Melanie at the reception. Her dress was black and sleeveless and her dark hair was swept up off her long neck. She was more than beautiful.

She was stunning.

A strange feeling, something like a tickle, shimmied up his spine.

''Something wrong?'' Melanie furrowed her brow. ''If you'd rather not—''

''Of course nothing's wrong.'' He shook the feeling off, reached for his leather jacket and slipped the picture into his pocket. "I'll have her delivered to you safe and sound and in one piece, m'lady."

"Thank you." Melanie grinned at him. "Oh, and Lucian?"

He'd already started for the door. "Yeah?"

"Would you mind taking my car?"

He lifted a brow. "What, the sophisticated city girl has a problem with trucks?"

Melanie shook her head. "It's just that the baby seat will fit better in the back seat of my car, that's all."

He turned slowly. "Baby seat?"

"Didn't I tell you?" she asked sweetly. "Raina's bringing her baby with her."

It felt good to be on steady ground again, Raina thought with a sigh of relief. The flight, though a short one, had been bumpy, and Emma, normally the sweetest-tempered child, had been unusually cranky. Raina tucked the now-sleeping child in the crook of one arm while she wheeled her carry-on bag with the other. If there was one thing she'd become an expert at after Emma had been born, it was the fine art of juggling. A baby in one hand and a diaper in the other, not to mention a career, time, money and sleep. Sleep being at the bottom of the list.

Hugging Emma close, Raina fell in step with the other passengers pouring off the plane. She'd worked sixteen-hour days this past month to get everything in place for the upcoming show of her new fall line of lingerie. While she was gone, Annelise, her assistant, would handle details, and Raina knew she had nothing to worry about.

But worry or not, Raina wouldn't have missed Melanie's baby shower for anything. After the wedding Melanie had gone on her honeymoon, and Raina had gone to Italy for fourteen months before relocating in New York. There'd been no opportunity to see each other, and between the time difference and the busy lives they both led, they'd only spoken a few, brief times.

But neither time or distance would ever break the bond between them. Melanie was the sister that Raina had never had. They'd grown up together, cried on each other's shoulders in bad times, laughed together in good times. Shared their deepest, darkest secrets.

Most of their secrets, Raina thought, and pressed a gentle kiss to the top of her daughter's soft head.

A man talking on his cell phone in front of her stopped suddenly and she stumbled, gasped when her foot caught on her suitcase. She might have gone down if someone on her left hadn't grabbed her elbow.

She turned with an embarrassed smile. "Thank you. I'm not quite—"

She froze.

Lucian. Lucian Sinclair.

No! her mind screamed. *I'm not ready for this. Not yet.*

Maybe not ever.

He looked at her, those incredible green eyes, and frowned. "Are you all right?"

Of course I'm not all right, damn you! What the hell are you doing here?

"Yes." She croaked the single word out, then cleared her throat. "Yes, of course."

She knew she'd have to see him sooner or later. He was Gabe's brother, after all, and she expected he might drop by the house sometime. She had prepared herself for that. But she'd never expected him here, at the airport. And she *definitely* wasn't prepared.

"Melanie was supposed to pick me up," she said weakly, still struggling to hold on to her composure, though her knees had turned to the consistency of mud, and her mind was still spinning.

"They're holding baby shower tribal council, and she asked me to fill in for her." He kept hold of her elbow while he reached for her suitcase. "Let me get that."

When she kept a death grip on the handle, he looked at her, one brow raised.

I don't want you to get anything for me. Ever, she thought.

"Oh, sorry." She pulled her hand away. "Thank you."

"It's just a suggestion," he said, and nodded at the other deplaning passengers spilling around them, "but we should probably keep moving."

"Right. Of course."

She tried to tug her elbow away from him, but with Emma sleeping in her arms and all the other passengers crowding around her, she had no room to maneuver. So his hand stayed on her, guided her through the river of people.

How well she remembered his hands. Large, callused hands that were strong yet amazingly gentle. Too many nights she'd dreamed of those hands, of his touch. And then she would waken, alone, her body coiled with frustration. With anger. With pain.

She'd remembered every stroke of those long, rough fingers, every breath-stealing kiss of his strong mouth, every sigh and gasp of pleasure. He had touched her where no man ever had before, made her want things she'd never wanted.

And he hadn't even remembered her name.

Lucian, this is Raina...

Raina? Raina who?

Remembering that phone call, the pain and humiliation of it, gave her strength. He'd disrupted her entire world, but she'd meant nothing more to him than a simple roll in the hay. And a forgettable one, at that. She'd be damned if she'd let him see that he'd hurt her. That the night they'd spent together had meant more to her than any other night of her entire life.

So much more, she thought as she hugged her baby closer.

"Do we need to go to baggage claim?" Lucian asked.

She slipped her arm from his hand as she shook her head. "I'm only staying a few days."

"That requires a steamer trunk for most women," he said with a grin.

How could he be so casual with her? Act as if nothing had ever happened?

The smile she gave him was stiff. "Well, I guess I'm not most women."

He raised his brows at her distinctly cool tone. *Dammit, dammit,* she cursed herself. It was one thing to be indifferent and quite another to be rude. If she didn't want him to question her, or to suspect that she felt there had been something more between them than a night of wild sex, then she couldn't very well walk around acting like a shrew.

"I'm sorry." She softened her smile. "It's been a long day, and Emma will be awake soon. If you don't mind, I'd really just like to get back to the house."

Lucian gestured toward the exits. "Your wish is my command."

Yeah, well, then eat dirt and—

The hand he slipped to the small of her back cut off her thought. How dare he put his hand on her so easily? she thought. As if it belonged there? She stiffened inwardly at his touch, pretended that she hadn't even noticed. When he told her that Melanie had put a baby seat in the car for Emma, Raina simply nodded and kept walking.

Thankfully the noise of the crowd inside the airport prevented any normal conversation, and with Emma asleep in her arms, yelling was definitely out of the question. So they walked together, his hand on her, as if they were a couple, which only increased Raina's anxiety level all the more. She didn't want anyone to think that they were together like that. Several women smiled at Emma as they passed. Several *other* women smiled at Lucian.

Why wouldn't they? she thought. He'd certainly blown her socks off when she'd first met him. Six foot four, muscular, broad shoulders and dark good looks. And those eyes of his. Lord, just one glance from those deep-green eyes and a woman could feel her bones melt. It was a handsome package, wrapped with rugged sensuality and tied up with a great big ribbon of pure masculine charm. A present no woman could resist.

She'd known his type well, before they'd met, been married to one. Which was exactly the reason she'd kept her distance at Gabe and Melanie's rehearsal dinner and at the wedding. Instinctively she'd known that this man had the power to hurt her.

Then he'd driven her back to Melanie's house that night. And they were alone. Alone in that great big house, with snow quietly falling outside. He reached for her, or she reached for him. She still wasn't sure. The only thing she was sure of was that once he touched her, once she touched him, there was no going back. She hadn't wanted to go back.

And the next morning he was gone.

"Is something wrong?"

She blinked, realized that they'd walked out of the airport and were standing in the cavern of a parking structure. Lucian held open the back seat door to a black Explorer. She groaned silently, wondered how long she'd been standing there as if she were a complete dimwit.

"No, of course not." She moved toward the open door, then reached inside to settle her still-sleeping daughter into the car seat. She tucked the baby's arms securely inside the shoulder straps, but her fingers were shaking so badly she couldn't manage to snap the metal buckle into place.

"Need some help?" Lucian asked.

Before she could say no, he'd already leaned down beside her and reached inside the car. Her breath caught at the brush of his muscled arm against hers, the touch of his fingers on her own.

Memories flooded back: a long, slow fall to the bed, urgent whispers, bare skin to bare skin. Even the smell of him, a masculine, spicy scent, was the same. Heat rushed up her arms, over her breasts, then spiraled through her body into her blood.

All that in the time it took him to snap the buckle.

Lucian knew he should move away, of course. He'd already clicked the buckle in place, and the baby was snug and secure in the car seat. For some reason he stayed where he was.

In his entire life he couldn't remember when he'd ever been more aware of a woman's presence. The moment he'd first caught sight of her coming off the plane, he'd felt his pulse jump. She'd been easy to spot, not only because every man within twenty feet had also been looking at her, but because she stood a good three inches taller than all the other women around her. And she wasn't even wearing heels. She was long and sleek, her tailored slacks black, her sleeveless turtleneck the color of wine. Her scent was light but exotic. Her dark, shiny hair was pulled back in a thick braid, her bangs a wispy fringe above eyes that made him think of dark-blue smoke.

She might *look* hot, Lucian thought, but good Lord, the woman was cold as an Arctic night. He'd never been attracted to snobs or snooty women before. If anything, the Ice Queen attitude had always been a major turn-off. For some reason, with this woman, it didn't seem to matter. Because here he was, in the most innocent situation, with nothing more than a harmless touch of shoulders and the slightest brush of his leg against hers, and he was aroused.

Down, boy, he reprimanded himself.

There was something about her. Something so incredibly…familiar. Even though he couldn't remember, he knew that he'd met her at the wedding. But this seemed so much more immediate. Much more *intense* than a casual meeting.

But he was certain it hadn't been anything more than that. According to everyone at the wedding, he and Raina had barely spoken. They'd never even been alone.

He'd have to rectify that situation, he decided, but this was hardly the time. Melanie would kill him if he came on to her friend before he even got her back to the house.

But there *was* later, he thought. He didn't know the situation with Raina, didn't know if there was someone in her life, maybe the baby's father or someone else she might be seeing. What he did know was that she was single, and as far as he was concerned, that made her fair game.

Rather than scare the woman off by coming on too strong, Lucian kept his attention on the baby, a dark-haired beauty with rosy cheeks and a turned-up nose. The pink sweater she wore covered a soft, white dress embroidered with pink flowers, and her tiny shoes were pink satin. Everything about her was delicate.

He smiled at the baby. "What's her name?"

"Emma." Raina's voice softened and warmed. She smoothed the front of her baby's sweater. "Emma Rose."

Lucian watched as Raina smoothed the front of Emma's tiny sweater. Her fingers were long and smooth, the stroke of her hand light as a butterfly's wings. He had to remind himself to breathe.

He forced his attention back to the baby. "She's going to break a few hearts."

Raina smiled. "That's what Teresa, Emma's nanny, keeps telling me. She told me to enroll her in a convent now."

The smile on her lips was the first real one he'd seen, Lucian noted. It didn't seem to matter that it wasn't for him. It captivated him all the same.

"If she were my daughter," Lucian teased, "I'm sure I'd feel the same way."

As if he'd flipped a switch, the light in Raina's eyes went dark. The smile was gone, as well.

What had he said?

"She'll be awake soon." Raina pulled away, took a step back from the car. "If she's hungry, the only thing she'll be breaking is your eardrums."

"Well then, we'd better get her home." Lucian had been around long enough to know a brush-off when he heard one. She'd let her guard slip for a moment, but the neon sign that flashed Keep Away was back on.

He quietly closed the back seat door, then opened the front passenger door. If she'd been any other woman, he would have just accepted her blatant rejection. It would certainly be the smart thing to do.

But wasn't she the one who'd told him that she wasn't like most women? And he wasn't always the smartest guy around, either.

With a grin, he closed the car door. If nothing else, Lucian predicted that Raina Sarbanes's visit to Bloomfield was going to make his life extremely interesting.

Two

Gabe and Melanie's house was as beautiful as Raina remembered. Nestled on five acres of pristine farmland, the two-story Victorian had recently been restored to its original beauty by Gabe himself. Outside there was a new coat of paint, Cape Cod blue, with a white porch and trim. Windows sparkled in the late-afternoon light, and daffodils bloomed in the front beds like little bursts of yellow sun. Raina knew that the inside was just as beautiful. High ceilings, shiny hardwood floors, huge fireplaces and a bright, airy kitchen. It was a spectacular house, filled with character and history. And romance, Raina thought with a smile. This house was where Melanie and Gabe had met and fallen in love.

This house, Raina remembered, was also where she and Lucian had made love. In a beautiful, antique, pine-carved four-poster bed, underneath a snowy-white down comforter, between soft-blue flannel sheets—

A bump in the road snapped her back to the moment, and she turned to check on her daughter. Emma had just woken up a couple of minutes ago and was still groggy from her nap. In a few minutes Raina knew that her daughter would be more than ready for a snack and a bottle.

The thirty-minute drive from the airport had been a quiet one. Lucian had been polite, pointing out a landmark here and there and a few more notable points of interest. Raina was relieved, as well as thankful, that he hadn't tried to lure her into anything more than superficial conversation.

Being alone in the car with him and Emma had stretched her nerves thin. The man filled her senses. The sound of his voice, the scent of his skin, the heat of his body. More than once she'd caught herself staring at him. His strong hands on the steering wheel, the square line of his jaw, the slight bend in his nose. Each time, she would jerk her eyes away and curse silently at her weakness.

Thank goodness they were finally here, she thought as he parked the car in front of the house and cut the engine. She'd had a distinct plan before she came to Bloomfield. If she'd had to be alone with Lucian five minutes more, maybe even five seconds more, she was afraid she might have completely blown that plan to smithereens.

She might have come here for Melanie's baby shower, but she had something else to accomplish while she was here. Something more important and more frightening than anything she'd ever faced before.

"Raina!"

Melanie was already out the front door and coming down the porch steps as Raina slid out of the car and rushed toward her. Laughing and with tears in their eyes, the women embraced.

"Oh, look at you, just look at you." Raina swallowed back the tightness in her throat as she touched Melanie's belly. "It's so wonderful."

"And you." Tears were streaming down Melanie's flushed cheeks. "Where is she?"

"Right here." Raina turned back toward the car. "She just woke up, so she may be a little crank—"

Raina went still at the sight of Lucian standing beside the car with Emma high in his arms. She felt as if the breath had been sucked out of her.

"She wanted out," Lucian said as he grinned at the baby. "Since you two were busy, I accommodated her."

Emma smiled back at her rescuer and touched his cheeks. Her hands were so tiny, so white and smooth against Lucian's darker skin.

No! You can't touch her, Raina wanted to scream, but she simply pressed her lips together and bit the inside of her mouth.

"Oh, Rae." Melanie clasped her fingers to her mouth. "Oh, my heavens."

In spite of the situation, Raina couldn't stop the swell of pride and love in her chest. She started to move toward Lucian to take her daughter from him, but Melanie beat her to it.

"Come to your Aunt Melanie." Melanie held out

her hands to the baby. Emma gurgled and smiled but seemed quite content to stay where she was.

"She likes me," Lucian announced, and bounced the baby. Emma giggled with delight.

"She just doesn't know any better." Melanie clapped her hands and coaxed Emma from Lucian's arms.

Now that Melanie was holding Emma, Raina could think clearly again. Slowly she released the breath that had caught in her lungs.

"Isn't she just the most beautiful thing you've ever seen?" Melanie cooed over the baby.

"Absolutely," Lucian said.

Raina glanced at Lucian. Her cheeks warmed as she realized that his gaze was not on Emma but on her. But then her blood warmed from anger. How could he look at her like that? Was he so damn arrogant to think that all he had to do was give her a smoldering I-want-you look and she'd rush right back through that revolving door to his bed and jump in the sack with him?

When he couldn't even remember her name?

She wouldn't respond to his comments or looks, she resolved. She had no regrets for the night they'd spent together, but whatever feelings she'd had for him were gone. Emma was all that mattered to her now. Emma was everything.

The sudden outpour of women from the front porch jarred Raina from her thoughts. Cara, holding her son, Abby and Sydney came rushing forward like a tidal wave. Raina had become close with the women in the two days she'd spent with them all during her last visit, and she looked forward to spending time with them again.

Women.

Lucian shifted awkwardly while they all embraced and gushed over each other, watched as they played musical babies with Matthew and Emma. He might not understand women, but he never tired of looking at them. And these five women were truly something to see. But it was the one he wasn't related to who truly caught his attention.

When she smiled, her face lit up and her eyes sparkled. So maybe ice water didn't run through the woman's veins, after all, he noted. Though she'd been stiff as a two-by-four since he'd picked her up from the airport, she now moved with the grace of a dancer. The sound of her laugh captivated as well as intrigued him. He'd heard that laugh before, he was certain of it. From the video tape of the wedding? Or was he drawing something up from that blank corner of his mind? Occasionally he would almost remember something from the two days he'd lost. A smell, a sound, an image. There'd even been a couple of vague dreams. But nothing had ever been quite this strong before.

Then, just as quickly as it had come on, the feeling was gone, and there was just this moment. Just the sound of a beautiful, though confusing, woman laughing.

Like a Ping-Pong ball, the comments between the women flew back and forth.

"She's got your nose."

"Matthew looks just like his daddy."

"Sydney, you and Reese got married! I'm so happy for you."

"Was Italy wonderful?"

"Abby, I love what you've done with your hair."

And so it went. With five of them, Lucian knew this could go on for quite a while. Sydney held little Emma now, and the baby seemed to be having a conversation of her own with Matthew, who was currently in Abby's arms. The women all laughed and fussed over the two infants. Shaking his head, Lucian turned away and reached into the car to retrieve Raina's luggage and diaper bag.

"You don't have to bother. I'll get that."

He glanced over his shoulder, saw Raina standing behind him. "No bother."

"No, really." She reached for her suitcase as he pulled it out of the car. "I can get it."

For a moment Lucian was distracted by the feel of her hand on his. Her fingers were amazingly soft, her skin smooth. He had the distinct feeling she felt that way all over.

"I'm sure you can." He held on to the suitcase. "But my mother taught me a few lessons in manners. The least I can do is carry a suitcase for a lady."

It was a little heavy-handed, Lucian knew, but it worked. Raina pressed her lips into a thin line, then moved her hand away.

"Thank you," she said, though it was obvious to Lucian it was forced. "But I'll need the diaper bag now."

He handed her the bag, and she hugged it to her. Her eyes met his, and for a moment it seemed as though she wanted to say something.

"I—"

At the sound of Emma's soft cry, Raina quickly glanced over. "It's past time for her snack and bottle," she said awkwardly, then looked back at him. "I...I just want to thank you for picking me up at the airport."

She turned and headed back to her baby. Lucian furrowed his brow as he watched her go. There was something odd about the woman. The way she'd treated him from the moment he'd picked her up at the airport, the way she looked at him, as if there was something on her mind, something she wanted to say. She kept herself composed and in control, but it almost seemed as if under the surface she were angry at him.

He was certain he hadn't done anything to upset the woman in the past hour. Which could only mean that she had to be bothered by something he'd done *before*.

Of course. That had to be it. He must have said something to her at the wedding, or maybe the rehearsal dinner, that had put a bee in her bonnet. But from what everyone had told him, he and Raina had barely spoken to each other.

Jeez, he couldn't very well apologize for something that he couldn't remember. If Raina was ticked off at him, then how difficult could it be to just say so?

He couldn't ask her now, not with everyone around. He'd have to find a moment when they could be alone, which didn't look as if it would be anytime soon. Raina had Emma in her arms, and all the women were heading back to the house, still babbling and fussing over each other. He closed the car door and followed.

"Oh, Lucian." Melanie turned and waited for him on the porch. "Dinner will be ready in a little while and you're staying. Abby made a pot roast, and Sydney made apple dumplings."

"You don't have to ask me twice." He grinned at his sister-in-law. "Where shall I put Raina's bag?"

"In the guest room upstairs." Smiling, she gave him a kiss on the cheek. "Thanks for picking her and Emma up from the airport. She's a very special friend."

"Any friend of yours is a friend of mine," he said, though Raina had been anything but friendly.

And since he was staying for dinner, Lucian thought as he followed Melanie into the house, this would be the perfect opportunity to get the woman alone sometime during the evening and find out why.

"I hit a home run, Mommy. Right off the tee. Daddy helped, but mostly I did it, didn't I, Daddy?"

"You sure did, slugger." Pride lit Gabe's face. "That ball almost went into space."

Kevin's grin widened, and his blue eyes sparkled. "It was way cool, Uncle Lucian. I wish you coulda been there to see me."

"I wish I could have too, pal. Next time for sure." The wink and grin that Lucian gave his nephew made Raina's heart flutter. Lucian had been listening patiently to Kevin since they'd sat down at the dinner table, even though the little boy had been talking nonstop. For a man who'd made it clear he never intended to have children, he certainly was good with them.

All the other women had gone home, leaving just Gabe, Melanie, Kevin, Lucian and herself to eat a huge pot roast and a giant bowl of potatoes and carrots. The food was delicious, but Raina's stomach was so tied up in knots that she had to force herself to eat. Next to her, sitting in a high chair, Emma squealed at Kevin when he stopped talking long enough to chew.

"I think Emma likes you, Kevin," Melanie teased her son.

"Aw, Mom." Kevin groaned like a true six-year-old. "She's a baby."

It was true, though, Raina thought with a smile. Emma had been enthralled with Kevin from the moment he'd walked in the front door. It seemed that all the Sinclair men had that effect on women.

Kevin, on the other hand, wasn't remotely interested in girls or babies. At the moment, baseball was the only thing on Kevin's mind.

And the only thing on Raina's mind was how quickly this meal could be over and how quickly Lucian would leave.

"How 'bout I come by tomorrow?" Lucian said to Kevin. "You can show me exactly how you hit that ball."

"That would be cool." The wide grin on Kevin's face quickly faded. "Oh, yeah, I forgot. I'm not gonna be here 'cause my mom's having a party for our new baby."

"We've been banished for the day." Gabe's sigh

was as exaggerated as it was phony. "From our own home."

"I told you that you could come to the shower if you want to." Melanie cut her son's meat into little pieces, then pointed her fork at Gabe. "You both declined the offer."

"That's 'cause we don't wanna be stuck here with a bunch of girls." Kevin made a face. "You wouldn't want to, would you, Uncle Lucian?"

"I happen to like girls," Lucian said with a grin and glanced at Raina. "Sometimes I like them a lot."

He'd made the comment casually enough, but Raina understood that he'd directed it at her. He was *flirting* with her, in this house, at the dinner table, with Gabe and Melanie watching. Fuming inside, she turned to Emma and offered a bite of potatoes.

The man was a blackheart!

"And they sure like you, too," Kevin said, though his tone was one of disgust. "Every time we go to the grocery store, Cindy Johnson asks my mom about you, and so does that redheaded lady at the post office who laughs real loud. Even Miss Shelly, my teacher at school always says, 'How's your uncle Lucian?' Jeez." Kevin shook his head. "Why don't you just marry one of 'em? Only not my teacher, 'cause I wouldn't wanna call her Aunt Shelly. The other kids would laugh at me."

Raina glanced at Lucian, who at least had the decency to look mildly uncomfortable with Kevin's sudden and excessive information regarding his love life. Not that she was surprised, of course. What else would she have expected from a man like Lucian? He probably threw darts at a board to see who the lucky girl would be for the night.

"As a matter of fact," Melanie said sweetly, "we were just talking about that very thing this morning. Weren't we, Lucian?"

The look Lucian shot Melanie warned her off. "I don't recall."

Amusement danced in Melanie's gray eyes. "Something about comforting all the women of Bloomfield since your brothers got married, I believe. Not wanting to disappoint any of those lonely, single women."

"How magnanimous," Raina said stiffly. When everyone looked at her, she cursed herself for speaking at all.

"We were kidding around." Lucian held out his hands in defense. "Weren't we, Mel?"

Melanie smiled. "So does that mean you *are* going to pop the question to Sally Lyn?"

Raina glanced up sharply at the same time Gabe started to choke. Lucian getting married? Her heart slammed in her chest.

"Sally Lyn?" Gabe hit his chest with his fist. "As in Sally Lyn Wetters? When were you planning to tell me about this?"

"What does pop the question mean?" Kevin asked.

"It means asking someone to marry you," Melanie said.

"Uncle Lucian's getting married?" Kevin's eyes were round with astonishment. "Are you gonna have a big party like my mommy and daddy did?"

"I am *not* getting married," Lucian said fiercely. "And definitely not to Sally Lyn."

"Oh, that's right, I forgot," Kevin went on as if he hadn't heard Lucian at all. "You can't remember my mommy and daddy's party 'cause of your accident. You had a good time, though. You danced with everyone. Even Aunt Raina. So can I come to your party?"

"Kevin," Lucian said with great patience. "I am not getting married and I'm not having—"

"What accident?"

The words were out before Raina could think. The bite of smashed carrots she'd been about to feed Emma hovered in the air. She wasn't sure whether it was the intensity in the tone of her voice or the stunned expression on her face, but everyone, including Kevin, turned to look at her.

"What accident?" she asked again.

"It was no big deal," Lucian protested.

Yes, yes, it is a big deal. Raina's mind raced. *A very big deal.*

"I told you about Lucian's accident the morning after the reception." Melanie furrowed her brow, then said with less certainty, "Didn't I?"

The morning after the reception...

"No." Blood pounded through her veins. "You didn't."

"They knew we'd have cut our honeymoon short if we'd found out he was in the hospital, so they didn't tell us until we got back," Melanie said.

"The hospital?" Raina whispered the two words, turned and stared at Lucian. "You were in the hospital?"

"Just for a couple of days."

Emma started to fuss about the bites coming so

slowly. Raina's fingers shook as she gave her daughter a spoonful of carrot.

"You were in Italy, Rae." Melanie looked apologetic. "And if you remember, we didn't talk for almost three months. I guess by that time, since Lucian was all right, I just didn't think to tell you."

Didn't think to tell me? Oh, dear Lord. Raina swallowed back the scream bubbling up in her throat, struggled to keep her voice calm. She looked at Lucian, held his gaze with her own. "What happened?"

He shook his head. "No idea."

"You mean—" she hesitated "—you don't remember?"

"The police report said that his truck spun out on an icy road sometime around 6:30 a.m." Gabe picked up the glass of merlot he'd been drinking and swirled the red liquid. "Based on the damage to his truck, he's a lucky boy that his injuries weren't worse than they were."

"But you don't remember? Nothing at all?" It was all she could do not to grab him by the shoulders and shake him. "Not even the wedding?"

"Nothing about the wedding, but I did make a toast at the reception that stuck in my head for some reason." Lucian shrugged. "Everyone tells me I had a great time, though, so I guess I'll have to believe them."

Oh, you had a great time, all right, Raina thought. And not just at the wedding. "What's the last thing you *do* remember?" she asked cautiously.

"Driving home after picking up my tux," Lucian said. "That was the day of the rehearsal dinner."

The day she'd come to town, Raina realized. She

and Lucian met for the first time that night, at the rehearsal dinner.

So he didn't remember her. Didn't remember meeting her, dancing with her, driving her back to Gabe and Melanie's…

Making love with her all night.

She suddenly wished she hadn't turned down the glass of wine Gabe had offered her.

"We still haven't figured out the mystery of what he was doing out at that hour of the morning. Especially why he was over at Jordan's Junction." Gabe stared at his glass of wine. "Though we do have a theory."

"Can it, Gabe," Lucian snarled.

"Oh?" Raina white-knuckled the fork in her hand. "And what is it?"

Gabe grinned, obviously enjoying his brother's discomfort. "Well, he still had his tux on, so it's doubtful he even went home. That implies a woman was involved."

"Do you *mind?*" Lucian's eyes narrowed.

"Reese, Callan and Ian had bets down on which one of the constant string of female visitors at the hospital might have been the one, but no one 'fessed up."

"Is that so?" Raina heard the sound of her voice, but it felt disembodied somehow. As if someone else were speaking.

"To this day," Gabe said, as he finished off his wine and set the glass on the table, "she still remains our mystery lady."

Three

———

It wasn't having too much time on his hands that was driving Lucian crazy. The construction business had always been that way, and he loved that part of his work. Fourteen-hour days for four months on end, then nothing for weeks. Between projects he had the extra hours to spend however he liked, whether it was working on his own house without interruption or jumping on his motorcycle and taking off for days at a time. He had the freedom to stop wherever he wanted, whenever he wanted, for as long as he wanted.

It was a great life. Simple and uncomplicated, with endless choices.

No, having too much time on his hands didn't make him crazy.

Raina Sarbanes was making him crazy. He couldn't

get the woman out of his mind. Even sitting here at the counter in his brother's tavern, with Ian on one side, Callan on the other and a basketball game on the overhead TV, Lucian was thinking about Melanie's best friend.

The woman confused the hell out of him. From the moment he'd picked her up at the airport she'd been cool and blatantly uninterested, then suddenly during dinner she'd shown surprising concern over the accident he'd had after the wedding. Was she just being polite, or had that been genuine concern?

And why would what had happened to him really matter to her at all?

He'd messed up his truck pretty bad, but the accident hadn't been a serious one. He'd had scrapes and bruises, a mild concussion and one hell of a headache for a couple of days, but that was it. Well, except for the fact he'd lost almost two days of his life. But the doctor had told him that memory loss of that nature was not abnormal with the type of head injury he'd sustained. He'd accepted that as no big deal.

But sometimes it *was* a big deal, he thought. Sometimes he had the strangest feeling that it was a *very* big deal.

He'd tried to get Raina alone last night after dinner to ask her if he'd offended her in some way at the wedding, but she'd conveniently disappeared upstairs with her baby and hadn't come back down. Today was the shower, so he couldn't go over there now, either.

Lucian frowned as he picked up the mug of beer he'd been nursing for the past half hour. Patience had never been his strong suit.

Cheers erupted all around him when Allen Iverson with the 76ers shot a buzzer beater to upset the favored New York Knicks. Callan and Ian both slapped Lucian on the back at the same time and beer sloshed out of his mug.

"Hey, careful when a man's got a beer in his hand," Lucian complained.

"And a woman on his mind." Reese stepped up from the other side of the bar and wiped up the spill.

"Who's the lucky lady today?" Callan handed Ian the five bucks he'd just lost on the game.

"What makes you think I've got a woman on my mind?" Lucian scowled at his brothers and brother-in-law. "There are other things that occupy my time and attention when I'm not working, you know."

The other three men looked at each other, then back at him.

"Was he watching the game?" Ian asked Callan.

"Nope."

"Was he working on his house today?" Ian asked Reese.

Reese shook his head. "Not that I know of."

"Has he even been drinking that beer Reese gave him a half hour ago?"

They looked at the full mug of beer, then at each other. "It's a woman," Ian, Callan and Reese said together.

"Come on, bro, out with it." Reese pulled the warm beer out of Lucian's hand and dumped it, then filled a fresh mug. "So what's up?"

"Nothing's up." Just to prove it, he took a long pull on the ice-cold amber brew.

Ian snagged a peanut from a bowl on the counter

and cracked it open. "Cara said you were tripping over your tongue when you brought Melanie's friend back from the airport. What's her name, Rita?"

"So I looked, so what?" He shrugged. "I'm not blind or dead, you know. And her name's *Raina*," he added, "not Rita."

"Raina, that's right."

Ian grinned at him, and Lucian knew he'd been had.

"Look, sorry to disappoint you girls." Lucian gave the other men a bored look and took another sip of his beer. "But it's just not there."

"It's not there on her part, anyway." Callan wasn't about to miss an opportunity to let a dig pass by. "Obviously, the woman is as smart as she is gorgeous."

Lucian gritted his teeth. Maybe, just maybe, he thought, if he ignored them they'd all go away. And if he believed that, he might as well go out and buy some beach property next to Sam Peterson's dairy farm.

If anything, Lucian knew from experience that they were just getting started.

"Uncle Ian! Uncle Callan! Uncle Reese! I hit a home run yesterday." Kevin came bounding up to the bar with Gabe close behind. The boy swung his arms in a reenactment. "You know, Uncle Lucian."

"Right outta the park, pal." Talk about timing, Lucian thought with a thankful smile. There was nothing like a loquacious six-year-old to curb a discussion about women. "I taught the boy everything he knows."

"I'd say that calls for a celebration." Reese caught

the eye of a petite redheaded waitress. "Marie, a burger and chocolate shake here for my nephew."

"Wow! Thanks Uncle Reese." Kevin climbed up on the bar stool. "And we should celebrate Uncle Lucian, too, since he's getting married."

Lucian nearly spit out the beer he'd just sipped. Except for the wail of a Willie Nelson song about being on the road—which was exactly where he'd like to be right now—it seemed as though the entire restaurant had gone quiet. Every head in the place turned and looked at him. Ian, Reese and Callan, brows raised, all stared.

Gabe, on the other hand, grinned and slipped onto the stool beside his son.

So much for curbing the conversation, Lucian thought with a sigh. With his luck, the headline of the *Bloomfield County Gazette* would be his impending marriage.

"I am *not* getting married," he said firmly and with as much patience as he could muster under the circumstances. "Not to anyone. You all got that?"

All the men gave each other a knowing look, then turned their attention back to Kevin, who'd thankfully changed the conversation back to baseball.

Lucian took another sip of beer and shook his head. For crying out loud, what was with all this marriage talk lately?

Married people just couldn't stand seeing single people happy, that was it. Couldn't believe that they were truly happy. Which he was. He *liked* being single and intended to stay that way for a very, very long time. Maybe forever.

It would take a very special woman to change his

mind, Lucian thought, and in his heart he truly didn't believe that woman existed.

"Oh, Rae, just look at this." Melanie's eyes shone brightly with tears as she clutched the tiny, white, knit hat in her hands. "Isn't this just the most precious thing you've ever seen?"

"It's lovely." Smiling, Raina set Emma down beside a pile of empty gift boxes, and the baby shrieked with delight. "See, Emma likes it, too."

"She was an angel today." Melanie offered the baby a bright red-and-blue rattle that had been on top of one of the packages. "Is she always that good around so many people?"

Raina sat down on the sofa beside Melanie, thankful for the quiet. The decibel level of thirty women at a baby shower was equal to that of a jet plane landing in a thunderstorm. The last person, including Melanie's sisters-in-law, had left just a few minutes ago, but Raina's ears were still ringing.

"She was practically born in a dressing room filled with models. She was adored by so many different women, I was afraid she wouldn't even know who her real mother was. I had to hire a nanny just so the child could have a little peace." Raina picked up a pale-green sleeper and felt a tug in her heart. "I can't even remember when she was this small."

"Rae." Melanie's smile faded as she took Raina's hand. "I'm so sorry I couldn't be there for you when you were pregnant with Emma. You know how much I wanted to be."

"Of course I know that." Raina gave her friend a hug. "I was in Italy, working sixteen-hour days. You were here, with Kevin and a brand-new husband. We were both where we belonged at that time, doing what we needed to be doing.''

Melanie nodded sadly, then leaned back and looked at Raina thoughtfully. "Why haven't we ever talked about it?"

Raina glanced away, watched Emma toss the rattle into an empty box and chortle with laughter. *We never talked because I'm a coward,* Raina wanted to say but couldn't.

Because I was terrified you'd ask who Emma's father was.

She hadn't even told Melanie that she was pregnant until she was six months along. Raina knew that had hurt Melanie, but she also knew that Melanie would understand, that she would forgive her and be patient. Melanie had always been all the things that Raina had not.

"I'm sorry," Raina said quietly. "I wasn't trying to shut you out. I didn't want you to worry about me, and I...I was confused. There were some things I wasn't ready to face."

"Are you ready now?"

Melanie's quiet question resonated through Raina. She glanced at her daughter, felt that same over-whelming wave of love wash over her.

Was she ready?

Her mind was still reeling from the bombshell that had been dropped on her last night at the dinner table: Lucian had been in an accident the morning after the wedding.

After she'd changed the bedding and straightened up any traces of Lucian having spent the night there,

Raina had packed her bags and called for a taxi to take her to the airport. She'd boarded her plane and left the country, all the time thinking that he'd walked out on her without even a thank-you-ma'am.

And three months later, when she'd made the most difficult phone call of her life...

Lucian, this is Raina...

Raina? Raina who?

The confusion in his voice, then the long silence that had followed had been like a knife in her heart. It was one thing to think he'd walked away from her without so much as a backward glance, but that he couldn't even remember her name was more than she could bear. Without another word she'd hung up the phone and never called back.

An *accident*. He'd left her and been in an accident.

She'd lain awake most of last night, tossing and turning in that same bed that she and Lucian had made love in. Images kept flashing in her mind: Lucian's truck spinning off an icy road. Lucian lying hurt and bleeding, alone in a ditch. Lucian lying in a hospital bed, his head bandaged and his body bruised.

He'd said at the dinner table that it was no big deal, but he had no idea how wrong he was. It *was* a big deal.

A very big deal.

She realized, of course, that she still had no idea what his intentions were when he'd left her that morning. If he'd come back, or if he'd called her. She would never know that now.

Because *he* didn't even know.

He couldn't remember. He didn't remember the night they'd spent together, didn't remember very much of the wedding, didn't even seem to remember meeting her, from what little she could gather.

She closed her eyes, struggled to breathe against the weight on her chest. All the hurt and anger she'd felt since that night turned to guilt. Somehow she had to make things right.

If only she knew how.

"Rae."

The sound of Melanie's soft voice snapped Raina out of her musings. Was she ready? Melanie had asked.

No. She wasn't ready. But she had no choice.

"There's something I have to do." Raina squeezed Melanie's hand. "Then I'll tell you everything before I leave here. I promise."

"I'll hold you to that," Melanie said, squeezing Raina's hand right back. "Now before Tornado Kevin and Gabe come blasting through the door, why don't we—" she stopped, listened "—too late. Hold on to your seat."

The front door flew open, and Kevin exploded into the room. Raina's heart skipped when hot on his heels came Lucian. Like two banshees, they ran through the living room into the kitchen.

Wide-eyed, Emma stared.

Gabe strolled in through the open door and closed it behind him. Smiling, he headed for his wife and bent down to give her a kiss.

"Let me guess," Melanie said. "They heard there was cake here."

"Yep. Word has it that it's chocolate with whipped cream."

"With raspberry filling," she added. "I hid a piece for you in the fridge."

"That's my girl." He kissed her again, then scooped Emma up off the floor. "And speaking of girls, how's my favorite little one?"

"Ready for a bath and bedtime," Raina answered. Now that Lucian had showed up, Raina was anxious to go upstairs. She knew they needed to speak, and soon, but this was hardly the time. "Come on, sweetie, let's give Uncle Gabe and Aunt Melanie a little alone time."

"Can we put her to bed?" Melanie asked, and grinned at her husband. "I'm out of practice, and Gabe could use a few lessons."

"You mean they don't come with an instruction book?" he asked, tickling Emma's belly. The baby giggled and grasped at Gabe's hand for more.

"Sure they do." It required a helping hand from Gabe, but Melanie managed to push herself out of the sofa. "And all the pages are blank. Same as that book titled, *What Men Know about Women*."

A loud thud came from the kitchen, a whoop of laughter, then Kevin came out a moment later, wiping chocolate crumbs from his face with the back of his hand. Melanie frowned at her son.

"I beat Uncle Lucian in an arm wrestle for the first piece of cake," Kevin announced proudly.

"Upstairs, young man," Melanie said firmly. "In the tub, then pj's on."

"Aw, Mom." Kevin headed for the stairs. "I'm not tired at all."

"Last time you said that you fell asleep on top of

your bed," Gabe said. "In your underwear, if I recall."

"Did not!" Kevin's face turned bright red as he looked from Raina to his father. "I was just resting."

He scampered up the stairs ahead of his parents, with Emma chattering at him. When Raina started to rise from the sofa, Melanie waved her back. "You just stay right here."

"But—"

"No buts," Melanie said as she slowly made her way up the stairs. "We'll be down as soon as Emma's asleep. You just relax until we get back."

Relax? Raina would have laughed if her throat wasn't so tight with nerves. With Lucian in the kitchen and everyone else upstairs, relaxation was the furthest thing from her mind.

"Hey."

She drew in a slow breath, then glanced over her shoulder at the sound of his voice behind her. Why did the man always have to look so damn appealing? she thought irritably. In her line of work she was constantly surrounded by men dressed in tailored, fashionable clothes, and all this man had to put on to look incredibly sexy was a pair of faded jeans and a snug black T-shirt.

She swallowed down the tightness in her throat and forced a smile. "Hello."

He held a paper plate with a hefty slice of cake in one hand and a fork in the other. He sauntered toward her, kept those incredible green eyes on her as he sat down on the sofa beside her.

"Looks like Melanie got a nice load of loot here." He gestured toward all the open presents lying around them, then pointed at a box sitting on the coffee table. "What's that thing?"

"A baby monitor." She busied herself by folding a white baby blanket, prayed that he wouldn't notice her hands were shaking. "It has dual receivers."

"No kidding? What will they think of next?" He grinned at her, took a bite of cake and groaned. "Damn, this is good."

It was making her crazy. Lucian sitting so close to her, grinning that Sinclair grin that made women weak. Even the way he ate that cake was sexy, she thought, all that chocolate and whipped cream he'd scooped into that handsome mouth of his, the way his eyes glinted with pleasure.

She remembered a night he'd looked at her that way, as if he'd wanted to gobble her up whole. She shivered at the memory.

"Cold?"

"Not at all," she said quickly, and reached for another baby blanket.

He nodded at a wicker bassinet sitting on the floor. "Don't tell me they're going to put my nephew in that oversize bread basket."

"What makes you think it's a boy?" Gabe and Melanie had chosen not to be told the baby's sex, but that didn't stop the family from speculating. "It could just as easily be a girl, you know."

"Could be, but I've got ten bucks down it's a boy." He looked at her thoughtfully. "Did you find out Emma was a girl before she was born?"

Raina felt her pulse quicken. This was definitely not an area of conversation she wanted to explore.

Not yet, anyway. She leaned forward to straighten the boxes Emma had been playing with on the floor.

"I knew."

"So you didn't want to be surprised?"

"No." She glanced up at the sound of water splashing from the bathtub upstairs, heard Emma's screech of pleasure, then Melanie and Gabe's laughter. "I think I should go—"

"Raina." He set his cake down on the coffee table, then reached out. "Wait."

The last thread of composure slipped when she felt his hand circle her wrist. She sat back down, but only because her knees wouldn't have supported her, anyway.

"What?" she said, and cursed the fact her voice sounded more like one of Cinderella's mice.

"Why do I make you so nervous?"

"I'm not nervous." *Big lie.* They both knew it.

"I've been thinking about you." His thumb brushed lightly back and forth over her wrist. "Wondering why you act so differently around me than anyone else. Was it something I did? Something I said at the wedding or before?"

"No." That at least was true. "It was nothing you said."

"Your pulse is racing," he murmured. "So it was something I did, then. Tell me. Please."

The soothing tone of his voice, the velvet touch of his thumb on her skin mesmerized her. "It…it wasn't at the wedding or before."

"So when was it?"

She closed her eyes, swallowed hard. "It was after."

Four

"**A**fter?" Based on the somber look on Raina's face and the serious look in her eyes, Lucian decided whatever he'd done, it must have been pretty bad. "Someone said you went back to Gabe and Melanie's house after the reception. I assumed that Cara and Ian took you back."

"They were going to," Raina said quietly. "But Cara was six months pregnant, and I could see she was exhausted. I told them to go ahead and I'd find a ride with someone else."

The implication hovered between them for a moment, then Lucian raised both brows. "Are you saying that *I* took you?"

"You were taking the wedding gifts over to Gabe and Melanie's, anyway. It made sense I would just ride along with you."

"But why didn't anyone know we left together?" he asked. "Someone must have seen us."

"You were loading your truck through the back door of the reception hall and we drove out from the back parking lot. Maybe in all the confusion of everyone leaving at once, they thought you'd left before me, instead of with me."

He hated this, having a blank spot in his brain. It had driven him nuts at first, but he'd simply accepted that other than the wedding toast he'd made to Gabe and Melanie, he would probably never remember anything about that night or the day before.

He felt the rapid-fire beat of her pulse under his fingertips, the icy chill of her skin. Like a punch in his gut, he realized what she was trying to tell him.

Oh, hell...

"Are you saying that I...that we...?"

She nodded. "We spent the night together."

Oh, hell.

"Raina, my God, I...I don't know what to say." He'd been in a situation or two, but nothing that ever came close to this. "I didn't, I mean, was I—"

Damn. He didn't know *what* to say.

They'd *slept* together. Spent the night together—here in this house.

"And you never said anything?" he finally managed. "Not even to Melanie?"

"There was no reason to tell Melanie. What happened was between you and me."

"But you never said anything to me, either." He struggled to find some kind of balance. "Why?"

"I was asleep when you left the next morning." She pulled her hand from his, tucked it under her leg.

"There was no note when I woke up and you didn't come back so I thought—"

"That I was a complete jerk. Jeez." Her hostility toward him at the airport made all the sense in the world. Good Lord, he was lucky she hadn't decked him one. "Look, Raina, I have no idea where I went, but I swear to you I wouldn't have just taken off like that without saying goodbye."

"I didn't know about your accident." She leaned toward him. "If I had, I never would have just left like I did, either."

He tried to absorb the impact of what she'd just told him, but it felt as if he'd been dealt a knockout blow and couldn't quite grab the ropes to pull himself up.

They'd made love. He still couldn't believe it.

And dammit to hell, he couldn't remember.

"Lucian." She glanced up at the muffled sound of Melanie singing "Rock-a-Bye Baby" to Emma, then looked back at him. "In spite of how this may sound to you, and the fact that we'd only just met, it wasn't casual sex. Impulsive, yes, unexpected, absolutely. But it wasn't casual."

"Damn." Shaking his head, he dragged a hand through his hair. "Of all the things I would never want to forget, it would be making love with you."

She blushed at his words. "Lucian—"

"So you're the mystery woman." He reached for the hand she'd tucked under her leg, glanced down as he traced the ridge of her knuckles with his thumb. "According to my family you were less than enamored with me. How did it…I mean, how did we—"

He paused. Damn, but this was awkward. He was

on unfamiliar territory here, not knowing what had happened or how, certainly not knowing what to say. How was he supposed to ask for details without sounding crude?

At the sound of a door closing upstairs, Raina quickly pulled her hand from his. "We need to talk, Lucian, but this isn't the right time."

He nodded. This was definitely not the right time. He heard Melanie and Gabe talking to Kevin in the hallway upstairs, and Lucian knew he'd better leave now, before they came back down. He was still dazed from what Raina had told him, and Gabe would know something was up.

"I'll be over in the morning. I promised Kevin we'd hit some balls out back."

He held her gaze as he stood and pulled her up with him. Unable to stop himself, he touched her cheek with his fingertip, noticed her sharp intake of breath and soft flutter of her lashes as she glanced down. Oh, yeah, he thought. There was something here, and it wasn't just on his side, either.

"Tomorrow," he whispered.

"Yes," she answered. "Tomorrow."

He left then, wondering how that single word could hold such promise and apprehension at the same time.

"Lucian is not going to like this one little bit." Shaking her head, Melanie pulled fresh, warm bagels out of a brown paper bag and set them in a basket on the kitchen table. "He hates surprises."

"That's what makes it so much fun," Cara said as she added sliced bananas to a bowl of mixed fruit. "He won't even know what hit him until he walks through that door. Ian," she called into the living room where the other men had gathered. "You have film in the camera?"

"All set," Ian called back to his wife.

Purple and red birthday balloons had replaced pink and blue baby shower decorations and a banner printed from Abby's computer read, Happy Birthday, Lucian. Sydney stood at the kitchen counter drizzling icing on the cinnamon rolls she'd baked, and Abby was at the stove frying bacon. The house was filled with all the wonderful scents and sounds of a family Sunday brunch.

If there was one thing that the Sinclair clan enjoyed, Raina noted as she watched all the hustle and bustle, it was a party. It didn't seem to matter that just yesterday they'd had a baby shower for Melanie. A birthday was a birthday, after all, and whether Lucian wanted it or not, his family intended to celebrate.

Not a moment had passed since he'd left last night that she hadn't thought about him. While her daughter had slept soundly in the bedroom next to her own, Raina had spent most of her night tossing and turning, listening to the soft hum of the new baby monitor Melanie had set up. The sound had been a soothing comfort to her while she struggled to find the right words to tell Lucian about Emma.

Tomorrow, she'd said to him.

And tomorrow was now today.

His birthday, no less. She hadn't known about that until last night when Melanie mentioned the surprise brunch they were giving him this morning. If she had known, she never would have promised to talk with him today.

Of all the days to tell a man he had a seven-month-old child.

Nerves clawed at her stomach, and she felt as if a fist had hold of her chest. She knew there was no way he would let her put it off. He wanted to know the truth about what had happened that night. She understood that; he had a right.

If only she'd known about the accident, that he'd been in the hospital and lost the memory of those precious hours they'd spent together the night before. Everything might have been so different....

But she hadn't known, and life was full of if-onlys. She could only deal with the here and now.

"Raina, will you please fill this and set it on the dining room table?" Melanie pulled a container of orange juice out of the refrigerator and set it next to a glass pitcher on the table. "He's going to be here any minute and I still need to get the coffee going."

Eager for any little job to occupy her mind and hands, Raina opened the carton, then filled the pitcher and went into the dining room. In the living room Reese was on guard for Lucian. Callan was holding Emma, and Gabe held Matthew. To both babies' delight, Kevin was jumping up and down and making faces.

She couldn't help but smile, felt her eyes tear up at the sound of her daughter's laughter.

"They do that to you," Cara said from behind her. "Make you weepy and emotional over the smallest things. I bawled like a baby myself the first time Matthew smiled at me."

Coffee creamer in hand, Melanie joined Cara and Raina. "I couldn't even speak when they handed

Kevin to me in the hospital." Melanie touched her stomach, then blinked furiously. "Oh, dear, here I go again with the waterworks. Gabe's nickname for me these days is Niagara."

Raina and Cara both smiled with understanding and wiped at their own tears as they all hugged. Melanie was the only family Raina had ever known. In spite of everything, it felt good to be back.

"He's here!"

Raina's pulse jumped at Reese's announcement. Laughing and whispering, everyone scrambled to gather in the living room. Raina took Emma from Callan and stood back.

Lucian opened the door.

"Surprise!"

He stood in the doorway, startled for a moment, then shook his head with a groan and looked heavenward. Ian snapped a picture.

"Lord save me from this crazy family," he said, but there was no bite to his words. Grinning, he hugged and kissed Cara and his sisters-in-law in turn, and endured the digs and back slapping from all the men.

Nervous and a little overwhelmed, Raina held back, smiling at the festivities, but not comfortable enough to jump into the middle of it all. When Lucian moved toward her with a grin on his face, panic gripped her.

Before she could recover, he had his arms around her and had pulled both her and Emma close.

The warmth of his body against her own, the masculine scent of his skin, the rock-solid feel of his arms around her, everything went straight to her head. It was impossible to breathe, to think, even to react. She heard the sound of voices around her, saw the flash of Ian's camera, but her entire focus was on Lucian.

When he lightly brushed his lips across her cheek, lingered there for just a moment, her heart slammed in her chest.

Emma touched his cheek and gurgled, and the camera flashed again.

"So you were in on this conspiracy, were you?" He pulled away from her, then poked a finger in Emma's soft belly. "Did you know your mommy was so sneaky?"

Still not fully recovered from the unexpected contact with Lucian, Raina simply smiled, did her best to look composed, when in reality she was shaking inside.

"Food's on."

Carrying a steaming metal pan of ham-and-cheese quiche, Sydney came into the dining room through the swinging kitchen door. All the men teased Lucian, who took the ribbing good-naturedly. Since he was the birthday boy, Lucian sat at the head of the table and the women filled his plate for him, but the rest of the men were on their own.

They were an exuberant bunch, Raina thought as she watched food exchange hands and jokes fly. When she'd come in for the wedding, there'd been no time for relaxed family get-togethers. The rehearsal dinner at Reese's tavern had been hectic, followed by the wedding and reception the next day. The two days had flown by.

And after the reception, Raina thought, that part of the night had passed *much* too quickly.

As if he'd read her thoughts, Lucian glanced up at

her, held her gaze while he nodded at Callan, who was discussing the architectural changes on an upcoming project their company was scheduled to build. She should have looked away, told herself to, but she couldn't. She stared back, mesmerized, as if they were the only two people in the room....

Raina blinked, realized that Abby, who was sitting beside her had asked her a question. "Excuse me?"

"Melanie mentioned that you have a show coming up in a few weeks," Abby repeated.

"Two weeks." Raina forced herself not to think about Lucian, or that the conversation had now turned to her. "It's a new fall line of lingerie."

All the mens' heads snapped to attention. Melanie frowned and pointed a finger at her husband. "Say one word, Gabe Sinclair, and you're sleeping on the sofa tonight."

"What?" Gabe's expression was one of complete innocence. "I was just going to ask for some watermelon."

Groans and laughter circled the table, and though she tried to look angry, Melanie just shook her head with exasperation. Raina watched the two of them, saw the special look they exchanged and couldn't remember when she'd ever seen two people more in love.

She realized that every couple sitting here seemed to have that special look for each other, that look that was only for their mate, a look of love and respect that no words could express.

She'd been married for one year when she was twenty-two. Nicholas Sarbanes. He'd been handsome, wealthy, charming. Too late she'd realized that Nicholas had only wanted a trophy wife, a woman to look good on his arm and impress everyone in his exclusive circle of wealthy friends. She'd been dazzled for a few weeks by all the glitz and glamour and attention, but it had worn off quickly after they were married, as had his so-called love for her. She'd only been one in a long string of models he couldn't seem to keep his hands off.

Nicholas had never once looked at her the way these men were looking at their wives. No man ever had. They had looked at her with lust or desire, but not with the kind of love surrounding her at the moment. A love that endured. A love that was as endless as it was timeless. Love that spoke volumes in one word or no word at all. Love that was a look only two people understood.

"What's lawngeray?" Kevin asked while pulling a cinnamon roll apart.

"It's underwear for women," Melanie answered.

"Oh." Kevin turned the same color as the watermelon in the fruit bowl. "Why would anyone wanna see a show for *that?*"

Everyone chuckled, but no one seemed to want to answer the six-year-old's question, so the conversation moved swiftly on to basketball play-offs and one-year checkups for babies.

"The Lakers will never do it this year. Not with two key players out with injuries."

"All those shots were a nightmare. I cried as hard as Matthew."

"The Knicks are a shoe-in this year. Their center is hot."

"We've got five more months before Emma's appointment. I'm already dreading it."

Lucian teeter-tottered between listening to discussions about basketball shots and babies' shots. If Raina hadn't been at the table, he would have concentrated completely on basketball, but he found himself wanting to know more about the woman.

He'd passed on a poker game with Reese and the McDougall brothers last night. Instead he spent his evening pacing and thinking about Raina. Lord knew he had a lot to think about.

He still couldn't believe that they'd made love. Well, he believed it. He had no doubt that Raina was telling the truth. Why would she lie about something like that? He just couldn't *believe* it.

Just his luck. He'd made love to the most beautiful woman he'd ever seen in his life and he couldn't remember one damn minute of it. God had one hell of a sense of humor.

She must have thought him a complete idiot when he never came back or even said goodbye to her. In spite of the rumors regarding his love life, he'd never been promiscuous and he'd never been cruel. That wasn't his style.

He had so many questions—questions that she'd promised to answer today. He was chomping at the bit to get her alone, but now that his family had planned a birthday party for him, he knew he would have to wait. It was making him nuts.

While Gabe and Callan argued over who'd sunk the most baskets so far this season, Lucian turned his attention from Raina to little Emma. She was every bit as beautiful as her mother, though now that he thought about it, the child didn't really have Raina's features. Other than Emma's dark curls, the child looked more like she would belong to his sister. Especially those big green eyes, Lucian thought. They were exactly the same shade as Cara's.

And Gabe's. And Reese's.

And...*his*.

He frowned, felt his heart skip a beat. Emma's hair wasn't the same shade as Raina's, either.

It was darker...like his.

Lucian looked at Matthew and Emma, sitting next to each other, both of them in high chairs. They were so close in age, they almost looked like twins.

Or cousins.

His heart started to pound a little faster. No. It wasn't possible. Emma was seven months old, the wedding was—he stopped, did the math.

Oh, God.

He stood suddenly, kept his narrowed gaze on Raina. She'd been talking, but stopped in the middle of a sentence as she watched him walk around the table toward her. Her eyes widened with confusion, then fear.

He took her by the arm, felt a tic jump in his temple as he said, "We need to talk."

"Lucian!" Melanie stared at him in shock. Frowning, Gabe started to stand.

"Gabe, you stay out of this," Lucian said tightly. "I'm sorry, Melanie, but you'll all have to excuse Raina and me."

Melanie opened her mouth to protest, but Raina shook her head. "It's all right, Mel."

Melanie pressed her lips into a thin line and leaned back in her chair. Everyone else just stared.

His hand circling her arm, he practically dragged her up the stairs into the first bedroom, which happened to be the nursery.

He closed the door behind them and ignored Raina's gasp of shock when he brought her up against him.

"Tell me," he said in a low growl. "Is Emma my child?"

Five

——

Raina felt the blood drain from her head. What had happened? One minute they'd all been sitting around the table laughing and talking, the next minute he'd come at her with an intensity in his eyes that had, quite literally, taken her breath away. She hadn't had time to prepare or think or react.

She blinked at him, unable to speak, then gasped when he tightened his hold on her arm.

"Is she?" he asked again.

She yanked away from him, rubbed her arm as she stepped back. Whatever the situation, she refused to be manhandled. "This is hardly the time to have this discussion."

"She is, isn't she?" He stared at her, disbelief etched sharply in the tight lines on his face. "When you told me last night that we slept together after the wedding, I should have realized immediately. It doesn't take a rocket scientist to add up the months and figure it out.''

''Lucian, I—''

''She's got my eyes, my hair.'' He dragged a hand through that hair as he shook his head. ''She's got Sinclair written all over her, and I didn't even see it until this minute. Dammit, Raina, why the *hell* didn't you tell me?''

''When?'' She felt her own anger rise. ''The next morning when I woke up and you were gone without a word? Oh, well, since I hardly knew I was pregnant then, I guess not.''

''You could have—''

''What? Called you when I found out?'' She narrowed her eyes. ''For your information, I did call you. You didn't even know who I was. 'Raina who?' you said. Have you any idea how that felt?''

''For God's sake.'' He threw his hands out in frustration. ''I didn't remember because I *couldn't* remember.''

''Will you please lower your voice?'' she hissed, then sucked in a breath. ''Lucian, I'm not clairvoyant. Since Melanie and I had never talked about it, I had no way of knowing about your accident. All I knew was that I was in Italy, unmarried, pregnant and the father of my baby couldn't even remember my name. I did what I had to do.''

A muscle worked in his jaw as he started to pace. ''Why didn't you at least tell Melanie about this?''

''As far as I knew, you couldn't even remember my name.'' Raina shook her head. ''Do you really think I would call my best friend and put her in the middle of a situation like that? Tell her that I had a wild night of sex with her brother-in-law, who had made it clear he wanted no commitments in his life? For the first time in her life, Melanie was—is—happy. She certainly doesn't need me putting any strain or stress on that happiness.''

Lips pressed in a hard line, he stopped his pacing and moved toward her. ''I had a right to know that I had a child.''

Raina closed her eyes and nodded. ''After that phone call, and even right after Emma was born, I admit that I wasn't going to tell you, but then—'' she paused, wanting to choose her words carefully ''—then I realized that you *needed* to know. I have no family. If anything ever happened to me, Emma would be alone. That thought terrified me.''

''You were going to tell me because you thought I *needed* to know, not because you thought I would *want* to know?''

''That night we both made it clear that we weren't looking for love or permanence or commitment in a relationship,'' she said carefully. ''No marriage plans, no children. Why would I think you'd changed your mind?''

The night might have started that way, she remembered, though it hadn't ended that way. At least, not for her. By the end of that night, she hadn't wanted it to end. She'd already fallen in love with him.

And then he was gone.

''Lucian.'' She said his name on a sigh. ''I had no idea what you wanted, but from the moment I learned I was pregnant, I wanted that baby more than anything I've ever wanted in my life. Emma is my world.''

Eyes narrowed, jaw tight, he stared at her but said nothing. The tension stretched, but still he said nothing.

The distant sound of Emma's cry from downstairs brought them both back to reality.

He stepped away, still staring at her with those cool green eyes, then turned and left the room.

Raina released the breath she'd been holding, waited a moment and followed. Her heart sank as she heard Lucian's truck start up then drive away.

At the insistent sound of Emma's cry, Raina had no choice but to go to her daughter and face Lucian's family.

She sucked in a breath, lifted her chin and walked downstairs. Everyone but Kevin and Gabe were still sitting in the dining room, and they all looked at her as she walked in.

''I...I'm sorry,'' she started to explain, though she had no idea what she was going to say. ''Lucian and I, we...''

''Raina, you don't have to say anything.'' Melanie stood with a tired, fussy Emma in her arms. ''I'm sorry. I turned it off, but not before, I mean, not before—''

Confused, Raina glanced in the direction that Melanie's gaze had drifted, to an oak sideboard in the dining room.

Oh, God.

Raina's heart stopped as she stared.

The baby monitor.

Dread raced through her as she looked back at

everyone. She had no idea exactly how much they'd heard, but it was clear they'd heard enough.

Oh, God.

"Now *that*—" Reese was the first to break the awkward, horrible silence "—is what I call a surprise party."

Lucian pulled a nail from the pouch at his waist, positioned it at the corner of the two-by-four and swung the hammer. The nail slammed into the wood in one smooth hit. He swore, set the next nail, swung the hammer again. And swore.

Another nail, another swing, another curse.

He'd been at it for nearly two hours. Hammering, swearing. Thinking.

I'm a father.

I have a daughter.

Emma is my baby.

Father. Daughter. Baby.

It had taken two hours, plus several dozen nails and four smashed knuckles for the reality to sink in: he was a father. Emma's father.

That was one hell of a birthday present.

With a heavy sigh he dropped the hammer into his work belt, then scrubbed a hand over his face. He'd barely had time to accept the bombshell that he and Raina had spent the night together before the second bomb had hit. He had a kid. He'd been a father for seven months and he hadn't even known.

"Dammit." He kicked a sawed-off block of wood off the porch and sent it sailing into the nearby woods. She should have told him. He'd had a right to know.

He'd gone over it in his mind, again and again, struggled to make sense of it, to understand. But it was damn hard when he couldn't remember a blasted thing about the night they'd spent together.

He tried to put himself in her place, picture everything that had happened from her point of view: they make love; she thinks he's ducked out on her; she finds out she's pregnant; she calls him; he doesn't remember her name; she decides to raise the baby herself and not tell him because she thinks that he wouldn't want a child.

But no matter how hard he tried, no matter how many times he went over the scenario, it came back to the same thing: Emma was *his* baby, too.

Raina might have thought him a louse, but to keep his own child from him—he felt a fresh wave of anger roll through him and kicked another block of wood.

No matter what the circumstances, that was unforgivable.

Dammit! If only he could remember even just one little thing about that night.

She said that they had talked, that he'd told her he wasn't interested in a relationship or getting married or having kids. No doubt that was all true. He'd never met a woman that had made him even consider taking that long walk down the aisle.

But he'd never met a woman like Raina before, either. From the moment he'd picked her up at the airport two days ago, something had felt different with her. Something that went beyond a beautiful face and killer body. He'd been drawn to her in a way he never had to another woman before. He still was, dammit.

Those feelings aside, at the moment he'd like to wring her neck. If he had stayed at Gabe's house one minute longer, he just might have.

He knew he'd have to explain everything to his family soon. No doubt they were more than aware that something was up, something big. But he'd needed some time to calm down, to sort out his feelings and think everything through. No one would have wanted to be around him these past two hours.

So he'd come here and pounded on nails. He felt a little calmer now, more clear-headed. He still had no idea how to handle this, or exactly what to say, but he and Raina were going to talk.

Emma was his daughter, his child, and no Sinclair ever walked away from blood.

"He'll be back, Rae. He just needs a little time." Melanie turned off the gas under the teapot on the stove, then poured the hot water into a cup. "Now will you please stop pacing and sit down?"

"It's been over two hours." Raina glanced at her wristwatch and kept moving between the back door and the kitchen sink. "Emma will be waking up from her nap any time now. I don't want him storming in here and frightening her."

"He won't do that." Melanie dropped a tea bag into the cup, then set it on the table. "But I promise you, I'll hit him myself with a frying pan if he does. Now sit."

Reluctantly Raina sat, but she was wound up tighter than Tigger on caffeine. This waiting was making her insane.

She'd never been more embarrassed in her entire

life, facing Lucian's family after they'd heard her tell
him that Emma was his baby. If Reese hadn't broken
that awful silence, she wasn't certain what she would
have done. But everyone had spoken at once after
that, and she'd been so overwhelmed, she could
barely get a word in.

She'd been thankful, at least, that Gabe had taken
Kevin outside right after Lucian's loaded question regarding Emma's parentage. Since the six-year-old
hadn't said anything, it didn't seem as though he'd
understood what had happened. The rest of the family, however, had fully understood.

The men had held back, a little uncertain what to
say or do, but Abby, Sydney, Cara and Melanie had
all hugged her. In spite of the circumstances, they all
seemed thrilled to have an addition to the family.
There'd been no recriminations, no judgments or ver-
dicts handed out. Raina had seen the questions in their
eyes, but they hadn't asked. They'd simply accepted.

The Sinclairs were an amazing bunch, Raina had
thought as she'd gone back upstairs to lay Emma
down for her nap. Truly amazing. By the time Raina
had finally gotten Emma to sleep, they'd all cleared
out, leaving her alone in the house with Melanie,
who'd been fussing over her ever since.

It had taken a while, but Raina had finally told
Melanie the truth. Other than the personal details of
the night she'd spent with Lucian, she'd explained
everything that had happened.

"Drink," Melanie said as she sat in the chair opposite Raina. "You're white as a sheet."

To give her restless hands something to do, Raina
picked up the cup Melanie had set down in front of

her. The heat felt good on her ice-cold hands, and she sipped the citrusy herbal tea.

"I'm sorry, Mel." Raina stared at the steam rising from her cup. "The last thing I'd ever want to do is upset you."

"Rae, I swear, if you apologize one more time, I just may have to hurt you."

"An empty threat, Mrs. Sinclair." Raina smiled. "We both know you've never hurt anyone in your entire life."

"Not true. Didn't I trip that bully Willie Thomas in seventh grade when he teased Mitsy Davidson for wearing thick glasses?"

"No. *I* tripped him," Raina reminded her.

"Well, it was my idea." Melanie lifted an indignant brow. "You were just closer."

Raina laughed at the memory, then sighed heavily. "Oh, Mel. I was going to tell you about Lucian and me, but I never intended for you to find out quite like this. I came here for your baby shower, not to bring you and your family grief."

"Sweetie, how can you look at your beautiful little girl and think that she could ever bring grief?"

Raina blinked back the moisture in her eyes. "She is beautiful, isn't she?"

"She most certainly is." Melanie smiled, then leaned back, her gaze thoughtful as she looked at Raina. "I did suspect, you know. About you and Lucian."

Raina's head snapped up. "You suspected? But how could you have?"

"I'd been so consumed with Gabe and Kevin and everything that had happened in those months before

I came to Bloomfield that I didn't see it at the wedding," Melanie said. "But when I saw you and Lucian together the other day, saw the way you looked at him, I knew there was something you weren't telling me. Something important that was troubling you deeply."

"Was I really that obvious?"

"Maybe not to anyone else. But you and I have been through a lot together, Rae. I know you better than you know yourself. And it was obvious that Lucian was more than a little interested in you, too."

"But still—" Raina shook her head "—that wouldn't mean that I, that we..." She still couldn't say it out loud to Melanie. "And it certainly wouldn't mean that Emma was Lucian's child."

Melanie smiled. "Like Lucian said, it didn't take a rocket scientist to figure it out. He was just a little slower with the calculations than I was. And let's face it. Emma looks like a Sinclair. Those eyes of hers alone would be enough to make a person wonder. And there was one other thing, something that confused me until today."

"What?"

"You changed the sheets and made up the bed you'd slept in when you stayed with me before. No one has slept in that room since then, so I thought I should freshen the bed before you got here two days ago." She pulled a slip of paper out of the pocket of her dress. "I found this."

Raina looked at the small piece of paper Melanie handed her:

"I'll be right back. Please don't leave. Lucian."

It felt as if the air had been sucked from her lungs.

He'd left a note? All this time she'd thought he'd left without a word.

She couldn't move, couldn't breathe. From the backyard, she heard the sound of Kevin's laughter as he played ball with Gabe and the distant moo of the neighboring farm's cows. The only sound she heard inside was the fierce pounding of her heart.

"I'll be right back."

He'd intended to come back? The words in front of her started to blur, and she blinked to bring them back into focus.

"Please don't leave."

What did that mean? Don't leave before I get back? Or could it have meant don't leave at all?

Her fingers shook. No. Of course it hadn't meant that. It was foolish to read more into a simple note than what was there.

What mattered was that he *had* left a note. That maybe she had meant more to him than a simple, one-night stand.

"I was asleep when he left," Raina whispered hoarsely. "I never saw this."

"It fell between the mattress and headboard. Apparently it's been there all this time." Melanie leaned forward and took Raina's hand. "Oh, Rae. If only you'd told me sooner. What you must have gone through, and all by yourself."

"Emma was worth every minute, every second." Raina closed her eyes. "You never really know until you hold your baby in your arms what it feels like. Nothing else in the world matters. Just that tiny little bundle. You know that you can survive anything as long as you have your child close."

"Can I see that?"

Raina jumped at the sound of Lucian's voice from the kitchen doorway. His denim shirt and jeans were streaked with dirt, his dark hair sprinkled with sawdust. He moved toward her and took the note from her hands, then stared at it. Slowly his dark-green gaze lifted to hers.

"Well—" Melanie stood, glanced from Raina to Lucian "—well, ah, you two obviously need to, ah…talk. I'll go upstairs and check on Emma."

"Melanie, you don't have—"

"Thanks, Mel." Lucian cut her off. "We appreciate it."

When Melanie left, Lucian pulled a chair from the table and placed it at an angle beside Raina, then sat.

His closeness overwhelmed her. The earthy scent of fresh-cut pine and pure male assaulted her senses.

"I'm sorry I left like I did."

"Which time?" she asked coolly.

A muscle jumped in his jaw, and he leaned close. "I just spent the past two hours pounding on nails so that you and I could talk calmly. But I assure you, Raina, I am anything but calm at the moment."

"I'm sorry. You didn't deserve that. I'm a little tense," she admitted. "This is difficult for both of us."

"I'd say that's a bit of an understatement." He sighed heavily, then glanced down at the note in his hand. "I need to know what happened that night."

I fell in love with you, she wanted to say. But she wouldn't. That wasn't what he was asking, or what he wanted to hear.

"We unloaded the presents," she said quietly. "It

had started to snow and I asked you if you wanted some coffee. You said sure, then we both just stood there looking at each other. The next thing I knew I was...we were—'' her cheeks warmed as she hesitated ''—in bed.''

''Of all the things I'm surprised about,'' he said, and leaned closer still, ''it's not that.''

The husky tone of his voice and his knees touching her thighs made it difficult for her to think. There was no question that the physical attraction between them was incredibly strong. Which was exactly the reason that she'd kept her distance from the moment she'd met him. Why she needed to keep her distance from him now.

''Raina.'' He held her with his gaze. ''Whatever I've done in my life, I've never been careless when it came to sex. I can't believe we spent an entire night together and we didn't use protection.''

The heat on her cheeks turned to fire now. She knew that these questions would come up and that she'd have to answer them, but that didn't make it any easier.

''Of course we did.'' She folded her hands between her legs and looked down. ''But we must have, well, it was more than...'' She closed her eyes. ''It was a long night, Lucian. I can only guess that one time we might not have been as careful as the others.''

''I see.''

She couldn't bring herself to look at him, didn't want to see the regret she was certain would be in his eyes. Because no matter what happened now, she would never regret that night or the beautiful child it had brought her.

So she kept talking, kept her voice level and controlled.

"The next couple of months I attributed my exhaustion to the move and the long hours I was putting in at work. By the third month I knew something wasn't right. A drugstore pregnancy test confirmed my suspicions."

"And you called me?"

She nodded. "I admit I was afraid, but I thought you should know."

"Until I said, 'Raina who?'" he added with a sigh.

"Yes."

He said nothing for a long moment, then he stood and walked to the kitchen sink, turned and faced her. His expression was somber, his mouth pressed into a hard line.

"As I see it," he said tightly, "there's only one solution to our problem."

Confused, she looked at him.

"We're getting married."

Six

Lucian watched Raina's expression leap from confused to shocked. He'd expected that. Hell, no one could be more shocked than him.

"*What* did you say?"

"We can get a license in the morning, have our blood tests done right after that, then as soon as the state allows, we can go see a justice of the peace."

She stared at him as if he'd grown a second nose. "You hit yourself in the head with that hammer, right? Or maybe that accident you had after the wedding did more to your brain than just lose you a few hours."

He'd expected reluctance, but he certainly hadn't expected sarcasm. "Look, I realize this is catching you off guard. I admit the idea took some getting used to, but if you think about it, you'll see it's the only sensible thing to do."

"If I *think* about it?"

"That's right."

"The *only* sensible thing to do?"

Why the hell did she keep repeating what he'd said? "Yes."

She turned away from him then and dropped her head in her hands. When her shoulders started to shake, he moved toward her. Good Lord, he hadn't meant to make her cry.

"Raina, it's for the best, we have Emma to think about and—" He stopped suddenly, narrowed his eyes. "Are you *laughing?*"

She lifted her head and waved a hand to signal she needed a moment, but a fresh round of laughter seemed to grip her and her head dropped back down again.

Folding his arms, he said through clenched teeth, "Are you just about finished?"

She visibly struggled to compose herself, then stood and faced him, still wiping tears from the corner of her eyes. "You think marrying you would be the *sensible* thing to do? That's got to be the most ridiculous thing I've ever heard."

"Oh, is that so?" He took a step closer to her. "And just why is our getting married so ridiculous?"

"This is the twenty-first century, Sinclair. Shotgun weddings are retrograde."

"No one's putting a gun to my head, dammit. Emma is my daughter, and I'm trying to do what's right."

"We can do what's right without getting married, for heaven's sake. We'll work this out, Lucian. It's not necessary for you to make the supreme sacrifice here.''

''Who the hell said it was a supreme sacrifice?'' he yelled. ''If you'd just—''

The sound of Emma's quiet whimper came through the baby monitor, then Melanie's soft croon. Raina pressed her lips together and narrowed her eyes, then moved so close they were nearly nose-to-nose.

''For the first ten years of my life,'' she said tightly, ''I lived with parents who were vocal enough about their dislike of each other that my family was on a first-name basis with the police. I understand you're angry about this. But I won't tolerate shouting when my daughter is in the same house, do you understand that?''

Frustrated, he stared down at her, then sighed heavily and dragged a hand through his hair. ''Look, I'm still trying to find my balance here. Whatever you might think of me, having a kid, being a father, is not something I take lightly. Emma is not just your daughter. She's mine, too. That means something to me, dammit.''

Slowly the tension eased from her face and her shoulders relaxed. ''Lucian,'' she said softly, ''I admit when I came here two days ago I might have thought you were less than admirable. If I had known you'd left a note or that you'd had an accident, things might have been different. But the fact is, that *is* what happened then, and this is now. Now is what we have to deal with.''

''Fine. I'll accept that,'' he said evenly. ''Now give me one good reason why we shouldn't get married.''

Exasperation rumbled deep in her throat. ''Have

you listened to a thing I've said here? I could give you a dozen reasons.''

"Are you living with someone?''

"Of course not.''

"Dating someone?''

"Not seriously.''

"Well, neither am I.''

She stared at him in disbelief. "And you think that because neither one of us is involved with anyone else at the moment that we should get married?''

"No, I think we should get married because we have a child. I don't want anyone to ever point a finger at our daughter or whisper behind her back.''

She faltered, then squared her shoulders. "Single women, and men, raise children all the time now.''

· She'd tried to hide it, but he'd seen the fleeting pain, the concern, in her smoky-blue eyes. And her voice hadn't been quite so strong or so sure. "And I applaud them as well as respect them. But there are small minds out there. There always will be. Do we want our daughter to be a target for them?''

She turned away, rubbed at her arms. "My friends, the people I know, aren't like that. I would never let anyone hurt her.''

"There'll be kids at school, maybe the people who live next door or the clerk at the grocery store. Just one comment, even an innocent one, could hurt her. Let me protect her from that.'' He moved up behind her, put his hands on her shoulders. "Emma's my daughter, Raina. While she's still a baby, let me give her my name.''

She shook her head, but didn't move away. "We don't love each other, Lucian. What kind of marriage is it when two people barely know each other and have nothing in common?"

"We can get to know each other." He felt the heat of her skin through her soft cotton blouse, smelled the faint floral scent of her perfume. "And we obviously do have something in common."

"So like a man." Ice edged her words as she turned and stepped back. "This isn't about sex, Lucian. This is about Emma."

"I was talking about Emma."

"Oh." She shifted awkwardly. "Well, good."

"But since you brought the subject up—" he closed the space she'd put between them "—let's talk about that."

"There's nothing to talk about."

"Isn't there?"

"Get over yourself, Sinclair." Her chin lifted. "It was one night."

He smiled, watched her eyes darken to the color of thick, blue smoke when he touched a finger to the collar of her blouse. Desire sparked, then flared bright. "Was it just one night?" he murmured. "Or was it something more?"

With the tip of his finger, he followed the open V of her collar down and circled the first white button. His gaze dropped to her mouth. Her lips parted softly and her breathing turned shallow.

"Something tells me that's what happened the first time," he said thoughtfully. "That you, maybe we both, denied it, until it just sort of exploded between us. Am I right?"

"No." The single word was breathless, edged with panic.

He lowered his mouth within a breath of hers, hovered there. "I think that's a lie, Raina," he whispered.

She blinked, did not move toward him or away. "No, Lucian. That's what a marriage between us would be. A lie."

He closed his eyes on a sigh and stepped back. "Dammit, it wouldn't be like that. We could—"

"No." She shook her head adamantly. "We can't. I'm going to be here for another four days." Her voice softened. "I want to be as fair as possible with you. You're welcome to spend as much time with Emma as you want. We can figure out some kind of visitation schedule before I leave, if you'd like to. I'm hoping we'll be able to do this without lawyers."

Visitation schedule? *Lawyers?* He wanted to tell her *exactly* what he thought of that, but there were times when he knew it was best to keep his mouth shut. "Fine," he snapped out.

"I'm going to check on Emma now." When she moved to step around him, he caught hold of her arm.

"I lost seven whole months of my daughter's life, Raina." He pulled her up against him. "Just tell me this, how *fair* is that?"

"I'm sorry, Lucian," she said quietly, and he could see that she meant it.

He swore silently, then let her go. He stared at the closed door for a long moment after she was gone, struggled not to follow her.

Damn stubborn woman.

She might have won the first round, he thought irritably, but round two would be coming soon. Very soon.

He intended to be ready.

* * *

"Look, sweetie," Melanie cooed to Emma when Raina walked into the nursery. "There's your mommy now."

"I can do that." Raina moved beside the changing table where Emma smiled and kicked her feet at the sight of her mother. "Hello, my darling. Did you have a nice nap?"

Her daughter's smile got her every time, Raina thought. Made her heart swell, her throat thicken. Made the stress of the day disappear, no matter how bad it was.

She desperately needed that smile at this moment.

Melanie handed Raina a diaper and raised one brow. "Well?"

"Well..." Raina slipped the diaper under her daughter and smoothly taped the sides. "He, ah, thinks that we should get married."

"He thinks *what?*"

"That we should get married." It surprised Raina how calm her voice sounded when inside she was still shaking. "Would you hand me that little pink T-shirt on top of the diaper bag, please?"

"Let me get this straight." Eyes wide, Melanie stared at her. "Lucian Sinclair, my brother-in-law, a man who cherishes his bachelor of bachelor arts degree, asked you to marry him and you say, 'hand me that T-shirt'?"

"Well, actually, to be more specific—" Raina took the T-shirt from Melanie "—I said 'hand me that little pink T-shirt.'"

"Raina, for heaven's sake. What did you say?"

"I said no."

"Well, of course you did." Melanie furrowed her brow. "What in the world was he thinking?"

"He was thinking of Emma." With a fresh diaper and change of clothes, Raina kissed her daughter, then picked her up and cuddled. "He wants her to have his name. To protect her from small-minded people."

Melanie frowned. "Small-minded people?"

Raina kissed the silky top of Emma's head and breathed in the baby scent of her soft skin. "People with mean spirits and ugly thoughts who are just looking for a reason to gossip."

"Lord knows I've met more than a few of them myself," Melanie said with a sigh. "But still, marriage?"

"In theory it makes sense." Just the thought of those kind of people had Raina clenching her teeth. "It was the one thing, probably the only thing, that he could have said to make me even consider such a ridiculous idea."

"Are you saying that you *are* considering his proposal?"

"Of course not." Raina shook her head firmly, but even she could hear the doubt in her voice. What if Lucian was right? What if people did point or whisper behind Emma's back? Even considering the possibility made her chest hurt. "I told him that he could spend as much time with Emma as he wants, and that we'd work out a visitation schedule."

"Oh, good heavens." Melanie's eyes went wide. "I can just imagine how well *that* went over."

"There was a significant amount of chest thumping." Raina nibbled on the finger that Emma was attempting to stick in her mouth. "But he agreed."

"Don't be so sure, Rae." Doubt narrowed Melanie's eyes. "The Sinclair men can be quite persuasive when they set their minds to something. Believe me, I know."

"It's different with you and Gabe," Raina said firmly. "You love each other. Lucian and I barely like each other."

Melanie laughed. "Right. You just keep telling yourself that, honey. Who knows, maybe you'll even start to believe it."

At the sound of Kevin's voice calling her from downstairs, Melanie headed for the door. "I've got to get down there before my son and husband decide that a snack before dinner means a piece of cake the size of a Volkswagen. Come down and join us when you're ready."

Raina frowned as she shifted her daughter from one hip to the other. She could resist Lucian Sinclair. She could.

But she *had* felt a moment of weakness in the kitchen. When he'd slid the tip of his finger over her collar down to the button of her shirt. And when he'd brought his mouth to within a whisper of hers. Her skin had felt tight and hot, her breasts had tingled. An image of another time, when he'd kissed her hard and long, when he'd touched her all over, had sprung into her mind. And she'd wanted his mouth on hers, his hands on her body again.

He was right. She had lied. That night had been everything he'd said. They'd denied themselves until they'd exploded with need for each other. It was the most powerful experience of her life, the most incredible.

And the worst of it was, she thought in despair, that it was still there. The building of tension under the surface, threatening to erupt once again if she wasn't careful.

I'll be careful, she resolved, and followed Melanie out of the room. She hesitated at the deep sound of Lucian's voice, realized that he hadn't left. Her pulse skipped.

Very, very careful, she told herself.

With a deep breath she squared her shoulders and moved down the stairs.

It was one thing to tickle and play peekaboo with a baby and quite another to give it a bath and change its diaper.

Sheer panic filled Lucian as he stared down at the squirming, half-naked baby he'd just laid down on the changing table. Good Lord, he'd felt less fear the first time he'd jumped out of an airplane to skydive.

He must have been insane to insist that Raina let him take over after she'd put Emma in the tub for her bath. He'd seen the worry in Raina's eyes, had reassured her he was more than capable. After all, how difficult could it be? he'd thought. He'd seen Cara give Matthew a bath before. She'd made it look easy enough.

About as easy as climbing a greased rope.

He had managed to get one arm into the tiny, white T-shirt, but Emma wouldn't quite cooperate with the second arm. And something was definitely wrong with the diaper he'd put on, though he wasn't sure what.

"Need some help?" Raina asked from behind him.

He glanced over his shoulder at her, saw her watching him from the doorway, a bottle in her hand. Her eyes held a mixture of amusement and concern.

"I got it." He managed to get the second arm in the T-shirt and felt a surge of pride.

"It's on backward," she said, moving closer.

"I know how to put a T-shirt on," he defended. "I do it every day. Tag goes in the back."

"I was talking about the diaper."

"Oh." He glanced down. So *that* was the problem.

"And it really would be easier if you put the T-shirt over her head before you try stuffing her arms in. She has a sweet temperament, but it can only be stretched so far."

There comes a time in every man's life when he has to admit defeat, Lucian thought in resignation. This was definitely one of those times.

"I would have figured it out," he muttered, but stepped to the side and let Raina move beside him.

"Yeah, but ten-year-olds don't wear diapers," she replied sweetly.

"Ha, ha." He blew a shock of hair from his forehead. "I would have had it down pat by age two, no later than three."

He watched Raina's slender fingers move swiftly to repair the damage he'd done with both the diaper and T-shirt. When she reached for the pajamas, he knew he couldn't have managed without reinforcements. Emma would have been traumatized for life if he'd attempted putting that garment on her.

"So she has my personality, does she?" he asked while Raina slipped Emma's foot into the soft fleece sleeper.

She glanced up at him, confused.

"You said she has a sweet temperament."

At his comment Emma pressed her lips together and made a wet, razzing sound, then softly burped.

"Well, there are one or two similarities, I suppose," Raina said with a smirk.

When Emma started to babble, Lucian couldn't hold back a grin. Seemed that he'd been doing a lot of that today, at least every time he looked at his daughter.

His *daughter*.

The words themselves were still foreign to him, but somehow Emma wasn't. He'd stayed for dinner, then he and Emma had spent the evening playing on the living room floor. He'd been around babies before and he'd thought they were pretty cute, but he'd never been mesmerized. Everything that Emma did fascinated him. From reaching for a rattle to trying to sit up by herself, he'd thought the child was brilliant.

"Time for night-night, sweetie." Raina picked Emma up and nuzzled her cheek, then reached for the bottle.

"Will she let me?" Lucian asked.

"I'm not sure. She's never had a man give her a bottle at bedtime before."

Those words gave Lucian tremendous pleasure. He hated the possibility that some guy might have held his daughter this way. It was strange to him that he'd known for fewer than twelve hours that he was a father, yet he already felt extremely possessive of his child.

And his child's mother, as well.

He didn't like the idea that another man would be there at bedtime—Emma's *or* Raina's.

She handed him the baby first, then the bottle. "Sit over here in the rocker."

After a moment of fidgeting on both their sides, Lucian settled into the rocking chair with Emma. Her little hands opened and closed on the bottle, and she made soft, mewling sounds as she happily drank her bedtime formula. All the while, her bright green eyes stayed on him.

Raina shut off the overhead light, then turned on the Winnie the Pooh lamp on the dresser. "She should fall asleep before she finishes the bottle," Raina said quietly as she walked backward toward the door. "Lay her on her back and cover her with the blanket in the crib."

"Raina, stay." Lucian nodded toward a step stool sitting beside the rocker. "Come sit with us. Tell me about Emma."

She hesitated, then moved beside him and sat. "What would you like to know?"

"Everything." He looked down at the baby, saw her eyelids growing heavy. "How much did she weigh? What does she like? Does she sleep through the night? Is she healthy? What do you—"

"Whoa, wait up." Raina put up a hand to stop him. "One question at a time."

With Emma asleep in his arms, they sat there in the dim light while Raina answered each question he asked. He chuckled when she told him how Emma made a face the first time she'd eaten peas, he frowned when he heard that she'd had an allergic reaction to an antibiotic for an ear infection. How he wished he'd been there for all of that, for every first. The first smile, the first laugh, the first bite of food.

Every question she answered, every story she told, made Emma more his than before, made those two words, *his baby,* more of a reality.

By the time he laid her in her crib, with Raina standing beside him, he knew that there was no going back. Emma was his child, his daughter.

She was going to have his name.

Seven

"Hold it. Right there. No, wait, move to your left."

Raina held back the groan hovering deep in her throat and shifted to the left.

"Wait, wait, stop right there. That's it, that's it. Now smile."

She swore she might scream if she heard that word one more time. But she smiled anyway. Whatever it took to get this over with as quickly as possible.

A brand-new father with a brand-new camera was a force to be reckoned with.

Lucian had shown up at Gabe and Melanie's doorstep an hour ago and dragged her and Emma out into the backyard, spread a blanket on the sun-warmed grass with a few of the new baby toys he'd bought over the past two days, then started shooting pictures. He'd gone through at least four rolls of film so far, crawled on his stomach and practically stood on his head while he busily snapped the shutter. There were grass marks on his faded jeans, smudges of dirt on his navy-blue T-shirt and fragments of twigs and spring leaves in his dark hair. And still his enthusiasm had not yet dimmed in the slightest.

Raina might not have minded the impromptu photo shoot so much if Lucian hadn't insisted she be in the pictures, too. She'd tried arguing that it wasn't necessary for her to be included, that dressed in a white cotton tank top and jeans she would look out of place against the pretty pink dress Emma wore. She'd even tried to get him to let her take the pictures, contended that it made more sense for him to be in the photos, not her.

But tenacity seemed to be the man's middle name. He wouldn't let her change her clothes or take even one picture. If there was one thing to be said about Lucian Sinclair, Raina thought, it was his capacity to throw himself completely into whatever it was he set his mind to do.

She respected that attribute as much as she feared it.

In the past two days, since their discussion about marriage, he hadn't once brought the subject up again. He hadn't said anything to her about visitations or schedules or what was going to happen after she and Emma left the day after tomorrow. He'd simply played endlessly with his daughter, asked every conceivable question about her life for the past seven months and even insisted on dressing and bathing her. While part of Raina felt relieved, part of her was suspicious. He was making this easy, Raina thought.

Too easy.

And *that* made her nervous.

"Perfect." Lucian hunkered down at the edge of the blanket, smiled at his daughter while he shook a waggle-eared stuffed dog named Blue. It was one of at least six stuffed animals he'd bought for Emma and it seemed to be her favorite. "Let's get a shot with her holding Blue."

"We did that shot already," Raina informed him dryly. "Five or six times, I believe. We should go in now."

"Why?" He reached for a new roll of film. "Blue skies, a few clouds in the distance, warm breeze. Emma's having a good time. What could be better than this?"

That was the problem. She couldn't think of anything better. And Emma wasn't the only one having a good time, Raina thought. *She* was having a good time, too. And that was a dangerous thing. The more time she spent with Lucian, the harder it was going to be to leave.

The harder it was to keep her hands off him.

He'd been a perfect gentleman with her these past two days, charming and funny, asked questions about the fashion business and exactly what it was that she did. He never mentioned the night they'd made love or asked questions, made no sexual advances toward her or even showed more interest in her than he probably did any other woman.

He confused the hell out of her.

He frustrated the hell out of her.

Every time he got close to her, every innocent brush of their shoulders or hands, turned her insides soft and warm. All he had to do was look at her with those eyes of his, smile at her with that intoxicating Sinclair smile, and her knees went weak.

He grinned at her now, and she was glad that she was sitting with Emma in her lap. That's all it took, just a look, and she was lost.

"What?" she asked a little more sharply than she'd intended.

He sat on the blanket beside her, stretched out those long, muscular legs of his and pulled Emma onto his knees. "I was just wondering if you used to be this difficult when you were posing for all those magazine ads."

She rolled her eyes. "Mister, if you think *I'm* difficult, come backstage to one of my shows sometime. Those girls give new meaning to the word *difficult*. And anyway—" she lifted her hair off her neck, enjoyed the feel of the cool breeze on her warm skin "—that was a long time ago."

"Why did you quit?" Lucian asked. "All that fame and glamour?"

She couldn't help but laugh at that. "Eight hours in a bikini, posing on top of a mountain where it's thirty degrees and the wind is blowing, or six hours in one-hundred-degree heat dressed in heavy hiking gear is about as far from glamorous as you can get."

Smiling, he bounced Emma on his knee and made her laugh. "Melanie said that if you'd stayed with it, the name Raina would have been as recognized as Naomi or Cindy or Christy. She said you were known for 'The Look.'"

"Melanie's my friend. She feels obligated to say that." She glanced away, plucked a small yellow flower from the lawn, then tickled her daughter's cheek with it. "And as far as 'The Look' goes, my entire career was based on three of them."

"Yeah?" He gathered Emma into his lap and picked up his camera. "Let me see them."

"Oh, no." She put out a hand and shook her head.

"Tell Mommy I'll stop taking pictures if she co-operates," Lucian said to Emma.

"Promise?"

"Promise."

"All right, then, here goes. This is the 'Who, me?' look. I just imagine I've won the lottery." She cocked her head, lifted her brows and pursed her lips in surprise. Lucian snapped the pose, then she stared blankly into the camera. "This is the 'I don't have a thought in my brain' look. I just think of what's inside a balloon."

He laughed as he snapped another picture. Emma stuck a rattle in her mouth and cooed.

"And this is the 'Come take me, I'm yours,' look." She dipped her head, glanced upward as she parted her lips. "I imagine I'm about to be kissed by—"

You.

He glanced over his camera at her. "By who?"

She felt her cheeks flush. "Ah…Harry Connick Jr."

"Harry Connick Jr.?" He looked at her doubtfully.

She nodded. "I'm crazy about Harry."

Shaking his head, he raised his camera again. "Don't move."

Her gaze drifted to Lucian's mouth, and she couldn't help but remember what wonderful things he could do with that mouth. The breeze skimmed over her warm skin; the sweet scent of spring hyacinths filled the air. And all she could think was how much she wanted to touch his lips with her own, felt herself leaning toward him....

"Hello. Anybody out here?"

Raina jumped at the sound of Melanie's voice from the back porch. She and Gabe had left for a doctor's appointment before Lucian had showed up at the house this morning. Apparently, they had returned.

"Out here," Lucian called, then turned and took a picture of Gabe and Melanie as they crossed the lawn.

Gabe scooped Emma up into his arms. Emma squealed with pleasure, and Lucian took another shot.

"Uh-oh." Melanie looked at the camera. "Looks like somebody bought himself a toy today."

"How was your appointment?" Raina asked.

"The doctor said everything's fine." Melanie smoothed her hands lovingly over her belly and smiled. "Won't be too much longer."

"Don't see how it could be," Gabe said. "If she gets any bigger, I'm going to have to widen the doorways."

"Why do you think I married you?" Melanie cocked her head and looked at her husband. "A woman never knows when she'll need a good carpenter or mechanic. Since Bill at the garage was already married, that left me with you."

"And here I thought you married me for my good looks and sense of humor," Gabe said with a wounded-puppy-dog look.

"Shoot, she would have married *me* if she wanted those things," Lucian quipped, then snapped another picture when Gabe glared at him.

"Come on, cutie-pie." Melanie enticed the baby from Gabe and headed for the house. "Emma and I are hungry, aren't we?"

"I think there's a side of beef in the outside freezer," Gabe teased as he followed his wife, then played innocent when Melanie shot him a look over her shoulder. Shaking her head, Raina started to rise.

"Wait." Lucian took hold of her arm once Gabe and Melanie were out of earshot.

"You promised no more pictures," she said firmly.

"I want to talk to you."

Her pulse picked up speed. She glanced down at his hand on her arm, felt the sizzle of his touch all the way to her toes. "About?"

"You know."

All morning there'd been a playfulness in his eyes and manner. But not now. Now his eyes were intent, his manner somber.

"All right." She settled back. "Go ahead."

"Not here, Raina." He kept those forest-green eyes on her. "We need to go someplace where we can be alone."

Lucian parked his truck and came around to open the door for Raina. He knew she was nervous, though he wasn't certain if she was worried about having a conversation about Emma, or if she was worried about being alone with him.

He suspected it was both.

She'd been quiet on the short drive from Gabe and Melanie's but hadn't asked him where they were going. She'd simply sat opposite him, her shoulders stiff and back rigid as she stared straight ahead, no doubt preparing herself for what she assumed would be the worst.

"Maybe I should call Melanie," Raina said when he opened the truck door. "Just to make sure she got Emma down for her nap all right."

"Emma's fine, Raina. And Gabe's there for the rest of the afternoon, too. So stop worrying."

The furrow on her brow gave way to surprise when she stepped out of the truck and looked up at the framed house. She glanced at him with questioning eyes.

He shrugged. "It's sort of a hobby."

"It's yours?"

"Mine and the bank's, but mostly mine. It doesn't look like much yet, but I'm almost finished with the framing." He took her arm. "Come on, I'll give you the nickel tour."

He'd designed the house himself, a mixture of contemporary and ranch-style, with raised front and back porches and double-wide entry doors that hadn't been set yet. He'd picked them out, though. A pair of oak beauties with beveled glass.

"I'm in between projects now with my company," he said as they moved up the front steps. "I'll get the drywall and windows in next."

"Is that how you work on it? A little here and there when you have the time?"

"Something like that." He paused at the open entry. "After you, madam."

She strolled inside, the sound of her low heels on the bare wooden floors echoing in the cavernous entry and living room. Her jaw went slack. "This is *huge*."

"Four thousand square feet." He grinned at her

sheepishly. "I got a little carried away with the plans."

She moved from the entry to the living room, shaking her head in awe, then went into the kitchen. He watched her face transform into a look of reverence.

"Oh, Lucian." She gasped, hurried to the empty frame where the window above the kitchen sink would be installed, then gasped again. "The view is incredible."

"It is, isn't it?" he said without modesty and came to stand beside her. "The living room, kitchen and master bedroom all have the same view of the woods."

A chilly wind suddenly swept through the open window, lifting the ends of her hair. Outside, thick, puffy clouds surrounded the midday sun. He watched her shiver, then rub her arms as she turned to look at him. "It's beautiful."

You're beautiful, he wanted to say, but knew better. She'd finally let down that carefully guarded wall she'd been hiding behind for the past few days, and he didn't want to spoil the moment. Right now she was looking at him with such pleasure and delight that he felt his chest tighten with need. He wanted desperately to take her in his arms, right here, with the wind in her hair and a chill on her mouth. Wanted to kiss that chill away, to hear his name on her lips and to feel her hands on his skin.

Instead, he jammed his hands into his jeans and just smiled. "Thanks. It's a work in progress, but I'm getting there." He frowned when she shivered again. "We can leave if you're too cold."

She shook her head. "I'm fine. And besides, you

promised the nickel tour, remember? I've still got about three cents left, I'd say.''

He showed her the rest of the downstairs, which included a game room, a room that would be an office and a guest bathroom. Upstairs, there were two more bedrooms with full baths, a loft, plus the master bedroom and bath.

He couldn't help but feel pride as he watched her ooh and ahh over a design feature or compliment him on the work he'd done. Other than the female members of his family, he'd never brought a woman here before. He'd always kept this part of his life separate from the women he'd dated. Raina was the first.

In more than one way, he realized, and the thought sobered him.

He'd spent the past two days with Emma, played with her, actually learned how to change a diaper that stayed put, feed her cereal and bottles and given her a bath. He had no words to describe the feeling in his chest every time he looked at his daughter, but he knew what it was. For the first time in his life, he felt something that went as deep as a feeling can go. Something that quite literally took his breath away, something that scared the hell out of him but made him feel warm and full at the same time.

He loved Emma. Loved her as much as if he'd been there every day with her since she'd been born. He'd missed out on so much already, he didn't want to miss even one more day. He wanted to be a part of her life.

He wanted her to have his name.

He'd given Raina space these past two days, but the clock was quickly ticking the minutes away before they would be back on a plane to New York. He'd spent the past two nights pacing in frustration, wracking his brain for a solution.

He couldn't let them leave, dammit. He *couldn't*.

Because he didn't just want Emma. He wanted Emma's mother, too.

He watched her inspect the large walk-in closet in the master bedroom, heard her squeak of approval over size. So what if it wasn't a conventional marriage? he thought. People married and lived together for reasons other than love. They liked each other— at least, most of the time, anyway. And there was no question they were physically attracted to each other, in spite of Raina's denial. So maybe he hadn't planned on settling down and doing the picket fence, forever thing. He had Emma to think about now. What was important now was what was good for her.

Thunder rattled the open eaves overhead and snapped him out of his wandering thoughts. Rain began to tap on the roof.

"Uh-oh." He took her hand and pulled her from the closet, then headed down the stairs. "We'd better get out of here."

By the time they hit the porch downstairs, the sky had opened up. They were halfway down the porch steps when Lucian heard the sound.

Damn.

"What is it?" she asked over a rumble of thunder.

Shaking his head, he pulled her back up onto the porch, under the eaves. "Stay there for a moment."

While she waited on the porch, he knelt down in the wet dirt and looked under the steps. Water was running underneath.

"Lucian, what is it?"

"There's a litter of kittens under the front porch," he called back. "The mother is wild and won't let me near, but I leave food out, so—hey, wait."

Before he could stop her, she was already down on her hands and knees beside him in the pouring rain. "I see the babies," she said excitedly, "but there's water dripping on them."

"She'll never come out," he yelled over a new crash of thunder. "I'll be right back."

He ran and grabbed a tarp that covered a large stack of concrete mix. He knew every bag would be ruined, but what the hell. So he'd buy more. He was back in one minute, had the steps covered in two.

"Okay." She waved a hand, then stood and grinned at him. "They're dry now."

Shaking his head, he grabbed her hand. They were both muddy and wet, and he knew Raina had to be freezing. "Let's get out of here."

He dragged her behind him about thirty yards through the woods, and they dashed to the thirty-two-foot trailer he'd parked on the property. It wasn't luxurious, but it could hardly be called roughing it, either.

They were both soaked through by the time they ran up the steps, then fell, laughing and gasping, through the door.

"Hold on." He left her shivering and dripping on the small tiled entry, grabbed a towel from a closet and was back in two seconds.

He dropped the towel over her head and scrubbed at her wet hair, then wrapped it around her shoulders.

"That was extremely heroic, Mr. Sinclair." She

wiped at her face. "Who would have guessed you have a soft spot not only for babies, but kittens, too?"

"Don't tell anyone." He raked his soaked hair back from his face. "I do have an image to maintain, you know."

"Ah, yes, your image," she said with a grin, then wiped at his face with the towel. "Tough guy."

Her cheeks were flushed from the run, her eyes bright and sparkling. Her smile faded as their eyes met; her hand stilled.

The towel dropped from her fingers, then cautiously she reached out and touched his cheek with her hand.

His heart slammed in his chest when her gaze dropped to his mouth, and she slowly closed the distance between them.

"Lucian…"

Eight

This is crazy, Raina told herself. Pure insanity mixed with foolishness.

And she just didn't give a damn.

The feel of his cheek under her fingertips was wet but warm, with a slight stubble of beard. They'd brought the scent of the rain in with them, but the storm pounding over their heads on the trailer roof was nothing compared to the storm that pounded inside her body.

"Lucian." She whispered his name again. Water dripped from his hair down his face. When she swept her thumb lightly over his lips to brush the raindrops away, she felt his jaw tighten.

His hand, rough and calloused, closed over her fingers; a glint, something primitive and dangerous and intensely sensual, shone in his narrowed eyes.

"I know this is, that we—"

His mouth slammed against hers, hard and demanding. In one swift move he forced her backward, pinning her body between his and the closed door. Flames of heat licked at her skin and raced through her blood. She clung to him, was certain her knees wouldn't hold her up if she didn't. She tasted the storm on his lips, his tongue, met every thrust of heat with her own.

Fire and rain, she thought, as dazed as she was aroused at the feel of his greedy lips on hers. A tiny voice of reason whispered from somewhere in the back of her mind, but she ignored it. What was happening between her and Lucian had nothing to do with reason. Nothing at all.

This was about pleasure. About a need so strong, so deep, it refused to be denied.

As it had been the first time, she thought. And every time after.

As it was now.

She pressed closer to him, felt the solid wall of his muscled chest, his broad shoulders, the force of his mouth on hers.

The hard proof of his own need for her.

Everything sent her senses spinning, excited her as only Lucian could. He was the only man who had ever made her feel this way, made her completely lose control, released a passion inside her that she'd never known existed.

A moment of despair filled her as she realized that he was the only man who *could* bring her to this, that even if he didn't love her, he would still be the only man.

Then he cupped her buttocks and lifted her against him, fitted her rain-drenched body to his, and she had no more thoughts other than him.

"Raina." He yanked his mouth from hers, dragged his lips across her jaw, then down her throat. "Tell me you want me as much as I do you."

Because she couldn't find her breath, she simply moaned and pressed closer.

He held back, brought his face up to look into her eyes. "You need to say it. I need to hear you say you want me."

She stared at him in bewilderment. How could he question such a thing? Maybe she hadn't come out and said it, but she was the one who'd instigated this, the one who'd practically begged him to take her.

"Say it," he repeated, his voice husky and strained. "I need you to say it."

"I want you, Lucian." She took his face in her hands. "You know I've wanted you from the first time I saw you."

He stared at her, his eyes the color of the woods outside. She felt a moment of fear, a fear of entering the uncertainty of that dark, deep forest, certain that she'd be lost there forever.

But it was too late to turn back, she knew. She was already hopelessly lost.

Once again she brought her mouth to his, gently this time, kissed him as she'd never kissed another man. With her lips, her heart, her soul.

The heat built again; every brush of her lips, every tiny nip of teeth, every soft, delicate slide of her tongue against his, stoked the flames of desire. The need grew restless, rattled at the lock of its cage and screamed to be released.

"Raina." His incredible, magical mouth moved down her neck again, teasing, tasting. "Wrap your legs around me."

She did, then groaned at the fire-hot feel of his lips nibbling below her earlobe. This was everything she'd remembered, everything she'd dreamed about since that night so long ago.

Everything and more.

"Put your head on my shoulder," he whispered as he tightly circled her with his arms and carried her. The ceiling was low, and when he moved toward a small bedroom to the right, he had to duck his head to clear the doorway.

He stood at the foot of his bed, still holding her, both of them oblivious to their rain-soaked clothes and hair. She grasped his head in her hands, brought her lips to his, not gently this time, but ruthlessly.

His tongue mated, swirled with hers; his strong arms held her. Struggling for breath, she pulled back, met his moss-green gaze with her own as she dragged her wet tank top over her head and tossed it down on the floor at the foot of the bed. A fierce, feral look glinted in his eyes as he looked at her.

And then he feasted.

His mouth closed over the tip of her breast, nipped through damp, white lace, then suckled. She gasped at the arrow of pleasure that shot through her.

While his mouth and teeth worked magic on her, she clasped his head and brought him closer still, raked her fingers through his scalp as she bit her lip to keep from crying out.

"Take this off," he murmured.

Her fingers shook as she unsnapped the front catch of her bra. His mouth was on her bare flesh before she could slip the straps from her shoulders; his tongue found her pebbled nipple even as the lace garment dropped to the floor. White-hot pleasure rippled through her body as he kneaded and caressed her breast with his mouth, his lips, his teeth.

And his tongue...oh, heavens...what he was doing to her.

He blazed kisses over the swell of one breast to the other. Again and again he assaulted her senses: flames of heat licked her body; cold shimmered over her still-damp skin; blood pounded in her temples and drowned out everything but the sound of her own soft cries and the sudden crash of thunder.

"Was that outside or in here?" she asked raggedly.

He chuckled, then whispered, "Put your arms around me and hang on."

She did, and his mouth caught her gasp as they fell backward onto the bed with her on top of him. Another clap of thunder shook the trailer and they rolled with it, clung to each other as the storm raged on.

"Your shirt." She was already tugging at the damp fabric. He yanked it off.

Shoes came next; they both alternately swore and laughed in the struggle to remove wet jeans.

And then they were bare skin to bare skin, mouth to mouth. The urgency built within even as the storm raged outside. Her body throbbed with need, a sweet ache that coiled tightly between her legs, increasing with every stroke of his hand, every brush of his lips, every nip of his teeth.

There was nothing gentle about his touch. He plundered and ravaged, and all she could think was *more.*

"Wait." His voice was raw as he jerked his mouth from hers. He rolled away for what felt like a lifetime, but it was only a few seconds. When he turned back to her, he dragged her close, then pulled her underneath him.

The storm was in his eyes now, a wild, crashing, deep-green sea of passion. She arched toward him, gave herself up to the waves, felt herself rising up with the crest.

"You're beautiful," he murmured as he gazed down at her, knew that the words sounded trite. He knew that she'd heard them hundreds of times. When she reached for him, he shook his head in frustration.

He wanted her to know, to understand, that she was special. That *this* was special.

"I'll always remember you like this," he said. "No matter what happens, I'll always remember."

Her eyes, glazed with desire, held his. She smiled softly. "So will I," she whispered. "So will I."

He linked hands with her then, raised her arms over her head, entered her slowly. Her lips parted, her eyes closed while her breasts rose and fell sharply.

When at last he was deep inside her, she whimpered softly and moved her hips upward.

"Lucian," she gasped his name. "Please."

With their hands still intertwined, he started to move. She murmured encouragement, a disjointed mix of pleasure and soft moans. Her head rolled from side to side, her body bowed.

"Let me touch you." Her voice was urgent, demanding. "I need to touch you."

He released her and she reached for him, scraped her fingernails over his shoulders as her arms hauled him closer. Her lips sought his and took possession of his mouth. When he slid his hands down to her hips and gripped her tightly to him, a soft moan rose from deep in her throat. His heart beat as wild and fierce as the storm that was now overhead.

"Open your eyes." He dragged his mouth from hers. "Look at me."

Her eyelids slowly fluttered open and through a thick haze of desire, she met his gaze.

"Lucian." His name was a breathless whisper of need on her kiss-swollen lips. "Lucian," she repeated. "Now, please."

Her soft plea nearly sent him to the edge, but still he held back. His skin was no longer damp from the rain, but from sweat as he struggled to prolong the intense sensations exploding in his body. Sensations that increased with every thrust of his hips, with every sweep of her restless hands.

Blinding need drove him on, until, like that first distant sound of thunder, he felt the shudder roll from her body into his. Crying out, she clutched at him. He shuddered with her, bodies entwined, and they tumbled over the edge together.

The rain settled to a soft drumming on the trailer roof. Under the comfort of a blue cotton blanket, Raina nestled in the crook of Lucian's arm, her head on his shoulder while she stroked the hard planes and angles of his chest. Lost in thought and the quiet aftermath of their tumultuous lovemaking, neither one of them had spoken.

For the first time since they'd tumbled into the trailer, Raina glanced around the small bedroom. It was tidy but sparse, with a built-in nightstand on one side of the king-size bed and a small, dark pine dresser on the other side with a stack of books and a baseball sitting on top. A navy-blue valance trimmed the narrow windows and multicolored throw rugs covered pale-blue carpeting. Through the doorway, into the living section of the trailer, past a narrow kitchen and eating area, was a small dark-blue couch and more built-in cupboards. She assumed the bathroom was the closed door next to the bedroom.

A sharp contrast to the spectacular house he was building, but cozy. Very cozy, she thought, and burrowed into the warmth of his arm.

He broke the silence first.

"Was that how it was before?" His voice was rough, edged with amazement.

After she'd told Lucian about Emma, Raina had known that questions about that first night would eventually come up. She'd dreaded having this discussion. Until now. Now it simply seemed natural.

She rose on her elbow, cradled her head in her hand while she made circles on his chest with her fingertips. "Before?"

"Don't be coy, sweetheart." He frowned at her, but there was amusement in his eyes. "You know exactly what I mean."

"Yes." The dark sprinkling of hair of his chest tickled her fingers. "That's exactly how it was."

He lifted both brows and blew out a breath. "Wow."

"Yeah." She smiled, would have purred if she were a cat. "Wow."

"Raina." His hand covered hers. "I'm sorry I wasn't there. When you woke up, I mean. I don't know why I left like I did, I may never know, but I'm sure I would have come back. The note proves that."

"It happened, Lucian," she said with a sigh. "We can't change it. Even if I could, I wouldn't. Every time I look at Emma, I'm so thankful for what that night gave me. Speaking of—" she sat and looked for a phone "—I need to call Melanie."

He reached beside the bed and came up with a cell phone that he'd been charging in the wall socket. He dialed for her, then handed her the phone. Melanie answered on the first ring.

"Mel, I'm so sorry," Raina said into the phone, tried not to notice that Lucian's hand had slipped back under the covers. "We got caught out in the open in the storm." She sucked in a breath when he found the curve of her breast. "*Yes,* I mean, yes, of course, we're fine. I was worried about Emma. Did the thunder wake her? Oh, good, I'm so glad."

He nipped at her neck, nibbled on her earlobe, all while his hand caressed and kneaded. Raina struggled to find her voice. "Oh, they are? Well, we…should be there…soon." She bit back a moan when his hand moved lower. "Very soon, I'm sure."

The texture of his rough hand sliding over her belly sent shivers of intense pleasure racing through her. She hadn't even hung up the phone before he slipped into her, stroking her gently…surely. Sparks danced and shimmered over her skin, and when his mouth blazed hot, wet kisses down her neck and continued south, the sparks ignited into fire.

"What did Melanie say?" he murmured.

"She—" Words bounced in her brain and she fought to grab them. "Emma's fine. Sydney and—" she gripped a handful of the soft comforter when his mouth closed over her hardened nipple "—Abby came over to visit for a while. Melanie said—" she arched upward as his hand and mouth seemed to move with the same rhythm "—to take our time."

He moved over her suddenly, a dark, primal look in his eyes as he pulled her underneath him and slid his hands up her thighs. "Is that what you want to do?" he asked roughly. "Take our time?"

"No," she gasped, and reached for him.

And there it was again. The fury. The raw, naked need. It moved through them like a tornado, uncontrollable and wild, as spectacular as it was thrilling.

They let it take them until, breathless and shattered, they collapsed in each other's arms.

"So this is where you live."

"Most of the time." Lucian pulled a jar of instant coffee from the cupboard beside his small stove and set it on the counter, then reached into a drawer for a spoon. Raina sat at the kitchen table behind him, her legs tucked under her. He'd put on dry clothes and given her a white button-down shirt of his to wear, but she'd had to struggle back into her damp jeans. At least the storm had moved on, and the mid-afternoon sun peeked through the parting clouds.

"When I'm working on a big construction project

I sleep in the trailer on the site,'' he said. ''But this is my home base.''

''Quite a place.''

He glanced over his shoulder to see if there was any sarcasm in her eyes, but there wasn't. She seemed genuinely interested and charmed by his humble abode. Her hair had dried and now fell in a tumbled mass of dark curls around her shoulders. At the sight of her sitting here, wearing his shirt, with her hair mussed and lips still swollen and rosy from his kisses, he felt something hitch in his chest.

''I get by.'' At the insistent beep of the microwave, he opened the door, pulled out two steaming mugs and dumped two spoonfuls of coffee in each one.

''Microwave, TV, electricity and plumbing,'' she said with a smile. ''I'd say you get by just fine.''

He set the mugs on the table and slid into the booth across from her. Damn, but she was beautiful, he thought, felt his gut tighten at the sight of her blowing on her coffee. Once again he cursed the fact that he couldn't remember the night they'd spent together. His mind and his body still reeled from their short afternoon of lovemaking, and he couldn't help but wonder what an entire night had been like. What it would *be* like.

He wanted to know. One afternoon with this woman wasn't enough.

He wanted more.

As if she read his thoughts, their eyes met. Her smile slowly faded and she looked down at her cup.

He reached for her hand and pulled it toward him. Lightly he traced her knuckles with his thumb, marveled at how soft her skin felt.

"Raina, I think we should get married."

"Why, Lucian?" she asked quietly. "Because we're good in bed together?"

"No." His hand tightened on hers, then he relaxed. "But that doesn't hurt, you know."

She pulled her hand away. "It's no reason to get married."

"Emma's a good reason."

"We've covered that ground already," she said evenly. "I told you that I won't ever keep Emma from you. She'll know who her father is. You can see her whenever you like."

"In New York?" He bit back the crude word that was on the tip of his tongue. "On holidays and vacations? A weekend here and there when it suits you? I want more than that, dammit."

"What are you saying? That you want joint custody?" The look in her eyes turned icy blue. "You think our daughter should live here? In this trailer, with God knows how many women coming through that revolving door of your bedroom?"

He went still at her comment, felt the anger ripple through him. He struggled to gain control, then slowly, carefully said, "I have never brought a woman here before. And I most certainly never would while my daughter was under the same roof. And since you brought up the subject, what about you? How do I know who'll be sleeping in your bed while my daughter's in the next room?"

Just the thought of it turned his anger white-hot, made his gut tighten. What would happen once she was back in New York?

He didn't want to think about it, dammit. He

couldn't. Not without yelling or slamming his fist into a wall.

"I deserve that." She closed her eyes, sighed heavily. "But I have to ask, Lucian. If Emma is going to come here for visits, especially when she comes without me, I have to know."

He took in a slow breath, waited a moment for the anger to dissipate. "I wasn't suggesting joint custody," he said evenly. "I don't believe in shuffling a kid back and forth between households. As much as I'd want to be with her, I wouldn't do that to her."

"I know you wouldn't." Her shoulders relaxed a bit. "I've watched you these past few days. You're terrific with her. She already adores you."

"Then marry me and let me give her my name." He leaned forward. "It could be temporary. For a year or two. When she's old enough to understand, she'll at least think that we cared enough about her to give it a try."

"And you think a divorce will make her feel better that her parents aren't together?" She shook her head. "Lucian, I married once for the wrong reasons. I can't ever do that again."

"And what if you do decide to get married again?" The idea made his blood turn hot. "What then? What rights will I have?"

"Nothing would change between you and Emma if I get married. She'll always be your daughter."

"See that you remember that. Because I'm always going to be in her life, Raina. Always. And that means I'll be in your life, too. Accept it."

"You might be in my life, Lucian," she said tightly. "But that doesn't mean you'll be in my bed every time you get the itch. That *you* had better accept. If you want a formal agreement between us, one of us can contact a lawyer to handle the paperwork.''

''I don't want a damn lawyer.'' It was all he could do not to shake her. ''I want to see Emma when *I* want. Not when some damn piece of paper says.''

''All right.'' She drew in a slow breath. ''You can come to New York as often as you want, and I'll come to Bloomfield at least every other month. As she gets older, we'll increase the length of time she can stay here. When she starts school, we'll discuss vacations and holidays. Now I have to get back.'' She slid out of the booth and pulled her shoes on. ''I've already been gone too long, and Emma will be up from her nap by now.''

Damn stubborn woman, he thought as he followed her out of the trailer. By the rigid set of her back and shoulders, he knew there'd be no more discussion for now. Which was probably for the best, since he also knew he would have started yelling if they had continued.

She climbed into the truck before he could help her, which only aggravated him all the more. He kept his hands tightly on the wheel and his jaw clenched on the ride home. She kept her arms folded and her eyes straight ahead. He snapped a Nirvana tape into the dash player and turned it up, effectively blocking out any chance of conversation.

When he parked in front of Gabe's house, she unhooked her seat belt and slid out of the truck. She was already on the front porch by the time he'd shut off the engine and caught up with her. Dammit, they hadn't even talked about money or medical insurance

Nine

Raina had always hated hospitals. The smell of antiseptic, the hushed tones, the stark, dimly lit halls and rooms. She'd only been eighteen the two weeks she'd spent at The City of Hope in Los Angeles, watching and waiting while her mother slowly gave in to the cancer. She'd tried to locate her father, but he'd moved away her freshman year of high school and she'd had no idea where he'd gone. She still had no idea. After she'd buried her mother, she'd gone off to college on a scholarship and modeled part-time and she'd never looked back.

Except for Melanie. Until Emma, Melanie had been her only family. And now Melanie was in the hospital.

Trembling with the cold fear that wracked her body, Raina sat stiffly on the waiting room chair, her eyes squeezed shut. The cold was suddenly replaced by a warm, strong arm that gently pulled her close.

"Raina—" she heard Lucian say her name "—she's going to be fine. They're both fine."

Still numb, she glanced up, turned toward him as she gripped the front of his denim jacket. "Melanie? And the baby, too?"

"Melanie's still groggy from the cesarean, but everything went well. And based on the way my new niece is hollering, I'd say she's more than fine."

"Oh, thank God, thank God." She couldn't stop the tears of relief. "A girl. A little girl. Are you sure she's all right?"

"All the tests came out perfect." He grinned at her. "If you have to worry about anyone, worry about Gabe. He looks like hell."

She laughed, let herself enjoy the comfort of his arms. "What happened?"

He shook his head. "Gabe's still a little dazed, but from what I could gather, it's something called an abruption. It could have been serious, but in her case, because it wasn't severe and he got her to the hospital so quickly, they were able to do a C-section before it became critical."

"I was so scared." She shuddered, pressed her face into his chest. "So incredibly scared."

"It's all right now, baby," he murmured and pulled her closer. "Everyone's fine. You have to come see my new niece. She's tiny and pink and beautiful. They named her Kayla."

"Kayla." She smiled, knew that Melanie and Gabe had already picked that name if they'd had a girl, and

Kyle if they'd had a boy. "We have to call Abby and Sydney. They must be worried sick."

"Callan already took care of that." He stroked her hair away from her face. "Stop worrying."

Sydney had gone to pick Kevin up from school and bring him back to the house and Abby had stayed with Emma. Cara and Ian were on their way from Philadelphia and Reese and Callan had shown up a few minutes ago, then gone to check on Gabe.

It amazed Raina how quickly everyone had pulled together for Melanie. Without question, there wasn't one Sinclair who wouldn't go the distance for a family member. Emma would be a part of that, Raina realized with a swell of joy. No matter what happened, every Sinclair would be there for Lucian's daughter. The bond between them all was as strong as it was fierce. Emma would always be loved unconditionally, and she would always be protected because she was a Sinclair.

A Sinclair.

In a heartbeat it became as sharp and as clear as cut crystal. She knew what she had to do. She couldn't think about herself anymore. What she wanted or needed didn't matter. Raina knew she had to think of Emma.

She straightened, drew in a deep breath as she looked into eyes that made her think of black emeralds.

"Lucian—" she surprised herself at how strong her voice sounded "—if you still want to get married, my answer is yes."

* * *

"Lucian, I swear, you clench that jaw of yours any tighter, you're gonna break a tooth."

Arms folded high on his chest, Lucian frowned darkly at Reese. "If you don't wipe that smirk off your face, bro, I'm gonna break one of *your* teeth."

"Sounds like someone's a little testy today." Callan pushed away from the porch railing and moved beside Reese. It was a beautiful spring afternoon. Clear, blue sky. Warm. The scent of roses drifted in the air.

"'Course, it being your wedding day," Reese said, "we'll forgive you."

Lucian had known it was coming, of course. The jokes and wisecracks. But that didn't mean he had to like it. Lord knew, he'd thrown more than a few well-placed digs at each of his brothers on their wedding day.

Payback was hell.

Pulling at the gray silk tie choking his neck, he took a threatening step toward his brothers. "Yeah, well, I've got your forgive—"

"Now, now, boys," Ian reprimanded in a school-teacher tone as he stepped from the house onto the front porch. "Your 'plays well with others' column is about to get a very low mark."

"Just what I need," Lucian said dryly. "Larry, Moe and Curly. What the hell is taking so long in there? We were supposed to start ten minutes ago."

"Five minutes ago, actually." Grinning, Ian slapped a hand on the groom's shoulder. "But, after catching a glimpse of your bride, I understand your impatience."

His bride.

Lucian felt his throat turn to dust; his chest squeezed the air out of his lungs. Dear Lord, he was actually getting *married.*

He wanted to. More than anything, he wanted Emma to legally have his name. Wanted her to know that she was completely accepted, not only by him, but by all the Sinclairs.

But was Emma the only one he truly wanted to have his name? he wondered.

He knew why Raina had changed her mind about marrying him four days ago and why she had re-scheduled her flight back to New York. The scare with Melanie and little Kayla had sent Raina's emotions into an upheaval. He'd felt it, too. He realized at that moment that being a parent, being responsible for another life, forced a person to face their own mortality. That realization had staggered him. Humbled him.

Empowered him.

He knew there was nothing he couldn't do, nothing he wouldn't do for his child.

Tomorrow Raina was taking Emma and going back to New York. They'd agreed he could visit anytime he wanted, and she'd assured him that she would come to Bloomfield as often as her business allowed.

It wasn't enough. It wasn't even close to being enough. But for now, at least, he knew it would have to do.

He blinked. The Three Stooges were staring at him, and he realized he'd been completely lost in his thoughts. ''What?'' he snapped, annoyed at the amusement on their faces.

"They just gave us the sign." Ian swept a hand toward the front door. "After you."

"Raina, for heaven's sake, stop fidgeting," Melanie said from the cushioned easy chair in her and Gabe's bedroom. Nestled in her mother's arms, baby Kayla slept peacefully in her pink romper. "And don't bite that fingernail, either. You'll mess up your lipstick and your nail polish."

"I'm not fidgeting." Raina jerked her finger away from her mouth and clasped her hands tightly in front of her. "I'm just anxious to get this over with, that's all."

"Spoken like a true bride. Here we go now." Sydney pulled up the zipper of the cream silk sheath dress Raina had on, then held up the matching short jacket. "This is perfect."

Raina slipped her arms into the jacket and smoothed the front. It was the same dress she'd worn at Emma's christening, and she'd had Teresa ship it to her overnight from New York. It had only been delivered three hours ago, which had put all the other women in near heart failure. Especially when Raina had pulled out a black dress she'd brought with her and told them she'd wear that instead. She'd been teasing—sort of—but even Raina had to admit she'd been relieved when the delivery man rang the doorbell.

"Oh, Raina, you look beautiful." Abby shifted Emma from one arm to the other. "Doesn't your mommy look pretty, sweetheart?"

Emma cooed approvingly, and all the women laughed.

Warmed by the compliment, and the other women's enthusiasm, Raina couldn't help but smile, too. In spite of the fact that it wasn't a real wedding or a real marriage, she'd wanted to look nice. Wanted to remember this as a special day.

All heads turned at the quiet knock at the door, and Cara slipped in, her cheeks flushed with excitement.

"The minister just got here," Cara said, then gasped. "Oh, Raina, you look stunning."

"I can't wait until Lucian sees her." Sydney straightened Raina's collar. "That man's jaw is going to hit the ground."

Just the mention of his name had her stomach doing backflips. Sudden overwhelming panic gripped her.

She hadn't wanted all this fuss. A justice of the peace would have been fine. But once word had spread in the family that Lucian was getting married, there'd been no stopping the Sinclair women. Lucian had gone along with it, and even Melanie, her best friend, had been a part of the conspiracy. So now there were twenty or so guests downstairs, people she didn't know. Friends and co-workers of Lucian's. A minister. All waiting for a wedding.

All waiting for her.

She couldn't breathe.

"Uh-oh." Sydney guided her toward the bed and eased her on to the edge. "Just put your head down, honey, and take slow, easy breaths."

"I...I'm sorry," she gasped between breaths. "This is...so unfair to you all. You shouldn't...have gone to...so much trouble. It's not...we're not—"

She dropped her face in her hands. She couldn't pretend, couldn't continue with this farce.

"We're only getting married for Emma," she whispered hoarsely and lifted her head in anguish. "Lucian and I don't love each other like all of you love your husbands."

The women all exchanged a knowing look, then smiled with patient understanding.

Cara took Raina's hand and squeezed. "It's perfectly normal to be nervous on your wedding day. I broke out in hives the morning of mine."

"But we don't love each other," Raina insisted. "Melanie knows it's true. You've all been so wonderful to me, I don't want to lie to you. We aren't going to live together, and in a year or two we're going to get divorced."

Sydney sat beside her and slipped an arm around her. "Well then, I guess we better enjoy the time we're sisters-in-law, shouldn't we?"

Emma babbled happily when Abby sat down on the bed next to Raina and slipped an arm around her, too. At the unexpected display of affection, Raina couldn't stop the tears.

"Hey, what about me?" Melanie complained. "I'm stuck over here."

Laughing, the women hurried over to Melanie and, careful not to disturb the sleeping baby, they all gently hugged.

"Tissue," Abby managed on a sob and reached for the box sitting on the dresser.

A knock at the door had them all turning.

"Hey," Gabe called from the hallway. "Lucian's

just about worn a hole in the rug downstairs. You ladies ready?''

Eyes wide, Raina shook her head.

''One more minute,'' Sydney called back and they all scrambled, pulling on high heels and dabbing at makeup.

''Something old.'' Melanie reached in her pocket and pulled out an antique tortoiseshell hair clip.

''Something new.'' Abby pressed a white lace handkerchief in Raina's hand.

''Something borrowed.'' Sydney clasped a beautiful pearl choker around Raina's neck.

''Something blue.'' Smiling, Cara swung a blue-and-white lace garter around her finger and before Raina could refuse, it was already on her leg.

Sydney moved to the door and opened it. Gabe stood on the other side with Kevin, who pulled at the collar of the starched white shirt under his suit.

Gabe's eyes went to his wife first, softened at the sight of her with their baby, then he glanced at Raina and winked.

Her eyes darted frantically around the room.

''Quick, close the window before she jumps out,'' Melanie teased.

Laughing, Gabe scooped up his wife and child in his arms. It would be at least two weeks, he'd flatly informed her when he'd brought her home from the hospital, before she would be walking up or down any stairs. ''Ready?''

No!

Abby and Sydney flanked her and led her to the top of the stairs. At the sound of the music, Raina tried to take a step back, but they gently held her in place. Sydney pressed a bouquet of white roses into her hands and kissed her cheek.

At the sound of the wedding march, she swallowed hard, then slowly, step by step, made her way down the stairs on legs that felt like wood.

And then there were no more steps.

Her eyes met his as she walked into the living room, between the white folding chairs and down the makeshift aisle. Toward him. She no longer heard the music, no longer saw the people surrounding her.

There was only Lucian.

His suit was deep charcoal, his silk tie dark gray against a soft gray shirt. She remembered the first time she'd laid eyes on him, the way her knees had turned to water and her insides to warm taffy. It was no different now, and she had to force herself to concentrate, to put one foot in front of the other and hold her head straight, or she'd make a fool of herself for certain.

More of a fool than she already had, anyway.

He watched her with those sharp, piercing, green eyes of his, took in every detail from head to toe, then back up again. A slow masculine perusal that made her skin heat up and her heart pound harder and faster than it already was.

Somehow she managed to say the words, to slip a band on his finger and accept the ring he'd slipped on hers. To close her eyes and press her lips to his in response to the customary "you may kiss the bride."

And she let herself pretend, for just those few minutes, that it wasn't smoke and mirrors.

"Where in the world did all these people come from?" Beer in hand, Lucian stood in the shadow of a large spruce. Beside him, Gabe leaned against the thick trunk of his backyard tree. "I don't remember inviting Mabel and Henry Binderby."

In fact, he didn't remember inviting at least half of the people who'd drifted in, slowly but surely, throughout the course of the evening. There'd been so many bodies in the house at one point, they'd all finally dragged a few tables and chairs outside and spilled into the backyard. Music pounded from Gabe's stereo system, and Sydney had candles and tablecloths sent over from her restaurant, along with additional trays of pasta primavera, salad and rolls. Reese called in for reinforcements from his tavern, and a truck with a fresh keg of beer and a case of champagne had shown up an hour ago.

So much for the small wedding his family had insisted on.

"People just want to be here for this great historical event," Gabe said. "Lucian Sinclair's wedding will keep the gossip lines burning up for weeks. I've already heard four different versions of how and where you proposed, not to mention the romantic honeymoon you're taking in St. Thomas. Hey, isn't that Sally Lyn Wetters with Laura Greenley?"

Lucian choked on the beer he'd been about to swallow. Good Lord, it was one thing to have regular townspeople here, but *girlfriends?* he thought in dismay. Well, ex-girlfriends, anyway.

Terrific. Sally Lyn had spotted him and was already headed his way. Her lips were as bright red as her dress, and any other time he would have appreciated the pretty blonde.

But the only woman on his mind at this moment was Raina.

From the moment she'd walked down that aisle toward him, looking like the heavens had opened up and she was his special gift, every other woman he'd ever known no longer existed. Just Raina. With her smoky-blue eyes fixed on his, her dark, glorious hair swept up off her long neck, her rosy lips curved softly in a smile, she was everything a man could have ever dreamed of wanting. She absolutely dazzled him.

He searched her out now, found her standing on the back porch, laughing with Rafe Barclay, Bloomfield's sheriff. Jealousy, as unwelcome as it was unfamiliar, speared through him. Rafe was single and good-looking—so the women told him—and he wasn't shy or reserved when it came to the female gender.

Rafe was also his friend; they'd gone all the way through school together. Went fishing at the lake every few weeks and played poker on Saturday nights if they weren't out on a date. There'd been lots of playful competition between them, but Lucian had never once been jealous.

Not until now, at least.

"Yoo-hoo, Lucian." Sally Lyn waved as she made her way closer. "Why are you hiding over here?"

Lucian tried not to think about what Rafe had said to make Raina laugh or her eyes sparkle the way they did. Instead he forced a smile and thought about how relieved he was that he'd never slept with Sally Lyn. Otherwise, this would be way too awkward.

"Gabe," Lucian whispered under his breath. "So

help me, if you value your life, don't you dare leave me alone.''

Chuckling, Gabe pushed away from the tree, then lifted his beer bottle in a silent toast as he walked off.

He'd kill him later, Lucian thought, then decided that since he had a wife and two kids, he'd simply maim him.

"Congratulations, Lucian," Sally Lyn purred as she sidled up next to him and kissed him square on the mouth. "I just want to wish you and your new wife the best.''

"Thanks.'' He shifted uncomfortably, not sure what to say.

"I must say, though.'' She pursed her lips into a perfect pout. "I am, well, surprised.''

"Life's a surprise, isn't it?'' His gaze went back to Raina, narrowed when both she and Rafe were gone. "You never know what's going to happen.''

"That is so true.'' She giggled and ran a finger down his suit lapel. "Especially with you, Lucian. You always were so impulsive.''

"Isn't he, though?''

Lucian turned at the sound of Raina's voice. He'd been so busy looking for her with Rafe, he hadn't seen her skirt the edge of the crowd and come up from the side. Sally Lyn dropped her hand away and stepped back.

"Raina,'' he said, more than a little uncomfortable. "This is Sally Lyn Wetters. Sally Lyn, Raina.''

Sally Lyn held out her hand. "Lucian and I are old…friends,'' she said with just enough emphasis on the word *friends* to raise one of Raina's brows.

"How nice for you.''

Four little words spoken with such cool, bored sophistication that Sally Lyn had no response.

"Yes, well—" Sally Lyn cleared her throat "—it was nice to meet you."

Raina nodded, smiled, but said nothing.

"Bye, Lucian." Sally Lyn glanced at him, then sighed and walked away.

"Raina—"

"They're going to cut the cake in a few minutes," she said evenly. "Since your family's gone to all this trouble, we should make an appearance."

"Raina—"

"You also might want to wipe Sally Lyn's lipstick from your mouth." She handed him a clean tissue from the pocket of her silk jacket. "It's not even close to my color."

Frowning, he took the tissue and wiped the lipstick from his mouth and stared at the red stain. What the hell was he feeling so guilty for? He hadn't done a damn thing.

"We used to date," he said tightly. "That's it. I never even slept with the woman."

"Did I ask?" Her gaze held his. "We might be married, but we both know it's for Emma. For however long we decide to stay married, I won't question what you do or with whom. In return, I expect the same courtesy."

A muscle jumped at the corner of his eye. He didn't like the direction of this conversation one little bit. And he definitely didn't like the implication that she might be dating or sleeping with someone else. Especially while she was married to him.

He took hold of her arm and pulled her close to him. "What the hell are you trying to say?"

"I thought I was pretty clear," she said calmly, though her breathing had deepened. "I'm not expecting you to be celibate, Lucian, though for appearances, you should at least be discreet."

"Well, how very generous of you." His hand tightened on her arm. "And I suppose you'll be 'discreet' as well."

"I can control myself."

"Is that so?" A fury built inside him at the very thought of her with someone else, a fury mixed with desire from wanting her so badly he thought he might go mad if he didn't have her. He dipped his head, brought his lips within a finger's width of hers. To his satisfaction, her lips parted. "Is that what you were doing in my bed a few days ago, sweetheart, controlling yourself?"

It took a moment for his words to register, then her shoulders went rigid. She glanced quickly away, then closed her eyes and sighed.

"I'm sorry, Lucian," she said quietly. "I don't want us to argue the last night I'm here. It's just been a long day and I'm a little out of sorts."

He nodded, then relaxed his hold on her. "I think it's safe to say it's been a long day for both of us."

"I have a ten-o'clock flight in the morning," she said awkwardly. "I can ask Gabe to take me and Emma to the airport, if you'd rather."

He wanted to shake her, tell her she was his *wife* and she damn well wasn't going anywhere. But he knew in the long run it would only make things worse. She would still leave and his pride would have holes from her high heels as she walked away.

"I'll take you," he said tightly.

She stepped away from him and smiled, though it never reached her eyes. "Shall we go cut the cake now?"

"Fine."

Frustrated, he waited a moment to calm down before he followed her. He'd cut the cake, he thought, gritting his teeth. A great big piece. And he'd smash every little crumb in her pretty little face.

Ten

"**J**anice, have Brandy take a tuck in that strap. Lidia, you're supposed to wear the blue push-up, not the black strapless and Jill, for heaven's sake, put some adhesive on under that bra."

Struggling to remain calm in the midst of chaos, Raina sat cross-legged on the floor of the backstage dressing area and snipped off a loose thread on the side seam of a silver satin nightgown. Deidre, the red-headed model wearing the nightgown, did a slow 360-degree turn while Raina inspected the hem.

"Twenty minutes." Annelise, Raina's assistant, hurried by, her arms filled with a cloud of white tulle.

The knot in Raina's stomach twisted tighter.

"Raina, ple-ease." Aurel, a blond model from the Bronx, stormed over, thrust her hands on her slender hips and stuck her lower lip out. "Please let me wear the spiked leather choker with the black camisole."

"Aurie," Raina said patiently after she'd counted to three. "We're not doing a shoot for *Babes on Bikes*. Now spit out your gum and stand up straight."

The woman might be gorgeous and knew how to work a crowd, Raina thought with a sigh, but she had no sense of fashion, and you could almost hear the echo if you spoke too close to her ear.

"Fifteen minutes." Annelise rushed by again, this time clutching a plush teddy bear that one of the sleepwear models would be carrying on her walk down the runway.

Breathe, Raina told herself. Slow, easy, breaths…
Slow, easy, breaths…

The same exact words that Sydney had used the day that Raina Sarbanes had become Mrs. Lucian Sinclair. The day her life had completely turned upside down and inside out.

That day seemed so long ago now, a lifetime, though it had actually only been eight days. Seven days since Lucian had driven her and Emma to the airport. They'd barely spoken more than a few polite words on the ride there, and the tension between them had been stretched taut as piano wire. He'd kissed and hugged Emma, and Raina had seen the frustration in his narrowed eyes when he'd handed their daughter back, but he'd said nothing. He hadn't touched her. He'd just nodded and given her a tight goodbye.

He hadn't called once.

Not that she'd been home very much since she and Emma had gotten back to New York. She'd been busy every minute getting ready for the show. Except for today, Raina had brought Emma and her nanny to the office with her every day this past week, so there'd been no one home. But she had a machine. He could have left a message if he'd called.

Or she could have called him.

She'd picked up the phone at least once a day for the past six days with the intention of calling him. Then hung up. Picked it up again.

Hung up again.

Why was it so damn hard to say she was sorry?

Blowing a strand of hair out of her eyes, she snipped another loose thread from the hem of the nightgown. She knew she'd apologized at the reception, but she needed to say it again. Maybe she *had* overreacted just a little to that pretty blonde hanging on him. But when she'd seen that, that *hussy* kiss Lucian right on the mouth and hang herself on him like a tacky red painting on a wall, well, for crying out loud, what was she supposed to feel? She'd wanted to scratch the woman's eyes out.

She still wanted to scratch the woman's eyes out.

After the reception, after everyone had finally left and everything was cleaned up, she knew he'd wanted her to invite him into the bedroom. But she hadn't. She'd been too keyed-up from the day. If they had slept in the same room, they would have made love.

She had felt too vulnerable to let him that close, was afraid she would lose the last thread of control and tell him that she loved him. That she didn't want to go. That she wanted a *real* marriage.

So he'd slept on the couch and she'd slept in that big four-poster bed, alone, letting the tears fall.

"Raina, did you want the three-inch black heels with the black embroidered bra or the satin under-wire?"

Raina glanced up at the sound of her assistant's question and blinked. "What?"

Annelise pushed her big, black horn-rimmed glasses up her nose, then held up two different bras. "Did you want the three-inch black heels with the—"

When Annelise stopped midsentence, Raina finished for her. "The three-inch for the satin underwire. Four-inch black T-strap for the embroidered."

When Annelise didn't respond or move away, Raina suddenly realized that not only had her assistant gone quiet, so had the entire room, which was unheard of in a room full of twenty women before a show.

Frowning, Raina looked up, noticed that every woman in the place was looking behind her.

She turned.

Oh, dear Lord.

Slow, deep breaths…

Lucian stood two feet away, looking a little flustered, but so incredibly, wonderfully handsome in a hunter-green dress shirt and black dress jeans and boots, that every woman in the place had to be licking her lips.

She knew she was.

"Lucian," she gasped, then stood up so quickly that he had to reach out and steady herself or she would have fallen over.

"Hey, handsome," one of the models called out. "Can you come over here and zip me up?"

To his credit Lucian did not respond. Carefully he kept his attention focused on Raina. "I'm sorry, I know this is bad timing. I was just going to sit out front, but when I told the hostess who I was, she ushered me back here.''

''Who are you, sweet-cheeks?'' Aurel asked and moved in like a cat on the prowl. A few of the other models had also moved in, circling like a pack of she-wolves.

''Don't you know, sugar?'' someone said with a fake Southern accent. ''He's my hero.''

The remark triggered a flurry of alternative suggestions regarding who the handsome stranger was, until Raina finally said quite loudly, ''He's my husband.''

Instant silence.

Well, at least everyone was staring at *her* now, Raina thought, instead of Lucian. Even her assistant's eyes were huge behind her glasses. Since Raina had neglected to mention the little fact that she'd gotten married while she was in Bloomfield, she could only imagine the shock she'd just given everyone. It might have been funny if it wasn't so distressing.

''Lucian, what are you doing here?'' she said as calmly as she could possibly manage. Her heart hammered furiously against her ribs.

''You said I could visit whenever I wanted.'' He glanced sideways at the scantily clad models who'd leaned in close to listen, then quickly looked back at Raina and swallowed hard. ''I, ah, forgot this was a lingerie show.''

''So you just show up?'' She was torn between throwing her arms around him and kissing him or booting him out. How could he just show up here like this? Looking so wonderful, so *magnificent.*

She knew what every woman in the room was

thinking because she was thinking exactly the same thing.

Hubba-hubba.

"I went to your apartment," he said. "The nanny wouldn't let me in, but she told me I could find you here."

"For heaven's sake, Lucian, I can't talk to you now. I've got a show in—" she glanced at her watch "—oh, my God! Three minutes! Everyone, get in place, get ready. Jamie, you're first, straighten that strap and put some more lip gloss on. Aurel, take that choker off right this minute. Annelise, see that my— that Mr. Sinclair is escorted out front, please."

Everyone scurried and shifted to work mode, though Raina couldn't help but notice the longing glances that followed Lucian out of the room. Lord knew that her own gaze lingered on those broad shoulders longer than she had intended.

The sound of the master of ceremonies welcoming everyone jolted Raina back to the show. The loud, heavy beat of ZZ Top's "She's Got Legs" signaled the start.

The first model sashayed out, and for the next thirty minutes, Raina somehow managed to keep her mind off Lucian Sinclair and on her work.

Champagne flowed freely in the twenty-first-floor executive suite of the Hilton Hotel and Towers. A tuxedo-clad waiter carried a silver tray of miniature bruschetta and goose pâté on crackers for the crowd. Several bodies swayed to a musical mix of jazz, latin and rock tunes, while others huddled around the bar, arguing fashion trends: who was in and who was out.

At the moment Raina's new line of lingerie called "Whisper," was definitely in.

Lucian stood next to a fake palm in the corner, content to simply watch as Raina, dressed in a simple, black silk evening dress, mingled with her guests, graciously and modestly accepting the exuberant praise from the critics, buyers and designers she'd invited to the party.

Three weeks ago he'd have thought himself the luckiest man on earth. He'd had a front row seat at a lingerie fashion show and was currently surrounded by tall, gorgeous women. Any other red-blooded male would have thought he'd died and gone to heaven.

But he wasn't any other man, and it wasn't three weeks ago. Three weeks ago his life had changed, and this past week, without Emma, without Raina, had been hell. Everything about his life now, about himself, felt different.

At this moment there was only one tall, gorgeous woman he wanted to be with.

His wife.

He wanted everyone else gone.

Especially Aurel, he thought with a silent sigh, the blond, gum-popping model who'd been talking to him for the past five minutes about the date she'd had on some TV show called *Blind Date*.

"So I said to the guy, I said, like, who do you think you are, like, Mel Gibson? And he says, who do you think *you* are, like, Julia Roberts? Can you imagine, comparing *me* to Julia Roberts, that was just way cool and then he said…"

He nodded, offered an occasional "hmm," or "really?" while Aurel continued with a minute-by-

minute description of her television debut, but he kept
his gaze on Raina, who was shaking the hand of a
dark-haired man wearing a black Armani suit. From
the few words Lucian managed to hear, he was certain
the man was Italian.

When the man leaned forward and whispered
something in Raina's ear, Lucian narrowed his eyes.
She smiled and her brow lifted in interest as the man
continued to speak softly to her, then with a sigh, she
looked back at the Italian and reluctantly shook her
head.

Bastard. Lucian gritted his teeth. The guy was trying to hit on Raina. And right under her own husband's nose, no less. He'd like to stuff the guy's fancy
gold cuff links down his throat and pull them out
his—

"Hey, sugar." A tall, buxom, raven-haired model,
"Kimmie who could shimmy"—so the announcer
had said as the woman had sauntered down the walk-
way—suddenly appeared with two glasses of champagne and moved in close. "Looks like you need
something to fill those big hands of yours."

With his back against the wall, Lucian had no place
to go. He smiled politely and accepted the glass of
champagne she offered, but made no attempt to accept anything else she might be suggesting. While
Aurel continued with her detailed account of her evening out on the town with some guy named Steve,
Lucian watched Raina take the Italian's arm and lead
him over to another group of people.

Dammit. How long did these things last anyway?

He still didn't know what had possessed him to
jump on a plane this morning and come here without

so much as a phone call. One minute he'd been framing the tub for the master bath, pounding away while he listened to Led Zeppelin, the next minute he was packing a bag and heading for the airport.

Not that he hadn't thought about coming here every minute of every day for the past week. But thinking about doing something and actually doing it were two entirely different things.

And yet, here he was, in New York.

And here she was.

Now if only he could get her alone....

Lucian suddenly realized that another woman had joined his small group, a redhead with big green eyes who had the looks of a model but not the height. She'd said something to him, but he had no idea what. He played it safe by simply smiling and nodding.

"Terrific." The woman pulled a card out of her pocket. "Just give me your name and number and I'll call you."

Oops. Damn, what had she said to him? "Ahh, well, I—"

"Call him for what?" Raina stepped out of the sea of people and smiled at the woman. "Hello, Phoebe."

Lucian wanted to kiss Raina, not just because she'd saved him, but because he wanted to kiss her. All he'd thought about since she'd left after the wedding was how much he wanted to be with her. To kiss her. To make love with her.

Since *that* was obviously out of the question at this moment, he simply feasted his eyes on her, breathed in the familiar scent of her and took a sip of champagne.

"Hey, Rae." Phoebe smiled back. "Long time no

see. And your friend here just agreed to a photo shoot. I've got a contract with Calvin Klein he'd be perfect for.''

Lucian nearly spit out the champagne in his mouth. Raina raised both brows and looked at him. "Oh, really?"

No, not really, he wanted to say, but he could hardly tell the woman he hadn't listened to a word she'd said. A *photo* shoot, for crying out loud. No way in hell he was doing that.

"I appreciate the offer—'' oh, hell, what was her name? Oh, yeah ''—Phoebe, but I'm afraid I can't, I'm not—''

"Phoebe." Raina cut him off. "This is my husband, Lucian Sinclair. Lucian, this is Phoebe Knight. She's a photographer.''

"Husband?'' Surprise widened Phoebe's eyes. She glanced from Raina to Lucian, then back at Raina. "It's been longer than I thought, Rae. We definitely need to do lunch.''

"We will." Raina slipped her arm into Lucian's. "Now if you'll excuse us, I'm just dying to get this man alone for a minute.''

"Just for a minute?'' Aurel said in her whisky-toned voice. "I'd go for at least ten, honey.''

Lucian smiled at the spread of pink on Raina's cheeks as she pulled him away, was certain he heard the buxom model say she'd go for an hour.

"Bless you." He slipped an arm around Raina's waist and whispered in her ear. "You saved me.''

"You have no idea," she said with a lift of her brow. "Those two would have eaten you alive.''

Which was, of course, exactly what *she* wanted to

do, Raina thought as she dragged Lucian into a bed-room. A Latin beat, something by Marc Anthony pounded through the door she closed behind them.

She couldn't even be annoyed with Aurel or Kim-mie. They were simply being who they were, sirens with a cause, which was to make every living, breathing man adore them. They might be beautiful, but she thought she knew Lucian well enough to guess they weren't his type.

Phoebe, on the other hand, *had* concerned her. She was smart, successful, beautiful, and she didn't inter-sperse every other word with ''like'' or ''whatever.''

''Why in the world would you tell Phoebe that you'd do a shoot for her?'' she asked, folding her arms.

He scratched at the back of his neck and shifted from one foot to the other. ''Well, I didn't exactly. I was just…I was—''

''Oh, never mind.'' She closed her eyes and sighed. ''It's none of my business, anyway.''

She'd told him at the reception that she wouldn't ask him any questions if he didn't ask her any. So what's the first thing she did when she finally got him alone? Like a jealous idiot, she'd started asking ques-tions.

Well, if he wanted to do a photo shoot with Phoebe, he could go right ahead. He could do a hundred if he wanted.

If Phoebe wasn't such a good friend, Raina thought she just might rip every pretty red hair out of her gorgeous head.

Suddenly too tired to even stand, she sank on the

edge of the bed. "It's been a long day, Lucian. I don't have the energy to argue with you."

"Good."

She felt the mattress sink as he sat down beside her on the bed. She might be tired, she realized, but she wasn't dead. Her body came alive at his closeness, and it was there once again—that shimmering awareness of him. The familiar, masculine scent that was his alone, the heat rippling from his long, muscular body, the sensuality that radiated like waves off a New York city street in August.

He looked a little tired, she thought, noticed a tinge of red in his eyes. Had he missed her these past few days? she wondered. Or had he simply been angry at her? As much as she wanted to know, she wouldn't, couldn't ask.

"Congratulations on a successful show," he said, breaking the silence between them. "I liked your stuff. Your designs, I mean."

Considering the women who'd modeled the lingerie, she doubted he'd noticed her designs. Still, she appreciated his effort at complimenting her, and she sure as hell wasn't about to let him see that nasty little streak of jealousy she'd already displayed one too many times when it came to women fawning over him.

"Thanks." She thought about all the orders she'd taken, more than she could have ever dreamed. Why didn't it feel as wonderful as she'd always imagined it would? "It's been a good day."

"I hope I didn't ruin anything by surprising you at the show," he said.

She laughed softly, rolled her sore neck. "My girls

were so pumped up from looking at you backstage they came on the runway like fireballs just to impress you. I do believe I heard the word *sizzling* at least a dozen times this evening, referring to both my designs and my husband.''

He glanced away from her, but not before she saw the blush rise up his neck. It amused and thoroughly charmed her that she'd actually embarrassed him.

They sat shoulder to shoulder, thigh to thigh, careful not to make contact. He wore his wedding band, she realized suddenly, and felt her pulse flutter at the sight. Not quite ready to answer questions from the people she worked with, Raina had slipped hers off when she'd come home. She didn't know if Lucian had noticed or if he cared, but she did know that the emotions between them were still raw, still sensitive, and they were both treading carefully on what could prove to be very thin ice.

''I went to see Emma today. Teresa wouldn't let me in.''

''I told her about you. That we'd gotten married.'' There was a tiny piece of lint on Lucian's black jeans and she had to fold her hands together to keep from plucking it off. ''But she's very cautious with people she doesn't know.''

''I showed her my driver's license, my blood donor card and an airline ticket,'' he said dryly. ''She told me Emma was napping and I should go see you, then slammed the door in my face.''

''She's wonderful with Emma.'' Teresa was like a mother to her, a grandmother to Emma, Raina thought. She didn't know what she would ever do without her. "Don't be angry with her for being careful."

"Angry?" He looked at her with surprise. "I was thinking about giving her a raise. It was comforting to know there's someone like her watching over Emma when you aren't there."

She laughed at his unexpected comment, then stared down at her hands and felt her smile fade.

"Lucian," she said his name softly, "why are you here?"

"To see Emma."

Her chest tightened. She knew, of course, that he'd come to see Emma, but she'd be lying if she couldn't admit, even to herself, that she'd hoped, just maybe, he might have come to see her, too. *Stupid, stupid,* she mentally kicked herself.

"She'll be happy to see you." She forced herself to smile again, then pushed up from the bed to rise. "She's asleep for the night now, but you can come over in the—"

He took hold of her arm and eased her back onto the bed. "And I came to see you, too."

Her heart skipped, then raced. She looked up. "To see me?"

"I didn't like the way things came down between us before you left. I thought I…well, I just want you to know that there really wasn't anything between me and Sally Lyn. That—"

"Lucian, please, I'm sorry I said what I did at the reception. I shouldn't have. And you really don't have to tell me anything that—"

He put his finger to her lips. "That we never even slept together, like I already told you. And I sure as hell never had any thoughts of marrying her, like you may have heard."

"Really?" She hated that she sounded so happy over that fact, but she couldn't help it. "Because if you did, if you think that you might—"

"Raina, for God's sake." He looked at the ceiling. "Will you just shut up? This is difficult enough."

Not sure what to say about that, she shut up, looked down at his hand on her arm. The texture of his callused palm on her skin sent shivers through her.

"I didn't want you to leave last week."

"I live in New York, Lucian." *Why didn't you want me to leave?* Was it just Emma? she wanted to know. Or had he missed her, too? "My work is here."

"I know, dammit." Frustration had him raking a hand through his hair. "Look, let me hang around for a few days. I need some time with Emma and—"

He paused and she waited, breath held.

"—I promise I won't get in your way."

Why had she let herself believe that he might want to spend time with her, too? The hope she'd felt swooped down like a kite caught in a downdraft. A wave of exhaustion rolled through her, as profound as it was heavy, and all she wanted to do was go home and crawl into bed.

"I told you that you could visit anytime you wanted," she said with a sigh, then eased her arm from his hand and stood. "Come over in the morning and—"

She stopped suddenly, listened.

"What?"

"Do you hear that?"

He narrowed his eyes. "I don't hear anything."

"Exactly." She marched to the door and opened it.

The suite was empty. Even the waiter had left.

Raina stared in shock at the deserted room, then glanced at the serving cart that had been rolled in front of the door. There was a note taped to a bottle of champagne chilling in an ice bucket beside two flutes of crystal, a bowl of strawberries and a can of whipped cream.

Lucian came up behind her as she snapped up the note and read: "Congratulations to the Bride and Groom! We're sure you can be as wonderfully creative with the strawberries and whipped cream as you are with your designs! Love, Everyone!"

Lucian chuckled.

She turned abruptly, nearly bumped into him and felt the heat start at her neck and work its way upward.

"They, ah, thought we would want to be alone."

"Imagine that." He reached for the whipped cream, squirted a dollop on his finger and looked at it. "Did you know that I have a weakness for whipped cream?"

When he licked the puffy white cloud of cream from his finger, Raina felt her toes curl. Her lips parted as she stared at his mouth. "I…didn't know that."

"You know what else I have a weakness for?" he said quietly, locking his green gaze on her blue one.

She could barely breathe. "Strawberries?"

He shook his head slowly, kept his gaze on hers as he set the can of whipped cream back down. "You."

Eleven

*Y*ou.

That single word thrilled her, raced through her mind and her body like a firestorm. Made her tremble with anticipation.

"If you want me to leave," he said, his gaze still on hers, "tell me now. Right now."

His voice was strained, quiet as the empty room they stood in. The tension stretched between them like a tightrope, a high-wire that she suddenly found herself on, struggling to keep her balance on what was logical and sane.

Did she want him to leave?

He watched her with those hungry green eyes, and she'd never felt so consumed by a look. It frightened and thrilled her at the same time.

Excited her.

Did she want him to leave?

Not in a million years.

"Stay."

When his arms came around her, when he dragged her against him and crushed his mouth to hers, she felt that rope slip from under her. The fall was as endless as it was exhilarating. Adrenaline pumped wildly through her veins, made her temples pound and her heart sing.

Dizzy from the fall, from the desire swirling through her, she clung to him. His kiss was hard and demanding; the taste of whipped cream and champagne on his tongue was heady. He slanted his head, moved his mouth over hers and deepened the kiss.

Pleasure coiled inside her like a living thing, tighter and tighter.

"Lucian," she gasped, dragging her mouth from his. "We should…the bedroom…"

But then his mouth caught hers again, and she couldn't get the words out. Forgot what the words were.

They moved toward the bedroom, a halting, intimate dance of anxious hands and urgent whispers. She kicked off her heels; he unzipped her dress; buttons opened.

She wanted his hands on her everywhere, wanted her hands on him. A molten river of heat poured through her body. Brazenly she slid her hands over his strong bare chest, down his flat belly, then lower, stroking, caressing. Up, down again.

He groaned, pressed his hardness against her while he dragged her dress from her shoulders and shoved the garment down. And then his hands were filled with her aching breasts and it was her turn to groan.

And gasp.

In one swift move, he had her on her back, on the bed underneath him. Her breath came in short ragged gulps of air. He straddled her, kept his intense gaze on hers as he shrugged out of his shirt, then unbuckled his belt. The hiss of a zipper, the thump of a boot on the floor, then another thump.

She watched, in awe, incapable of speech. He had the body of a man who worked hard at his job: thick, muscled arms; large, callused hands; solid, wide chest. Power and strength emanated from him and quite literally took her breath away.

You.

That single word again. Did he truly have a weakness for her? she wanted to know. And was it only for the physical, or could it possibly be more?

Did she dare hope that it could be?

He moved over her, slid his hands up her thighs and stopped when he hit a sliver of black floral lace.

And smiled.

"Sexy," he murmured as he slowly ran one fingertip along the scalloped edge of her panties, from the outside of her leg to the inside.

"They're called—" she sucked in a breath when he reached the juncture of her thighs "—Shameless."

His finger hesitated, then moved back and forth over the soft mound of lace-covered curls. She bit her lip at the jolt of intense pleasure that shot through her. Heat coiled tightly between her legs, throbbing.

His finger slid underneath lace. "I don't remember this one from the show."

"No, I— Next month's. This is…what you would call a—" her heart stuttered when he slipped inside her "—private showing. Dammit, Lucian," she said on a moan. "If you keep talking, I'm going to have to hurt you."

Chuckling, he dipped his head and sent her reeling.

She clutched at his shoulders, arching upward on a gasp. His hands gripped her hips, held her steady while he moved over her. The heat built, curled upward, higher and higher, tighter. She begged him to stop in one breath, pleaded with him to continue in the next.

"Lucian, please," she sobbed. "I want you inside me. I need you inside me."

And then he was. Deep inside her. Not just in her body, she thought in a daze, but in her heart and in her soul.

Where he'd always been. Where he would always be.

She met him with every thrust, felt his muscles tighten and coil under her eager hands. The tempo increased until they both were panting, both falling together, then shuddering from the violent force of release….

"I swear to you I didn't come here for that."

Lucian held her close, brushed his lips over the top of her soft hair. They'd both been quiet in the aftermath of their lovemaking, both lost in their own thoughts. He really hadn't meant for that particular thought to be the first thing out of his mouth, but somehow it just popped out.

"You're lousy at pillow talk, Lucian." She turned

her head into his chest and nipped with her teeth. "I was hoping for something more like, 'amazing,' or 'unbelievable.'"

He rolled so he could look down at her. She smiled, a satisfied, content smile, like a cat who'd just polished off a bowl of cream. "Those words would pale," he said, tucking a strand of hair behind her ear.

A pretty shade of pink rushed over her cheeks. Her gaze dropped. "So what are you saying, that you're sorry we just made love?"

"Good grief, no." Looking at her like this, with her hair fanned out on the pillow, her lips still full and rosy from his kisses, her eyes glazed and smoky with desire, made it hard to remember what he'd been trying to say at all. "I've never been sorry about making love with you. I'm only sorry I can't remember that first time. It frustrates the hell out of me."

"Nothing like that…like you…" she said, keeping her eyes averted from his, "had ever happened to me before. It was like we'd been caught in a tornado." Her finger traced a slow circle on his chest. "It's still like that, Lucian," she said softly. "I could play games and deny it, but coy has never been my style. Sex with you is incredible."

Sex? Why did her casual use of the word suddenly annoy him? Was that all they were doing? Having sex?

Or was it more?

He'd never felt anything like this, for any woman. It confused the hell out of him, made him…nervous.

Whatever it was, he knew that he wanted Raina. In bed and out. And not simply because she was the mother of his child or because she was a beautiful woman. But because she was Raina. He'd missed her this past week. Missed her smile, the sound of her laugh, the way her eyes danced when she held Emma and played with her. He'd felt an emptiness he'd never known before.

He'd felt…lonely.

Jeez, that sounded pathetic. Since when had he ever been lonely? He had a big family, nephews, a niece, friends. And Emma. Just the thought of her made his chest tighten. He had it all. Damn, but he was getting sappy. If he wasn't careful, he'd be writing poetry and cutting out little lace hearts.

He shook off his thoughts, turned his attention back to the moment and the woman in his arms. Her fingertips were still moving over his chest, and her touch stirred the heat again, made his heart beat faster and his blood race.

"Raina." He said her name softly. "I have some time, a week or two, before we break ground on our next project. I can get a hotel room close to your place, spend some time with Emma."

And you, he said silently.

Her fingers hesitated, then moved again. "She'd love that."

"Great." Why had he wanted her to say *we? We'd* love that?

"What about the cat?"

He frowned at her. "Cat?"

"The cat under your porch and her kittens. Who's watching out for them?"

"Oh. That cat." He slid his hand up and down her arm. "They're living in my trailer now. I left the door open one afternoon and next thing I knew, they'd moved in. Abby's taking care of them while I'm gone.''

He felt her smile against his chest and snuggle closer.

''Lucian?''

''Yeah?''

There was a long pause before she finally lifted her gaze to his. ''You don't have to get a hotel.''

His heart jumped. He could see the uncertainty in her eyes. They were being so damn cautious, circling around each other. Why couldn't they just say what they were thinking? he wondered.

''You have a guest room?''

Her hands, soft and warm and smooth, moved down his sides. ''No.''

''A big sofa?''

''Only five feet.''

''Why, Mrs. Sinclair,'' he drawled, ''are you suggesting that I sleep in your bed?''

Her eyelashes fluttered down and she blushed. ''It's a big bed. And it would be convenient.'' Her blush deepened. ''To be close to Emma, I mean.''

''Well, we certainly want what's best for Emma now, don't we?'' He smiled, felt as if his entire body were grinning with him. ''What about Teresa?''

''We *are* married, you know,'' she said. ''Though we may have to show her the license before she approves.''

He brought his mouth close to hers. ''You sure I won't be in the way?''

''I think that's kinda the idea, Lucian,'' she murmured, parting her lips.

"What about your Italian friend?" he asked, part of him teasing, part of him wanting to know.

"Italian friend?"

"The man you were talking to earlier in the suit. Armani, gold cuff links. Will he be upset if I'm there?"

She opened her eyes. "Antonio Barducci? He's a columnist with *New York Sophisticate.*"

"He was whispering in your ear." Lucian nibbled on her earlobe. "I didn't like it."

Her laughter started somewhere deep in her chest, then rose like bubbles in champagne. Frowning, he lifted his head. "What's so funny?"

"He—" she turned her head into the pillow, then rolled out from under him. "He asked me if you were available. He said you were *bellissimo.*"

Heat flashed up Lucian's neck. "That's not funny."

She sat on the edge of the bed, still laughing. "It's hysterical."

"The hell it is," he muttered irritably. "What did you tell him?"

"I gave him your phone number."

"What!"

"I'm kidding." She reached for his shirt and tugged it on. "I told him you were my husband and to back off."

He heaved a sigh of relief. "Good."

She glanced over her shoulder at him and grinned. "I told him I thought you were *bellissimo,* too."

"Yeah?" He grinned back at her, then fluffed the pillows and patted the bed. "Come back here and say that again. It turned me on."

She bounced off the bed.

"Hey. Where are you going?"

She disappeared through the door before he even had a chance to admire those incredible legs of hers. Frowning, he tossed the sheet off and started to follow.

When she came back through the doorway, his heart leaped in his throat, then every drop of blood above his waist went south. She sauntered toward him, his unbuttoned shirt showing more than a glimpse of her long, naked body. In one hand she held a bottle of champagne, in the other, the canister of whipped cream.

"I know something else that might turn you on." A smile touched her lips as she moved closer. "What do you think?"

He couldn't think at all, but it didn't matter. It wasn't a question that required a response with words.

For the next week, the New York fashion world buzzed over Raina's new line of lingerie. *Inventive, sexy* and *trendsetting* were just a few of the adjectives being bantered around in trade publications and newspapers. Not to mention word-of-mouth. Orders were pouring in, and the phones at her office never stopped. Even now, as she rode up the elevator to her apartment, her ears still seemed to be ringing. She was thrilled by all the brouhaha, but exhausted at the same time.

Pretty much the same feelings she had toward Lucian.

They had gone back to her apartment together early the next morning after they'd made love that first night. Emma had still been asleep, and Lucian had stood over his daughter's crib, watching her, waiting anxiously for her to stir. At the first sign of movement, he'd picked her up and cuddled, then said, "Good morning, sweetheart," as if he'd been doing it her entire life.

Raina's chest ached at the sight of Emma's welcoming smile, the way she hugged her body close to Lucian's and put her head on his shoulder. At that moment Raina knew that if she hadn't already loved him, she would have fallen for him all over again right then and there.

But she did love him. She always had, she always would.

She'd hoped in the time they'd spent together that he might come to love her, too. But he'd never said the words to her she so desperately needed to hear. He seemed perfectly content with everything as it was. While she was gone at work, he spent his days with Emma.

The nights, Raina thought with a mixture of pleasure and pain, he spent with her, in her bed. She'd had so little sleep this week, she was running on sheer adrenaline. Not that she'd complained, she thought with a smile. If anything, she'd been the one who couldn't keep her hands off him. It had been an incredible, wild, thrilling week.

And it was about to come to an end.

Keys in her hand, she paused outside her apartment door, needing a moment to find her balance. She knew she shouldn't be upset with him because he hadn't offered more to her. She was the one who'd invited him into her home, into her bed. She hadn't asked for more, or anything at all in return. That would have required courage.

But the fact was, she wanted more. Needed more.

She'd enjoyed every minute of the time they'd spent together these past few days, but she wouldn't do this again. Couldn't go through the hurt every time he would have to leave.

They could be friends, they needed to be, for Emma's sake. But Raina knew now that she couldn't settle for anything less than a real marriage with Lucian. It wasn't enough for her to love him. She needed him to love her back.

She sighed, pressed her forehead to the doorjamb and closed her eyes. When the time was right, in a few months, maybe a year, she would file for divorce.

Sucking in a deep breath, she quietly opened her apartment door, saw Lucian playing "Itsy-Bitsy Spider" with Emma on the carpet in the living room.

Her heart ached at the sight of them, this six-foot-four man rippling his fingers and singing "down came the rain" to his tiny daughter.

"Something smells good." She stepped inside and sniffed the air. Teresa's spaghetti sauce, Raina was certain. Forcing a smile, she closed the door behind her. "Hello, sweetheart."

Lucian looked up at Raina's greeting. The endearment wasn't for him, of course, it was for Emma. Still, that single word, spoken with such tenderness and pleasure, brought a strange hitch in his chest. He smiled at her, then scooped Emma up in his arms and stood. "Give Mommy a kiss hello."

Raina kissed Emma's cheek, then nuzzled her neck, which brought a burst of giggles from the baby. When

Lucian bent to kiss Raina's neck, he felt her stiffen and move away.

"Have you eaten?" she asked.

She looked tired, he thought. And tense. He thought of a dozen ways to ease that tension. "Emma had some mashed rigatoni. She wanted to share, but I told her I was waiting for you."

Raina slipped her coat off and hung it up in the closet. There was a pause, a slight hesitation before she turned around.

"Something wrong?" he asked carefully.

"Bath time!"

Teresa came out of the bathroom, where Lucian could hear the water already running. He'd become fond of the tiny, silver-haired Greek nanny these past few days. She was a stern woman, all business, but her love not only for Emma, but for Raina, as well, was evident in the way she constantly fussed over them. It had taken him a day or two to get her to warm up to him, but he'd finally succeeded by bringing her a wedge of baklava from Nick's Greek Bakery across town. The next morning and every morning since, there'd been a fresh pot of coffee brewing for him when he'd come out of the bathroom. And whenever he got back from taking Emma on her walk, lunch would be waiting on the table. Yesterday she'd even made chocolate-chip cookies after she'd heard him mention to Raina that they were his favorite.

A terrific woman, he thought with a smile as he handed Emma over to the nanny.

"I'll come help," Raina offered, but Teresa waved her off, tickling Emma's belly with a stuffed terrycloth duck for the bath as they headed for the bathroom.

"I've never seen that duck before." Raina lifted a brow as she looked at him. "Have you been out shopping again?"

"I haven't got anything else to do while she's napping. And I bought something for you, too." Grinning, he pulled two tickets out of his shirt pocket. "*Dark Water.* Friday night. Eight o'clock. You and me."

He'd been anxious to see the expression on Raina's face when he showed her the tickets. The play was the hottest new thing on Broadway. He'd nearly had to sell his soul and do back flips to get the seats with only two days' notice.

"Thank you." She smiled weakly. "It's a wonderful thought."

Thank you? It's a wonderful thought? Hardly the response he'd been expecting. He furrowed his brow, watched her move into the kitchen and lift the lid off the pot on the stove. Steam rose along with the rich, spicy scent of tomatoes and herbs. She looked more than tired, he thought. She looked exhausted.

She'd had a busy week since the show last week, he reasoned. And she hadn't had much sleep at night, either, which was definitely his fault.

He'd make sure she got to bed early tonight, he told himself. To *sleep.*

He came up behind her, slid his hands up her arms. "It's a wonderful thought, but?"

She leaned back against him for a moment, then turned and stepped away. "But I can't go."

Something was wrong. Something more than long hours at work and lack of sleep.

Like a fist, an uneasiness settled in his gut. "You wanna tell me what's going on?"

"Lucian—" She hesitated, then drew in a long breath. "I've been offered a contract with Rossina Designs in Florence."

"Rossina Designs?" Though he'd never bought anything from the upscale clothing company, he'd certainly heard of them. Unless you lived in a cave, everyone had. "As in Florence, Italy?"

"Yes."

"Contracts are usually something to celebrate," he said evenly. "You wanna tell me why you look as if you just ran over a puppy?"

"The contract is for me to go to Florence and work with them there."

The fist in his gut tightened. "You're going to Italy? When?"

"Tomorrow."

"Tomorrow?"

"I'm sorry." Her voice shook slightly. "I know this is short notice. Everything has just happened so fast."

"I'd say that's a bit of an understatement." He told himself to be calm, then very carefully said, "All right. I can stick around here with Emma for a few more days until you get back."

She folded her arms tightly, as if she were cold, then closed her eyes. When she opened them again, she said, "Lucian, I'm taking Emma. We'll be gone for six months."

He went still, and the fist in his gut turned ice cold.

"You're going to Florence, *tomorrow*, for *six* months, and you're taking my daughter with you? Just like that?"

"It's an incredible opportunity that could mean a great deal for my business. I can't turn it down."

"Like hell you can't." He bit back the adjectives threatening to spill out. "You can do anything you want."

"I've worked hard for three years on my own to build a name for my designs." She looked directly at him, held her gaze steady with his. "Why would I say no to something like this?"

Why would she? he thought, clenching his jaw. She *had* worked hard to build her business and reputation in the fashion world, he'd learned that much from talking to her associates at the party. But *six* months?

"Six months will go by quickly," she said. "When we get back—"

"Dammit, Raina, you aren't going!" He swung away from her, raked a hand through his hair. "You can't just take Emma and leave like this. She's my daughter, and in case you've forgotten, we happen to be married."

"Signing a license and wearing rings doesn't make this a marriage," she said quietly. "We agreed to marry to give Emma your name. We also agreed that at some point our marriage would be dissolved. As far as I've seen, nothing's changed."

He could barely hear her words over the roar of blood rushing through his brain. Anger washed over him, and he struggled to keep his voice down. *Dammit!*

"Fine," he ground out. "Go to Florence. But leave Emma with me."

Shock registered on her face, but she quickly recovered. "Out of the question."

"Why? You'll be working all day. I'll take six months off. Callan and Gabe can run things for me, and I'll take care of Emma."

She advanced on him then, her lips pressed into a thin line. "Emma is my life. I love her. I would *never, ever,* leave her. She stays with me."

The fierce love that shone in Raina's narrowed eyes, the tone in her voice that resembled a lioness protecting her cub, took some of the heat out of Lucian's temper. In his gut he knew she was right, that Emma should stay with her, but his heart was telling him something different. He just didn't know exactly what.

"I love her, too," he said through gritted teeth. "Doesn't what I want count for anything here?"

"More than you know," she said softly. "You'll love her forever, Lucian. She's part of you and she always will be. Don't you know that?"

At the sound of Emma's splashing and laughter from the bathroom, they both turned.

It took every ounce of willpower he possessed not to yell, not to put his hands on Raina and shake her, then kiss her senseless and *make* her change her mind.

But he could see the determination in her eyes. She wouldn't change her mind. She was going. With Emma.

And there wasn't a damn thing he could do about it.

Jaw tight, lips pressed into a thin line, he turned

back to her. "I'm going to dress Emma and put her to bed. You eat."

He turned away from her, thankful that she didn't argue. After he dressed his daughter, after he rocked her to sleep and covered her with a blanket, then quietly crept out of her bedroom, he grabbed his jacket and headed for the front door.

He intended to find the closest bar and order a tall, stiff drink.

Or maybe two.

Twelve

With a diaper bag slung over one shoulder and tote bag on the other, Raina followed Teresa and a sleeping Emma through the sea of people in the noisy terminal. She always allowed plenty of time at the airport, and today, with short lines at the ticket counter, plus a thirty-minute delay on her flight, they still had an hour before their plane took off. Normally all that extra time would calm her, but today all she'd wanted to do was leave.

Except she *didn't* want to leave. She could hardly bear the thought of actually getting on that plane and leaving Lucian.

She swallowed back the sickness in her throat and moved with the river of people flowing through the corridors, felt as if she was surrounded by happy, smiling faces. Couples holding hands or walking arm in arm, excitement dancing in their eyes as they prepared to board their planes. A man and woman, obviously just reunited, stood by a money exchange machine and embraced, oblivious to the crowd around them. It was a tender scene, one that would make most people smile or feel warm inside.

It made Raina want to cry like a baby.

Maybe it wouldn't have been so bad if she'd at least been able to speak with Lucian before they'd left. If they hadn't argued last night. If he hadn't left as he had, angry and frustrated.

If he hadn't come in drunk as a skunk at 3:00 a.m.

She was certain he had no recollection of her helping him to the sofa, not an easy feat considering his size. But somehow she'd managed, then taken off his shoes as he'd curled up on the sofa.

She'd looked at him then, lying there so helpless, and she'd wanted desperately to cancel her trip. To forget the contract the designer had proposed, or at least offer to send Annelise in her place. Her assistant was eager and talented. Between fax, phone, computers and maybe one or two short trips to Florence, Raina could have made it work.

But the moment had passed quickly. If Lucian couldn't ask her to stay, if he couldn't say the words to her that she so badly needed to hear, there was no reason to stay. No reason to try.

I love you.

That was what she wanted, what she needed. He might be content to keep things as they were: a wedding ring but no commitment, sex but no love. She couldn't.

She wouldn't.

Not anymore.

Still, she wasn't sorry she married him. Emma would have her daddy's name, and no one would ever whisper or point fingers at her. She would know more love from Lucian and his family than Raina could ever have hoped for her daughter to have. Emma would always be safe.

But the pain of loving Lucian and not being loved in return would destroy her, Raina knew. She also knew that she would never love anyone again as much as she loved him. She could never come close.

She'd tried to wake him this morning, had called his name and shaken his arm, but he hadn't stirred. Not even when the doorbell had rung, or when the driver had carried their luggage out. Not even when she'd lightly kissed him on his forehead. She'd left a note on the kitchen counter, saying goodbye and giving him her hotel information and phone number in Florence, but she hadn't left him her flight information.

Maybe it was better this way, she thought. Better to leave the way she had, quietly. If he had wakened and they'd argued, it would only have been worse. More heartache, that was all she would have brought away with her.

If it were possible to have more, she thought, blinking back the threatening tears.

When Lucian woke he felt as if the Macy's Day Parade had set up its route directly inside his head. Crowds screamed, tubas blasted, bands marched right through the center of his brain. His mouth felt like cotton candy, minus the candy, and his stomach lurched like one of those giant blowup figures caught in the wind.

If he'd had a cork in his head, Lucian thought, there was no doubt it would blow off right about now.

Carefully he opened his eyes, groaned, then slammed them shut again.

The morning sun burned straight through his eyeballs, giving new meaning to the term "liquid fire." Pain bounced like pinballs inside his skull, complete with bells and whistles.

If he lived—and he wasn't so certain he wanted to—he never wanted to hear the term "race beers" again.

Still wearing the same clothes from last night, he unfolded his bent knees very, very slowly and sat, had to grip the side of the mattress to keep himself from falling flat on his face off the edge of the bed.

Not a bed, he realized as his eyes slitted open again.

The couch.

No wonder his body felt as if he'd been stuffed inside a washing machine and set on heavy-load cycle. His joints popped as he stretched, and the dull, heavy pounding inside his head turned needle sharp.

Stupid. Stupid. Stupid.

He had intended to cut the edge of his frustration, but he hadn't intended to drink as much as he had. He hadn't even ordered anything hard, as he'd originally intended. But one beer had led to another, and before he knew it, he'd been commiserating with several of the other patrons there and they'd all wanted to buy him drinks. Fortunately, a couple of his new-found pals had helped him back to the apartment, though he wasn't sure what time that had been.

He glanced at his wristwatch, waited a moment for the dial to come into focus. *Dammit*. It was almost eleven.

The apartment was quiet. Too quiet. And he knew. Knew that they'd already left.

He had no idea which airline or what time their flight was leaving. All she had said was afternoon.

Dammit, dammit, *dammit*.

The last morning he would have had to spend time with his daughter for six months and he blew it by lying around in a drunken stupor.

And Raina.

It was the last chance he had to see her for six months, too. He rubbed at the tightness in his chest and knew it had nothing to do with too many beers.

They were leaving today. Flying off to Florence.

He closed his eyes and hauled in a slow breath, then dragged his hands through his hair. Even that slight movement made his head pulsate. The only other time he'd ever woken up feeling like this was the morning after his accident and he'd found himself lying in a hospital bed. That hadn't been a great deal of fun, either.

Ironic, wasn't it, that both occasions revolved around Raina. He'd only wanted to go out and buy the woman some flowers, for God's sake, a few roses or—

His eyes flew open and he glanced up sharply, ignoring the pain that shot through his temple.

Flowers.

He'd gone out to buy her flowers. It had been too

early on a Sunday morning for the florist to be open, so he'd taken the back road leading to Sydney's restaurant, hoping that she'd have some extra roses. It had snowed the night before...the roads were slick. He'd been lost in thought, thinking about Raina...the truck slid on a patch of ice and then—

Nothing.

Dammit! He couldn't remember what happened after that. Blackness. Absolute, complete darkness.

He closed his eyes, pushed out every other thought and simply let his mind take him....

Gabe and Melanie's wedding...the sound of silverware clinking on champagne glasses. *To the bride and groom,* he could hear himself saying...

But he'd already remembered that little snippet of the wedding, Lucian thought in frustration. The toast he'd made to the bride and groom.

He forced himself to relax...saw himself standing in the back of the ballroom...Raina beside him...

Why don't I drive you back? I've got to take these presents over to the house, anyway.

At Gabe's house, brushing the snow off his jacket after the last present had been brought in....

Would you like some coffee?

Sure.

They'd stared at each other, only inches apart...and then she was in his arms, he was kissing her, both of them drunk, not from champagne, but each other.

Oh, God. He remembered. Not details, but most of it. Staggering up the stairs, struggling with clothes, the desperation to make love with her.

The morning after.

Be back in fifteen. Please don't leave.

He hadn't wanted her to go. He'd wanted her to stay. With him.

Just like now.

Panic filled him. How could this be happening twice?

I'm leaving for Florence Friday morning. I'll be gone six months.

Through the thick fog covering his brain, her words from last night came rushing back to him.

Why would I say no to something like this? she'd asked him and he hadn't had an answer.

Signing a license and wearing rings doesn't make this a marriage...as far as I've seen, nothing's changed.

Why would I say no to something like this...?

Nothing's changed....

His skull nearly broke in two at the sudden explosion of bells inside his head. The phone, he realized, and grimaced at the persistent shrieking.

The phone! It had to be Raina. It had to be!

He tripped over his feet, half stumbled, half crawled to the kitchen phone and snatched the receiver off its cradle.

"Raina!" he shouted into the phone. "Raina, is that you?"

"'Fraid not," Melanie said at the other end of the line. "Guess you'll just have to talk to me instead."

The call for her flight's departure brought Raina's head up from the game of peekaboo she'd been playing with Emma. Beside her, Teresa stood, then held her hands out to the baby, who smiled brightly and pumped her arms in excitement.

"Time to go, sweetheart," Raina said as she kissed her daughter, then handed her to Teresa.

With a sigh Raina gathered the diaper bag and her tote, then followed Teresa and Emma toward the gate entrance with all the other boarding passengers. Outside the tall, glass window, Raina saw their plane, heard the loud whir of its engine.

The finality of it, knowing that she was really leaving, made her chest ache.

Blinking back the threatening tears, she reached into her bag for their boarding passes, pulled them out and started to hand them to a pretty blond gate attendant—

"Raina! Stop!"

Her head jerked up at the frantic call.

"Please, stop, just stop!"

Her heart did stop.

Lucian.

He came running through the crowd of people, barreling his way through the bodies surrounding him, yelling her name.

Her heart kicked into high gear, hammering against her ribs. All she could do was stare as he came at her like a quarterback with a football.

"Lucian?"

Out of breath, he slammed to a stop in front of her. His face was flushed and unshaven, his hair spiked on the top, and he was still wearing the same wrinkled blue shirt and jeans he'd had on this morning. He smelled like strong coffee and peppermint.

"Raina," he gasped between breaths. "You can't leave."

"What are you doing here?" She wasn't certain

her knees would hold her, they were shaking so badly. "How did you know how to even find me?"

"Melanie," he said, still breathing heavy. "She called this morning. She knew. You can't leave, Raina. You can't."

Raina glanced around at all the faces staring curiously at them. Even Teresa watched, one brow lifted. "Lucian, we've been through this. Nothing's changed."

"Excuse me," the gate attendant said a bit impatiently, "are you coming through?"

"Yes." Raina held the tickets out.

"No." He snatched them away.

"Hey!" She narrowed a gaze at him. "Give those back to me."

He looked over at Teresa. "Teresa, please, just wait right there," he said, then took hold of Raina's shoulders and pulled her aside to let other passengers go by. "Raina, please, you've got to at least listen to me."

"You've got thirty seconds." Any longer than that, and she knew she'd crumble, that she'd say yes to anything as long as she could be with him.

"You're wrong."

Her heart sank. "You came all the way down here to tell me I'm wrong? Goodbye, Lucian."

She tried to pull away, but he tightened his hold. "Will you just listen to me? I came here to tell you that you're wrong about nothing changing. It *has* changed, dammit. Everything has changed."

She went still at the urgency in his voice and the desperation in his eyes. And there was something else, something she dared not even think...

"You were wrong when you said there was no reason for you to stay." His hands gentled on her arms, and his voice softened. "And you were wrong when you said our marriage was nothing more than a license and rings. You're wrong, Raina. There's every reason for you to stay."

"What, Lucian?" she heard her own breathless whisper. "What reason?"

"I love you."

The breath she'd been holding shuddered out. She looked into his eyes and it *was* there, what she'd thought she'd seen. She had to swallow the thickness in her throat before she could speak.

"You love me?"

"I've loved you from the moment I first laid eyes on you."

"You mean at the airport in Philadelphia?"

He shook his head. "No. I mean the *first* time."

"But you don't...you couldn't remember."

"I couldn't, until this morning. I'm still fuzzy on a lot, but the one thing I remember with clarity is the most important. I admit I resisted, that I even denied it to myself, but it's the truth, sweetheart. I fell head over heels in love with you at first sight. I didn't want you to leave after Gabe and Melanie's wedding. I wanted you to stay with me."

As worked up as he was, as frantic as he was, Raina was surprised that airport security hadn't already dragged him away. But it seemed as if everyone around them was simply watching, waiting with bated breath to see how this real-life drama would unfold.

She still wasn't sure herself.

"What are you saying, Lucian?" she asked carefully, needed to be very, very sure that she wasn't misunderstanding.

"Stay with me." He took her hand, brought it to his lips. "You and Emma. We can live anyplace you want. Bloomfield, New York, Florence. Timbuktu. I don't give a damn as long as you let me love you. As long as you give me a chance to make you love me, too."

Too staggered to speak, she stared at him. He didn't know? He couldn't see?

"Are you blind, Lucian?" she finally managed to say, then started to laugh. "You big idiot. Of course I love you!"

Relief poured through Lucian. *She loves me,* he thought, delirious with joy. Like the love-happy idiot he truly was, he gave a shout and picked her up. Her bags dropped to the ground, and he swung her around. Laughing, she wrapped her arms around his neck.

When he set her back down again, he kissed her, a long, deep, lingering kiss.

"Ah, excuse me," the gate attendant said awkwardly. Even she had a hopeful look on her face. "But we're going to have to close the gate. Are you staying?"

"If you can't stay," he said roughly, felt the words rip at his gut, "I'll catch the next flight. I can't be without you and Emma, I can't live without either one of you. Not even six hours, let alone six months. God, I need you both."

"You don't have to go anywhere, Lucian." She cupped his face in her hands. "I'm staying. Of course, I'm staying."

At the sound of scattered applause, Lucian glanced

up. Several women had wistful expressions on their faces, and a few of the men were grinning. Even Teresa had tears in her eyes. With a nod of approval, the nanny walked over and placed his sleeping daughter into his arms.

He had to swallow the tightness in his throat, was certain his heart was about to swell and burst with the love he felt for the child in his arms and the woman at his side.

"What about Florence?" he asked, afraid to give her an opportunity to change her mind, but knew that he had to. "What will happen if you don't go?"

"I'll have to make a lot of phone calls, but I can make it work," she said. "Looks like my assistant is going to get that trip to Italy she's always wanted."

"I can move to New York," he said firmly. "My brothers can take over my end of the business. I can sell the house once it's finished—"

"Sell our house?" She frowned and shook her head. "Not on your life. I've already got my office picked out, first bedroom on the upstairs right. Our daughter's bedroom will be across the hall."

"And the other two bedrooms?" He lifted a brow. "What do you suggest we do with those?"

"Well," she said, curving her lips, "it *would* be a shame to waste all that wonderful space, now wouldn't it?"

"Yeah, it would." He wondered how fast he could finish the house, if it were possible for his daughter to say her first word or take her first step in their new home together. He'd have help, he knew. Callan and Gabe and Reese, they'd all pull together for him. Together they could make it happen.

But the thought of his brothers also made him wince.

"Lord help me if my brothers ever catch wind of what I did here today," he said with a chuckle. "They would rib me ruthlessly for the rest of my life."

Amusement and love shone in Raina's deep-blue eyes as she slipped an arm through his and leaned over to kiss her daughter's cheek. "Just as long as we're around to see it."

"Oh, you're going to be around, all right." He deepened the kiss. "For the rest of my life, darlin'."

"You think you can remember that, Lucian?" She leaned toward him, pressed her lips lightly to his.

"I'll remember." He deepened the kiss and smiled. "Trust me, I'll remember."

* * * * *

HIS BABY SURPRISE

by
Kathie DeNosky

KATHIE DeNOSKY

lives in deep Southern Illinois and enjoys dining out, shopping, travelling through the southern and south-western states and collecting Native American pottery. After reading and enjoying Silhouette Desires for many years, she is ecstatic about being able to share her stories with others as a Silhouette author. She often starts her day at 2:00 am so she can write without interruption, before the rest of the family is up and about.

You may write to Kathie at PO Box 2064, Herrin, Il 62948-5264, USA.

To Wayne Jordan, for answering
my endless questions.

One

"**W**hat's wrong now, Martha?" Tyler Braden asked, sighing heavily.

He picked up a patient file from the top of the well-worn counter. In the three days since his arrival in Dixie Ridge, Tennessee, Ty had learned a very important lesson about Nurse Payne. Whatever thoughts she had, she freely shared.

"Are you gonna wear your Sunday-go-to-meetin' clothes every day of the week, Doc?"

Ty opened his lab coat to look down at his white shirt, striped tie and charcoal dress slacks. "What's wrong with the way I'm dressed?"

Martha looked at him over the top of her wire-rimmed glasses as if she thought he might be a bit simpleminded. "Around here, folks don't get gussied up like that unless they're gettin' married or buried."

Ty arched a brow. "What would *you* suggest I wear, Martha?"

She patted the thick, gray bun at the base of her neck—a gesture he'd quickly come to recognize as Martha's preamble to a lecture. When she walked around the counter to stand in front of him, her gaze raking him from head to toe, he had to fight the urge to reach down and make sure his fly was closed. A quick glance south of his belt buckle assured him it was.

"First of all, you need to lose the tie and white shirt. They make you look like you're about to choke." Martha looked thoughtful. "Doc Fletcher wears sports shirts, but you ain't as long in the tooth as Doc, so a T-shirt or sweater would suit you best." She pointed to his crisply pressed slacks, the creases razor sharp. "And while you're at it, you might want to buy yourself some jeans and save those for church." She shrugged. "Course it's up to you. But I'm warnin' you. Folks around here don't care too much for somebody puttin' on airs."

"But I'm not—"

"If you don't want to know, don't ask." Having pronounced judgment, Martha walked back around the counter and picked up the ringing phone. "Dixie Ridge Health Clinic."

Ty bit the inside of his cheek to keep his epithet to himself. When he'd first phoned Dr. Fletcher to discuss temporarily taking over the clinic, the older man had warned him about the crusty nurse.

"Old Martha will be your most valuable asset, but she'll also be your worst critic. Be sure to stay on her good side."

But mere words could never have prepared Ty for

the reality of Martha Payne. With a pleasant, grand-motherly face and the voice of a drill sergeant, she ran the clinic like a well-oiled machine. Serving as both receptionist and nurse, she demonstrated an efficiency that astounded Ty as much as her outspokenness irritated the hell out of him. Since his arrival, he'd been subjected to lectures ranging from his waste of gauze and tape to the appropriate way of answering the clinic phone. Now it appeared her opinions were taking a more personal turn.

Ty had noticed a quiet reserve about the patients. But preoccupied with their symptoms and complaints, he'd assumed it was because they didn't know him. He'd never dreamed it could be because of the clothes he wore. Pulling at the knot of his tie, he yanked it free and stuffed it into the pocket of his lab coat. Thank God, when his six months here were finished, he'd head back to Chicago and not have to listen to Martha reiterate his shortcomings.

Fifteen minutes later Ty bid farewell to Harv Jenkins with a reminder to take his medication regularly, then walked up to the reception counter. "Is that it for the day?"

Martha shook her head and shoved a chart across the counter. "Freddie Hatfield just brought Lexi in. Her water broke and contractions are two minutes apart. She's in the birthin' room and I'd say it won't be too long before it's showtime."

"Has she had any problems during the pregnancy?" Ty asked, scanning the chart. Dr. Fletcher had made few notations aside from the patient's weight and blood pressure.

"Nope. I've known Lexi Hatfield all her life and she's always been as healthy as a horse."

"Has she expressed any concerns about the delivery?"

"Nope." Beaming, Martha rounded the end of the counter. "She's doin' pretty good for a first-timer. But Freddie couldn't get past the front door."

"Nervous wreck?" Ty asked, following Martha down the narrow hall leading to the infirmary.

"Unless it's a matter of life and death, Freddie Hatfield avoids this place like a bachelor avoids a widow's convention." Martha shook her head and laughed. "Always has been delicate. Faints dead away at the smell of antiseptic."

Delicate?

Ty frowned at Martha's description of Fred Hatfield. Of all the terms he thought she might use to describe a man with a weak stomach, delicate wasn't among them.

A low moan from the infirmary broke through his musing. While Martha went to check the patient, Ty entered the locker room to change clothes.

All in all, he'd had a pretty good day, he decided, pulling on the blue scrubs. He hadn't seen anything more serious than Harv Jenkins's sore joints, and anticipated a routine birth.

Rotating his shoulders, Ty found much of the tension that had plagued him in recent weeks had begun to dissipate. Now if he could just get the nightmares under control....

Shaking off the guilt and regret, Ty scrubbed, plastered a smile on his face and shouldered open the door to the birthing room. He wasn't about to let the tragic events that led to his being here intrude on his good mood.

"Where's Freddie?" the patient asked.

Martha laughed. "Where do you think?"

"Over at the Blue Bird."

A tingle raced the length of Ty's spine at the patient's familiar soft southern drawl. Only one woman's voice had ever affected him that way. He glanced over at the bed, but Martha blocked his view. If he didn't know better, he'd swear—

He shook his head at the ridiculous thought.

"Freddie took off out of here like a scalded dog," Martha said.

As he tied the bottom strings of the mask around his neck, Ty listened to the patient groan, then huff and puff her way through a contraction. When it finally eased, she blew out a deep cleansing breath.

"Freddie's a big wimp," she said, her voice raspy.

He couldn't have said it better. No matter how queasy old Fred was, the guy could at least try to be present for the birth of his child.

"O-o-oh, why do they…have to come…so close together?" the woman moaned a split second before she began panting her way through another pain.

His disdain for the weak-kneed Fred increased. Compelled to reassure his patient, Ty walked over to the side of the bed. "You'll do just…"

His voice trailed off as he stared openmouthed at the woman in the final stages of labor. Alexis Madison, popular talk radio hostess and, until almost a year ago, Ty's next door neighbor, was about to give birth in a rural health clinic in eastern Tennessee.

The last time he'd seen Alexis had been the night before she left Chicago. Due to a station buyout, she'd been told to move her show to Los Angeles or find work elsewhere. She'd chosen to quit and move back to Tennessee. In fact, she was one of the reasons he'd taken the job in Dixie Ridge. When he'd been looking for a place to hide from the media, he remembered her talking about the peace and quiet of the Smoky Mountains. After sending out a few feelers, he'd jumped at the chance to temporarily take over the clinic.

The disappointment tightening his chest surprised him. He'd been more than a little attracted to her from the moment they met and had intended to look her up while he was here in the hopes of becoming better acquainted. But there wasn't any reason to do that now. She'd obviously found some guy named Fred as soon as she moved back, gotten married and started a family.

He forced a smile as he gazed down at her. "Hello, Alexis."

Lexi figured it had to be the pain causing hallucinations. It had been almost ten long months since she'd heard Tyler Braden's rich baritone. Besides, the location was all wrong. She was back home in the mountains of Tennessee, not the concrete jungle of Chicago.

But when she opened her eyes, the metallic taste of fear spread through her suddenly dry mouth and she let out a horrified moan. "N-o-o-o…not you!"

"You knew Doc Fletcher wouldn't be here for the delivery," Martha reminded her. She reached up to pat Ty's shoulder. "This here's Doc Braden. He's fillin' in."

Panic swept through Lexi and she grabbed the front of Martha's white uniform. "Get him away from me!"

"Simmer down, Lexi." Martha disengaged herself

and turned to Ty. "Don't take offense. They all act like they're devil possessed by the time they reach this stage of the game."

"Please, Martha," Lexi pleaded. She had to make the woman understand she didn't want Tyler Braden anywhere near her. "I don't want *him* delivering my baby."

"Lexi, you know there ain't another doctor within thirty miles of here," Martha said, her voice stern.

"Then you do it!"

"Now, cut that out." Martha shook her finger. "You know the only time I catch a baby is when the doctor can't get here in time."

"Then go tell Freddie to get the car…and take me to Granny Applegate!" Lexi felt like a beached whale as she struggled to sit up.

"Who the hell is Granny Applegate?" Ty asked.

"An old woman up on Piney Knob," Martha said, pushing Lexi's shoulders back down when she finally managed to prop herself up on her elbows. "Granny takes care of some of the folks around here with her home remedies. And she's delivered more babies than a porcupine has quills or time to count 'em."

Upset and completely unprepared for the next contraction, Lexi moaned. Pain pulled at her insides, demanding her body take action. Closing her eyes, a guttural sound rumbled in the back of her throat as she strained with all her might to push her baby into the world.

When the contraction ended, she opened her eyes to see Ty shaking his head. "Don't be ridiculous, Alexis. There's no other choice. You wouldn't make it as far as the front door before you give birth."

"You two know each other?" Martha asked curiously, her keen eyes assessing the situation.

"We've met," Ty said, a muscle along his lean jaw tightening.

"A long time ago-o-o," Lexi added as her body demanded another push.

Ty frowned and stepped to the end of the bed. "Unless I miss my guess, your protest is about to become a moot point. How long have you been having contractions, Alexis?"

When he tried to lift the sheet, Lexi planted her feet on the end of it. "My name is Lexi. And leave that sheet alone."

He pulled at the linen. She pressed her feet down more firmly.

"All right, Lexi. How long have you been in labor?"

"Since early this morning." She couldn't think of a more humiliating situation than her current position, and where Ty was about to look. They were really no more than casual acquaintances. "Get away from me."

He ignored her protest, freed the sheet and arranged it over her bent knees. "Why did you wait so long before you came to the clinic?"

"I didn't realize…I was in labor-r-r." Another wave of pain swept over her and she completely forgot her embarrassment as she rode the swell of the contraction. "I just…had a backache…until my water broke. That's when…the pain really became intense."

Ty's examination confirmed his earlier suspicions. Alexis was fully dilated and the fetus had entered the birth canal. "We'll have to put this argument on hold for a while, Lexi. You're about to have your baby."

Pushing his personal feelings aside, Ty's physician instincts took control. "We need to get her feet in the stirrups, Martha."

Martha nodded and moved the retractable equipment into place. "These new birthin' beds are the best thing to come along since penicillin. Maybe we'll get more maternity cases here at the clinic now that we have this little jewel."

"Where do most of the women go?" Ty asked as he tied his mask in place. "Granny Applegate?"

"Yep. Most of the women on the mountain have Granny come to their house." Martha chuckled at his disapproving frown. "Now, don't go gettin' your shorts in a bunch, Doc. She's a licensed midwife and when she runs into trouble, she always gives us a holler."

Ty didn't have time to respond to Martha's explanation when Alexis moaned and voluntarily lifted her feet to brace them in the stirrups. As he positioned himself at the end of the bed, his gaze locked with hers. Limp from perspiration, her golden brown hair had been pulled back with some type of clip, drawing his attention to the exhaustion marring her beautiful face. His chest tightened at the tears filling her emerald eyes, the trembling of her perfect lips, and the bright spots of color staining her creamy cheeks. She was extremely tired, in tremendous pain and understandably frightened. She needed the baby's father at her side, lending his strength, letting her know he was there for her when she needed him most.

"You're doing great, Lexi," he encouraged. "I can see the baby's head."

She nodded and squeezed her eyes shut. "It really hurts, Ty."

He felt her pain all the way to his soul. On impulse, he reached out, took her hand in his and gave it a gentle squeeze. "It won't be much longer. I promise."

The simple act of reassurance quickly had his insides churning with emotions he didn't have the time, nor the inclination, to sort through. Another contraction demanded their attention.

Supporting the baby's emerging head, he automatically urged, "I need you to give me one more big push and it will all be over."

As Alexis pushed with all her might, first one shoulder, then the other slipped free and the baby slid into Ty's waiting hands. Quickly suctioning the mucus and blood from the baby's mouth and nose, he watched the infant stare at him bleary-eyed for a moment, scrunch its little face, open its mouth and wail at the top of its tiny lungs.

The kid had the temper of a Chicago cab driver and enough volume to put a banshee to shame.

Ty smiled. "Martha, mark the time of birth," he said, clamping the umbilical cord in two places.

"It's a boy, Lexi!" Martha said happily, recording the numbers.

Alexis laughed. "Are you sure? I just knew I'd have a girl."

"Unless little girls have started comin' with extra plumbing, that's a boy," Martha said, chuckling. "What are you gonna name him?"

"Matthew."

Ty barely heard the two women as a crushing tightness filled his chest. No matter how many times he

witnessed the miracle of birth, it never failed to fill
him with a humbling sense of wonder, as well as a
twinge of regret. Since he didn't intend to have children, he'd never have a moment like this to call his
own.

Fred the Cream Puff was one hell of a lucky man.
And the wimpy little jerk wasn't even here to realize
it.

A mist clouding his eyes, Ty examined the squirming infant. Ten fingers. Ten toes. He grinned. An im-
pressive sprinkler system.

But as Ty looked more closely at the baby, his
smile faded and he felt the blood drain from his face.
A tiny dimple dented the infant's chin, an inch of
black hair covered his head and a small cowlick at
his forehead caused his hair to part on one side.

Ty thought back to that night in Chicago. The one
and only night he and Alexis had—

He stared in awe at the miracle he held, his gut
clenching painfully as realization slammed into him
with the force of a physical blow. The resemblance
was more than just coincidental. It was undeniable.
And that telltale little cowlick proved it. It had been
a family trait for generations.

Tyler Braden had just delivered his own son.

Two

Ty handed Lexi her son, and while he dealt with the usual postpartum procedures, she focused her attention on the squirming infant in her arms. Matthew Hatfield's tiny fists flailed the air like a frustrated prizefighter, and his displeasure with the whole business of being born was written all over his little red face.

Love like she'd never known surged through her.

With a full head of black hair, a tiny dimple in his chin and a cowlick at the edge of his forehead, he was the most beautiful baby she'd ever seen—and the spitting image of his father.

The realization caused Lexi to glance up at the man who had unwittingly helped create the infant she held. How could fate be so cruel? Of all the hundreds of thousands of licensed physicians in the world, why did Tyler Braden have to be the one to take over the

Dixie Ridge Health Clinic while Doc Fletcher had his knee replacement surgery?

Ty was an experienced trauma specialist, for heaven's sake. One of the best in his field. Why wasn't he in some huge hospital, taking care of real emergencies? Why wasn't he seven hundred miles away—in Chicago—where he belonged?

A mixture of fear and apprehension filled Lexi to the depths of her soul as she watched Ty. Was he aware the miracle he'd participated in just happened to be the birth of his own son? And if he did realize the baby she held had been the result of their only night together, how would he react? Would he even care?

He hadn't said anything, but that did little to alleviate her fears. She didn't know him well enough to know how he'd react. He might be the type of man who could be a seething caldron of rage on the inside, yet appear to be the epitome of calm. She just didn't know.

When Ty reached over to lift the now sleeping infant and place him into Martha's outstretched arms, Lexi tensed. "Where are you taking my son?" She'd tried to keep her voice steady, but exhaustion and panic sharpened her tone.

"Don't worry, Lexi," Martha reassured. She hefted the baby onto her ample bosom and headed for the door. "I'm just gonna give this little man his first bath. Then, after Doc checks him over, I'll bring him in for you to nurse."

Lexi quietly watched Ty take her blood pressure and listen to her heart, when what she really wanted to do was jump out of bed, grab her son and put as much distance as possible between them and the clinic. Draping the stethoscope around his neck, Ty reached down to place his fingers on her wrist. Her skin tingled at the contact and her breathing became shallow.

Dear heavens, had she lost her mind? She'd just had a baby and her body felt as if she'd pushed a bowling ball through a keyhole. That should be enough to make her swear off men for life. The very last thing she should be feeling was any kind of awareness.

But whether she should or not, there was no denying its presence, or its cause. Ty had always had that effect on her. She could still remember the first time he'd spoken to her in the elevator of their apartment building. It had been the day he'd moved in. When he'd said, "Hi. I'm your new neighbor," his smooth baritone had surrounded her like a soft velvet cape. And it had taken her a good fifteen minutes to get her pulse back down to normal.

After that they'd rarely seen each other. Until the night she'd lost her job and—

No. She wouldn't—couldn't—think about that now. If she did, panic would set in and she might give away her secret. At the moment, she was at his mercy and there wasn't any way she could get away from him.

"When will the baby and I be able to go home?" she asked cautiously.

Ty ignored her question as he fought the turmoil raging within. He gritted his teeth and tried to ignore the feel of her soft skin beneath his fingers, the heated current traveling the length of his arm and exploding in his gut. How could he feel anything but contempt for Alexis after what she'd done? The shock of finding that he was the father of her child had damn near brought him to his knees only minutes ago.

"Everything appears to be fine with you and the baby," he finally managed to say. "Looks like the two of you will be going home in a couple of days." He hurriedly scribbled notations on her chart, snapped it shut and headed for the door. He had to get away from her before his cool facade cracked and his tangled emotions spilled out with the force of a raging river. "I'll be in to check on you later."

Knees that threatened to buckle carried him from the room, down the hall and into his office. Closing the door behind him, Ty leaned heavily against it.

He wanted answers and he wanted them now, but reason won out. Alexis needed to rest, and an upsetting confrontation at this point would be counterproductive. Besides, he wasn't sure he could talk to her without a serious breach of his professionalism.

A light tap on the door signaled that Martha had finished bathing the baby.

"He's ready for your examination, Doc," Martha called from the other side. "We'll be in exam room one."

Ty tossed the chart on the desk, then sank down in the chair behind it. "Bring him in here, Martha."

"While you get acquainted with our newest patient, I'm gonna run over to the Blue Bird Cafe and tell Freddie that everything went just fine," Martha said as she entered the room and handed Ty the precious bundle she carried. She paused for a moment, watching him cradle the infant to his chest. "I know this sounds like I ain't got the brains God gave a squirrel, but that baby sorta looks like you."

Ty couldn't have responded if his life depended on

it. When Martha quietly closed the door behind her as she left, he barely noticed. A lump the size of his fist clogged his throat, and the moisture suddenly misting his eyes was dangerously close to spilling down his cheeks. When the baby wrapped tiny fingers around one of his own, the lump in Ty's throat felt as if it grew to the size of a basketball.

Love, so fierce it was almost debilitating, raced through him as he stared down at his son. Ty had never allowed himself to believe a moment like this would be his to treasure. Never let himself entertain the thought of having a child of his own.

But no matter what reasons Alexis had for keeping her pregnancy a secret, Tyler Braden did have a son. And he'd be damned before he sat idly by and watched another man take his place in raising the boy.

For all he cared, the very squeamish, thoroughly inadequate Fred Hatfield could take a short leap off a tall cliff.

As long as it was in his power to prevent it, history would not repeat itself. Unlike Ty, Matthew was going to know his father and never feel the social inferiority that Ty had always felt.

He placed a kiss on the baby's forehead and made a solemn promise to himself and his son. "You're going to know I love you and that I'll always be there for you." He hugged the baby close. "And I'll walk through hell before I let Fred Hatfield or your mother stand in my way."

Lexi woke with a start, her heart pounding. She sat up and frantically searched the dimly lit room for the wicker bassinet Martha had placed Matthew in after he finished nursing.

It was nowhere in sight.

Panic tearing at her insides, Lexi reached for the call button, but her hands trembled so badly she couldn't engage the switch. Tossing it aside, she threw back the sheet and tried to get out of bed.

Her sore body protested the rapid movement and her knees threatened to give way when she stood, but she ignored the warnings. She had to find her baby.

By the time she crossed the room and made it down the long corridor to the deserted reception area, her flagging strength was all but spent and she had to lean against the wall for support.

"Martha—"

"Lexi, what in the name of all that's holy are you doin' out of bed?" Martha sent her swivel chair skating backward as she rose and hurried to Lexi's side. "I told you the first time you got up, I had to be there in case you needed help."

The room began a sickening swirl and Lexi felt herself start to sag. "Where's…my baby?"

"Doc, get out here," Martha yelled when Lexi leaned heavily against her. "Now!"

Just before Lexi lost her battle with the dark curtain closing around her, strong arms scooped her up and lifted her to a wide chest. Her nostrils filled with the essence of the man holding her. He smelled of spice cologne and…baby powder.

He must have been holding the baby when Martha called for help. The thought instantly cleared her fog-filled head.

Strength flowed from Ty's body to hers as he cradled her to him, and Lexi squeezed her eyes shut against the wave of emotion welling up inside her.

"Please, put me down."

"No."

"I can walk," she insisted.

"Yeah, right." Ty laughed, but the sound held little humor. "Trying to walk is what damned near had you kissing the floor."

Without another word, he carried her down the corridor to her room and tucked her into bed. At the loss of contact, Lexi suddenly felt cold and abandoned. It was a ridiculous feeling, considering the circumstances, but it was still very real.

With calm efficiency, Ty wrapped a blood pressure cuff around her upper arm, pumped air into it, then slowly released the valve as he listened with his stethoscope. Apparently satisfied with the reading, he took her pulse, recorded the numbers on her chart, then folded his arms across his chest to stare down at her.

"It isn't called labor for nothing, Alexis," he said, his voice stern. "Your body had to work very hard and use a lot of energy in order for you to give birth. And although I don't advise a patient staying in bed more than a few hours following a routine delivery, I do expect her to listen to orders."

Lexi ground her teeth to keep from screaming that it was his fault she'd gotten up, that she'd had a terrible nightmare in which he'd taken her baby. But caution forced her to remain silent. In no way did she want to arouse Ty's suspicions.

"As you recently found out, feeling faint is not uncommon the first time a woman tries to walk after giving birth," Ty continued to lecture. "That's why you were told to wait for Martha's assistance."

Lexi glared at him. "Are you quite finished, Dr. Braden?" When he gave her a slight nod, she asked the question foremost on her mind. "Where's my son?"

"He's right here," Martha said, wheeling the bassinet to the side of Lexi's bed. "He's been visitin' with Doc while you took a nap." Turning to Ty, she asked, "Are you sure you don't want me to stay?"

"Go ahead, Martha," Ty said, nodding. "I can handle things from here."

"Doc Fletcher always wanted me to be here when we had an overnight patient," she said, clearly miffed.

Ty shrugged. "Dr. Fletcher had a wife to go home to. I don't. Besides, I'll be here anyway. I have to get caught up on some paperwork and it'll take most of the night to get it done."

Hoping Martha proved to be as stubborn as always, Lexi's heart sank when she saw Martha hesitate. "Are you sure?"

"I promise I'll take good care of them," Ty said, smiling. "Now go home and get some rest."

Lexi watched with growing horror as Martha finally nodded and walked toward the door. "If you need me, you've got the number," Martha said, waving goodbye.

The very last thing Lexi wanted was to be left alone with Ty. In fact, she didn't want to be anywhere near him. The more time they spent together, the bigger the chance he'd realize he was Matthew's father.

As if to draw attention to that very fact, the baby let loose with a lusty cry.

"It appears somebody wants his dinner," Ty said. He picked the infant up, but seemed in no hurry to place him in Lexi's outstretched arms. "You said his name is Matthew?"

"Yes." Her apprehension intensified as Ty smiled fondly at the angry baby he continued to hold.

"Have you and Fred picked out a middle name?" he asked without looking at her.

Watching him stare down at the baby, Lexi frowned. "Did you meet Freddie this afternoon?"

"No." Ty chuckled when Matthew tried to find nourishment from the tip of his little finger. "I was with a patient. Maybe Fred and I will have the chance to get acquainted when he comes to take you and the baby home."

"Maybe," Lexi agreed.

All she had to do was keep the two from meeting. It shouldn't be hard, Lexi decided. She was quite confident that Freddie would be more than happy to wait outside the clinic.

"So, does this little guy have a middle name?" Ty asked again, interrupting Lexi's thoughts.

She searched his face, but his expression gave no indication of what he might be thinking. "Scott," she answered cautiously. "Why do you want to know?"

Ty finally handed the baby to her when Matthew found Ty's finger to be less than satisfying. "I need his full name for the birth certificate."

Relieved, Lexi managed a weak smile as she held her son close. "His name is Matthew Scott *Hatfield*."

"Of course," Ty agreed. Then, to her immense relief, he turned and left the room.

His son cradled to his chest, Ty sat in the darkened room, his eyes fixed on the sleeping woman in front of him. The months since she'd left Chicago had done nothing to lessen the effect she had on him. From the first time he'd laid eyes on her that day in the elevator, Alexis had taken his breath away with her beauty, had made his heart skip a beat when she spoke. She still did.

And earlier, when he'd carried her back to bed, the bittersweet memories of their night together had been overwhelming. The feel of her softness against him, the sweet smell of her honeysuckle-scented hair where it brushed his cheek, had made him feel as if he'd go up in flames.

But Alexis was off-limits now, married to another man. A man she was trying to pass off as Matthew's father. His jaw tightened involuntarily. Ty didn't think he'd ever forgive her for that.

He gazed down at the baby he held. Alexis may have replaced *him* with someone else, but Ty would never stand by and watch his son call another man "Daddy."

He smiled as his tension eased. He fully intended to let Alexis know he was aware of the truth.

And Ty knew exactly how to go about telling her.

Lexi's nerves were stretched to the breaking point. Time was slipping away. Fast.

If Freddie didn't show up soon to take her and the baby home, Ty would be back from his house calls. Her whole plan hinged on being gone before that happened.

When Martha walked into the room carrying an armload of fresh linens, Lexi tried to keep the anxiety from her voice as she asked, "Is Freddie out in the reception area?"

Setting the sheets on the bedside table, the older woman shook her head and began stripping the bed.

"Ain't seen hide nor hair of Freddie. And unless I miss my guess, we won't either."

Martha was right.

The smell of antiseptic and Freddie's delicate stomach were a dangerous combination. It would take a matter of life or death before Freddie Hatfield risked coming anywhere near the inside of the clinic.

Lexi walked over to the window on the far side of the room and parted the calico curtains. The sight of Freddie pacing uncertainly between the car and the clinic door made Lexi smile with relief. "I wonder how long Freddie's been out there."

Martha came over to peer out the window. "No tellin'." She laughed when Freddie stopped, glanced at the clinic door, then shook her head and started pacing again. "Goin' back and forth like that, Freddie's gonna wear a trench in the pavement."

As they watched Freddie's obvious dilemma, a shiny, red four-wheel-drive pulled into the parking lot. When the driver got out, pulled a black bag from the back seat and walked over to where Freddie stood looking helpless and forlorn, Lexi's blood turned as cold as ice.

Ty had returned and it appeared he was going to exchange polite conversation with her "husband," Freddie.

"Is something wrong?" Ty asked the obviously nervous woman.

"No," the blonde answered. A rosy glow tinged her cheeks when Ty's expression turned skeptical. "Well…sort of." She pointed a shaky finger at the clinic door. "I need to go in there…but I can't."

"Why not?" Ty asked, confused. "The clinic is open to everyone."

Her blush deepened as she struggled to explain. "It's…well, you see…I have this problem."

"What is it?" he gently coaxed. "I'm Dr. Braden. Maybe I can help."

"I don't think so," she said, her ponytail swaying from side to side as she vigorously shook her head. "I've tried to get over it. Really, I have." Her eyes pleaded for his understanding. "But there isn't anything I can do about it. It's a curse."

"What makes you think you're cursed?" Ty asked. He made a mental note to check the list of psychiatrists in Chattanooga. He just might be sending one of them a referral.

The woman closed her eyes, took a deep breath and blurted, "Aw, hell, Doc. The place makes me sick."

Ty wasn't sure what explanation he'd expected, but this wasn't it. "Excuse me?"

"It's the smell of antiseptic," she explained, clearly embarrassed. Her anxiety increasing, she twisted her hands into a tight knot. "Just one whiff of that stuff and I'll hurl in all directions."

Ty coughed to keep from laughing at her impassioned description. "I can see where that would present a problem," he agreed. "But I can't examine you out here in the parking lot."

"Oh, I'm not here to see you," the woman said hastily. "When I need a doctor, I go see Granny Applegate up on Piney Knob."

Ty frowned. Every time he heard the old woman's name or thought about her approach to medicine, he envisioned black cats and a steaming caldron of witch's brew. How could a young, seemingly intelligent woman place herself in the care of a quack like that?

"If you're not here to see me, then—"

"I'm here to take my sister-in-law and her new baby home," the woman interrupted. She gave the building a nervous glance. "But I can't let her know I'm here unless I go inside. And if I do that—"

"You'll get sick," Ty finished for her.

She seemed pleased he understood. "If you could just tell Lexi I'm here, I'd really appreciate it."

"Sure," Ty said, heading for the clinic entrance.

His disgust for Alexis's husband grew by leaps and bounds as he thought of the pretty blonde's dilemma. Evidently queasiness plagued the whole Hatfield family. Good old Fred had to have known the kind of anxiety his sister would suffer.

But did the man care how much hell he put the women in his life through? No. The ever-concerned Fred was a complete washout in the sensitivity department. How could any woman be attracted to a jerk like that?

Ty shook his head as he entered the clinic. There were some things about women he guessed he'd just never understand. He was beginning to think he didn't even want to.

Lexi turned away from the window, walked over to the bassinet and picked up the baby. In a few minutes Ty would be in to confront her with what he'd learned about her "husband." From there, it would be easy for him to figure out the rest of what she'd tried so hard to keep hidden.

She drew in a shuddering breath as she lowered

herself into the rocking chair and, holding Matthew close, set the chair in motion.

It wasn't that she wanted to keep Ty in the dark forever about his son. She'd never wanted that. But fear had kept her silent through the long months of her pregnancy, and now she needed time to come to grips with all that had happened. How was she supposed to tell a man who never intended to have a child that he'd fathered one?

"Lexi, do you feel all right?" Martha asked, concerned. "You look like you've seen a saint."

She wished what she'd just witnessed *had* been an apparition. At the moment, seeing a ghost sounded far more appealing than facing Ty.

"I'm fine," she answered, her voice far more calm than she felt. "I just want to take Matthew and go home."

"Can't say I blame you. Everybody rests better in their own bed." Martha finished tucking the corners of the sheet. "I'll get the birth certificate and a discharge paper for you to sign. Then you and that little angel can be on your way."

"I've taken care of it, Martha," Ty said, walking into the room.

Martha propped her hands on her ample hips. "If you keep doin' my job for me, we're gonna be havin' another long talk." Her menacing glare never wavered as she breezed past him.

"Great," Ty muttered, drawing Lexi's attention. "Another lecture."

Lexi's breath lodged in her throat at the sight of Ty, her fears and anxiety fading as she watched him cross the room.

Ty was, and probably always would be, the sexiest

man Lexi had ever seen. In a suit and tie he was sexy. But in jeans and a T-shirt, the man was downright sinful. The knit fabric, stretched across his wide shoulders and upper arms, drew attention to his well-formed chest muscles and bulging biceps. The royal blue color highlighted his deep, azure eyes.

. The faded denim of his jeans hugged his long, muscular legs and emphasized his narrow hips. But from her seated position, it put certain other outlined areas on eye level as well.

Lexi swallowed hard when her pulse took off at an alarming rate. She had to have some kind of record-breaking hormonal imbalance. After the ordeal of giving birth not forty-eight hours ago, she shouldn't want a man within a hundred miles of her—and especially not Tyler Braden.

"I need you to sign this release form before you go," Ty said, handing her a paper and pen.

He reached down to take the baby and Lexi watched him cradle her son—their son—in the crook of his arm. Ty smiled when he put his index finger close to the baby's hand and Matthew wrapped his own tiny fingers around it. The sight was so poignant, Lexi had to look away.

Tears filled her eyes as she signed the release form Ty had given her. She wanted to tell him Matthew was his son, wanted Ty to be as happy about the baby as she was. But he'd told her once that he never wanted a child. And he'd been quite adamant about it.

When she'd asked him why he felt that way, his eyes had taken on a fierce gleam and he'd mumbled something about not being good with children. But watching him with Matthew now, Lexi knew for certain that wasn't the case.

"Your sister-in-law is waiting for you in the parking lot," Ty said.

Prepared to face the music, Lexi took a deep breath, rose from the rocking chair and handed him the paper. The moment of truth had arrived. She'd known a showdown with Ty was inevitable once he learned Freddie wasn't her husband. But she'd hoped for more time, hoped to put things in perspective before they discussed their son's birth and the bizarre circumstances of meeting again.

"Freddie has a real problem with the clinic—"

"I know," Ty interrupted, his disgust evident. "Doesn't he realize his sister suffers from a weak stomach, too?"

Shocked, Lexi barely managed to keep her mouth from dropping open. Evidently, Freddie hadn't introduced herself.

Lexi knew she was opting for the coward's way out, but at the moment, a hasty exit was far more appealing than a confrontation she wasn't prepared to deal with.

"I'm, uh, pretty sure Freddie knows the effect the clinic has on her." Lexi tried to keep her voice even as she reached for her son. "We'd better not keep your aunt waiting, Matthew."

When Ty continued to hold the baby, their eyes locked for a long, tense moment before he finally said, "You have to wait for a wheelchair."

"I don't need—"

"It's standard policy, Alexis."

"But that's ridiculous," Lexi protested. She waited for Ty to place Matthew in her arms, but when he just stood there glaring at her, she waved her hand to encompass the room. "Look around, Ty. You're in the Dixie Ridge Health Clinic. This place is a million miles away from the protocol that dictates a big city hospital. Besides, I'm perfectly capable of walking out of here."

"That may be, but for insurance purposes we have to follow procedure," he argued.

Martha wheeled the chair into the room, her expression revealing how she felt on the subject. "For what it's worth, Lexi, I think it's pretty silly myself." She gave Ty a withering glare. "Doc Fletcher never got bent out of shape when I let a patient walk out of here on their own steam."

"I'm not Dr. Fletcher," Ty stated flatly. He turned back to Lexi. "Now, if you'll have a seat, I'll take you and Matthew out to the car."

Desperation clawed at Lexi's insides. She didn't want to run the risk of Ty talking to Freddie again. With each meeting, the odds increased that he'd learn the truth. And although she fully intended to tell him everything, she didn't want or need the added complication of explaining in front of her sister-in-law.

"Alexis?"

"I told you my name is Lexi."

"All right, *Lexi*," Ty said, emphasizing her name. "Sit down."

Lexi glared at him. "And if I refuse?"

A gleam of determination lit his dark blue eyes. "I'll pick you up and carry you out."

"You wouldn't."

"Try me." His smooth baritone carried just enough edge to it that Lexi had no doubt he meant exactly what he said.

Several tense seconds stretched between them before she reluctantly gave in and lowered herself into the chair. ''Now are you satisfied?''

He placed the baby in her waiting arms and didn't even try to hide his smug smile. She felt like punching him.

When Ty moved to take hold of the rubber grips on the back of the chair, Martha shook her head. ''I'll take care of getting Lexi and the baby out to the car, Doc. It's *my* job. You're needed in exam room two, anyway. A thump rod on one of Carl Morgan's barrels popped loose and he's gonna need a couple of stitches to close a cut on his hand.''

Ty looked bewildered. ''Thump rod?''

Martha winked and Lexi smiled in spite of herself. ''You can tell he's a city boy, can't you, Martha?''

Laughing, Martha nodded. ''Stands out like Harv Jenkins's big toe when his gout's actin' up.''

''You still haven't answered my question,'' Ty said stubbornly.

Relieved Ty wouldn't be taking her and the baby out to Freddie's car, Lexi managed to grin. ''A thump rod is a part on Carl's...boiler.''

''It's a technical term used by people in Carl's line of work,'' Martha added, her eyes twinkling merrily.

Ty frowned. ''What line of work is Carl in?''

Lexi glanced at Martha, but the woman just shrugged. How much should they tell Ty? After all, he wasn't from the mountains and he certainly wasn't accustomed to mountain ways.

''He raises pigs,'' she said, finally settling on a half-truth.

''Then why would he need a boiler?''

''He uses it to cook up pig feed, Doc,'' Martha

answered. Her air of innocence almost made Lexi laugh out loud.

When Ty didn't make a motion to leave, Lexi asked, "Was there something else?"

He suddenly flashed a smile that sent a warm, fluttery feeling all the way to the pit of her stomach, then handed her an oversize envelope. "Here's Matthew's birth certificate."

The warmth remained with her all the way out to the base of Piney Knob Mountain. Freddie turned the car off the main highway and announced, "Mary Ann Simmons was right. That doctor is a real hunk."

"I suppose," Lexi said, trying to sound completely indifferent. Her attempt failed, but fortunately Freddie didn't seem to notice.

"He's real understandin', too." Freddie glanced in the rearview mirror at Lexi, where she sat next to the baby's car seat. "He didn't even bat an eye when I told him how I couldn't go inside the clinic because of the place makin' me sick."

"That's nice," Lexi said absently. Listening to Freddie extol Ty's many virtues was the last thing she wanted or needed to hear. To distract herself from her sister-in-law's chatter, Lexi removed the decorative parchment from the large envelope Ty had given her earlier.

Scanning the document, she felt her heart lurch to a stop, then take off at an erratic gallop. It wasn't the official birth record. That would be filed at the county clerk's office. But the complimentary certificate did reflect Ty's intentions.

And they couldn't have been more clear.

Matthew's surname had been recorded as Braden. And Ty had listed himself as the baby's father.

Three

Fall had always been Lexi's favorite time of year, but as she stared out of the car window, she saw none of the fall colors painting the mountain. One question kept swirling through her mind, screaming for an answer, blinding her with its implications.

What did Ty intend to do next?

By listing himself as Matthew's father on the birth certificate, he'd let her know—in no uncertain terms—he had something in mind. But what?

He thought she was married. Didn't he care about the problems his actions could cause if she really did have a husband?

"Lexi, are you all right?" Freddie asked when she opened the car door and peered into the back seat. "You look like you stuck your finger in a light socket."

Dazed, Lexi looked around. They'd driven up the

narrow, winding road to her cabin and parked without her even noticing.

The leaves on the maple and oak trees continued their daily transformation from green to shades of rust and gold. The marigolds she'd planted at the beginning of summer still bloomed heartily despite the crispness of the early fall nights. Birds still sang with the sweet purity of freedom. The chipmunk living under her front porch still scurried about, gathering acorns for the upcoming winter.

When so much in her life had changed, how could everything look just as it had only two days before?

"Oh, Freddie, nothing is ever going to be the same," Lexi said helplessly.

"Of course it won't," Freddie agreed. She unbuckled the seat belt holding the baby's car seat and lifted it from the back seat. "But don't worry. I'm sure every first-time mother feels a little overwhelmed at the thought of taking care of her baby."

Lexi glanced down at the birth certificate she still held. "I wish that was my only worry."

"You know Jeff and I will help." When Lexi made no move to get out of the car, Freddie gave her an exasperated look. "What's gotten into you, Lexi? You couldn't wait to get away from the clinic. Now you act like you don't want to go inside the house."

Sliding the parchment back into the envelope, Lexi slowly got out of the car. She'd fully prepared herself to shoulder the responsibility of being a single mother, had completely accepted how things had to be.

But the rules of the game had changed radically with Ty's unexpected reappearance in her life. By listing himself as the baby's father, did he expect to help her raise their son? Would he try to obtain custody of Matthew?

The thought sent a chill all the way to her soul. She needed someone to confide in. Someone who would listen and at least try to understand.

Lexi stared at Freddie for several seconds as Grandma Hatfield's sage words whispered through her mind. "A burden is sometimes easier to carry if you share it with someone you trust."

She had a burden, all right, and it weighed a ton.

Taking the handle of the baby carrier in her right hand, she hooked her left arm through Freddie's. When she spoke, her voice sounded surprisingly steady, considering her insides quivered like a bowl of gelatin in an off-the-scale earthquake. "Let's go inside, Freddie. There's something I need to tell you."

It wasn't as difficult as Lexi had thought it would be, and by the time they walked into the living room, Freddie was gaping at her.

"He's what?"

"You heard me," Lexi said calmly. "Tyler Braden is Matthew's father."

Freddie collapsed on the couch, her eyes wide. "But when did you two—I mean, where—"

Lexi placed the baby in the antique cradle that had held four generations of Hatfield infants. "When? Nine months, two weeks, and four days ago. Where? Chicago." She turned to give her sister-in-law a sardonic smile. "And before you ask how—the usual way."

Her sister-in-law shook her head as if to clear it. "You mean to tell me he's a doctor and he didn't recognize the symptoms of pregnancy?"

"We..." Lexi hesitated. No matter how she said it, it was going to sound bad. "We only spent one night together." She tiredly lowered herself into the rocking chair beside the cradle. She felt as if the weight of the world rested squarely on her shoulders. "It was the night before I left to come back home."

"But what about birth control?" Freddie asked. "I mean, him bein' a doctor and all, you'd think—"

"We did use something," Lexi interrupted. She shrugged helplessly. "But there isn't any method that's one hundred percent effective."

"Except abstinence," Freddie corrected. "And if you'd picked that method—"

"We wouldn't be having this conversation," Lexi finished.

Freddie rose from the couch and began to pace the length of the room. "Does he realize Matthew is his?"

"Yes."

When Freddie whirled around, her long, blonde ponytail slapped the side of her face. "I thought you told me he didn't know about the pregnancy." Her eyes narrowed and she propped her fists on her hips. "That woodpecker knew and waited all this time—"

"No," Lexi interrupted. "I haven't said anything to Ty."

"Then, how are you sure he knows?"

Lexi handed Freddie the birth certificate. "He must have figured it out, because he listed himself as the baby's father and Matthew's last name as Braden."

Freddie scanned the document, an incredulous expression crossing her delicate features. "Granny's garters! What do you think he'll do now?"

"I wish I knew." Lexi closed her eyes and rested

her head against the high back of the rocking chair. "But that's not all."

"There's more?" Freddie looked at Lexi as if she'd sprouted horns and a tail.

Lexi nodded. Any other time, they'd find humor in Ty's assumption about her marital status. But at the moment, Lexi couldn't find anything even remotely funny about the situation.

When Lexi remained silent, Freddie frowned. "I'm not going to like this, am I?"

"Probably not." Lexi grimaced as she struggled for the courage to meet Freddie's suspicious gaze. "He thinks I'm married to *you*."

Freddie looked as if she'd been pinched. "Grandpa's long johns! Where did he get a goofy idea like that?"

"Ty heard Martha and me talking about you," Lexi explained. "I guess he assumed by the name that 'Freddie' was a man and my husband."

"And you didn't set him straight." It was more an accusation than a question.

Lexi shook her head and stared down at her tightly laced fingers. "No."

Clearly confused, Freddie plopped back down on the couch. "Why not?"

Biting her lower lip, Lexi tried to keep a sob from escaping. When she finally gained control of her emotions, her voice quavered. "I guess I was trying to buy some time…until I could figure out what to do." Tears filled her eyes as she met her sister-in-law's disbelieving gaze. "Oh, Freddie, how could I have made such a mess of things? And why couldn't he have stayed in Chicago where he belongs?"

Freddie left the couch, knelt beside the rocking

chair and put her arms around Lexi. "Do you love him?" she asked gently.

"To tell the truth, I'd have to say I don't even know him," Lexi sobbed.

"Oh, holy cow! This just gets more and more bizarre every time you open your mouth."

Tears spilled down Lexi's cheeks, and she tried to swipe them away with the back of her hand. "Ty and I were neighbors. He lived down the hall and we rarely ever saw each other. We'd pass in the hall and speak, or say 'hello' as we got on or off the elevator. But that was it. Until…the night I quit the radio station."

"What made that night different?" Freddie asked.

Lexi took a deep breath. She'd started explaining things. She might as well finish. Besides, keeping secrets was precisely what got her into this mess to begin with.

"After a meeting with the corporate wonder boy in charge of restructuring the radio station, I decided there was no way I'd move my show to L.A. I didn't want to move that far from home, so I turned in my resignation—effective immediately—and cleared out my office. Everything I'd worked to build in the last five years had just disintegrated in less than thirty minutes, and I doubt I could have felt any lower." She sniffed back a sob. "When I went back to my apartment to pack, Ty had just gotten off duty at the hospital. He looked even worse than I felt."

Freddie nodded. "But how did you two get together?"

"He said he'd had a really bad day in the E.R. and I told him about losing my job." Lexi gave her sister-in-law a watery smile. "Ty suggested that we share

dinner and a bottle of wine, since we'd both had a
rotten day. I should have refused, but I didn't feel like
being alone. So I accepted.''

"Who ended up where? Was the deed done at your
place or his?''

"Freddie!''

"Sorry, Lex, but this is just like a soap opera.''

Lexi shrugged. "My apartment had a gas fireplace
and we picnicked in front of the hearth. He brought
two bottles of wine and I supplied the cheese. We
talked about being disillusioned with life and I told
him about the peace I'd always found in these mountains and how I intended to come back here. Somehow, one thing led to another, and before either of us
knew what happened, we were gathering our clothes
and saying an awkward goodbye.''

Sitting back on her heels, Freddie shook her head.
"Geez, when I have a bad day, I feel lucky if Jeff
plays a Garth Brooks CD and pops a pizza in the
microwave so I don't have to cook supper.''

They remained silent for several minutes as the
gravity of the situation sank in.

"I wonder what he'll do now,'' Freddie finally
said.

"I'd like it if he just left me and the baby alone.''
Lexi wiped at a tear as it slid down her cheek. "Forty-
eight hours ago all I had to worry about was having
a baby. Then, in less than a split second, my whole
world is turned inside out.''

Freddie nodded sympathetically. "I can imagine it
was a real shock to find out the daddy of your baby
was gonna be the one to do the deliverin'.''

"You have no idea.'' Lexi hiccuped. "There I was,
ready to give birth, when Ty walked in. What was I

going to say? Oh, by the way, you just happen to be the father of the baby you're about to deliver. A child—'' her voice caught ''—you never wanted.''

''Now hold it.'' Freddie's pixielike features mirrored her confusion. ''How do you know he never wanted kids?''

''He told me that night.'' Lexi closed her eyes to hold back the threatening tears. ''Ty didn't say why, but I'm sure it had something to do with what he sees every day in the E.R.''

Suddenly overwhelmed, Lexi finally gave into the wave of emotion she'd held back since seeing Ty again. She cried for the circumstances surrounding their son's birth and the uncertainty of what Ty intended next.

Freddie held her while she sobbed, then handed her a tissue once the tears finally subsided. ''Maybe you're wrong about him not wantin' a baby.''

''I don't think so,'' Lexi said, wiping her cheeks.

''Jeff is never gonna believe this.''

''No!'' Her voice desperate, Lexi pleaded, ''Please don't tell anyone. And especially not Jeff. At least not until I have a chance to work this out with Ty.''

Her sister-in-law's hazel eyes filled with understanding. ''That would probably be best. Knowin' your brother, he'd go after the man with his double-barrel shotgun—''

''And all hell would break loose,'' Lexi finished for her.

They sat in silence for a time before Freddie asked, ''What's he doin' in Dixie Ridge, anyway?''

Lexi shook her head. ''I wondered that myself.''

Freddie rose to her feet. ''When do you think he'll let you know what his intentions are?''

"I don't know." Lexi rubbed at the pounding in her temples. "But I don't think I'll have too long to wait. I think what he did with the birth certificate is proof enough that Ty isn't the type of man to bide his time once he's decided on a plan of action."

Ty started counting mailboxes when he spotted the old wagon wheel leaning against a rail fence. In the city, he'd used building numbers, street names and well-known landmarks to find his way around. But here in the mountains, addresses weren't always that easy. He found himself looking for stumps and wagon wheels, counting mailboxes and relying on a tremendous amount of luck to find where he needed to go.

He turned onto the steep lane past the sixth box, a self-deprecating smile curving the corners of his mouth. When Martha informed him that he'd have to make house calls in order to treat a few of his older, less mobile patients, he'd thought the practice inefficient and outdated.

He'd been wrong.

The more he drove the winding roads snaking their way up the side of Piney Knob, the more Ty appreciated the morning ritual, felt a little more tension drain away. For the first time in more years than he cared to count, he was taking life at a slower pace, paying attention to things he'd never had time to notice before. He was beginning to like the difference in the way it made him feel, too. He liked being able to gear down and lower his guard. Not only was he getting to know the people on Piney Knob, he was beginning to know himself.

Ty gazed out the windshield at the panoramic view. Making house calls gave him the chance to enjoy the earthy tones of autumn painting the mountains with their rich hues, to see the ancient peaks and valleys shrouded with the smoky mists the area had been named for. He found he liked the frosty bite of the morning air, the clean smell of pine, instead of the sulfuric smog of the city. And this morning the practice provided another bonus.

Glancing at the packages in the passenger seat, his smile widened. Every patient on this morning's list of house calls had heard about the baby and asked if he would mind taking their gifts to Lexi. In doing so, they'd inadvertently handed him the perfect excuse to check on his son.

"Not that I need one," he muttered.

As far as he was concerned, being Matthew's father was reason enough for him to stop by the Hatfield place any time he damn well pleased.

He steered the truck around a sharp bend in the road, pulled to a stop in front of a small rustic cabin and looked around.

The place was nothing like he'd thought it would be.

In Chicago, Alexis's apartment had been highly fashionable, ultra modern and very expensive. But Lexi's house was humble and unassuming. The place looked like it had been constructed of giant Lincoln logs and might possibly have a little shed out back with a crescent moon carved in the door.

Ty shook his head as he got out of the truck and walked around to the passenger side to retrieve the gifts. He was having a hard time assimilating the two completely different lifestyles of the same woman. How could Lexi Hatfield be so different from her alter ego, Alexis Madison?

He heard the screen door squeak a moment before Lexi asked, "What are you doing here, Ty?"

He finished gathering the packages from the front seat before turning to face her. She didn't look happy that he'd dropped by. But that didn't matter. He had a right to see his son.

His arms loaded with presents, he walked toward the wide porch. "Some of my patients asked if I'd deliver their baby gifts."

"You could have taken them back to the clinic and had Martha call me." He watched her protectively fold her arms beneath her breasts. "Freddie would have picked them up."

Ty ground his teeth at the mention of Fred the Fearless. "I was in the area." Unable to hide his contempt for the man, Ty finished, "Besides, we both know good old Fred wouldn't make it past the front door." He started up the steps. "By the way, is he at home this morning?"

"No."

"Good."

"Ty—"

Their gazes locked for several tense moments as Lexi blocked his way. The wariness in her beautiful green eyes, the protective way she folded her arms in front of her, quickly had compassion tugging at Ty's insides. Fear was an emotion he'd never wanted or expected to solicit from any woman.

"These gifts are getting heavy," he said gently. When he saw indecision cross her flawless features, he urged, "Let's go inside."

Lexi hesitated before she finally opened the door and allowed him to enter. "You can put those on the table," she said, pointing to the kitchen area of the great room. "I'll look at them later."

Ty placed the packages where she'd indicated, then turned to study the rest of the house. The rustic log walls, crocheted rag rugs scattered across the polished hardwood floor, and large stone fireplace created a warm, cozy atmosphere. As he stared at the flagstone hearth, memories of their night together swamped him. A cold winter evening spent in front of a crackling fire, the flames illuminating the fine sheen of perspiration coating his and Lexi's bodies as they made love.

He shook his head and frowned. Remembering that night was wasted time and energy. She was married. If she spent any time snuggled against a man in front of a fireplace these days, it certainly wouldn't be with Tyler Braden.

"It was nice of you to take the time to bring the gifts," Lexi said from behind him. "But I'm sure you need to get back to the clinic."

"Not really." Anger surged through him. She could try dismissing him all she wanted, but he'd walk through hell before he allowed her to eliminate his presence in Matthew's life. "I've finished my house calls for the day and I don't have any appointments scheduled until later this afternoon." Careful to keep his expression as congenial as possible, he turned to face her. "Besides, I think it's time we had a long talk, Alexis."

"I told you my name is Lexi."

Ty smiled coldly. "Ah, yes. Alexis is your city name, isn't it?"

"Ty, don't—"

She looked so vulnerable, so wounded, Ty had to

stuff his hands into his jeans pockets to keep from reaching for her. He reminded himself of what she'd done, how she'd tried to keep Matthew from him.

"Where's the baby?" he asked, surprising even himself at the harsh tone of his voice.

As if on cue, a soft mewling sound began and quickly grew into an impatient cry.

He watched her glance nervously at the hall. "I'm sure you can find your way out."

When she turned and started down the hall, Ty followed. "I'd like to see how my son is doing."

He could tell by the stiffening of her slender shoulders, the balling of her fists at her sides, that his statement had touched a nerve.

Well, that was just too damned bad. Finding out she hadn't bothered to tell him about his child had tapped a few nerves of his own.

Lexi suddenly spun around to face him, her eyes snapping green fire. "Why are you here, Ty?"

"I told you, I want to see my son." He glared back at her. If she thought she was going to keep him from seeing the only child he never expected to have, she had a lot to learn. "What's the matter? Are you afraid old Freddy boy will get angry about my being here?"

"Freddie has nothing to do with this."

"You got that right," he shot back. "I'm glad to hear you admit it."

"You're impossible."

When she turned away from him to storm through a door at the end of the hall, Ty followed. Stopping just inside the room, he glanced at the big double bed, his mouth tightening into a flat line. He didn't want to think about another man sharing that bed with her, holding her close, loving her beneath the colorful patchwork quilt. He knew it was ridiculous, but it caused a primitive, territorial feeling to race through him.

He turned to watch Lexi pick up Matthew and cradle him to her. She kissed the top of the baby's head and murmured something soft and soothing, then shifted her attention back to Ty.

"You'll have to come back another time," she said. "Matthew wants to nurse."

Ty shrugged. "So, let him. It's not like I've never seen a woman breast-feed." Why he dropped the hard edge to his voice, he wasn't sure, but the next thing he knew his tone sounded suspiciously seductive when he added, "Besides, I've seen your breasts before."

Her cheeks colored a rosy pink. "Ty, please don't—"

"Please don't what? Don't remember how beautiful your body was that night? How perfect your breasts are?" He shook his head. "There are some things a man never forgets."

"You'd better try."

Ty stepped forward to free the top button of her loose cotton dress. "Not in this lifetime, honey."

He didn't have any idea what the hell had gotten into him, but he couldn't seem to stop himself from releasing the second and third buttons. His fingertips grazing her satiny skin beneath the soft calico made him swallow hard and caused his body to tighten. He brought his hand up to caress her cheek, to trace her lips with the pad of his thumb.

Why couldn't things have been different? Why hadn't she contacted him when she discovered she was pregnant?

Obviously hungry and impatient, Matthew suddenly let out a loud wail.

The baby's cry brought Ty back to his senses as effectively as a bucket of ice water. He immediately dropped his hand and took a step back.

What the hell had he been thinking? She belonged to another man. And that was one boundary Ty had never, nor would he ever, cross. Besides, she'd intended to cut him out of his son's life.

"He's going to mutiny if you don't feed him," Ty said, his voice harsh.

She hesitated. "You aren't going to stay."

Ty nodded. "I want to spend some time with my son."

She gave him a look that would have sent a lesser man packing. Ty stood his ground.

But as she walked the short distance to the rocking chair in the far corner of the room, the gentle sway of her hips caused the muscles to tighten along his jaw as he fought against the familiar stir of desire. Having a baby hadn't diminished her alluring figure or detracted from her sensuous beauty in any way. In fact, it added a softness Ty found absolutely fascinating.

If he had any sense, he'd get in his truck, drive back down the mountain and take a dip in the ice-cold river flowing through the middle of Dixie Ridge. Instead, he shoved his hands into his jeans pockets, leaned a shoulder against the tall post at the end of the bed and hoped his smile looked less forced than it felt.

With her silky golden brown hair loosely tied back, her soft cotton dress moving gently around her perfect calves and her bare feet padding across the hardwood floor, Lexi looked like the quintessential earth mother. When she seated herself, unfastened the cup of her bra and guided her breast to the baby's eager mouth, Ty felt as if his insides had been set afire.

The intimacy of watching her nurse their child was overwhelming. And he knew for certain he'd never witnessed a more beautiful or poignant sight.

It changed nothing. She'd intended to keep the existence of his child from him. He'd do well to remember she couldn't be trusted.

Lexi cursed her crazy hormones as she settled back in the big, antique chair. When Ty had reached out to unbutton her dress and his fingers brushed the slope of her overly sensitive breast, her knees had threatened to buckle and her pulse had started pounding like an out-of-control jackhammer.

She heard his sharp intake of breath, could feel his intense gaze as he watched their son take her nipple into his mouth. But she refused to look at Ty, refused to allow him a glimpse of the tears threatening to spill down her cheeks.

When she'd been pregnant, she'd dreamed of sharing a moment like this with a husband, longed for the closeness the simple act could create between a couple. But the reality of the current circumstances was more of a nightmare than any kind of romantic fantasy.

"Does Fred know I'm Matthew's father?" he asked.

"Yes. But I told you, Freddie—"

"Good," Ty interrupted. His tight smile caused Lexi to shiver. "Then he won't be too surprised when you tell him I'm demanding joint custody."

She'd known from the moment Ty walked into the birthing room over a week ago that this conversation was inevitable. But she hadn't wanted it to be like this. Not with her breast exposed and him looming over her like a wild animal ready to pounce.

Her nerves stretched to the breaking point, she jumped when the pager clipped to Ty's belt beeped. She watched him press a button on the side and read the transmission on the tiny screen.

"We'll have to talk about this later," Ty said, his expression grim. "I'm needed at the clinic."

"I'm sure you can find your way out," Lexi said, careful to keep her voice even.

Their gazes met for a long tense moment before Ty promised, "I'll be back."

"I know."

Relief flowed through her when Ty finally turned and walked down the hall. She listened as he crossed the great room and left the house. Only then did she release the breath she hadn't been aware she was holding.

When Matthew finished nursing, Lexi changed his diaper, then placed her sleeping son in the cradle for a nap. "If your daddy thinks he can come in here making all kinds of demands, he's in for a rude awakening," she whispered.

Her emotions a tangled mix of anger, fear and anticipation, Lexi went to the front door to stare at the lane Ty had driven down only minutes before. Within the next few days, he'd be back to settle things once and for all. He'd have a lot of questions and want just as many answers.

Four

$\mathbf{A}$ week and a half later, Ty had just stepped onto Lexi's porch when he heard it. It wasn't loud, and if the door hadn't been partially ajar, he probably wouldn't have noticed it at all. But once a man heard that sound, it left a permanent impression. Nothing sent a chill racing up a man's spine faster than the sound of a woman's heartbroken sobs.

He'd never in his entire life entered a house uninvited, but he didn't give the matter a second thought when he threw open the door and rushed into the great room of Lexi's small cabin. The late-afternoon shadows forced him to stop as his eyes adjusted to the muted light. He cursed even that small delay as he frantically searched for her.

Fear like he'd never known coursed through him when he found her curled up on one end of the large couch, Matthew cradled close to her breast. As a physician, he knew all too well the complications that could develop in an infant's first few weeks of life.

He knelt down in front of her. "What is it, Lexi? Is Matthew all right?"

She nodded, but when she raised her eyes to look at him, sobs wracked her slender body and a fresh wave of tears began to course down her cheeks.

"Is everything all right?" he repeated.

Nodding, she handed him the baby, covered her face with her hands and cried harder.

Ty checked Matthew to be sure and found him sleeping peacefully.

"Why are you crying?" Ty asked, thoroughly perplexed.

"I...don't...know," Lexi wailed, her face still buried in her hands. "But...I...can't stop."

Ty's confusion quickly gave way to understanding and an overwhelming sense of relief. He had a good idea what the problem was and the reason for the uncontrollable weeping. Lexi had a case of the "baby blues."

"I'll be right back," he said, rising to his feet. He walked down the hall to Lexi's room, settled his sleeping son in the cradle beside the bed, then made a detour into the small adjoining bathroom for a damp cloth.

It wasn't at all uncommon for a woman to experience unexplainable bouts of crying for several weeks after having a baby. Sudden hormonal changes combined with the responsibility and stress of taking care of an infant often overwhelmed a first-time mother. It was something a woman had no control over.

Glancing at the image of himself in the mirror above the sink, he felt guilt stab at his gut.

Great timing, hotshot.

Lexi was still trying to find her way as a new mother. A week and a half ago, he'd shown up demanding joint custody, adding a tremendous amount of tension to an already stressful situation.

That was something *he* could have controlled.

When he returned to the great room, Ty seated himself on the couch beside her and gently pulled Lexi into his arms. He bathed her face with the washcloth, but the gesture only made the tears fall faster. He finally abandoned his efforts and simply held her while her tears ran their course.

His guilt increased with each sob, and it wouldn't have surprised him to learn his picture would be inserted next to the word *jerk* in all future editions of *Webster's Dictionary*. It had been inconsiderate and insensitive to show up demanding his rights only a few days after she'd given birth. As a doctor, he should have known better. But as a first-time father, he was discovering that emotions often overrode years of training and common sense.

And his emotions weren't the only thing he was having trouble controlling. At the moment, with Lexi's face pressed to his shoulder, her warm breath feathering across the pulse at the base of his throat, his own hormones were doing their best to overpower his good intentions.

He'd only taken her into his arms to offer comfort. But his body wanted to offer a whole lot more.

Ty gritted his teeth and tried to think of something to cool the heat building inside him. Anything.

An image of the river flowing through the middle

of Dixie Ridge came to mind. The creeks and streams that ran down the mountain, and eventually emptied into it, were fed by underground springs. The water was ice-cold.

Ty mentally stripped off his clothes and dived in.

It didn't work.

He tried to think of Lexi's husband.

Snuggling on the couch with another man's wife wasn't the smartest thing he'd ever done. What if Fred walked in and found her in Ty's arms?

No help there.

The thought of Fred trying to take Ty's place as Matthew's father added an element of anger to the fire building in his gut. Nothing would please Ty more than the opportunity of taking a punch at the elusive man's nose.

He realized Lexi's tears had subsided when she sniffed and tried to push out of his arms. He tightened his hold. "Feel better?"

She nodded. "I'm…sorry. I don't know why that happened."

"It's pretty common."

Ty rubbed his cheek against her honeysuckle-scented hair. God, he didn't think he'd ever smelled a more heavenly scent.

"Please tell me…it won't happen again," Lexi said, her voice reflecting her embarrassment.

When she spoke, her lips brushed the column of his throat. His lower body reminded him the last time he'd made love had been with the woman he held.

"Normally, the mood swings don't last more than a week or two."

He stroked the length of her back and tried to tell himself he was only offering consolation. But deep down Ty knew the real reason he continued to hold Lexi, knew exactly why he didn't want to let her go. It felt so damned good to have her back in his arms, to have her soft, warm body pressed to his. How many times since that winter night in the city had he wished they'd had more time together?

Lexi felt Ty's warmth surround her, and a sense of coming home lit within her soul. He placed a finger beneath her chin, tilted her head back and kissed away the moisture still clinging to her lashes. Her pulse kicked into overdrive. His lips skimmed her forehead with aching tenderness. Her toes curled.

"It tears me apart to see you cry," he said, his voice rough.

The sound of his rich baritone sent tingles of anticipation skipping over every nerve in her body.

Lexi slowly met Ty's gaze. The look of raw hunger in his dark blue eyes took her breath.

"Hey, Lex, whose truck is that parked in the driveway?" a male voice called from the porch.

The man entering the cabin came to a dead stop at the sight of the couple cuddling on the couch.

Lexi jumped at the intrusion and quickly moved out of Ty's arms. She'd forgotten all about Jeff stopping by to fix the kitchen faucet.

She stood to face her brother. "I didn't expect you this early."

"That's obvious," Jeff said tersely, scrutinizing her appearance. She knew there was absolutely no way he'd miss the heightened color of her cheeks, her mussed hair or her labored breathing.

Ty slowly rose from the couch to stand beside her. "The SUV belongs to me."

"And just who the hell are you?" Jeff demanded, his accusing glare narrowed on Ty.

"Tyler Braden."

"He's the new doctor down in Dixie Ridge," Lexi added.

"My wife mentioned how helpful you were when she was at the clinic," Jeff growled. "But she didn't say anything about how friendly you are." He pointed to the couch. "Do you cozy up to all your female patients that way?"

Lexi glanced from her brother to Ty. Both men were eyeing each other like a couple of prizefighters competing for a title belt.

Jeff she could understand. He'd always been the overly protective older brother. But Ty?

Then, like a bolt of lightning, it hit her. Ty thought Jeff was her fictitious husband, Fred.

Great! This was just what her frayed nerves needed. She'd wanted a calm, private conversation with Ty about the birth of their son. Now she faced an explosive confrontation with the added bonus of an audience.

She had to do something. Fast. Once Jeff learned that Ty was Matthew's father, her brother would start throwing punches first and ask questions later.

"Ty, would you please check on the baby?" When he acted as if he intended to stay rooted to the spot, Lexi added a heartfelt, "Please?"

He looked as if he wanted to protest, but finally nodded and walked down the hall. She could tell by his stiff back that he wasn't at all happy about it.

Lexi watched until Ty was safely out of earshot, then turned to Jeff. Careful to keep her voice low, she pleaded, "Could you please come back later?"

Jeff rolled up the sleeves of his plaid flannel shirt, then folded his arms across his wide chest. "There's no way in hell I'm leavin' you alone with that guy."

"Why not?"

"Doctor or not, any man who puts the moves on a woman less than three weeks after she's had a baby can't be up to any good."

Lexi groaned. She recognized that stubborn look on her brother's face. Hell would freeze over before Jeff left without an explanation.

But she had to try. "I promise to explain everything later."

"No."

She watched him flex the well-developed muscles in his forearms. To get Jeff to leave now would take nothing short of a full-fledged miracle complete with thunder, lightning and a booming voice from above.

Or a feisty little pixie with fire in her eyes.

"Where's Freddie?"

Clearly confused by the unexpected question, Jeff gave her a look that said he thought she might be a few bricks shy of a full load. "At home. Why?"

She didn't bother to enlighten him as she walked over to the phone and punched in the number. To her relief, her sister-in-law answered on the second ring.

"Freddie, get over here," Lexi blurted. "Now."

"What's wrong?"

"Ty dropped by for a visit."

Freddie gasped. "And Jeff showed up to fix the faucet."

"You got it."

"Granny's garters! Have they started throwin' punches yet?"

Lexi glanced over her shoulder at her brother's

dark frown. "No, but you know Jeff. If he finds out about you-know-what before I can explain…"

"Hang on. I'll be right there."

Lexi hung up the phone, cursing her crazy hormones and men in general. Tears blurred her vision, then streamed down her cheeks to drop silently from her chin. What a perfect time for another crying jag, she thought disgustedly as she turned to face her bewildered brother.

"I'm going to have to ask a favor of you, little man," Ty said, leaning over the cradle to change his son's diaper. "I need for you to be a good boy while I settle things with your mom and Fred. Think you can do that for me?"

Matthew gazed up at Ty, waved his fists, kicked his feet and noisily sucked at the pacifier in his mouth.

"Good." Ty fastened the last tape on the diaper, then rocked the cradle gently. In less than a minute the baby's eyes closed and his pacifier stopped bobbing. "I knew I could count on your help," Ty whispered to his now sleeping son.

By the time he walked back into the living room, Lexi was sobbing uncontrollably and her husband was standing over her, looking like he faced the hangman's noose with no hope of escape.

"What the hell's wrong with her?" he asked, sounding desperate. "One minute she looked like she was ready to tear my head off, then all of a sudden she opened her mouth and started bawlin' like a baby."

Ty rubbed the tension at the back of his neck. "Hormone imbalance."

The man's cheeks colored a bright red and his mouth formed an *O* as understanding dawned. "Sorta like that monthly PMS stuff?"

Ty shrugged. "I guess that's a fair comparison."

He looked miserable. "What can we do to make her stop? I'd rather climb a barbed wire fence buck naked than listen to a woman cry."

Ty's stomach clenched. It would have been easy to take great satisfaction in the guy's misery, had it not been for the obvious concern written all over his face. Any fool could see Fred loved Lexi with all his heart and her tears were tearing him apart.

"What on earth have you two done to this poor girl?"

At the sound of the angry feminine voice, Ty looked up to see the blonde he'd met at the clinic throw open the door and rush into the house.

"Nothin'," the big man said quickly. When she glared at him, he looked beseechingly at Ty. "Tell her."

Before Ty could add his reassurance, the petite blonde put her arms around Lexi and led her to the couch. Turning on the men, she pointed to the door. "Outside! Both of you. And I better not hear your voices raised above a whisper. Is that understood?"

When they hesitated, she treated them to a look that had both men heading for the door with no thought of arguing the point further.

Ty raised a brow and shot the guy a startled glance when he muttered a subdued, "Yes, sweetpea," as they both tried to shoulder through the door at the same time.

Once outside, Ty sized up the man seated next to him on the porch steps. Fred the Cream Puff didn't look anything like Ty had imagined. Instead of a wimpy little guy with a sickly look, the man was every bit as tall as Ty, outweighed him by at least twenty pounds and appeared to be as healthy as the proverbial horse.

Ty stared at the thick stand of pines surrounding the yard. A flash of bright blue drew his attention, but he found no pleasure in his first glimpse of a mountain bluebird. He couldn't feel much of anything, beyond a numbing sense of guilt.

He'd tried to tell himself Fred was a complete jerk with no redeeming qualities at all. But Ty had just witnessed how much the guy cared for Lexi, how her tears had damned near brought the big man to his knees.

"I learned a long time ago not to cross my wife when she's in a snit," the man said. He grinned sheepishly. "It could be hazardous to my health."

"Sometimes retreat is the better part of valor," Ty agreed.

"You better believe it." The man blew out a deep breath. "My better half may be tiny, but I'll be the first to admit, dynamite comes in small packages."

Lexi was slender, but at five foot seven she certainly couldn't be considered petite. "Who are you talking about?" Ty asked, frowning.

"My wife. She may look like an angel come to earth, but when she gets on a rampage she can send the devil runnin' for cover." He laughed. "We're lucky she didn't have the time to work up a full head of steam before she threw us out."

Ty's mouth dropped open. "You're married to the blonde?"

"For the past seven years," the man said proudly.

He glanced toward the door, his smile loving. "She's really somethin', ain't she?"

Ty looked more closely at the man beside him. Although his hair was more a dark blond than golden brown, there was no denying the resemblance. He wondered why he hadn't noticed it immediately.

"You're Lexi's brother."

The man nodded as he pumped Ty's hand. "I'm Jeff Hatfield."

"I thought you were Fred."

Shaking his head, Jeff laughed. "Nope. Freddie's my wife."

Ty couldn't have responded if his life depended on it.

"Well, actually, her name is Winifred Mae Stanton-Hatfield," Jeff explained. "But she hates it. And don't even think about callin' her Winnie or Freddie Mae. You'll be sportin' a shiner in two seconds flat." He laughed and shook his head. "If you know what's good for you, you'll call her Freddie, same as everybody else."

Ty's logical mind tried to assimilate what Jeff had just told him. "Lexi isn't married," he said incredulously.

Mottled spots of anger crept across Jeff's cheeks. "No. She came home near ten months ago, single and jobless. When we found out she was pregnant to boot, Freddie and I tried to get her to tell us who left her high and dry, but she flat out refused. I even told her I'd go after the bastard with my double barrel and see that he done right by her."

Ty stiffened at the all too familiar term, but recovered enough to ask, "What did she say to that?"

"She told me it was none of my business," Jeff

said, clearly exasperated. "Can you believe that? Some city slicker leads my only sister down the primrose path and I'm supposed to forget all about it."

Staring at his hands clasped loosely between his knees, Ty took a deep breath, then met Jeff's angry gaze head on. "She apparently felt the same way about the baby's father."

"What do you mean?"

"She didn't tell me either."

Jeff looked as if he'd been smacked between the eyes with a baseball bat. "You...you're the lowdown, no good—"

"Yes."

Jeff jumped to his feet, his hands balled into tight fists. "Oh, I get it. My sister was good enough to take to bed, but not good enough to walk down the aisle. What kind of man are you? How could you just stand back and let her go through all this by herself?"

Ty stood to face Jeff, his own fists ready. "I wouldn't have if I'd known—"

When the punch came, Ty was ready for it. Using a survival trick he'd learned in his teens, he moved swiftly to block the right cross, then twisted Jeff's arm behind his back and held it as he tried to reason with the man.

"I didn't know anything about the pregnancy. In fact, until the day I delivered the baby, I hadn't seen or heard from your sister since she left Chicago."

Jeff struggled to free himself, then turned to face Ty. The fight seemed to drain away as he recognized the truth in Ty's steady gaze.

"Damn! You really didn't have any idea she was pregnant, did you?"

"Not a clue."

"Lexi Gail Hatfield! Get out here."

Seconds later the door opened, but instead of Lexi, Freddie stepped out onto the porch. Planting her hands on her hips, she warned, "Jeff Hatfield, I thought I made it clear I didn't want to hear your voice raised."

"That sister of mine has a lot of explainin' to do," Jeff growled. He pointed to Ty. "Braden is the baby's daddy and she didn't even bother to tell him."

"I know," Freddie said calmly.

Caught off guard by his wife's admission, Jeff opened and closed his mouth several times before he could speak. "And you didn't tell me?"

Freddie smiled. "No."

Jeff folded his arms across his chest as he glared at his wife. "Why not?"

"Lexi made me promise." Freddie's eyes lit with mischief. "Besides, Love Dumplin', there are some things men just don't need to know."

The horror on Jeff's face at Freddie's use of the obviously private endearment had Ty clearing his throat to keep from laughing out loud. But when she blew Jeff a kiss as she went back inside, Ty couldn't keep from smiling.

"Love Dumpling?"

"You didn't hear that," Jeff warned.

Ty's grin widened. "Hear what?"

Jeff slumped down on the steps, his cheeks bright red. "Women!"

"There's no figuring them out," Ty commiserated. He sat beside Jeff and stared off into the distance. "I still can't understand why Lexi didn't get in touch with me as soon as she found out she was pregnant."

"That must have been a hell of a shock when she finally did tell you."

"She didn't," Ty said, his tone reflecting the betrayal he still felt. "I had to figure it out on my own."

"Then how do you know for sure the baby is yours?"

"There's no doubt about it. The timing is right and he looks just like me."

Jeff chuckled. "With all that red, wrinkled skin, how can you tell? To me, all babies look alike."

"He also has a cowlick just slightly left of the center of his forehead. Just like mine. It's a family trait."

They sat in silence for several minutes as Jeff digested what Ty had told him.

"Did Lexi finally fess up and tell you why she didn't say anything?" Jeff asked.

"No." Ty heaved a sigh. "But you can bet I intend to find out."

Lexi sat on the couch, dabbing at the last of her tears with a crumpled tissue. "What are they doing now, beating each other to a bloody pulp?"

From her vantage point at the window, Freddie gave a disgusted snort. "It looks like they're laughin'." She shook her head as she walked over and plopped down in the rocking chair. "If I didn't know better, I'd swear they were long lost buddies. But you know Jeff. He could be plannin' just about anything."

"Men," Lexi muttered.

"You can't live with 'em and you can't shoot 'em," Freddie agreed, heaving an exaggerated sigh.

Both women nodded in solemn agreement, then burst out laughing.

"Thanks," Lexi said. "I needed that."

"I figured you did." Freddie glanced at the door. "How long do you think it will be before Ty comes in here demandin' answers?"

Lexi shrugged. "I'd say just about any time. By now I'm sure Jeff has explained that you're Freddie and enlightened Ty about my marital status."

"Do you want me and Jeff to stick around in case you need moral support?" Freddie offered.

Tempted, Lexi finally shook her head. "It would be best if we worked this out on our own." She stood, straightened her shoulders, then started for the door. "He's not the only one with questions."

"Atta girl, Lex," Freddie said, grinning. "Take the bull by the horns."

Lexi winked. "Or the doctor by his stethoscope."

"Oooh, that sounds kinky." Her expression turning serious, Freddie rose to leave. "I hope you get the answers you want."

Her voice little more than a whisper, Lexi said, "Me, too."

"If you need us, all you have to do is pick up the phone. We can be here in less than five minutes." Freddie hugged Lexi close for several seconds, then opened the door to announce, "Jeff, it's time for us to go home."

Ty and Jeff stood to face the two women as they walked out of the house.

Jeff stubbornly placed his hands on his hips. "But Lexi and Braden—"

"Have things they need to talk over," Freddie stated. "And they don't need us to do it."

Jeff looked as if he wanted to protest, but his wife's don't-even-think-about-it frown stopped him short.

Turning, he extended his hand to Ty. "Good luck, Braden."

"Thanks." Ty shook Jeff's hand, then glanced at Lexi. The determination he saw sparkling in her dark green eyes had him adding, "I have a feeling I'm going to need it."

When her husband continued to linger, Freddie prompted, "Come on, Jeff. You've got work to do at home."

Jeff looked confused. "I do?"

Freddie nodded. "Granny Applegate said the moon is right for makin' a baby tonight, Love Dumplin'." She walked up to wrap her arms around his waist. "And I can't do it by myself, big guy."

Jeff gave Ty a wicked grin. "Aw, hell. It's a dirty job, but somebody's got to do it." Reaching out he grabbed Freddie's hand and hurried her along as he headed for the path leading down the mountain. "See y'all later."

Ty watched the couple disappear into the thick forest at the edge of the yard, before turning to face Lexi. She looked thoroughly exhausted.

"I suppose you'd like some answers," she said, motioning for him to follow her into the house.

"Are you sure you're up to this?" he asked, closing the door behind them.

"No. But I don't think waiting will make it any easier."

Ty walked over to where she stood. "You're probably right."

She looked tired, but so damned determined, he didn't think twice about taking her into his arms. He'd always admired strength and independence, found it incredibly sexy in a woman.

Pulling her close, he gazed down at her. "Do you have any idea what a relief it is to find out you aren't married?" he asked, his voice husky. "For the past few weeks, I've been on one hell of a guilt trip."

"Why?"

"Lusting after another man's wife has never been my style," Ty said. He lowered his head. "And because I've wanted to do this since I walked into the birthing room weeks ago."

Five

Ty crushed Lexi's lips beneath his, chastising her for the deception. But as his mouth moved across hers with bruising pressure, desire quickly erased his feelings of betrayal and he eased the kiss to trace her lips with his tongue.

She was soft, warm and, to his satisfaction, very receptive to his gentle probing. Teasing, encouraging her to allow him entry, he reacquainted himself with the sweetness he'd found the night they'd conceived Matthew.

He tightened his hold and fitted her more fully to him. The scent of honeysuckle and sunshine filled his nostrils. He didn't think he'd ever smelled anything quite so sexy. Her full breasts pressed to his chest, her softness melting against his hard contours, and her moan of desire made Ty's body grow tight with need.

His immediate and totally predictable response caused his jeans to feel as if they'd shrunk.

The discomfort helped to restore some of his sanity. He wanted her, had wanted her from the first day they'd met. But she couldn't make love this soon after giving birth. Besides, there were too many unresolved issues between them. Too many questions he deserved to have answered.

Summoning every ounce of strength he possessed, he broke the kiss. He forced himself to pull back and turn away to keep from reaching for her again.

"Before this goes any further, we'd better talk," he said, his voice less than steady.

Lexi's knees felt like the tendons had been replaced with stretched out rubber bands as she walked over to the rocking chair. If she didn't sit down, and soon, she knew for certain she'd collapse in a heap on the floor.

Ty's kisses had been potent that night in her apartment. But today they had gone way beyond powerful. Today they had been downright debilitating.

The moment his lips touched hers, she'd forgotten all about the problems they faced now, or how they would resolve them. He'd taken all that from her and left her with nothing but the ability to feel.

Lowering herself into the chair, she watched him settle himself on the couch. He leaned his head back against the soft leather, obviously struggling with what he wanted to know first.

She knew this had to be very hard for him. But then, she found it no less difficult.

"It's not like I got pregnant on purpose, Ty," she stated, deciding to get things started.

He shook his head. "I never thought you did."

"I didn't find out until several weeks after I returned home."

"I figured as much." He sat forward, the only outward sign of his emotions reflected in the tightening of his jaw. "But it doesn't explain why you failed to tell me about the pregnancy. Didn't you think I had the right to know?"

"I wanted to tell you."

"Then why didn't you?" He shot up from the couch and began to pace. "Didn't it occur to you that I might want to have a say in the choices you made?"

Lexi took a deep breath. "I knew exactly how I wanted to handle the situation."

He whirled around to face her. "And my input wasn't needed?"

"I didn't say that."

He stopped in front of her, the color on his lean cheeks heightened by his anger. "What *are* you saying?"

Lexi sighed. "I wanted my baby, Ty."

"*Our* baby. He's my child, too."

"Yes."

She'd known their discussion would be arduous at best, but she still hated having to vocalize what she'd feared all those months ago. Folding her hands in her lap to keep them from trembling, she steadily met his furious gaze. "I thought you might try to convince me to terminate the pregnancy."

He sucked in a sharp breath. "What made you think I'd want that?"

"What else was I to think?" she asked. "You made it perfectly clear that night that you never intended to father a child."

Ty felt his anger drain away as his words came

back to haunt him. He had felt that way. He still would, if he hadn't known about Matthew. But Ty did know. And that changed everything.

He rubbed the tension building at the base of his neck. "Circumstances are different now."

Lexi stood to face him. "Because you know about the baby?"

"Yes."

"Why didn't you want a child, Ty?" She placed her hand on his arm. "I've seen you with Matthew, and I can tell you like children."

He ignored her question. He wasn't ready to share his reasons, to watch the disgust fill her emerald gaze. "Whether I ever intended to or not, I did father a child. And I'm going to take responsibility for him." Ty met her questioning look. "You deprived me of the knowledge I was going to be a father, but you won't keep me from being a major part of his life, Lexi."

"What makes you think I'd want to do that?" she asked, looking shocked.

"Because you've had ample opportunity to set the record straight." Unable to keep a hard edge from his voice, he continued, "But you didn't. And if I hadn't put everything together, you would have let me continue to believe that Matthew belonged to another man."

Obviously startled by his impassioned statement, she gasped. "No."

He placed his hands on her shoulders as he gazed down at her. "Why did you lie to me, Lexi?"

"I didn't lie," she insisted, her slender body trembling beneath his hands.

Ty ground his back teeth as he struggled for control. Losing his temper wouldn't accomplish anything. "No, but your omission of the facts was the same as if you had lied. You knew I thought you were married. And not once did you try to set the record straight. Hell, I didn't even know your real name. I thought you were Alexis Madison."

"That was my on-air name. The radio station thought Lexi Hatfield sounded too country."

"So Alexis Madison was born," Ty guessed. He knew it was unreasonable to expect more of her than he was willing to give himself. But at the moment he wasn't feeling very rational. "You were ashamed of your background?"

"No." She glared at him. "I'm not the least bit embarrassed that my father was a carpenter with an eighth-grade education. Or that my mother went straight from high school graduation to changing diapers. I come from good, honest people and I'm proud of them."

"How did they feel about the concessions you made for your career?"

"They were killed in a car accident when I was fifteen," she said sadly. She paused a moment before she gave him a defiant look. "But had they lived, I'm confident they'd have understood and supported my decision to go along with the name change. Just as I'm sure your parents supported your decision to become a doctor."

Lexi watched Ty stiffen at the mention of his family, watched him shutter his emotions as effectively as if he'd lowered a curtain.

Anger, swift and hot, swept through her. She placed her fists on her hips. "Oh, so that's the way it is, huh? We can dissect my family. We can question my decisions and motivations. But yours are off limits.''

His expression indicated that she was correct in her assessment of the situation. ''Why should my background matter?'' he asked defensively.

''It's part of my son's—''

''Our son.''

''*Our* son's heritage. He'll want to know your family, want to know how their influence made you the man you are.''

His stony silence and guarded expression spoke volumes. If she hadn't realized it before, she did now. Ty wanted to be part of Matthew's life, but not hers.

''Can you at least explain what you're doing here?'' she asked.

''I wanted to see my son.''

Lexi shook her head. ''No. I mean why did you come to Tennessee? You're one of the top trauma specialists in Chicago, Ty. Why did you take over something as tame as the Dixie Ridge Health Clinic?''

''It's only temporary. I'll be going back to the city in a few months.''

''I know. But why did you leave Chicago in the first place?''

''Does it matter?''

He was hiding something. She was sure of it. Was his reluctance to talk about his past or his present plans a way to keep her from finding out that he intended to take her son with him when he left Dixie Ridge? Where they might go if he did?

Feeling a chill spread throughout her soul, Lexi took a deep, steadying breath. ''I see no reason to carry this any further. You seem to feel my life should be an open book, but yours is off-limits. But it doesn't work that way.'' She walked to the door. ''I think it would be best if you leave, Ty.''

He looked as if he wanted to argue the point, but when she opened the door and stood beside it, he walked out onto the porch. ''I'll come back another time to finish our discussion about joint custody.''

As he descended the steps, Lexi advised, ''From now on, when you want to see Matthew, I'd appreciate if you'd call before you drop by.''

After finishing his morning house calls, Ty drove down Piney Knob. He paid little attention to the picture-postcard scenery or the crisp smell of autumn on the October breeze. He wasn't even able to manage more than a curious glance when he passed Carl Morgan on his way up the mountain, the man's truck piled high with bulging burlap bags and crates of plastic gallon jugs. For the past week, Ty had been desensitized to anything except the heavy feeling of regret that followed his conversation with Lexi.

Her accusations about his reserve had been right on the mark. He did keep certain aspects of his life locked deep inside. But it was more a measure of damage control than anything else. He'd learned long ago that if he didn't want to hear the inevitable condemnation that would surely accompany his revelation, silence was his best defense. He'd only revealed his secret to one woman in his life—a woman he'd thought cared deeply for him—and he'd never forget the sting of rejection that had followed.

Steering the truck into the clinic parking lot, he got out and reached into the back seat for his medical bag. Some things were better buried, never to be exhumed. He wanted to keep it that way. He didn't want to face the inevitable ridicule that would accompany his confessions. Or, worse yet, the accusations. He saw enough of those each night in his dreams.

Forcing the disturbing thoughts from his mind, he pushed open the clinic door.

Martha glanced up from the book she'd been reading. "You look like somethin' the dog dragged up and the cat wouldn't have. Haven't you been gettin' enough sleep?"

"I'm fine, Martha."

He should have known the eagle-eyed nurse would notice, and feel it her duty to comment on, his haggard appearance. Hoping to divert her inevitable questions, he asked, "What does it look like today? Do we have many appointments?"

"Nope." Martha checked the few folders in the wall pocket beside the desk. "Looks like the rest of the mornin' is free and clear. Your first patient isn't scheduled until afternoon."

Ty nodded and walked past her. "If you need me for anything, I'll be in my office." When the ample nurse followed him into the small room at the back of the clinic, he frowned. "Was there something else, Martha?"

He almost groaned aloud when Martha patted the thick roll of gray hair at the base of her neck and straightened her pristine smock. He didn't feel up to another lecture. But whether he wanted to hear it or not, once she started the ritual, Martha was impossible to stop.

He shrugged out of his jacket. "What have I done this time, Martha?"

"I like you, Doc." She eyed him over the top of

her glasses. "You've still got a ways to go, mind you. But for a city boy, you're showin' a lot of promise."

"Thank you, Martha," Ty said, surprised. He could have sworn the woman thought him a total incompetent. "Coming from you, I consider that quite a compliment."

"That's why I'm gonna have my say," she stated, her look defying protest.

Apprehension plucked at the hairs on the back of Ty's neck as he hung his blazer on the coat tree, then moved to the chair behind his desk. He had the distinct sensation of waiting for the other shoe to drop. Knowing Martha, he didn't figure he'd have long to wait.

He didn't.

"Just how much time are you gonna waste before you do right by Lexi Hatfield?" she asked, placing her hands on her wide hips.

Ty was grateful he'd been in the process of seating himself. Otherwise, he might have landed on the floor. If he thought he'd been surprised by Martha's backhanded compliment, it was nothing compared to the shock racing through him at that very moment. How had she discovered the truth?

At his obviously dumbfounded expression, Martha nodded. "That's right. I know you're that baby's daddy. Now what are you gonna do about it?"

Ty cleared his throat and tried to regain both his voice and composure. "Who—"

"Nobody had to tell me," Martha interrupted. She tapped her glasses with a wrinkled finger. "I may have to wear bifocals, but I ain't blind. That fuss Lexi kicked up when she found out you'd taken over the clinic was enough to raise my antennae. Then you admitted the two of you had met before.'' She shrugged. ''It didn't take a genius to figure out the rest. Besides, any fool can see that child looks more like you every day.''

Ty felt as if the breath had been knocked out of him. ''How long have you known?''

''About as long as you.'' Martha gave him a sympathetic smile.

''But you haven't said anything.'' He rubbed at the tension creasing his forehead. ''That's not like you, Martha.''

She settled herself in the chair across the desk from him. ''I figured you and Lexi would get things straightened out, go see Preacher Green and everything would be put to rights. But for the past week you've moped around like a bloodhound that's lost his nose.'' Her keen eyes assessed him once again. ''What happened? Did she turn you down?''

Ty winced. Martha wasn't going to like his answer. ''I didn't ask.''

''And why not?'' Compassionate before, Martha's eyes had turned to glittering chips of blue ice.

''It's complicated.''

Martha snorted. ''Only because the two of you make it that way. Did you love her?''

Ty stared at the crusty nurse. Hell, he didn't even really know Lexi. Oh, he'd liked her immediately when they first met in the elevator of their apartment building two years ago. And he'd wanted her almost just as long. But love?

''Well, did you?'' Martha persisted.

Discussing his acquaintance with Lexi wasn't going to be easy without making it sound exactly like what it had been—a one-night stand. ''No, I can't honestly say that I loved Lexi. I liked her. A lot.'' He chose his next words carefully. "But she left to come back here and we didn't have a chance to explore anything further.''

Martha looked grim. "Well, I've known lots of folks that started out with less. I guess you can learn to love each other after the deed's done.''

"What are you talking about, Martha?'' Ty wasn't at all comfortable with the direction Martha was taking the conversation.

"I'm talkin' about the two of you doin' the right thing.'' She folded her arms beneath her ample bosom. "When are you gonna marry her?''

Ty stared at the older woman for several seconds. An image of Lexi in his arms as he made love to her every night for the rest of their lives, holding her while she cried out his name, flashed through his mind. Blood surged to the lower region of his body, making him light-headed.

He gulped hard and shook his head to clear his wayward thoughts. "Have you lost your mind, Martha? I just told you that we liked each other, but we aren't in love.''

"I ain't deaf. I know what you said. But right is right. I've seen a lot of marriages based on a whole lot less than the couple likin' each other.''

"But—''

"No buts about it,'' Martha interrupted. "I've known Lexi Hatfield all her life. You can bet your bottom dollar if she liked you enough to sleep with you, her feelings could run deeper, given the time. Now get the lead outta your shorts and pop the question.''

"I know what her answer would be if I did.'' Ty

shook his head. He couldn't believe he was actually giving the idea consideration.

"Think she'd say no, huh?"

"I don't *think*, Martha. I *know*."

"Then you need help."

Apprehension once again tingled across his scalp. "I don't think—"

Martha ignored him. "Does Jeff Hatfield know you're the baby's daddy?"

"Yes, but—"

"I'm surprised he hasn't already thought of it," she said, grinning.

Ty's hair felt as if it stood straight up. He had a feeling he knew what she had in mind. "Don't even think about it, Martha."

She laughed and treated him to a conspiratorial wink. "Ever heard of a shotgun weddin', Doc?"

"Freddie, I don't need a new dress," Lexi protested as they drove down Main Street. "I have more clothes now than I'll ever wear."

"Those are city clothes," her sister-in-law insisted. "Since you're not goin' back to Chicago, you need country duds."

Lexi pointed to her T-shirt and jeans. "In case you hadn't noticed, I'm wearing the same thing you are."

"But I don't have some designer's name plastered across my butt," Freddie shot back. She parked the car in front of Miss Eunice's Dress Shop. "Besides, you've been cooped up in the house with the baby for the last month and a half. You need to get out, even if it is just for a couple of hours."

"But I feel guilty about being away from Matthew."

"We both know Martha will take good care of him," Freddie said, clearly losing patience.

"She'll spoil him rotten," Lexi muttered.

"No more than I already have." Freddie got out of the car and came around to open the passenger door. "Now get your butt outta that seat so we can try on some clothes."

Lexi reluctantly left the car. She'd never seen Freddie so persistent. If she didn't know better, she'd swear her sister-in-law was up to something. But for the life of her, Lexi couldn't imagine what it would be.

Sighing, she opened the shop's door. It didn't matter. How much trouble could Freddie get her into in Miss Eunice's Dress Shop anyway?

Miss Eunice McMillan parted the curtain behind the counter to peer at the three men in her stockroom. "They just pulled up out front."

His grin wide, Jeff checked his watch, then winked at Ty. "Right on time."

Ty watched the elderly woman's head slip back through the curtain as the bell over the door tinkled merrily. His stomach did a backflip when he thought of what they were about to do. This had to be the craziest stunt he'd ever been involved in. And he still couldn't believe he'd gone along with it. But the more he'd thought about it, the more he'd warmed up to the idea. He'd not only get to be a full-time father, he'd share his life with the most alluring woman he'd ever known. That is, *if* he could convince her to return to Chicago with him. He didn't want to think about what would happen if she wouldn't.

He eyed the double-barrel shotgun Jeff held and

rubbed his hands against the legs of his trousers to dry his sweaty palms. At one point, Ty had tried to back out of the scheme, reasoning that it would be better to go the more traditional route of courting Lexi, then asking her to marry him. But his soon-to-be brother-in-law wouldn't hear of it.

"Are you certain that gun isn't loaded?" Ty asked for the tenth time since they'd taken their places in the storeroom.

Jeff chuckled as he released the catch, broke the gun down and revealed two empty chambers. "Don't worry, Braden," he said, his voice hushed. "I couldn't shoot you, even if I wanted to." He snapped the gun back together, then held it out for Ty's inspection. "Both triggers are broke off. The only reason I keep it is because it belonged to my granddaddy." He narrowed his eyes. "But don't go gettin' any ideas. I've got one at home that works just fine."

Unwilling to put Jeff to the test, Ty nodded and turned his thoughts to more pressing matters. He hoped the seams of the ill-fitting tuxedo jacket held just a little while longer. Used for the shop's wedding display, the damn thing had to be twenty years old and two sizes too small.

For the past two weeks, Martha, Freddie and Miss Eunice insisted everything was under control, that he didn't have a thing to worry about. They'd made all the arrangements, planned down to the very last detail and selected everyone's clothes. Martha had even pulled in a few favors down at the county courthouse and made arrangements for the marriage license without Lexi having to be present to obtain it.

At the time, Ty had been more than happy to let them handle things. The less he knew about the plan,

the less he had to deny. Now, standing in a tuxedo
that threatened to burst at the seams across his shoulders and was way too tight in certain sensitive regions
below his belt, he wished they'd at least consulted
him about his size.

"What are they doing now?" Preacher Green
asked from behind Ty.

Jeff peeked through the part in the curtain. "Lexi's
gettin' ready to try on the dress Freddie picked out."
He clapped Ty on the back. "As soon as she gives
the signal, we'll get this show on the road."

"Looks like everybody's here," Preacher Green
announced when the back door opened and Martha
hurried inside with the baby.

"I got here as soon as I could," Martha said,
breathlessly. "Does Lexi suspect anything?"

Ty shook his head. "No. If she did, I'm sure she'd
be out of here in a flash."

Martha placed a reassuring hand on Ty's arm. "Relax, Doc. If I wasn't sure this is the right thing to do,
I wouldn't have any part in it."

"Martha's right," Jeff agreed. "Sometimes Lexi
don't know beans from buckshot about what's good
for her." His grin wide, he held up the shotgun.
"That's why we've got ol' Betsy here. To convince
her."

Ty looked from Jeff to Martha. He hoped like hell
they were right.

"Freddie, I don't see any reason to try on these
shoes," Lexi protested when her sister-in-law pushed
a pair of ivory satin pumps into the tiny dressing cu-
bicle.

"You have to," Freddie insisted.

"Why?"

Freddie blinked owlishly as if searching for an answer. "Because…because…" She looked at the elderly shop owner hovering beside her. "Feel free to jump in here anytime, Miss Eunice. Why does Lexi have to try on the shoes?"

The older woman stepped forward, her smile confident. "You have to put on the shoes so we can make sure the hem is just the right length, Lexi."

Lexi thought the reason sounded lame. But if it would hurry things along, she'd do whatever they asked. The sooner she finished trying on a dress she didn't want, need, or intend to buy, the sooner she could get back to the baby.

Slipping the pumps on, Lexi stepped out of the dressing room to stare at her image in the full-length mirror. She should have paid more attention to the dress Freddie had shoved into her hands and insisted she try on.

Made of soft ivory satin overlaid with delicate white lace, the garment had a sweetheart neckline, a dropped waist bodice adorned with seed pearls and a midcalf handkerchief hem. It was utterly stunning and looked just like a—

Lexi whirled around to face Freddie and Miss Eunice. "This is a wedding dress!"

"Oh, Lexi, it's perfect," Freddie exclaimed, tears filling her eyes. "You look beautiful."

"Let's see how these flowers look with the dress," Miss Eunice said.

Before Lexi could protest, the elderly woman shoved a bouquet of brightly colored wildflowers into her hands, plopped a matching garland on top of her head and fastened a string of pearls around her neck.

"What on earth—"

Lexi stopped short and blinked against the bright flashes of light as Freddie clicked off several pictures with the camera she'd pulled from her shoulder bag. Momentarily blinded and caught completely off guard, she teetered precariously when Freddie lifted her foot and slipped a blue garter up her leg to just above the knee.

Despite the fact that Lexi was off balance and seeing colorful spots dancing before her eyes, movement at the back of the shop caught her attention. She stared openmouthed at the sight of Ty, Jeff, Preacher Green and Martha, with the baby in tow, emerging single file from Miss Eunice's stockroom.

Lexi felt the blood drain from her face when she realized where they were headed.

Miss Eunice's wedding display, complete with fake marble columns, matching candelabras and brass arch, decorated with cheap plastic greenery, was ominously empty of its bride and groom mannequins.

Six

"**Y**ou're supposed to be a nervous bridegroom, Braden," Jeff said under his breath. "Act like one."

His hands raised in surrender, Ty felt a trickle of sweat make its way from his temple to the edge of his jaw as they marched toward the brass arch. "Believe me, that won't be much of a stretch."

"Lexi, get over here," Jeff bellowed. He poked Ty's back with the shotgun. "Braden and I had a long talk and he's finally come around to my way of thinkin'."

Ty glanced at Lexi and wished with all his heart he hadn't. He'd been right about her not liking the situation. In less than a split second, her expression had changed from shock to absolute fury.

Oh, he hadn't deluded himself into thinking she'd readily embrace the idea of a shotgun wedding. At first, he hadn't either. But when Martha took it upon herself to mention the scheme to Jeff and Freddie, the three had presented a very convincing argument. Once they were legally married, Ty would not only get to be a full-time father, he and Lexi might be more inclined to renew their acquaintance and explore what they might have had together if she'd remained in Chicago.

At the time it seemed the perfect solution. Now it sounded like the most ridiculous scheme he'd ever heard.

Marriage was a hard enough proposition when both parties were willing. But a forced marriage? And a groom with a past that the bride might never be able to understand or forgive?

"Jeff, have you lost your mind?" Lexi shrieked, drawing Ty back to the present. "Put that gun down."

"No way." Jeff motioned for Ty to take his place beneath the vine-covered arch. "Braden's gonna do what he should have in the first place. He's gonna do right by you and the baby."

Lexi turned her furious gaze on Freddie. "You obviously had a hand in all of this. I don't suppose I can count on you to talk some sense into that bone-headed brother of mine?"

Freddie looked anything but repentant. "Nope." She put her arm around Lexi's shoulders to urge her forward. "We've all talked it over and everybody agreed. The three of you need to be a family."

Lexi felt color flood her cheeks as she watched Martha, Preacher Green and Miss Eunice bob their heads in complete agreement. "They were in on this, too?"

"You bet." Martha looked proud as punch. "I'm the one who suggested it."

"Well, it's not going to work," Lexi retorted. She threw the bouquet at Freddie and moved to take the baby from Martha. "Matthew and I are going home. And if you're all lucky, I may forget all this in about fifty years."

"Don't even think about it, Sis," Jeff said, his expression grim. He drew back first one hammer on the gun, then the other. "At this range, I could hit Braden with both eyes closed."

The sound stopped Lexi in her tracks. "Jeff Hatfield, you wouldn't dare."

He gave her a one-shouldered shrug as he continued to aim the gun at Ty's back. "Try me."

"Under the circumstances, I'd rather you didn't test him, Lexi," Ty said through clenched teeth.

Lexi bit her lower lip to keep from uttering a most unladylike word in front of Preacher Green. She turned her attention back to the gun Jeff held. She didn't think he would carry through on his threat. But she wasn't sure. Jeff had an unshakable opinion of right and wrong when it came to marriage and babies. If he'd made up his mind that Ty should marry her, nothing would change it.

Her gaze narrowed on Ty. His voice sounded surprisingly calm, all things considered. As a doctor, surely he'd seen the damage a shotgun could do. If he had any sense he should be scared half out of his mind. But to her way of thinking, he looked a little too composed for a man with a double-barrel poking him in the back.

"You're willing to go through with this?" she asked him.

Ty glanced over his shoulder at the gun Jeff held,

then back at her. His smile tense, he nodded. "More than willing."

Freddie took advantage of Lexi's hesitation. "See, Lex. He wants to marry you." She shoved the wild-flowers into Lexi's hands and pushed her forward. Whispering close to her ear, Freddie added, "Here's your chance for the happily-ever-after you always talked about when we were kids."

Lexi glared at her sister-in-law. "I'll never tell you another thing as long as I live. In fact, you'll be lucky if I ever speak to you again."

"Oh, you'll talk to me." Freddie laughed as she positioned Lexi next to Ty beneath the arch. "And I'm bettin' it won't be too long before you're fallin' all over yourself to say thanks, too."

"Don't hold your breath," Lexi muttered.

"This is truly a joyous day," Preacher Green pronounced, stepping in front of Lexi and Ty.

"I just love weddins," Miss Eunice blubbered into her lace-edged hanky.

"Aw, shut up, Eunice," Martha said, her own voice quavering. "Let Preacher Green get the deed done before one of these two bolts for the door."

"Dearly beloved…"

Ty's chest tightened when he looked at his beautiful bride. He'd have liked to start their union on better terms. But since that didn't seem possible, Ty would take what he could get and hope their differences could be worked out later.

"Join hands and face each other as you repeat after me," Preacher Green commanded.

Ty watched Lexi hand her bouquet to Freddie, then turn to face him. Her green eyes sparkled with anger and her slender fingers trembled, but she didn't hes-

itate. When she placed her hands in his, he felt like
he'd been handed a rare and precious gift.

"I, Tyler Braden, take thee, Lexi Hatfield—"

Lexi listened to Ty's rich baritone as he repeated
the sacred vows. His strong, sure hands wrapped protectively around hers, his warm smile as he gazed
down at her, made her insides feel warm and quivery.

She mentally gave herself a good shaking. That
didn't change one darned thing. As soon as they were
finished, she fully intended to walk right out of Miss
Eunice's Dress Shop and straight across the street to
the office of Warren Jacobs, Attorney at Law.

"The ring, please?" Preacher Green requested.

Smiling in spite of her tears, Martha stepped forward with Matthew. "Not every little boy will be able
to say he was the ring bearer at his mama and daddy's
weddin'."

That was when Lexi noticed the matching gold
wedding bands tied to the slender white ribbons of
the baby's sacque. The sight caused her own tears to
threaten as she watched Ty unfasten one of the rings
and take her hand in his.

"With this ring…"

His gaze held her captive while he pledged his
faithfulness and slipped the wide band over her finger.
When he tenderly rubbed the pad of his thumb over
the shiny gold, warming the ring—warming her—
Lexi's toes curled inside the ivory pumps.

She jerked her hand from his. She'd better watch
it. His touch could almost soften her resolve. And she
fully intended to see the marriage annulled before the
ink had a chance to dry on the certificate.

Preacher Green cleared his throat for the second
time.

"Lexi?"

His smile warm, Ty extended his left hand. "Your turn."

Lexi blinked. She'd been so caught up in her own thoughts, she'd lost track of what would happen next.

Her hands trembled as she unfastened Ty's ring from the ribbon on Matthew's short jacket and tersely repeated the words everyone expected to hear. But the moment she slipped the ring on Ty's finger and he closed his hands over hers, her pulse took off at a gallop and her breath came in short little puffs.

"By the power vested in me by God and the State of Tennessee, I now pronounce you husband and wife," Preacher Green said, sounding very pleased. "You may kiss the bride."

When Ty continued to gaze at her, Preacher Green chuckled and tapped him on the shoulder. "Kiss your bride, son."

Ty grinned, then gently drew her forward to seal their union with the traditional kiss. She watched him slowly, deliberately, lower his head until their lips met, his mouth covering hers in tender exploration.

Her legs began to tremble.

His tongue stroked her lips apart, then thrust inside in a possessive claiming.

Her knees failed completely.

When she sagged against him, he tightened his arms and drew her even closer. The feel of his obvious desire pressed to her lower belly caused her heart to race and her head to spin. Heat shot through her as he gently stroked her tongue with his, imitating the movements of more intimate lovemaking.

In the confines of her borrowed satin shoes, her toes curled, straightened and curled again.

"Save it for the honeymoon, Braden," Jeff said, pulling Lexi from Ty's arms. He wrapped her in a brotherly bear hug. "Congratulations, Sis."

Dazed from Ty's kiss, Lexi could only nod.

"I'm glad you finally caved in and went along with this," Jeff said close to her ear.

Lexi blinked as reality slowly returned. "Why?"

"Well, first of all, it was the right thing to do," he stated emphatically. "And second, it could have proven mighty embarrassin'."

She pulled back to meet her brother's relieved gaze. "What on earth are you talking about, Jeff?"

"I don't know what I would have done if you'd recognized ol' Betsy," he admitted.

Lexi stared at the gun in Jeff's hands. "You mean you forced us to get married with a shotgun that won't even fire?"

Jeff nodded, his grin wide. "You didn't think I'd take the chance on turnin' you into a widow before you became a wife, did you?"

"I swear if it's the last thing I do, I'll get even with you for this, Jeff Hatfield," Lexi said. Fixing her gaze on the lawyer's office across the street, she marched toward the door.

Dixie Ridge seemed strangely vacant when Ty steered the SUV away from the curb in front of Miss Eunice's Dress Shop. The old shoes and tin cans tied to the back of the truck thumped and pinged the pavement, the sound amplified by the unnatural quiet.

Ty barely noticed.

His attention was focused on the silent woman beside him. Lexi's pensive mood bothered him. She hadn't said two words to him since Preacher Green pronounced them husband and wife. Was she already trying to think of a way to get out of their marriage?

Freddie had assured him Lexi would protest, but once she'd said her vows, she'd do her best to stick to them. Had Freddie been wrong?

Or did Lexi think he felt trapped? Should he admit that it had all been a setup? That he'd willingly gone along with the plan? That he'd even insisted the wedding date be set far enough past the baby's birth so they could have a real wedding night?

As he turned the truck onto the road leading up the side of the mountain, Ty weighed his options. Maybe he'd tell her on their fiftieth wedding anniversary, but he didn't think it would be wise to inform her of the ruse now.

He reached for her hand to reassure himself she really was seated beside him. He smiled when his thumb grazed the gold band he'd recently placed on his wife's finger.

His wife.

Ty liked the sound of those words. He'd long ago given up on ever having a wife and family, wouldn't allow himself to think about something he knew he could never have. Now it seemed a very real possibility, and what he wanted more than he could have ever imagined.

"I don't know much about being a husband and father," he admitted to the silent woman beside him. "But I promise, I'll do my best. We can make this work, Lexi."

Lexi tensed at the sincerity she detected in Ty's voice. He sounded as if he wanted them to stay together. Nothing would make her happier than to have a loving husband and a good father for Matthew.

She glanced over at the profile of her handsome husband. In the weeks following their son's birth, she'd witnessed firsthand that Ty was a good, caring father. But a loving husband? Oh, she knew he was as attracted to her as she was to him. But that didn't mean they'd be able to build a lasting relationship. And a marriage at gunpoint wasn't the same as starting a life together based on love and mutual respect. Besides, he'd be going back to Chicago and she had no intention of returning to the city. She wanted to raise Matthew right here in the mountains of Tennessee. It would be best for all concerned to end the marriage with a quiet annulment before news of the wedding had a chance to get out. She'd already have things underway if Warren Jacobs's office hadn't been closed on Saturdays.

"What the hell is this all about?" Ty asked, drawing her out of her pensive mood.

He'd turned the truck into the drive leading up to her cabin, but the narrow lane was blocked by a horse-drawn carriage with a "Just Hitched" sign attached to the back.

When Ty stopped the SUV, Harv Jenkins jumped down from the front seat of the surrey and motioned for Ty to roll down the window. "Afternoon, Doc," he said, tipping his hat. "Just park over to the side of the driveway and I'll give you and the new Missus a ride up to the house." His toothless grin wide, he added, "You make a mighty pretty bride, Miss Lexi."

"What's going on?" Ty asked, parking the truck where Harv indicated.

"I'm not sure." Lexi got out of the truck and slammed the door as Jeff pulled his truck in behind the carriage. She pointed a finger at her brother and

Freddie, who got out to drive the SUV up to the cabin. "Those two are toast. When they insisted the baby had to ride with them, I should have known they had something else up their sleeves."

Ty helped her get seated in the carriage, then slid in beside her. "What do you think they're up to now?"

"No good, if I know that brother of mine," Lexi stated flatly.

Harv slapped the big, gray horse on the rump with the reins and the carriage lurched forward. The rollicking sounds of music and laughter reached them just before they rounded the curve in the lane and pulled to a stop at the edge of Lexi's yard.

"It looks like a carnival," Ty grumbled.

Struck speechless by the large crowd milling around her yard, Lexi could only nod. In little more than an hour, her tidy lawn had been turned into an elaborate outdoor wedding reception.

White crepe paper streamers and expandable tissue bells hung from every tree. Tables and chairs, borrowed from the Methodist church down in town, had been set up banquet fashion in front of a head table. They'd been decorated with wildflower centerpieces that matched the bouquet she still held.

More than a little dazed, Lexi watched the edge of a long, white tablecloth flutter in the breeze. The buffet table, piled high with assorted dishes and platters of delicious-smelling homemade food, had been constructed of sawhorses and a sheet of plywood. Similar tables had been set up to hold a huge punch bowl, wedding cake and gifts. Her neighbors had even taken down the wooden swing on her front porch in order to make room for a small band.

She might have found it all very touching had she
not felt as if her life had gone into a flat spin with no
hope of recovery. This morning she'd been a single
mother with nothing more on her mind than trying to
get out of a shopping trip with her persistent sister-in-
law. Now she found herself married, facing a wedding
reception that looked as if it could go on well into the
night, and forced into altering her annulment plans.

Her idea of keeping things quiet had just been
blown to smithereens. With the whole mountain celebrating her nuptials, there was no way she could end
the charade of a marriage now. She'd already fed the
local gossips enough ammunition when she came
home pregnant from Chicago. They'd all called her
"that poor little gal up on Piney Knob some city
slicker led astray." She certainly didn't intend to give
them reason to start up the rumor mill again.

"I don't remember this being part of the plan," Ty
muttered.

"What was that?" Lexi asked, distracted. With all
of her neighbors descending on the carriage, she
wasn't sure she'd heard him correctly.

He cleared his throat. "I said, I don't remember
seeing such a clan."

She gave him a suspicious look. Something told
her he knew a whole lot more about the day's events
than a groom at a shotgun wedding should. But she
didn't have time to dwell on the fact. A stream of
well-wishers surrounded the carriage and before she
knew what was happening, Ty jumped to the ground
and helped her down.

His hands still at her waist, Ty watched the crowd
part to allow an old woman the honor of being the

first to congratulate the bride and groom. "Lexi, you're just about the prettiest bride I ever did see," the old woman stated. She wrapped Lexi in a loving embrace, then stepped back, her gaze raking Ty from head to toe. "Boy, you don't hardly look old enough to spawn a baby, let alone help birth one."

Lexi laughed. "Ty, this is Granny Applegate."

He stared in disbelief at the tiny, old woman in front of him. When he'd first heard of Granny Applegate, he'd pictured an old crony in a flowing black cape, with stringy gray hair and a wart on the end of her nose. But in reality, the elderly lady wore a brightly colored housedress, had short, snow-white curls and one of the kindest faces he'd ever seen.

"Boy, if you don't shut your mouth right quick, you're gonna catch a bug," Granny cackled.

"It's nice to meet you," he said, finally getting his vocal cords to work.

She patted his arm with a bony hand, her smile warm. "Later on, me and you are gonna have a talk, son."

"We are?"

Granny nodded so vigorously, her white curls bobbed. "I'm gettin' on in years and I'm thinkin' you might be a good one to take over birthin' the babies here on Piney Knob. But we'll talk about that some other time." She patted his arm again. "Welcome to the mountain, son."

Ty didn't have time to tell the old woman he'd be leaving in a few short months. For the next twenty minutes, he and Lexi were deluged with neighbors and friends expressing their heartfelt congratulations.

"You've got to see the decorations," one of the women said, tugging Lexi from his side.

He regretfully watched a group of women lead his new wife across the yard to show her their handiwork. When Jeff and Freddie insisted they take the baby for the evening so he and Lexi could be alone, he had immediately started making plans for their wedding night. And they definitely hadn't included a large, boisterous crowd.

"I wish you'd told me when I was at the clinic last month that you were lookin' for a wife," a young woman said, sauntering up to him. She pursed her bright red lips in an obviously well-practiced pout, batted her false eyelashes and ran a perfectly manicured, fake red fingernail along the satin lapel of his tux. "I'd have been more than happy to apply for the job."

Ty was saved from having to comment when Jeff came to stand beside him. "Mary Ann, I saw Jake Sanders over by the punch bowl a few minutes ago. He was lookin' mighty lonely and I think I heard him ask where you were." Jeff winked as he place Matthew into Ty's arms.

The dark-haired young woman brightened instantly. "See you later, boys," she called, hurrying across the yard.

"Thanks," Ty said, grateful for Jeff's intervention. He cradled his son to his chest as he watched Mary Ann zero in on her next unsuspecting victim. "Don't you think one of us should warn Jake?"

"Naw. Those two have been carryin' on for years." Jeff chuckled as they watched the voluptuous woman separate Jake from the group of men standing around the punch bowl, take him by the hand and hurry him into the woods. "One of these days he'll get up the nerve to ask her to marry him. Then all the men on the mountain can breathe easy again.''

"I know of at least one wife who'll be glad to see that happen,'' Freddie added from her husband's side.

"Now, darlin', you know you don't have a thing to worry about,'' Jeff said, draping his arm around Freddie's shoulders. "I'm a one-woman man.'' He kissed the top of her head. "And you're the only woman for me.''

Ty felt a stab of envy at their affectionate banter. Would Lexi feel the same when the flirtatious woman was no longer single? Did she even care that Mary Ann had openly flirted with him?

Mary Ann Simmons leaned her full bosom against Ty and Lexi saw red. Mary Ann could flirt with every other man on the mountain in her attempt to get Jake Sanders to propose, but she'd better leave Ty alone. Lexi wasn't sure why she felt that way, since she had no intention of staying married to the man. But that didn't matter. Right now Ty *was* her husband.

Her husband.

She still couldn't believe she and Ty were married. But thanks to her brother's highhandedness, she now found herself legally wed to the father of her child. And by forcing the marriage, Jeff had unwittingly added one more obstacle for them to overcome before they could reach an amicable agreement on joint custody of Matthew.

Lexi watched Ty hold their son as he talked with Jeff and Freddie. He looked completely at ease and not at all like a man who had just been forced into doing something he didn't want to do.

The baby wrapped his fingers around one of Ty's and she watched him smile down at their son. They were forming a strong bond, and one that she hoped would remain strong after Ty went back to Chicago.

Lost in thought, it took her a moment to realize someone was ringing a bell. The majority of the crowd soon produced bells of their own and joined in. Lexi suddenly found herself being ushered to the middle of the yard.

"They won't stop until you two kiss," Helen McKinney told Ty. She gave Lexi a conspiratorial wink. "And it better be a good one."

Lexi watched her brother nudge Ty. Nodding, he shrugged out of the tux jacket, handed it to Jeff, then rolled up the sleeves on his white shirt. He started toward her, and as he drew closer, her heart skipped a beat. His eyes had darkened to navy, and the promising smile curving his firm lips took her breath away.

The crowd closed in for a better look when Ty stepped close and folded her into his arms. His strength held her captive, his warmth surrounded her, making her legs tremble.

Lexi placed her hands on Ty's broad chest to steady herself. If her knees didn't stop wobbling, she'd have to have the problem checked out by a doctor.

Her stomach fluttered wildly as an image of Ty's strong, talented hands gliding along her legs flashed through her mind.

"Are you two gonna moon-eye each other all day?" someone shouted.

"Plant one on her, Doc," Harv urged. "We ain't gonna stop ringin' these bells till you do."

Ty gazed down at Lexi a moment before dipping

his head to do as the crowd requested. Slowly, thoroughly, he tasted her peach-flavored lip gloss, savored her tenderness as she returned his caress. His tongue coaxed, teased, then parted her lips to enter the sweet, warm recesses of her mouth.

He tried to remind himself they were standing in front of at least a hundred people. His body could have cared less. Her soft sigh as he deepened the kiss, her tongue stroking his, caused heat to gather in his loins and his body to strain against the fabric of his trousers.

"Way to go, Doc!" a teenage boy yelled.

Lexi started to pull away, but Ty held her close. "Give me a minute," he said, his voice husky.

"What's wrong?" she asked, her breasts brushing his chest as they rose and fell with her labored breathing.

"Just stay close," he whispered against her hair. The smell of her honeysuckle shampoo teased his nostrils and Ty pulled back to keep from making matters worse. "Something came up," he growled.

Lexi's eyes twinkled. "Oh, really? And what would that be, Dr. Braden?"

Feeling his body begin to relax, Ty gave her a quick, hard kiss, then set her away from him. His grin wicked, he promised, "I'll show you later, *Mrs. Braden.*"

Seven

Ty stood on the porch beside Lexi as they waved goodbye to the last of their guests. He'd really enjoyed getting better acquainted with the people of Piney Knob. He liked watching them leave even more.

He'd wanted to be alone with Lexi all day. But once started, the wedding reception seemed to go on forever. And it might have, if not for Carl Morgan's very pregnant wife, Lydia, going into labor.

For the first time since arriving in the mountains, Ty was glad to hear the woman preferred Granny Applegate attending to the delivery and not him. He had plans for the rest of the evening, and they certainly didn't include using his medical degree.

"Do you think Matthew will be all right?" Lexi asked, giggling.

He watched the taillights of Jeff and Freddie's car

disappear around the bend in the drive. "Matthew will be just fine with your brother and Freddie. If they need us, they'll call."

Lexi hiccuped, then in a stage whisper added, "I'm a little tipsy. I think someone might have spiked the punch."

"I don't think they did, honey, I *know* they did." He placed his arm around her shoulders and steered her into the house.

Throughout the day, Carl Morgan and Harv Jenkins dug into their coat pockets for fruit jars filled with moonshine, which they poured into the frothy orange punch. Fortunately, when Mary Ann Simmons separated Jake Sanders from the pack of men guarding the large bowl, Ty noticed what was taking place. From that point on, he'd opted to drink iced tea instead.

He closed the door and secured the lock before turning to face Lexi. He didn't want her to get the idea he was rushing her, but the day had taken its toll. Throughout the afternoon and well into the evening, he'd held Lexi close, kissed her when the crowd rang the bells, and ached a little more each time he had to let her go.

"Come here, Mrs. Braden," he said, reaching for her.

"Ty, we need to talk—"

"Not tonight, honey." Pulling her close, he buried his face in her honeysuckle-scented hair. "I've had a hell of a day and talking isn't what's going to make it better."

Ty's lips caressed her temple, her ear, then trailed tiny kisses to the wildly fluttering pulse at the base of her throat. She'd had just enough punch to make her brain foggy and her will to resist him almost powerless.

He tightened his embrace and the evidence of his hunger pressing against her lower belly made her tingle all over. His spicy aftershave intoxicated her with its musky scent. The knot of desire, building inside her from the moment he sealed their union with a kiss at the end of their marriage ceremony, tightened into an almost painful ache. He lowered his lips to hers in a kiss so tender, it brought tears to her eyes. The feel of his tongue claiming hers sent heat coursing through her veins.

Just when she thought she would surely go into total meltdown, Ty ended the kiss. Taking her hand in his, he started toward the hall.

"Let's go to bed, Mrs. Braden."

Lexi allowed Ty to lead her down the hall and into her bedroom. Her heart and traitorous body told her to throw caution to the wind and make love with her husband. Her fuzzy mind tried to remind her they wouldn't be married long, but for the life of her, she couldn't remember why.

He stopped to turn on the lamp beside the bed. His smile promising, he reached out to trace his finger along the lace edge of her neckline. "This dress is beautiful, but I'm sure it will look much nicer hanging in the closet."

His low, soft-spoken comment made her heart skip a beat. Consummating their marriage would only add more complications, but the combination of Ty's lovemaking and the spiked punch put reason and logic beyond her capabilities.

He turned her away from him, arranged her hair over her shoulder and pulled down the zipper. The raspy sound caused tingles of anticipation to skip along every nerve ending in her body and she felt her knees begin to tremble.

Ty pressed his lips to her nape as he slid his hands inside the dress to caress her shoulders, then slowly eased the garment down her arms. Tremors of excitement coursed through her and her breathing became shallow at his featherlight touch.

When the dress lay around her feet in a pool of shiny satin and frothy lace, Ty wrapped his arms around her to pull her back against him. The feel of his solid frame, the scent of his musky cologne, caused heat to pool deep in her belly. When her head fell back against his shoulder, he pressed tiny kisses to the exposed column of her neck.

"Ty..."

"Yes."

"The light..."

"What about it?" he asked, his arms wrapping around her as he continued to nibble his way across her shoulder.

"Please, turn it off."

His cheek pressed close to her ear, he whispered, "You weren't shy with me before, honey. What's wrong?"

Her breath caught as his hands slid down the length of her sides, then back up to the swell of her breasts. "I...was in shape then."

"Honey, you're more beautiful today than the day we met," he said, his voice husky. Reaching out, he switched off the lamp. "But I want you to feel comfortable with me."

Lost in the sound of his deep voice and the feel of his firm lips on her sensitive skin, Lexi couldn't have responded if her life depended on it. Muted light from the sliver of moon outside intimately surrounded them, and the warmth of Ty's hands closing over her breasts caused waves of longing to course through her. She briefly wondered when he'd removed the rest of her clothing, but when he turned her to face him, the sight of hungry desire in his navy eyes and the sound of his ragged breathing stole her breath.

She ran her fingernail over one of the shiny black studs holding his shirt closed. "You looked very handsome in this tux today, Dr. Braden."

Ty's body tightened further with each one of Lexi's throaty words. He'd wanted to take things slow, to make their first time together as man and wife very special. But the velvet rasp of desire in her voice very nearly sent him over the edge.

Impatient to feel her silky skin against his own, he brushed her fingers aside, grasped the edges of the shirt and tugged. Polished black studs flew in all directions. He couldn't have cared less. He pulled her to him and the feel of her firm breasts heating his chest, her hardened nipples pressing into his skin, had him thinking he just might have a coronary right then and there.

"Honey, this feels almost too good." He shuddered as he tried to catch hold of his rapidly deteriorating control. "It's been a long time. I'm not sure I'll be able to take things as slow as I had intended."

"Ty—"

Although she hadn't moved, he felt her withdrawal as surely as if she'd pulled from his arms. He knew what ran through her mind, the question she couldn't bring herself to ask.

He placed his finger beneath her chin and tilted her

head until their gazes locked. "There hasn't been anyone since you left Chicago, Lexi. You're the only woman I've made love to in the last year."

"Since that night," she whispered.

Nodding, he smiled. "That's right, honey. And I vowed today that you'll be the only woman for the rest of my life."

He lowered his head to seal the promise with a kiss and felt her apprehension drain away on a soft sigh.

"Ty."

His name on her lips, her warm breath feathering his skin as she spoke, had his body pulsing with urgent need. He moved them closer to the bed, but the tuxedo trousers slid down around his ankles, causing him to stumble. His arms still holding Lexi against him, they fell across the four-poster bed in an undignified heap.

No sooner had they landed on the mattress than a horrible clanging split the air.

"What the hell is that?" he asked, trying to kick free of the slacks. The more he struggled, the louder the noise became.

Lexi suddenly burst out laughing. "I'd wondered where Jeff and Freddie disappeared to right after the band started playing. Now I know."

With every clang, Lexi's laughter increased.

He stopped trying to free himself and gave her a suspicious look. The deafening sound quieted, but Lexi continued to laugh.

"Jeff…Freddie…cowbells," she gasped.

Ty frowned. She must have had more punch than he'd thought. "Lexi, honey, you're not making sense," he said patiently. "What do Jeff and Freddie have to do with cowbells?"

When she continued to laugh, he shifted to gaze down at her. His movement only caused the noise to begin again and her laughter to increase.

Tears rolled down Lexi's cheeks as she shook her head. "They tied cowbells...to the bottom of the bed."

"That's what the clanging is?"

She nodded and the noise commenced again. So did her laughter.

Ty cursed as he sat up and switched on the lamp. Wrestling his legs free of the slacks, he knelt down to peer under the bed. Over a dozen bells in assorted sizes dangled from the springs.

Stretching out on his back, he inched his way beneath the bed. "Why the hell would they tie cowbells to the bottom of the bed?"

Giggling, Lexi wrapped herself in the quilt and peered over the side of the mattress at him. "So we'd have to stop what we were doing and untie them. Harassing newlyweds on their wedding night is a mountain tradition."

He yanked the string free on the last bell and hauled himself from under the bed. "Why?"

"It has something to do with—"

"Causing a hell of a lot of frustration for the couple?"

She nodded, her grin wide. "It certainly seems to have worked in your case."

Ty rose to his feet, switched off the light, then hooked his thumbs in the waistband of his white cotton briefs. "Fortunately, I'm very resil—"

His words stopped abruptly at a horrendous sound from outside. "What now?" he bellowed, switching on the light again.

Lexi scrambled from the bed. "It's a shivaree."

"What the hell is a shivaree?" he shouted above the whoops, catcalls and banging of pots and pans coming from the yard.

"Another one of those mountain customs," she answered, rushing to collect her clothes. "Now quick, get dressed."

"What will it take to make them stop?"

"We'll have to go out onto the front porch to greet the crowd," she said, sounding breathless from her haste to get dressed.

Pulling on the tuxedo slacks, Ty muttered a phrase that would have blistered the ears of a seasoned sailor. "We've been with these people all day. Wasn't that enough? Surely they have love lives of their own. Why do they feel the need to ruin ours?"

"It's hard to explain," Lexi said, struggling to zip the dress Ty had removed earlier. "But I promise, this is the last of the harassment. A shivaree is the grand finale."

"Good. The sooner it's over, the sooner they leave." He fastened the waistband of his trousers, then grabbed her hand. "Come on. Let's get this over with."

Lexi trotted along behind him. Poor guy had no idea how the shivaree would end, or the lasting effects it would have. "Ty, you don't understand—"

"Hey, Doc, you're lookin' a mite flustered," Harv Jenkins shouted when Ty flung open the door.

"Where'd you leave your shirt, Doc?" someone else called.

"Why did the light keep goin' on and off?" Jeff asked, his grin knowing.

"Lexi, how did you manage to turn your dress inside out?'' Freddie asked. Her hazel eyes sparkling with mischief, she pointed to Lexi's right arm. ''And why is your bra hangin' from the sleeve?''

As the group howled with laughter, Lexi looked at Ty. He wore nothing more than the tuxedo trousers and a frown. Glancing down at her dress, she groaned. In her haste she'd not only put the garment on inside out, the hook of her bra had caught on a thread and hung from her shoulder like a droopy flag.

''What happens now?'' Ty asked.

She felt a stab of guilt at what was about to happen, but there wasn't a thing she could do to stop it. ''We either serve them all a drink or they'll ride you around the yard in a wheelbarrow—''

''If that's all it takes to get them to leave, I'll be more than happy to play this silly game,'' Ty said, releasing her hand and vaulting off the porch.

Lexi started to tell him how the ride would end, but he was immediately cut off from her, surrounded by the laughing crowd. She watched helplessly as they led him over to where Jeff stood holding the handles of a one-wheeled cart.

''He doesn't know what's going to happen, does he?'' Freddie asked, climbing the steps of the porch to stand next to Lexi.

Lexi shook her head and watched Ty allow the men to seat him in the wheelbarrow. ''He doesn't have a clue.''

Obviously shocked, Freddie asked, ''Why didn't you tell him?''

''I tried, but he was so intent on getting it over with, he wouldn't listen.''

''I figured he was in the dark about it when he

willingly jumped off the porch,'' Freddie said, laughing.

"Is Martha watching the baby?'' Lexi asked as the procession began.

Freddie nodded. "We dropped them off at our house. Jeff will take her home when we get back.''

Lexi watched Ty being wheeled around the yard in a random pattern. "He thinks they'll ride him around for a few minutes and that'll be it.''

Jeff pushed Ty in a wide sweep around the front yard, the crowd running along behind, laughing and banging their pots and pans. When the parade started around the side of the house toward the small creek at the back of her property, Lexi glanced at her sister-in-law. "Time for the main event.''

Freddie turned to enter the house. "I'll go get some towels.''

Lexi ran down the steps and headed in the direction the crowd had taken Ty. "And start the hot water running in the shower.''

Ty gripped the sides of the wheelbarrow and wondered if he had somehow been transported to the Twilight Zone. Since his arrival in Dixie Ridge, he'd encountered some rather strange differences in culture and traditions. But this was without a doubt the most bizarre.

His rear end bounced up, then landed hard on the metal bottom of the cart as the wild ride continued around the side of the house, toward the back of Lexi's property. The crowd's laughter seemed almost maniacal and they beat their pots and pans harder the closer they got to the creek. He felt a tingle of apprehension run the length of his spine.

Turning to look over his shoulder, he tried to shout above the noise. "Jeff, you want to turn this thing around?"

"Hang on, Braden," Jeff said, grinning. "It's just about over."

"That's what I'm afraid of," Ty ground out between bone-jarring bumps. They were getting closer to the ice-cold stream than he felt comfortable with, and he had a sinking feeling he knew exactly how this strange ritual would end.

Closing his eyes, he held his breath and braced himself for the inevitable.

Ty's teeth chattered and he shivered uncontrollably as he stood beneath the spray of hot water. Steam filled the shower stall and rolled out to fog every corner of the small bathroom. He didn't care. He was colder than he'd ever been in his life. And try as he might, he couldn't erase the feel of icy water closing around him.

He closed his eyes and tried to stop shivering as he mentally ran through every curse word he'd ever heard. That done, he made up a few new ones.

He'd had big plans for the evening. He'd wanted to make love to Lexi all through the night, to show her how good they could be together. But when the crowd dumped him into the cold mountain stream, that idea had come to a swift and frigid end.

His teeth clicked together as another wave of goose bumps rose to the surface of his chilled skin. He'd never been one to feel sorry for himself, but he couldn't seem to keep the gloomy thoughts at bay.

He opened his eyes and glanced back down at his lower body. He wondered if certain parts of his anatomy would ever function normally again. As a doctor, he knew they would. But as a man facing his wedding night with no hope of loving his wife properly, Ty couldn't keep from feeling morose.

Just as the water began to turn tepid, Lexi's shadow appeared on the other side of the frosted glass door. ''Ty, are you ready to get out? I've put the electric blanket on the bed and turned it up to high. It should be warm now.''

He hurriedly shut off the tap, stepped out of the shower and grabbed the towel she'd warmed in the clothes dryer. He vigorously rubbed his chilled skin with the heated terrycloth.

''Put this on,'' she commanded, handing him a bathrobe.

''N-no…w-way.'' He tried to sound firm, but his teeth clicked together like a set of the chattering choppers sold in novelty stores and his staunch refusal lost all effect.

''It's just from the bathroom to the bedroom,'' Lexi said patiently. She draped the robe around his shoulders, then winked. ''Besides, I promise not to tell your patients how good you look in pink chenille.''

Ty might have protested further, but she'd heated the robe with the towel and he couldn't bear to give up the warmth it provided. ''Th-thank y-you.''

Once he was settled beneath the layers of several quilts and the electric blanket, his teeth still chattered, but his body was racked with only an occasional chill.

Lexi lay down beside him and snuggled close to share her body heat.

Nothing.

He pulled her closer.

His mind responded. His body remained dormant.

When she moved against him, Ty ground his teeth. He hated to admit it. It just wasn't something a man wanted to think about. Ever. And especially on his wedding night. But he might as well face facts. There was no way in hell his traumatized body was going to perform.

"Lexi, honey, I..." He paused as he searched for a less humiliating reason than admitting his predicament. Closing his eyes, he groaned. "I have a headache."

Eight

At the first ring of the phone, Ty reached across Lexi to the bedside table. He'd learned during the early days of his internship to awaken clearheaded and completely alert. His profession demanded it. All too often the snap decisions he had to make meant the difference between life and death.

"Dr. Braden speaking," he said, keeping his voice low. He didn't want to disturb Lexi.

"Doc, I know this is your weddin' night, and I hate to do this to you, but you're needed up here at the Morgan place," Martha said. "Granny ran into some problems. She called me to come help, but there's nothin' I can do. The baby's breech."

Ty looked at the clock and groaned. Why did so many infants decide to make their grand entrance at two or three in the morning?

After questioning Martha about the woman's condition, he determined it would be safe to move her. "Have Carl take her to the clinic," he said, throwing the covers back and sitting up on the side of the bed. "If the baby doesn't turn and Lydia can't deliver naturally, I may have to perform a C-section. If that happens, I want a sterile environment."

Martha's voice was all business. "We'll meet you at the clinic and I'll get things set up."

He once again glanced at the clock and did a quick mental calculation. "I should be there in fifteen minutes."

Hanging up the cordless phone, Ty glanced down at Lexi. She looked beautiful in sleep. Her long, dark lashes rested on her porcelain cheeks like tiny, wispy feathers. He wanted to kiss them. Her golden brown hair spread out across the pillow made him want to run his fingers through the silky strands as he made slow, passionate love to her. He felt his body react.

Great. Now that his body had finally thawed out and he experienced the first stirrings of desire, he had to go deliver a baby. Shaking his head, he slowly rose to his feet. "Some wedding night."

"Ty?" Lexi murmured sleepily. "Is it Freddie calling about Matthew?"

"The baby's fine," he said, pulling on the tuxedo trousers. He had no choice but to wear the ill-fitting suit. It was all he had to put on. He'd planned to move his things from the small apartment he'd rented above the Blue Bird Cafe sometime later today. Now he wished he'd thought to throw a pair of jeans and a T-shirt in the truck before the wedding yesterday.

"What's wrong?" she asked, sitting up.

"Granny can't deliver Lydia Morgan's baby," Ty said, stuffing the shirttail into his pants. "It's a breech presentation and I may have to perform an emergency Cesarean."

Lexi pushed the hair from her eyes and got out of bed. "I'm going with you."

"There's no sense in you missing sleep," he argued. "If everything goes well, I should be back in a few hours."

"I want to go," she said. Rummaging around in the closet, she selected a pair of jeans and a lightweight sweater. "I might be able to help."

Ty caught her around the waist and pulled her to him. "Honey, Martha and I will take care of Lydia." He gave her a quick kiss. "There's nothing you can do."

"You don't know Carl," she argued, stepping back and heading for the bathroom. "He acts first and thinks about it later. I'll try to keep him in the waiting room, and have fresh coffee ready for anyone who wants it."

When she returned, Ty watched her tie her sneakers, then put her hair up in a ponytail. "Are you sure?" he asked, stepping into his own shoes.

"Yes."

Maybe if he allowed her to see what his job entailed, she'd better understand the times when he'd be called away or have to work terribly long hours. Smiling, he planted a quick kiss on her lips and threaded his arm through hers. "Come on. Let's go deliver a baby."

"Carl, I'm sure everything is going well," Lexi said, watching the big man pace the length of the waiting area.

She'd already had to talk him out of barging into

the tiny operating room once. She seriously doubted she could prevent him from entering the room if he really set his mind to it.

"Ty will do everything he can for Lydia and the baby," she said, hoping Carl listened.

When he turned to face her, his shoulders slumped and his brown eyes reflected the depth of his anguish. "I love Liddy more than life itself. If somethin' happens to her, I'll never forgive myself."

Envy pierced Lexi's heart. Why couldn't she have a relationship like that?

Restless, she left her chair. "Let's step outside and get a breath of fresh air, Carl. Maybe you'll feel a little better."

"But what if they need me?"

"Ty will send Martha to find you if something happens," Lexi said, pushing open the glass door that led to the parking lot.

As they stood watching signs of the approaching dawn, the inky darkness of the night sky dulled to the pale gray of early morning and the stars above seemed to blink out one by one. The lights over in the Blue Bird Cafe came on. Helen McKinney had arrived to start baking biscuits and making gravy for the breakfast crowd.

"Miss Lexi?"

She turned her attention back to the man beside her. "Feeling better, Carl?"

He took a deep shuddering breath. "If y'all don't mind, could I be by myself for a few minutes?" he asked, his voice rough with emotion.

"Of course, Carl." She reached out to touch his arm. "I'll be in the waiting room."

Tears blurring her vision, Lexi pushed through the

clinic door. She didn't have to look back to know that Carl had already knelt down, clasped his hands in front of him and thrown back his head to face the heavens as he prayed for his wife and unborn child.

It was clear Carl Morgan loved Lydia with all his heart and the possibility of something happening to his wife had literally brought the big man to his knees.

Lexi had always wanted a relationship like that, wanted her husband to love her with all his heart and soul. But thanks to her brother and his meddling ways, she found herself married to a man she hardly knew.

Oh, she'd always been attracted to Ty and he'd made no secret of the fact that the attraction was mutual. But that wasn't the same as love.

She pulled a tissue from the box on the reception counter and wiped the tears from her cheeks. Ty had made it clear that he intended to be a good husband and father and that he wanted them to stay married.

Lexi had no doubt that she could grow to love Ty. Just watching the way he cared for their son, she wasn't far from the emotion now. But would Ty ever be able to love her in return? He wanted to be a part of Matthew's life, but that didn't mean he wanted to be a part of hers as well. They'd married because he'd had a shotgun to his back, not because he'd fallen in love with her. Should she try, for their son's sake, to make their marriage work? Would that be enough for her?

"Martha, mark the time of birth," Ty said, placing the newborn across Lydia's stomach.

"Is my baby all right?" Lydia asked, her voice weak.

"Everything is fine," Ty assured her. "You have a beautiful daughter."

"Oh my!" Tears coursed down the woman's cheeks. "I've waited so long for a girl."

Ty smiled against the paper mask as he finished the postpartum procedures. Fortunately, the baby had turned herself in the womb and Lydia had delivered naturally.

"How many brothers does she have?" he asked.

"Five," Lydia said proudly.

Ty chuckled. "A basketball team."

Martha wrapped the baby in a pink receiving blanket, then placed her in her mother's arms. She took hold of the gurney to wheel it into one of the patient rooms at the back of the clinic. "Looks like you're startin' on the cheerleadin' squad now, Liddy."

"Oh, no I'm not," Lydia said, shaking her head. "After what I went through this time, there won't be a next time. Carl's gonna get fixed."

While Martha settled their patient in her room, Ty removed the mask and headed for the waiting area. Smiling, he shook his head. He didn't blame the woman after the difficult time she'd had giving birth, but he wondered if Carl would be all that eager to go along with his wife's solution to family planning.

"Where's Carl?" he asked, entering the small waiting area. Lexi sat by herself, her arms wrapped protectively around her middle.

"He stepped outside for some air." She rose to stand in front of him. "He's been half out of his mind with worry. It was all I could do to keep him out of there."

Ty nodded. He wanted to take her in his arms and ask what was wrong, why she looked at him with such sadness. But he needed to find Carl and alleviate the man's fears about Lydia. "I'll go talk to him."

"How did things go?"

"Everything went just fine." His gaze zeroed in on the plain gold band circling her left finger. For some reason, he'd needed the assurance that she still wore his ring. "I'll tell you all about it after I've talked to Carl."

Ty stepped out into the pale light of dawn and, glancing around, found Carl on his knees a few feet from the door, his wide shoulders shaking with silent sobs. Ty hesitated as he thought of Lexi and their own son's recent birth. Until a month and a half ago, he hadn't given any thought to how he'd feel if a woman had a difficult time delivering his child. It simply hadn't been an issue. But now, for the first time in his life, Ty fully understood the agony the man must have gone through while awaiting word about his wife and baby.

"Carl?"

The man was on his feet immediately. Unashamed of the tears still coursing down his cheeks, he demanded, "How's Liddy? Is she—"

Smiling, Ty placed his hand on Carl's shoulder. It felt wonderful to be delivering good news for a change, instead of offering hollow condolences. "We didn't have to perform a C-section, Carl. Lydia delivered naturally. She and your daughter are waiting for you to come in and see them."

"Daughter?" Clearly shocked, Carl's eyes widened. "Well, I'll be damned. Liddy's been wantin' a little girl for years." He quickly wiped the moisture from his cheeks with his shirt sleeve, then stuck out his hand to clasp Ty's. "I sure do appreciate everything you did for them, Doc."

Ty shook his head when Carl vigorously pumped his arm. "No need to thank me. I'm glad I was here to help."

Carl's mouth split into a wide grin as he released Ty's hand and headed for the door. "I'll make sure you don't regret comin' to Dixie Ridge, Doc. I surely will."

Ty followed the man inside the clinic. Every time one of his patients said something similar, he ended up with jars of home-canned pickles and jellies, or cakes or pies. He had no idea what Carl would show up with in the next few days. But Ty had no doubt the man would find some way to convey his appreciation.

He shook his head and started for the waiting room where he'd left Lexi. If the good people of Dixie Ridge gave him a choice, he'd be happy to have some uninterrupted time alone with his wife.

"You can hang your clothes on this side," Lexi said, pointing to the space she'd created in the closet. She watched Ty hang several pairs of jeans where she'd indicated, before she turned to the dresser. "I'll clear a drawer for your other things, then go down to Jeff's and Freddie's to pick up the baby."

Her mind straying back to what she'd witnessed at the clinic, Lexi absently removed the contents of the drawer, while he finished hanging his shirts.

"Tired?" Ty asked, his arms coming from behind to pull her back against him.

Lexi's pulse quickened and her breath caught at the

feel of his solid chest against her back, the strength of his arms wrapped around her. "Ty, we need to talk," she said, her voice not nearly as convincing as she would have liked. She cleared her throat and tried again. "We both—"

"Not now, honey." Ty's lips caressed her ear. "We've been married almost twenty-four hours and it's past time we became man and wife."

Drawing from an inner strength she hadn't known she possessed, Lexi stepped away from him. "No, Ty."

"Why?"

She took a deep breath before she turned to face him. "We may be married, but we aren't going to become man and wife. After a reasonable amount of time, we'll quietly get the marriage annulled, then go on with our separate lives."

She watched a shadow of emotion cross his face a moment before he folded his arms over his wide chest. "That's not acceptable."

"Why?" she asked, incredulous. "You couldn't possibly be any happier than I am about being forced into this charade."

He shrugged. "I'm willing to give it a try."

Tears threatened, but she blinked them back. "I want more in my marriage than for my husband to just 'give it a try.' I want him to be committed to the relationship. To give all of himself, and to settle for no less from me." Lexi shook her head. "Ty, do you realize how little I even know about you?"

"That works both ways, Lexi," Ty said evasively.

She'd be darned if she let him dodge the issue this time. She waved her hand, encompassing the room. "Look around, Ty. My life is an open book. What you see in this room, and throughout this cabin, is who I am. Where I come from.'' She pointed to the bed. ''The antique quilt my great-grandmother made over fifty years ago says I'm sentimental. The cradle Matthew sleeps in has been in my family for five generations. That says I value tradition. The picture of my parents hanging in the living room says I'm proud to have been their daughter.'' She propped her fists on her hips. ''You're the one who never talks about your family or your background. I don't even know your parents' names. Have you even bothered to tell them about Matthew?''

He tilted his head to stare at the ceiling a moment, took a deep breath, then meeting her gaze, answered. ''My mother's name was Mary. She died while I was in med school.''

Lexi could tell by the pain she heard in his voice that they'd been close. ''I'm sorry. What happened?'' she asked quietly.

''She suffered a fatal head injury during a mugging.''

''Is that why you became a trauma specialist?''

He nodded. ''I'd been leaning toward specializing in emergency medicine, but that more or less finalized my decision.''

''What about your father? Is he still alive?''

''I don't know.'' Ty's expression changed from sadness, to self-protection, then to deep regret. ''I have no idea who the man was.''

Lexi felt his pain as deeply as if it were her own. ''You were—''

''A bastard.'' The edge in his voice made her wince.

''I was going to say illegitimate,'' she said gently.

Ty's hollow laughter echoed through the room. "That's the nicest way anyone's ever put it."

"You're ashamed of it?" she asked, unable to understand why he thought it mattered.

"I've learned to live with it," he answered, his tone guarded. "But when I was growing up, I also learned very quickly not to let the fact be known."

"You were taunted because of it?" she guessed, feeling as if her heart would break. The loneliness and hurt he must have suffered as a child had to have been devastating. "Children can be very cruel."

Ty shrugged. "They only repeated what they'd heard their parents call me."

"Things are different now, Ty. It's more acceptable for a woman to choose single motherhood."

"Yes. But thirty-five years ago it wasn't widely accepted," he reminded her. "Sure, times were changing, but not in the neighborhood where I grew up. I was the only kid on the block without a father."

"Did your mother—"

Ty nodded. "She knew who he was, but she never would tell me. Apparently, their relationship ended on bad terms. Whenever I asked about him, all she'd ever say was that he wasn't worth knowing." He gave her a meaningful look. "And she didn't bother telling him about me either."

Realization slammed into Lexi, taking her breath. "If you hadn't taken over the clinic—"

"History would have repeated itself," he finished for her. "I might never have known I had a son."

Lexi didn't hesitate. She stepped forward and wrapped her arms around his stiff shoulders. "I always intended for our son to know who you are and for the two of you to meet. But I wanted to wait until he was old enough to understand.''

''Does my less than complete pedigree bother you?'' he asked.

Lexi's gaze locked with his. She could tell by the intensity in his deep blue eyes that her answer mattered a great deal to him.

''No. Why should it?''

''I have no heritage to pass along to Matthew,'' he said cautiously. ''I didn't even know my maternal grandparents. They refused to have anything to do with me, or my mother. They said I was a constant reminder of the shame she'd brought to their family.''

Understanding suddenly dawned as she stared at him. ''That's the reason you never wanted to have children, isn't it? You didn't feel you had anything to offer them?''

He nodded. ''I have no idea what kind of genes I'll be passing on.''

''Ty, none of that will matter to Matthew,'' she said firmly. ''He'll love you for the man you are. All that will matter to him is that you return his love.''

Ty reached out to pull her to him. ''What about you, Lexi? How does it make you feel to know your husband is a—''

She placed her fingers to his lips to keep him from saying the ugly word. ''Don't ever call yourself that again.'' She searched his face. ''Why would I care?''

''I've only shared this with one other woman and her reaction was anything but understanding.''

Lexi couldn't believe that such a trivial thing as illegitimacy would matter to anyone. ''She was a complete fool.''

He let out a deep, shuddering breath. "It's a relief to have that out in the open."

Loosening her ponytail, he arranged her hair around her shoulders, then placed his forefinger beneath her chin. He tilted her head so their gazes met. "Please, Lexi, give our marriage a chance. Let me be part of a whole family for the first time in my life."

Lexi closed her eyes to his beseeching look. She felt like she was teetering on the edge of a cliff. The next step she took, whether forward or back, could very well be the biggest mistake of her life.

"I have another confession to make, honey." His lips tenderly skimmed her cheek. "At the wedding yesterday, I was a willing participant. You were the only one present who didn't have prior knowledge of the plan."

Before she could comment, his mouth came down on hers in the gentlest of kisses.

"Let me be your husband, Lexi," he whispered against her lips. "Let me hold you, feel you take me inside, and watch you touch the stars."

She heard the passion in his voice, saw the raw desire darken his eyes to navy. He pressed his lower body to hers and allowed her to feel how much he wanted to claim her as his. Her own body responded with a fevered ache.

He hadn't been forced to marry her, after all. He did want to share his life with her. Did she really want an annulment?

Ty gave her a smile that made her heart flutter. "Let me make love to you for the first time as my wife, Lexi."

Her knees began to wobble as the sound of his deep, hypnotic baritone wrapped around her. If he set his mind to it, Tyler Braden could melt the polar ice caps with his voice. She expected the emergency warning system to post flood advisories at any moment.

"You're not playing fair," she said breathlessly.

"I know," he said, brushing his lips across hers. "But I'm not feeling very fair right now."

The moment his mouth met hers, Lexi knew her body had overruled her mind in the matter. She'd hungered for Ty's touch, for his lovemaking, since that winter night in front of her fireplace in Chicago.

Ty slipped his hands beneath her sweater and pulled her closer. His palms whispered over her skin as he traced the part in her lips with his tongue, coaxing her to allow him entry. But instead of deepening the kiss, he continued to tease. His tentative touch caused a restlessness to build within her and Lexi moaned and moved against him. She wanted him to end the sweet torment, to satisfy the hunger he was creating.

"What do you want, honey?" he asked, pressing tiny kisses along her jaw, then down to her collarbones.

"I want you to kiss me, Ty," she said, her voice husky. "Really kiss me."

He raised his head to look down at her. "Is that all you want me to do?"

"No."

"What else do you want, Lexi?"

Lexi didn't have to think twice as Ty's talented hands continued to stroke her back and ribs. "I want you to make love to me, Ty."

Nine

Satisfaction flowed through Ty at her husky request. When her eyes drifted shut and her head fell back to expose the silky column of her neck, he wasted no time in taking advantage of her position. Gathering her sweater in his suddenly unsteady hands, he pulled it over her head. His normally capable fingers felt useless as he fumbled with the clasp of her bra. Once he'd released the hook and tossed it on the floor with her shirt, he was rewarded with the sight of her full breasts, the peaks tight for his touch.

He lowered his head, his tongue swirling one dark coral nipple as his thumb traced the other. When she shivered against him, he nibbled at the beaded tip before drawing it into his mouth, first chafing, then soothing. By the time he raised his head, Lexi's porcelain cheeks wore the rosy blush of desire and his own skin was coated with a fine sheen of perspiration.

The visible proof of her excitement fueled his own. He wanted to give to her as he'd never given to a woman before, but apparently Lexi had other plans. She gave him a smile filled with promise as she placed her hands on his chest and her fingers found his own sensitive flesh.

She traced the nubs with her nails. His breath rushed out in a harsh whoosh. She lowered her head to nip and tease. He stopped breathing all together.

When she raised her head to look at him, her busy fingers slid down the length of his chest and tugged at his jeans. Her seductive smile, the desire he saw darkening her eyes, caused his heart to pound and his body to strain against the denim.

Liquid fire flowed through his veins as she released the snap and slowly lowered the zipper. But when she touched the hard ridge straining at his cotton briefs, Ty felt like he just might burst into flames.

He caught her hands in his, placed them on his shoulders and reached out to slide the first button through the hole at the band of her button-fly jeans. Pure male satisfaction flowed through him as he watched her eyes glaze, heard her sharp intake of breath when his fingers dipped into the open vee to slip each button free. Releasing the last one, he slid the jeans and her silk panties down her slender legs and added them to the pile of clothes lying on the floor.

Reaching up to take Lexi's hands from his shoulders, he guided them to his waist. Lightning, keen and hot, flashed and sizzled across every nerve in his body as she lowered his jeans and briefs. By the time she'd finished the task, Ty's teeth were clenched so tightly, his jaw felt welded shut.

Her hands, as they skimmed down his hips and thighs, had almost brought him to the point of no return. But when she found him and circled his fevered flesh with her soft hands, he sucked in some much needed oxygen and stopped her delightful exploration.

"Honey, I'm not going to be able to take much more of this," he said, his mouth feeling like he could spit cotton. "It's just been too damned long."

"Then make love to me, Ty." The sound of her throaty reply bathed him with waves of heated excitement.

Ty pulled her to him and buried his face in the cloud of her golden brown hair. He shuddered at the sweet smell of honeysuckle, the feel of skin against skin and the taste of desire on her parted lips. Sweeping her into his arms, he carried her the few steps to the bed and gently placed her on top of the antique quilt.

He stared in awe at the perfection of her. "You're the most beautiful woman I've ever seen, Lexi. And you're mine. My wife. The mother of my son."

Joining her on the bed, Ty took her into his arms and kissed her with all the awe and wonder of a man who realized what a precious gift he'd been given.

She threaded her slender fingers in his hair and the fire inside him began to build even hotter. Exploring, reacquainting himself with her body, he stroked her dewy softness. Her complete readiness for him, the arching of her hips as she met each caress, caused the flames to flare out of control.

Desire, hot and urgent, thrummed through his veins, but Ty somehow managed to find the strength to leave her for a moment. The preventive measure in place, he gathered her to him, covered her body with his and nudged her knees apart. Their gazes met and locked as he slowly eased himself inside.

He heard her breath catch, saw the rapture reflected in her expressive eyes as he filled her completely. There was so much he wanted to tell her. So many things he needed to say. But with his body held intimately inside hers, and with passion illuminating her beautiful face, words were simply impossible.

"Lexi," was all he could get out as he lowered his mouth to hers.

The sweet taste of desire on her perfect lips, the feel of her softness surrounding him, unleashed the taut energy he'd fought to control. Spirals of hunger and need wrapped around them as in perfect unison they yielded to the ultimate dance of love. Together they reached for the stars and they both cried out at the beauty of it when their souls found heaven awaiting in one brilliant burst of heat and light.

His breathing slowly returned to normal and Ty eased himself to her side. He wrapped his arms around her and she murmured his name a moment before falling asleep. Being up most of the night had taken its toll on both of them. His last thought before sleep overtook him was how good it felt to have her back in his arms.

"Ty, wake up," Lexi said gently shaking his shoulder. "You're having a nightmare."

Ty sat up with his back to her. Coated with cold sweat, his body trembled and his heart pounded as if it were going to leap from his chest. Taking deep breaths, he tried to regain his composure before he faced her.

"What were you dreaming about?" she asked, clearly concerned. "It must have been terrible."

He jerked around to face her. "Did I say anything?"

She looked startled at his harsh tone. "Yes. But I couldn't understand what it was. You were pretty incoherent."

Ty ran a hand over his face and tried to rub the images from his mind.

"It was just a dream, Ty." She placed her hand on his shoulder. "Do you want to tell me about it?"

"No!" Without another word, he left the bed and stalked into the bathroom.

Bracing his hands on the bathroom sink, he bowed his head and took several deep breaths. When he finally felt steady enough to glance at the mirror, he barely recognized the haggard man staring back at him.

He'd never before thought of himself as a coward. Hell, he'd stared death in the face more times than he cared to count in the course of treating young gang members and deranged addicts. But staring down the barrel of a Saturday night special or watching the polished, steel point of a switchblade slash the air hadn't caused him a fraction of the terror that twisted at his gut now.

If he told Lexi what happened that snowy evening almost a year ago—the night they'd made love—why he'd been desperate to be held, and why he'd recently had to leave Chicago, he might lose her and their son for good. He gritted his teeth against the thought of her reaction. He couldn't bear to watch condemnation glaze her eyes.

Or worse yet, fear. He'd rather die than to have her be afraid of him.

But maintaining his silence wasn't the answer either. By his response when she asked him to talk about the dream, she had to know he was hiding something.

Ty shut his eyes against the battle raging within. Either way, he ran the risk of losing her.

When she left Chicago almost a year ago, it had taken him several months to stop looking for her each time he stepped into the elevator, to keep from laying in bed each night wondering what would have happened if she'd stayed in the city. But this time he knew for certain it wouldn't be as simple as that. If she sent him away, this time he doubted he'd survive.

"Lexi, you haven't heard a word I've said," Freddie complained, removing a sheet from the clothesline.

"I'm sorry." Lexi gave her sister-in-law an apologetic smile. "I guess I'm a little tired."

"Well, I would hope so." Freddie grinned. "After all, you are a newlywed."

Tears threatened as Lexi glanced down at her son snuggled close to her breast. She'd taken the baby for a walk and found herself at Jeff and Freddie's house. She knew deep down it wasn't by accident that her walk had her visiting her sister-in-law. Lexi needed someone to talk to and Freddie had been her confidante since they'd been seated next to each other in Miss Barnes's first-grade class at Dixie Ridge Grade School.

But from the moment Lexi arrived, Freddie had chattered a mile a minute about what a lovely family the three of them made. And with each comment, Lexi felt her heart break just a little more.

She bit her lower lip to keep it from trembling. "My fatigue isn't from what you think," she finally said.

Freddie folded the sheet, then placed it in a large wicker basket, her bright smile fading. "Things aren't goin' well?"

"Not really."

Freddie gave her a measuring look before heading toward the house. "Why don't you put Matthew down for a nap in the spare bedroom, while I make a pot of coffee?"

Following her sister-in-law into the house, Lexi made sure Matthew was asleep before joining Freddie at the kitchen table.

"So, what's wrong?" Freddie asked, placing a steamy cup of coffee in front of Lexi. "You look like your favorite bird dog died."

Lexi wiped at a lone tear making a trail down her cheek. "I'm afraid it's not going to work, Freddie."

Freddie reached out to place her hand on Lexi's arm. "I'm sure in time things will work out."

"You don't understand." Lexi shook her head as she stared down at the cup clutched tightly between her palms. "It's not anything as simple as adjusting to him leaving his socks on the bathroom floor or the cap off the toothpaste. Ty is hiding something that's tearing him apart, but he won't let me help." Her gaze met Freddie's. "A few days ago he had this horrible nightmare, and I could tell he was reliving something terrible. But when I tried to get him to talk to me, he flat-out refused."

Freddie looked thoughtful. "Did you stop to think it might be too painful for him to talk about?"

"That's possible," Lexi conceded. "He did tell me about his family, so he is opening up."

"Give him a little more time," Freddie suggested. "You've only been married a few days. Some things take longer to share. You can't expect him to just unload everything all at once." She gave Lexi a wink. "I have faith in you, girl. You'll bring him around."

Lexi took a deep breath. "I hope you're right."

"I know I am." Freddie checked her watch. "Granny's garters! Jeff will be home in an hour and I haven't even thought about what to fix for supper."

When she rose from her chair, the color drained from Freddie's face and she gripped the table to keep from falling.

Lexi jumped to her feet and put her arm around her sister-in-law's shoulders. "What's wrong?"

"I'm okay." Freddie grinned sheepishly. "I've just got to learn not to move so fast, that's all."

"Are you sure you're all right?" Lexi asked, not at all convinced. Freddie's face was still a pasty white and her breathing seemed labored.

"I couldn't be better," Freddie assured a moment before her eyes fluttered shut and she completely lost her battle with consciousness.

Lexi rose from the chair when she heard Jeff's truck come to a sliding halt in front of the house. It didn't surprise her in the least that her brother had made the forty-minute drive from Gatlinburg in a little over twenty. When she'd called his cabinet shop and explained the situation, she'd immediately found herself talking to an open line.

The front door crashed open with a resounding thud as Jeff's long strides carried him well into the room. "Where's Freddie?" he demanded.

"In the bedroom," Lexi said. She caught hold of his arm when he started toward the hall. "Ty's with her now."

Jeff glanced down at the hand Lexi placed on his forearm, then looked at her as if seeing her for the first time. He took a deep shuddering breath before he finally asked, "What happened?"

Lexi explained what had taken place, then added, "She refused to go to the clinic, so I called Ty."

Jeff's tight nod was almost imperceptible. "How long has he been in there with her?"

She checked the clock on the mantle. "About ten minutes. It shouldn't be much longer."

"I can't understand it. She's always been healthy as a…" Jeff's voice trailed off at the sound of a door opening and two people coming down the hall.

When they walked into the living room, Ty was smiling and Freddie looked absolutely radiant.

At his wife's side in a heartbeat, Jeff put his arm around her shoulders for support. "What happened, sweetheart? Are you all right?"

Lexi watched Freddie glance at Ty and grin before she wrapped her arms around Jeff's waist. "I couldn't be better, Love Dumplin'. I just got a little woozy, that's all."

Jeff's cheeks turned red. "I asked you not to call me that in front of people," he muttered. He hugged his wife close and turned to Ty. "Why did she faint?"

Ty grinned. "I think I'll let your wife tell you."

"Well, somebody better tell me," Jeff said, clearly losing patience. "And damned quick."

Freddie giggled. "Don't get your shorts in a bunch, big guy. Ty said feelin' faint sometimes happens to pregnant ladies."

The silence that accompanied Freddie's announcement lasted only a split second before Jeff swept his petite wife into his arms and let out a whoop that could have raised the dead. "We're gonna have a baby."

"That's wonderful," Lexi exclaimed, relieved that nothing was seriously wrong.

She glanced at Ty and felt a twinge of regret. When she'd found out Matthew was on the way, she hadn't been able to make such a joyous announcement. She'd gone home in a state of shock to an empty house and tried to make plans for her future as a single mother.

Ty's intense blue gaze met hers from across the room and they stared at each other for several long moments. She could see the regret, and knew he was thinking of what he'd missed during her pregnancy with Matthew.

She wanted more than anything for their marriage to work. Maybe Freddie was right. Maybe if she gave him more time, he'd open up, allow her to help, and they could start building a future together.

"Thanks for comin' here to the house," Jeff said, interrupting her thoughts. He reached out to shake Ty's hand. "Freddie wouldn't go inside the clinic unless it was a matter of life and death."

Ty shrugged. "No problem. I'd just seen my last patient for the day when Lexi called."

"I'm so happy for both of you," Lexi said, smiling. "You've waited a long time for this."

"We sure have," Jeff said. He tucked Freddie

close to his side and grinned down at her. "We've got some celebratin' to do, sweetheart."

Lexi watched her brother gaze lovingly at his wife. She had a good idea what Jeff had planned for the evening and it certainly didn't include her and Ty.

An ache settled around her heart. In time, maybe Ty could learn to love her the way Jeff loved Freddie. He'd said he wanted to give their marriage a chance, to work at being a whole family. Wasn't that what she wanted too? He had shared his illegitimacy with her—something that had been very difficult for him. It wasn't everything, but it was a start. In time, maybe he could learn to love and trust her with whatever haunted him. But she'd never know if she didn't try.

"It's almost time for Matthew's dinner, isn't it, Lexi?" Ty asked, winking.

She smiled. "As a matter of fact, I think it is."

When she, Ty and the baby left Jeff's and Freddie's house, Lexi doubted that either one of the pair even noticed.

"There must have been something to Granny Applegate's prediction last month," Ty said steering the SUV onto the road.

"Which one was that?" Lexi asked.

He laughed. "The one about the moon being right for women becoming pregnant. Freddie's is the third pregnancy I've diagnosed today."

"A baby boom on Piney Knob."

"Looks like it," he agreed.

They fell into an uneasy silence as they drove up the lane to the cabin.

He hated the strained atmosphere between them, the caution. He knew he was only postponing the inevitable. There were things that, as his wife, Lexi had a right to know.

When he parked the truck in front of the house, Lexi surprised him by getting out of the back seat and getting into the bucket seat on the passenger side. Turning to face him, she reached out to hug him.

''Honey—''

''It doesn't matter right now, Ty. We'll take things one step at a time. I'll be here to listen when you're ready.''

Incapable of finding the right words to express how he felt at her gentle reassurance, he kissed her.

Heat shot through him when her lips met his. Her fingers threaded through the hair at the base of his neck and urged him closer. Allowing her to take control of the kiss, he felt a jolt of desire as strong as an electric current course through him. She stroked his lips with her tongue, then nipped at them with her teeth. Never in his wildest dreams could he think of anything more provocative than Lexi taking the role of seductress.

The fire she was building inside him with her tentative exploration heightened his senses and caused his body to tighten to an almost painful state. When she urged him to open for her, he groaned at the sweet taste of her, the tantalizing smell of honeysuckle as it seductively wrapped around him.

His mind and body zeroing in on one thought, it took him several seconds to realize a truck horn blared from somewhere behind them. Breaking the kiss, he glanced in the rearview mirror to see Carl Morgan climb down from the cab of his truck and start toward them.

"Damn!" He reached for the door handle. "Don't these people have lives of their own?"

"I used to think so," Lexi said. She got out of the truck, then opening the rear door, released the catch on the baby's protective carrier. "I'll take Matthew inside, while you see what Carl wants."

Ty cursed vehemently, got out of the Blazer and slammed the door. How the hell did these people ever expect a newly married couple to find happiness when they wouldn't leave them alone?

"What can I do for you, Carl?" he asked impatiently.

Not at all put off by Ty's abrupt tone, Carl grinned. "Sorry 'bout hornin' in on your business there, Doc. I promise I'll let you get back to Lexi in just a few minutes. But I wanted to stop by and bring you somethin' to show how much I appreciate all you did for Liddy and the baby the other night."

Ty heaved a sigh. He felt like a heel. "It's not necessary, Carl."

"Yes, it is," the big man insisted. He motioned for Ty to follow him. Walking to the back of his truck he pointed to the bed. "I promised you I'd make sure you didn't regret comin' to Dixie Ridge and I never go back on my word."

Ty started to say he wouldn't regret coming to the mountains if everyone would just leave him and Lexi alone. Instead, he found himself counting to ten as he tried to regain some of his usual patience.

"Carl, I was just doing what I came here to do. You don't have to—"

The words died in Ty's throat when he saw what Carl had in mind. There in the middle of the truck bed, a big red bow tied around its neck, a black-and-white pig the size of a cocker spaniel sat as regal as any monarch.

"This here's Dempsey," Carl said, grinning. "He's a registered Hampshire."

"Dempsey?"

"Yeah, but don't blame me for callin' him that. The boys name 'em as soon as they're born." Carl shrugged. "Anyway, Dempsey is yours now."

"Mine?" Ty shook his head. He didn't want to insult the man, but he needed a pig about as much as the North Pole needed ice cubes. "I appreciate the gesture, but I can't accept him, Carl. I'll be going back to the city in a few months. Besides, I don't know the first thing about taking care of a pig. I don't even know what they eat."

"Pigs are easy to get the hang of," Carl said, lowering the tailgate. He unloaded a huge pail and carried it to the porch. "And don't worry none about what to feed him. I'll keep you supplied with plenty of my special recipe." He patted the top of the bucket with his big, beefy hand. "Just give him a scoop of this a couple of times a day and he'll be fine."

"Carl, I can't let you do this," Ty insisted. "I told you I'll be going back to Chicago."

The man just grinned, tied a rope around Dempsey's neck for a leash, then placed the pig in Ty's arms. He slammed the tailgate shut and headed for the driver's side door. "Welcome to Piney Knob, Doc."

"I don't have a place to keep him," Ty tried, feeling desperate. What the hell was he going to do with a pig?

"He'll be fine right back there," Carl said, pointing to the shed behind the cabin. Having solved that problem, the man crawled into the cab, turned the truck around and waved as he drove out of sight.

Dempsey grunted and squirmed, then emitted a large burp.

Ty glanced down at the small pig tucked in his arms. He felt like he'd entered the Twilight Zone for the second time in a week.

Five minutes ago he was well on his way to making love to his wife. Now he stood, holding a squinty-eyed little pig that appeared to have digestive problems.

He cursed and set Dempsey on his feet. Ty watched the pig's wobbly trot as he led the animal to the shed. Great! Dempsey probably had inner ear trouble to go along with his gassy stomach.

Ty decided he'd worry later about a remedy for the little porker's problem. He wanted to get back to Lexi before someone else showed up to ruin what had started out to be a promising evening with his wife.

Ten

Lexi finished nursing Matthew, then placed her sleeping son in the cradle. She wondered what was taking Ty so long. She hoped he wasn't being called away on another emergency.

They needed time together. Time to talk. Time to start building a foundation of trust between them.

She walked into the great room just as Ty entered the house. "What did Carl want?"

Ty rolled his eyes and shook his head. "I can't believe it. We are now the proud owners of a black and white pig named Dempsey."

"Carl gave you one of his registered Hampshires?" she asked incredulously. "He must really be grateful. Those animals are quite valuable."

"Only if you make a movie about him talking to sheep," Ty muttered.

She shook her head. "Wrong breed of pig."

"Whatever."

Lexi might have laughed had it not been for Ty's exasperated expression. "What did you do with him?"

"I put him in the shed." He wrinkled his nose and shook his head in disgust. "Along with a really foul-smelling bucket of pig food."

That did it. She couldn't contain her laughter any longer. "You don't want to own a pig?"

"No." He crossed the room and took her into his arms. Lowering his head, he brushed her lips with his. "And I don't want to think about it now."

Ty's kiss made her pulse race and her stomach flutter. She didn't want to think about a pig named Dempsey either.

"Is Matthew asleep?" he asked when he raised his head. His blue eyes had darkened with desire, and the hunger she saw there took her breath away.

"Yes."

She watched the pulse at the base of his throat quicken and she leaned forward to kiss it. The slight movement against her lips sent tingles over every nerve in her body.

"He should sleep for a couple of hours," she offered.

Ty traced his finger along her cheek as he stared down at her. "I'm going to take a shower. I'll only be a few minutes."

Lexi nodded and watched Ty walk down the hall. She waited patiently until he closed the bathroom door, then followed him. When she heard the water running, she grinned. He hadn't asked her to join him, but some things were more provocative when done on impulse.

Her breath caught when she entered the bathroom and watched Ty's masculine form silhouetted through the frosty glass of the shower doors.

She quickly shed her clothes, opened the door and stepped inside. "I'll wash your back, if you wash mine."

"What took you so long?" he asked, his voice low and suggestive as he reached for her.

Ty's arms closed around her to pull her forward. If she could remember what he'd asked, she might have answered. But the feel of his hard, wet maleness pressed to her sent ribbons of desire threading their way through every part of her, and she forgot her own name, let alone anything she'd been about to say.

His hands ran the length of her back to the curve of her bottom, then up her sides to the swell of her breasts. He supported the heaviness he'd created there as he lowered his lips to sip the water droplets from her skin. Her body tingled. He took one beaded tip into his mouth, then the other to tease them with his strong teeth and slightly rough tongue. When he raised his head, he kissed her like she'd never been kissed before, and the taste of his passion left her weak and wanting.

Lexi ran her hands over his shoulders, his wide chest, his flanks. She wanted to give to him as he gave to her. When she touched him, her fingers closed around his length and she was rewarded with his groan of pleasure as she tested his strength, soothed him with her palm.

He caught her hands in his and placed them on his shoulders as he knelt before her. "You're beautiful," he said, his lips skimming her satin skin.

His hands slid over her hips to her inner thighs and

when he found her, she felt as if she might go up in flames. Heat threatened to consume her as Ty's finger dipped inside to tease, caress, stroke. He treated her to the same sweet torture she'd subjected him to only moments before.

When she thought she'd surely die from the pleasure of his touch, he rose to his feet and lifted her to him. Their gazes locked as Lexi circled his shoulders with her arms and wrapped her legs around him. Without a word, he braced himself against the shower wall and slid himself inside her.

Lexi gasped at the intense pleasure of being filled by him. She closed her eyes and her head fell back as she arched against him, taking all he had to give, trying to absorb his body with hers.

Ty moved and the coil of need in her belly tightened, the exquisite pleasure almost more than she could bear. With each powerful stroke the pressure increased and she found herself clinging to the moment, responding in ways she'd never before experienced. He must have sensed her readiness, her fierce need of fulfillment because he brought his hands down to cup her bottom, holding her more tightly to him as he increased the rhythm.

Just when she thought she could take no more, spirals of heat and light raced through her and Lexi clung to Ty as her body shattered into a million pieces. She felt him stiffen a moment before he joined her in the all-consuming pleasure, releasing his essence deep inside her.

Lexi slowly drifted back to earth as Ty slid them to a sitting position on the floor of the shower. Exhausted, water cascading over both of them, she lowered her forehead to his shoulder.

"It's never been like that," she whispered.

Ty shook his head as he stroked her wet hair. "For me, either."

She leaned back to look at him. "I think I'm falling in love with you."

It hurt that he wasn't returning her confession of love, but his eyes darkened to navy a moment before he lowered his mouth to hers. He kissed her with a tenderness that stole her breath and chased away all thought.

When the kiss ended, he reached up to turn off the water. "Let's find a more comfortable place to continue this, honey."

Nodding, Lexi rose to her feet, opened the door and reached for one of the thick towels on the rack beside the shower. She blotted the water from Ty's wide chest and shoulders, but when she started to dry his legs, her breath caught and her stomach fluttered at the sight of his rapidly changing body.

"You seem to have a recurring problem, Dr. Braden."

"Looks like it." He grinned suggestively. "Want to help me find the cure?"

"Well, I don't have any formal medical training," Lexi said, returning his smile.

He took her hand in his and led her into the bedroom. Taking her into his arms, he whispered close to her ear, "Sometimes there's no better way to learn than hands-on training."

And, as his hands once again began to work their magic, Lexi decided she had to agree.

"It appears you have your days and nights mixed up," Ty said, picking up his smiling son.

He glanced over at the bed to see if Matthew's cooing had awakened Lexi. She slept peacefully.

Ty cradled the baby to him and quietly walked down the hall. "We don't want to disturb Mommy. She's really tired."

Walking into the living room, he turned on a lamp, then settled himself and the baby in the rocking chair. "I want to thank you for being a good boy and taking such a long nap this evening," Ty said, kissing the baby's soft cheek. "It gave Daddy a chance to spend some time with Mommy."

Matthew gave him a toothless baby smile and gurgled.

Ty chuckled. "You understand, don't you, little man?"

The baby's tiny hand bumped against Ty's ring finger and curled around it in a surprisingly strong grip.

Ty gazed down at his son's hand so close to the gold ring circling his finger. He'd never allowed himself to think of what it would be like to be a husband and father. Never thought he'd feel the kind of love he experienced at this moment. He wanted it to last forever.

Being away from the stress and tremendous pressure he'd been under for the last several years, he'd had time to think. He wasn't sure what the future held, but he knew for certain he wouldn't be going back to the E.R. when he returned to Chicago. Treating the patients of Dixie Ridge, he'd discovered he liked the more relaxed pace of private practice.

Setting up an office in a quiet suburb would be something to consider. Then maybe Lexi would be receptive to going back with him.

He glanced at the hall, then leaned his head back

and closed his eyes. Before that happened, Lexi deserved to know about the man she'd married. The man who'd fathered her child.

Time was running out. Dr. Fletcher would be returning to resume his practice at the Dixie Ridge Health Clinic in a few months and Ty would be leaving. If Lexi and Matthew went back to Chicago with him, she'd learn all too soon about the sins of the man she'd married.

And it scared the hell out of him.

"Honey, could you come here?" Ty called from outside.

Concerned by the worry she detected in his voice, Lexi shifted Matthew to her shoulder and hurried out onto the porch. She found Ty standing in the yard with Dempsey.

"What's the problem?"

"Call Jeff and tell him I won't be going fishing with him today."

"Why not?"

Ty glanced down at the pig and frowned. "Something's wrong with Dempsey."

She watched the little pig stagger closer to Ty. "What makes you think that?" she asked, barely able to keep a straight face.

The little pig chose that moment to sit down and lean his head against Ty's leg.

"I fed him about an hour ago and now he can barely stand up." He reached down to give Dempsey a sympathetic pat on the head. "I'd better take the poor thing to a vet."

Dempsey emitted a loud burp, grunted contentedly and gave Lexi a glassy-eyed stare.

She tried not to laugh, but it was no use. She knew exactly what Dempsey's problem was. "Ty, you don't have anything to worry about. There's nothing wrong with that pig that time won't take care of."

He looked skeptical. "Are you sure? From the smell of that stuff Carl gave me to feed him, I think he might have food poisoning."

When Dempsey lay down on his side and immediately started snoring, Lexi laughed so hard, tears filled her eyes.

Ty glanced down at Dempsey again, then gave her a long, measuring look. "Why do I get the idea you know something I don't? This pig isn't sick, is he?"

She shook her head as she came to stand next to him. "How much of that feed did you give him?"

"Carl said to feed him one scoop twice a day." Ty frowned. "But he still seemed hungry so I gave him another scoop."

Lexi nodded. "That's what I thought. Carl doesn't raise hogs for his main source of income, although they do contribute to it. He keeps them to get rid of the by-product created by his real line of work."

Ty raised one dark brown. "And that would be?"

Smiling, she kissed his cheek. "Carl runs one of the most productive stills on Piney Knob."

"He makes moonshine?"

Lexi laughed at his incredulous expression. "Yes, and it's a well-known fact that pigs love the taste of fermented corn. That's why Carl keeps them."

Understanding crossed Ty's handsome face. "They dispose of the grain once it's been used to make the liquor. When I gave Dempsey extra, it was more than he's used to."

Grinning, she nodded. "You exceeded Dempsey's tolerance level."

Ty looked thoroughly disgusted. "Bottom line, I got Dempsey drunk."

"Yes, Dr. Braden." Lexi laughed. "You're guilty of contributing to the delinquency of a pig."

"I'm not sure this is such a good idea," Ty said, following Jeff through the woods. "I know even less about fishing than I do about feeding pigs."

Jeff laughed. "Don't worry about that pig. He'll sleep it off. Besides, goin' fishin' is just an excuse."

"For what?" Ty ducked and barely avoided being slapped across the face by the low-hanging branch Jeff had shoved aside. "You want to enlighten me on the real reason we're out here in the woods, risking life and limb?"

"I've got some things I want to ask you about Freddie's condition," Jeff called over his shoulder, continuing up the path. "I don't want Freddie or Lexi gettin' wind of how little I know about pregnant ladies. They'd never let me live it down."

"There's no big mystery," Ty said, trying to keep up with Jeff and dodge the sharp briars snatching at his clothes.

"That's easy for you to say," Jeff retorted. "You've been to school for stuff like this."

"What is it you want to know?" Ty asked, stopping to unsnag his sleeve from a briar.

"Am I gonna be gettin' up in the middle of the night to drive over to Gatlinburg for stuff like pickles and ice cream or some other ungodly combination of food?"

Ty chuckled. "There are no guarantees. Some

women do crave strange things. But it's not set in stone that Freddie will be one of them. She might not have any cravings at all."

"That makes me feel a little better," Jeff grumbled. He shuddered visibly. "I don't much cotton to the idea of havin' to watch her eat that stuff."

They walked on in silence for several yards, before Ty asked, "Was there anything else you wanted to know?"

Jeff stopped abruptly and turned to face him. "Yes, there is."

From the expression on the man's face, Ty could tell Jeff wanted to discuss more important matters than Freddie's future eating habits.

"Have you ever considered doin' home deliveries?" Jeff asked, point-blank. "I wouldn't be askin', but we both know how Freddie feels about goin' inside the clinic."

"No, I've never considered it. But it's a moot point anyway." Ty rubbed at the tension building at the base of his neck. Lately, every time he thought of going back to the city, his muscles tensed and his gut twisted. "I'll be going back to Chicago well before Freddie gives birth. Besides, I thought Freddie preferred Granny Applegate."

"Maybe she does. But I don't." His expression determined, Jeff explained, "Don't get me wrong. Granny is a real fine woman, but she's been talkin' lately about retirin'. I doubt she'll even be midwifin' when Freddie needs her."

"She mentioned something about that at the wedding reception," Ty said, nodding.

Jeff shrugged. "I just want the best for my wife

and baby. I'd feel better about a doctor takin' care of Freddie when her time comes.''

Ty fully understood Jeff's concerns. ''I don't blame you. Talk to Dr. Fletcher when he returns. Maybe you can make some kind of arrangement with him.''

Jeff nodded. ''I guess I can try.''

Ty met his brother-in-law's concerned gaze. ''I'm making no promises, but I'll talk to Fletcher and ask him to give it serious consideration.''

Jeff grinned. ''That'd be great. Thanks.''

They started back up the path, but a sharp, loud crack stopped them both in their tracks.

Ty heard a dull thud as something hit the tree beside him. ''What the hell was that?'' he asked, brushing chips of bark from his hair.

''Get down!'' Jeff shouted, turning to grab Ty by the arm.

No sooner had Jeff taken hold of his arm than a second crack split the air and Ty felt the ground rush up to meet him. The outside of his upper left arm felt as if it had been set on fire and he automatically reached up to soothe the burning. He must have hit it on something when Jeff pulled him down, he decided, rubbing the area.

''You okay?'' Jeff asked.

''Yes. What's going on?''

Jeff looked around the now eerily silent woods. ''In case you hadn't noticed, we're being shot at.''

''Who would—''

''I'm not sure,'' Jeff interrupted. ''But we need to get out of here.''

Ty put his left hand down to push himself to his knees, but white-hot pain suddenly shot up his arm and he glanced at the spot to see his shirt was torn.

Shock and revulsion coursed through him at the surreal sight of his own blood rapidly soaking the fabric. Throughout his years in an inner-city hospital emergency room, he'd faced all kinds of threats, but never once had he actually been injured.

"Let's get back to the truck," Jeff said, rising to his feet. He began gathering their fishing rods and tackle box. "Whoever fired that gun must have cleared out, and I think we'd better do the same before he comes back with some buddies."

Ty put his right hand over the wound and attempted to regain his footing, but slightly off balance, he sank back to his knees. "You're going to have to help me get up," he said through clenched teeth. "I've been shot."

Jeff dropped the fishing gear and knelt beside him. "Damn! How bad is it?"

"There isn't enough blood for it to have severed an artery," Ty said. "I think it's just a flesh wound. But it burns like hell."

"Let me take a look," Jeff said.

Ty removed his hand for Jeff to peel back the torn edges of his shirtsleeve. The bullet had cut a path across the outside of Ty's upper arm, but the damage seemed minimal.

"It's going to take a few stitches to close, but otherwise it isn't bad," Ty said, feeling somewhat detached as his physician's eyes assessed the wound.

At that moment, the sound of brush being pushed aside and heavy footsteps caused them to look up. Carl Morgan, rifle in hand, was bearing down on them like a charging bull.

"Aw hell, Doc, I didn't know it was you and Jeff," he said, dropping to his knees beside Ty. "I wasn't meanin' to hit anybody. I was just tryin' to warn y'all away from—''

''You thought we were the authorities comin' to bust up your still, didn't you?'' Jeff accused, removing his handkerchief from his hip pocket and winding it around Ty's arm.

Carl's shoulders drooped. ''Yeah. They've been lookin' for my boiler for the past six months,'' he admitted. ''But I've always stayed one step ahead of 'em. This bein' my last batch and all, I just wanted to get it jugged and out of here before I busted up the cooker.''

''You're going to stop making moonshine?'' Ty asked.

Carl nodded. ''I promised Liddy that if we ever had a baby girl, I'd quit runnin' shine and go to raisin' hogs full-time.''

''Why does havin' a daughter make a difference?'' Jeff asked, securing the makeshift bandage on Ty's arm.

''Little girls are special,'' Carl said simply. A wondrous expression crossed his face as he hooked his thumbs in the straps of his overalls and explained. ''I don't want to take a chance of bein' caught makin' white lightnin' and get myself thrown in jail. I don't want little Carly ashamed of her daddy.'' His expression turned to one of pure misery when he glanced down at Ty's arm. ''Now this had to happen. You're gonna have to report this, ain't you, Doc?''

Ty stared off into the distance as he pondered what he would do. In Chicago, he'd viewed things as black and white. Right and wrong. Legal and illegal. And he wouldn't have thought twice about turning Carl in to the authorities.

But here in the mountains, it was a different story. Since being here in Dixie Ridge, Ty had learned to be flexible, to take into account the gray areas as well as the black and white of a situation.

Carl wasn't just a nameless face in the crowd. He was a friend. A neighbor. A loving husband and father. A man who deserved a chance to mend his ways.

Ty had no idea why a daughter's opinion meant more than a son's, but he wasn't going to question Carl's logic. The fact that the man was going to quit the illegal activity was all that mattered.

"As a doctor, I'm supposed to report any kind of gunshot wound," Ty admitted. "But I think I can overlook this, *if* you keep your word and cease making moonshine."

Carl brightened. "You have my word. I won't make another drop." Glancing at the handkerchief wrapped around Ty's arm, blood already staining the pristine white, his expression turned dark once again. "Damn! Lexi's gonna have my hide for shootin' you."

"It wasn't your fault," Ty said, shrugging.

Jeff and Carl gave him a look that stated quite clearly they both thought he'd lost his mind.

Ty grinned. "I have no idea who fired the gun or why."

Jeff chuckled as he caught on to Ty's meaning. "I don't either."

His voice suspiciously hoarse, Carl got to his feet. "I owe you both. I'll see that you don't regret it."

Ty quickly shook his head. "No more pigs, Carl. Just get rid of that still and we'll call it even."

"Thanks, Doc," Carl said, reaching out to shake Ty's hand. "I won't forget this."

"I'll take Ty down to the clinic so Martha can clean and bandage his arm," Jeff said, helping Ty to his feet. "Carl, you get your 'shine jugged, then bust up that boiler."

"I surely will," Carl said a moment before he picked up his rifle and disappeared back into the dense woods.

"We'll stop by the cabin and get Lexi on our way down to Dixie Ridge," Jeff stated, gathering their fishing gear.

Ty shook his head. "No. She's probably busy with the baby. Besides, it's no big deal."

Jeff stopped to give him a knowing grin. "You don't know much about women, do you?"

"I know enough," Ty said as they started back down Piney Knob.

"No, you don't," Jeff retorted. "Wives make a big deal out of everything."

"Lexi won't. She's levelheaded and I'm sure she'll understand."

Jeff's laugh echoed through the woods. "I hope you remember that while she's readin' you the riot act."

Lexi stopped doing sit-ups to stare at her sister-in-law. "Mary Ann Simmons and Jake Sanders are finally getting married?"

"That's what Miss Eunice was tellin' me when I stopped by to see about orderin' some maternity clothes." Her hazel eyes dancing merrily, Freddie plopped down on the exercise mat beside Lexi. "And you'll never guess where they've decided to get hitched."

"Where?"

"You remember how Mary Ann always tried to copy everything you did when we were in school?" Freddie asked.

Lexi sat up to blot perspiration from her face with a soft towel. "Don't tell me—"

Laughing, Freddie nodded. "She's insistin' she wants a weddin' just like yours. She's asked Miss Eunice if it would be all right for them to be married in the dress shop and use the weddin' display, just like you and Ty."

"Oh, good grief!" When she finally stopped laughing, Lexi shook her head. "I can't believe it. I figured Mary Ann would still be chasing Jake around Dixie Ridge when they were both too old to run."

Freddie grinned. "Well, she might have been, if the moon hadn't been right."

Lexi's mouth fell open. "She's pregnant?"

"Yep. And Jake's struttin' around like a peacock with his tail fanned. I stopped by the Blue Bird after I left the dress shop, and he was grinnin' from ear to ear."

"Ty mentioned that he'd diagnosed several maternity cases lately," Lexi said thoughtfully. "I wonder who else is pregnant."

Freddie shrugged. "I don't know. But rumor has it that Granny Applegate has decided to quit deliverin' babies."

"Oh, Freddie," Lexi said, her tone sympathetic. "What will you do?"

"Jeff is talkin' to Ty right now about startin' home deliveries." Freddie smiled. "He told me he wants the best for me and the baby." Her eyes filled with tears. "Isn't that just the sweetest thing?"

Lexi didn't have the heart to remind her sister-in-law of Ty's imminent departure when Doc Fletcher returned. She hadn't wanted to think about it herself.

Ty would go back to Chicago and she'd stay here to raise Matthew in the unhurried pace of the mountains. She'd like nothing more than to give her marriage to Ty a chance, but no matter how much she loved him, it didn't change the fact that he obviously didn't return her feelings.

Biting her lower lip to keep it from trembling, she reached out to hug Freddie. "It doesn't surprise me in the least that Jeff's talking to Ty about home delivery. That brother of mine loves you with all his heart and soul."

And I wish with all my heart that Ty felt the same way about me.

When the phone rang, Lexi groaned and slowly rose to her feet. "Now where on earth did I put that cordless phone?" she asked, sniffing back tears as she searched the end tables.

"Ours always manages to slip down between the couch cushions," Freddie said, joining the search.

Just as Lexi found the phone, the answering machine picked up.

"Lexi, get down here as soon as you can." Martha's worried voice filtered into the room. "Doc's been hurt. Jeff just brought him into the clinic."

Eleven

"**W**here's Ty?" Lexi demanded when she found her brother in the clinic's small reception area.

Jeff lounged in one of the chairs, his long legs stretched out in front of him, ankles crossed. He didn't look like he had a care in the world.

"Martha's got him back there in one of the exam rooms, stitchin' up his arm," he said, then had the audacity to yawn.

Trying to get the details from her brother about what had taken place was proving as difficult as pulling a hen's teeth. Never in her entire life had Lexi wanted to hit someone as much as she wanted to punch Jeff at that moment. She might have too, had she not been holding Matthew.

"Jeff Hatfield, you'd better answer your sister," Freddie said, stepping around Lexi. "And you'd better do it right now."

At the sight of his wife standing inside the walls of the clinic, Jeff was on his feet in a split second, his mouth agape. "Freddie, sweetheart, what the hell are you doing in here?"

Had it not been for the gravity of the situation, Lexi might have laughed at the startled expression on her brother's face. But at the moment her main concern was Ty.

"What happened?" she asked impatiently. "When Martha called all she said was that Ty had been hurt."

Jeff shifted from one foot to the other. "I should have known Martha wouldn't let her shirttail hit her backside until she called and got you all riled up."

"Dammit, Jeff, I'm beginnin' to lose patience with you," Freddie warned, taking the baby from Lexi.

"Uh, well, he got shot," Jeff finally stammered.

Tears filled Lexi's eyes and she began to shake uncontrollably. "Oh, dear Lord!"

"It's okay, Sis." Jeff folded her into his arms. "It's just a flesh wound. He's okay."

"I've got to see for myself," Lexi said. Pulling away, she turned to Freddie. "Could you—"

"Don't worry about Matthew," Freddie said, shifting the baby to her shoulder. "We'll take care of him. You go check on Ty."

Nodding, Lexi hurried down the hall. When she heard voices behind one of the exam room doors, she didn't think twice about walking right in.

"I figured it was about time for you to get here," Martha said. She tied and clipped a suture, then glanced at the clock on the wall. "Tied the record coming down Piney Knob, too. Freddie must have been drivin'."

Ty sat shirtless on the exam table, a scowl crossing his handsome face. "I told Jeff not to call."

"He didn't," Lexi said, her gaze running over every inch of her husband. Other than the nasty-looking wound Martha attended to on his upper left arm, Ty looked to be all right.

"I didn't want you— Ouch! Dammit, Martha, will you take it easy?"

Lexi felt her heart shatter into a million pieces, along with her hopes of making their marriage work. He didn't have to finish what he'd started to say. It was perfectly clear Ty didn't want her with him.

Tears threatened, but she somehow found the strength to force them back. "I thought you might need me with you," she stated, thankful that her voice remained steady despite the huge lump clogging her throat. "Apparently I was wrong. Have Jeff give you a ride home."

"Lexi, I didn't mean—"

But Ty found himself talking to an empty doorway. He cursed under his breath. He'd tried to tell her he hadn't wanted to worry her.

"I'm the one who called," Martha admitted, reaching for a roll of gauze. She began wrapping it around his arm. "And if somethin' like this happens in the future, you can bet your bottom dollar, I'll do it again."

Ty's frown deepened. "Why? It wasn't anything serious."

"I can see you're gonna have to be set straight on a few things about women," Martha said. She stopped her bandaging to shake her finger at him. "A woman's place is at her man's side when he's sick or hurt. No matter how minor it is, that's where she wants to be and that's where a man needs her to be.''

He winced when Martha resumed wrapping the gauze around his arm. If he didn't know better, he'd swear she drew the bandage extra tight on purpose. ''I could have told her all about it once I got home.''

Martha shook her head. ''A wife doesn't want to hear somethin' like this secondhand. She wants to know what's goin' on right now.'' She took Ty's shirt from the hook on the back of the door and handed it to him. ''And that's her right. When she married you, Lexi promised to be at your side in sickness as well as in health, to face the good times with you as well as the bad.'' She shrugged. ''That's called trust, son. Without it, your marriage won't have a whisper in a whirlwind's chance of lastin'.''

Trust.

Ty felt his gut clench as he mulled over the word. He'd given Lexi his name, but that was about all he'd given her when they'd repeated their wedding vows. The day they were married, she'd gifted him with her trust just by placing her hands in his. But he hadn't believed her feelings for him could be strong enough to see past his parentage, hadn't had the faith that she would understand and love him anyway. He'd been wrong. She'd accepted his illegitimacy much easier than he had.

He closed his eyes and took a deep breath. Trust. One little word that could either make or break their marriage. And the one he had to accept, or risk losing Lexi forever.

Put that way, he really didn't see that he had any other choice. The time had come to lay his soul bare. He had to tell her what he'd kept hidden for so long, what had eventually driven him to temporarily leave Chicago.

He just hoped Lexi could accept it as easily as she had his parentage. And love him in spite of it all.

"There somethin' you gotta do before you go try to make things right with Lexi," Martha said, breaking into his thoughts.

Ty sighed heavily. "What's that, Martha?"

"You have to call Doc Fletcher. He says it's important and he needs to talk to you pronto."

Ty got out of Jeff's truck, then watched it disappear back down the long drive before turning to face the cabin. His arm ached, but the physical discomfort was nothing compared to the mixture of excitement and fear twisting his gut. He knew what he had to do, what he should have done when he'd had the nightmare a week ago.

Ty took a deep breath and slowly walked up the steps of the porch. He just hoped like hell it wasn't too late for them already.

"Lexi?" he called, entering the cabin.

Nothing.

His fear increased as he crossed the room and headed down the hall. What if he *was* too late?

Relief flooded him when he reached the door to the bedroom and heard Lexi's soft voice as she talked to their son.

"Lexi, honey, I—"

Ty stopped short at the sight of her clothes spread across the bed. The knot in his stomach tightened painfully. Walking over to the closet, he grabbed a clean shirt.

"Are you going somewhere?" he asked, careful to keep his voice even, in spite of the panic he felt.

He shrugged out of the bloody shirt and pulled on the clean one as he watched her finish changing Matthew's diaper. She placed the baby in the cradle before turning to face him.

That was when he saw the evidence of tears on her pale cheeks, the guarded look in her expressive green eyes. He hated that he'd been the cause of her anguish, hated to think that what he was about to tell her might cause her even more.

"I'm not the one who will be leaving," she said, her voice thick with tears. "But would it matter to you at all if one of us did?"

"Yes," he said, buttoning the soft flannel. He turned to face her. He didn't care anymore if he looked or sounded desperate. All that mattered was for Lexi to know the truth, to give him another chance. "I don't think I'd survive losing you, Lexi."

"Why?"

Ty rubbed at the tension building at the back of his neck. The look she'd given him spoke volumes. If he didn't tell her everything this time, he'd lose her for sure.

"We need to talk, Lexi."

"It's past time," she said, her voice reflecting her hurt.

Matthew began to make happy baby noises. The sound was one of the sweetest Ty had ever heard. A lump the size of his fist clogged his throat when he thought about how much he had at stake, what his admission might cost him.

"You look tired. Why don't you go into the living room and put your feet up?" he suggested, walking over to the cradle. He picked up Matthew, then turned to face her. "I'll join you as soon as I get the baby to sleep."

When Lexi nodded and left the room, Ty glanced down at his smiling son. "Wish me luck, little man."

Matthew gurgled and wrapped his tiny hand around Ty's finger.

"Thanks for the moral support," Ty said a moment before he closed his eyes against the emotions threatening to overwhelm him. "Daddy feels like he's about to take a blind leap off the side of the mountain."

Lexi watched Ty walk into the great room and, without a word, go over to the picture window. He stood for several long moments, staring at the mountains beyond. From his profile, she could tell he saw none of the scenic view.

"I didn't mean to hurt your feelings this afternoon at the clinic," he finally said. "I thought you'd be busy with the baby. I knew it wasn't serious and I couldn't see any reason to upset you."

"I'm not some hothouse flower, Ty. I don't need to be sheltered from reality." She stared at his broad shoulders, wishing he'd turn to face her. "I'm your wife. I'm supposed to know what's going on and be with you, not hear about these things later."

He gave her a short nod.

When he remained silent, she asked, "How is your arm?"

"It hurts like hell."

"Have you taken anything for it?"

He shook his head. "It's nothing I can't handle." He dragged in a ragged breath and turned to look at her. "Besides, I want to be sure I have a clear head for what I'm about to tell you."

Lexi's heart thudded against her ribs as she watched him straighten his wide shoulders, then turn to face her. She could tell that whatever he was about to say would be the most difficult thing he'd ever told anyone. Was he going to tell her he no longer wanted their marriage to work? Was he going to say goodbye?

"What would you like to know first?" he asked.

"Whatever you'd like to tell me," she answered quietly.

Ty shrugged. "I suppose we could start out with why I'm here in Dixie Ridge and not back in Chicago."

"Yes, Ty. We could."

She watched emotion cloud his clear blue gaze before he turned back to the window. "When we were together that night in your apartment, you talked about the beauty of the Smoky Mountains, how peaceful and laid-back the pace is here," he said, his voice even. "A few months ago I needed to get away for a while and decided to put out some feelers to see if there might be a community in the region in need of a doctor."

"About the same time Doc Fletcher was looking for someone to take over the clinic while he had surgery?" Lexi guessed.

Ty nodded. "He heard I was looking for a temporary position and got in touch with me."

"But I thought you liked your job."

"I did." He took a deep breath, then turned back to her. "But I've decided I can't continue as a trauma specialist any longer, Lexi."

"Why not? You're one of the best."

His face reflected his inner struggle, when he admitted, "I found, more times than I care to count, that I'm not." He jammed his hands into his jeans pockets, then shook his head. "The burnout rate for trauma specialists is high. I would have had to give it up eventually." He swallowed hard. "I think I could have handled it for a while longer, if it hadn't been for—"

She watched him squeeze his eyes shut on the memory. When he opened them, his bleak gaze was testament to how deeply he had been affected.

"Ty?"

"God, Lexi, I've seen too many kids die," he said, his voice raw with pent-up emotion. He took a deep shuddering breath. "I can't bear to stand over another gurney and have a child's eyes stare up at me with hope and trust, then watch them grow clouded and dull as life drains away."

Lexi bit her lower lip to keep it from trembling. She could tell it had taken a great deal of courage for him to admit what he viewed as a weakness, a failing. "I never realized what E.R. doctors have to deal with every day."

He sighed heavily. "I was arrogant enough to think I could handle it and remain detached." He shook his head. "I found out differently."

"I'm sure you saw some pretty horrendous things," she said gently. "Maybe after being away you'll feel differently when you go back, Ty."

"No. I've decided I can't go back to being a trauma specialist."

"I never—" Lexi's voice caught and she had to

pause a moment before she could continue. "I never realized how difficult it must be for you."

He ran a hand over his face as if to erase the dark memories. "Believe me, you wouldn't want to hear the ugly details."

Lexi felt her heart swell with love. Ty had tried to protect her from what he was going through—the tragic side of his profession—with his silence.

"You should have told me," she said firmly. "I've never been, nor will I ever be, someone who runs from the unpleasant aspects of life."

"It's a moot point now," he said, shrugging. He stared at her a moment before he added, "There's something else you need to know."

From the look on his face, Lexi knew his previous confession would pale in comparison to what he was about to tell her now.

He took a deep breath. "It happened the night we spent together," he said, his voice taking on a distant quality. "Nothing unusual for a weeknight. A couple of injuries from MVA's—car accidents. A knife wound." He paused. "Nothing major."

She could tell by his expression that whatever had taken place that evening had changed his life forever. "Ty?"

After several long minutes, he continued. "Everything was quiet, so I decided to go up to ICU to check on a patient I'd treated a few days earlier. I'd just stepped off the elevator when they paged me to get back down to E.R., stat."

He paused, his emotional pain obvious. The sight broke her heart.

"I arrived downstairs at the same time the ambulance pulled in," he finally said. "Everything was going our way. We had the kid out of the ambulance and wheeled into a treatment room in record time. He had a gunshot wound, but he was conscious and responsive. One of the nurses cut his shirt off, and I had just stepped up beside him when he went into cardiac arrest.''

She watched Ty walk over to the fireplace to brace both hands on the mantel as he struggled with the memory. When he finally turned to meet her gaze, his voice was suspiciously hoarse. ''My best just wasn't good enough.''

Tears flooded her eyes at the sight of his pain. ''Oh, Ty. I'm so sorry.''

He nodded. ''When I went out to talk to his family, the boy's brother lost it and pulled a gun.'' Ty took another deep breath before he could continue, his voice raw with emotion. ''It was clear the kid was high, but there was no reasoning with him. Hell, I doubt he even heard me. He was waving the gun, threatening to shoot everyone in the waiting area. But when he pointed it at a little girl, I knew I had to do something. I jumped him and while I tried to get the gun, it went off. He was hit.'' His big body shuddered. ''We started working on him right there on the waiting room floor.'' He closed his eyes. When he opened them, his gaze begged for her understanding. ''I swear, Lexi, I did everything I could to save him. But his mother started screaming that I'd let her son die on purpose.''

She wished she could make things easier for him. But she sensed there wasn't anything she could say or do to take away the memory of that fateful night.

''She was overwrought,'' Lexi said gently. ''She didn't know what—''

Lexi winced at the tortured look that crossed his face. "The woman knew exactly what she was accusing me of," he said bleakly.

Despite the warmth from the fire she'd built to chase away the early evening chill, Lexi shivered. Tears streaming down her cheeks, she left the couch to walk over to him.

She put her arms around his stiff shoulders. "How do you know she meant what she said?"

"Even after the investigation cleared me of any wrongdoing, she continued to pursue me through the media." He swallowed hard. "For nine months she called into radio talk shows, sent editorials to the newspapers, and even called the hospital administrator daily to demand that I be fired. When she didn't give up, the administration suggested I take a leave of absence and drop out of sight to see if that would stop her."

"Oh, Ty." Lexi felt his pain as deeply as if it were her own. There wasn't a doubt in her mind of his innocence. Putting her arms around him again, she held him close. "You didn't mean for it to happen. The police cleared you of any charges."

His gaze intense, he took a deep shuddering breath and placed his hands on her shoulders. "Can you love a man who's killed another human being, Lexi?"

"Ty, it wasn't your fault," she said, placing her hand on his cheek. "You could have just as easily been the one shot."

"Yes, but—"

"I know you, Ty. You would never harm someone intentionally." Taking his hands in hers, she asked, "How many lives have these hands saved, Ty? How many people are alive today because you were on duty when they arrived in the E.R.?''

When he shrugged, she looked directly into his deep blue eyes. ''It was an accident, Ty. You're no more at fault in that boy's death than he was himself. You have to forgive yourself.''

''I've learned to live with what happened,'' he said, his tone guarded. ''But I thought you might not—''

''You know what your problem is, Dr. Braden?'' she interrupted. ''You think too much.''

The disbelieving frown on his handsome face made her realize how deeply his doubts ran.

She walked over to the door and turned the lock. ''It looks like I'll just have to show you that I mean what I'm saying.''

Ty watched Lexi cross the room to stand before him. His arm ached, but he paid little attention to the pain as he took her into his embrace. He'd seen compassion in her eyes, but none of the accusations he'd feared. Hope began to flare as he stared down at her.

''What did you have in mind, Mrs. Braden?''

''You'll see,'' she said, pulling away from him. She took him by the hand and led him over to the fireplace. Reaching up, she pushed the top button of his shirt through the button hole.

''I just put this on.''

''I know.''

''And you're going to take it off?''

''Um-hmm.'' She loosened the rest of the buttons and carefully removed the garment from his injured arm. ''I can't show you what country lovin' is all about if I don't.''

''I didn't realize there was a difference between

city and country loving," he said, his body responding to her soft touch.

"Oh, yes." She gave him a look that made his
mouth go dry. "There's a *big* difference."

Ty allowed her to pull him down onto the braided
rug in front of the hearth. "Do you think I'll like it?"

"Absolutely."

Feeling more free than he'd ever felt in his life, he
found he was more than ready to put into words what
he'd known from the moment they met. "I love you,
Lexi. I've always loved you."

She gave him a smile that sent his blood pressure
skyrocketing. "Now I'm going to prove to you once
and for all that *I* love you. I'm going to fulfill one of
your fantasies, and by the time I'm finished, there
won't be a doubt left about my believing you. Or the
way I feel about you."

To Ty's utter amazement, she did just that.

Lexi smiled up at Ty when he handed Matthew to
her. Guiding her breast to the baby's searching mouth,
she asked, "Do you think you could get used to country lovin', Dr. Braden?"

"Definitely." He grinned as he settled beside Lexi
on the big leather couch, then wrapped his arms
around her and their son. "I'm finding I like all aspects of country life. Especially the loving."

"I'm glad to hear that," she said, her tone leaving
no doubt in his mind about her contentment.

Ty kissed the top of her head. "How did you know
I fantasized about making love to you in front of the
fireplace?"

She smiled. "I saw the look on your face the first

day you stopped by here. You couldn't take your eyes off it."

"I was pretty transparent, huh?"

"As a pane of glass."

They were silent for a time as Ty watched his son nursing at her breast. He felt like the luckiest man alive.

"Will you set up a private practice when we return to Chicago?" Lexi asked.

He stared at her intently. "You'd go back with me?"

"Of course." She gave him a reassuring smile. "A family should be together."

He kissed the top of her head. She was willing to go with him, even though he knew raising their son in the city wasn't what she wanted to do. "We're not going back."

Her expression reflecting her happiness, she pulled back to stare at him. "We're staying here?"

Ty nodded. "After you left the clinic this afternoon, Martha gave me a message to call Dr. Fletcher. Seems he's enjoyed being home so much, he's decided to retire. He's asked me to take over his practice here in Dixie Ridge."

"Do you like living here, Ty?" she asked cautiously. "It's a lot different than you're used to."

He chuckled. "I have to admit, I thought places like this only existed on television or in the movies."

"Culture shock?" she asked, laughing with him.

He nodded. "Some of the quirky neighbors and their odd customs take a while to get used to. But I'm finding I like being part of this community. And I like being a country doctor."

Lexi smiled. "Good. This is where I want to raise our children."

Ty felt some of his anxiety return. "You don't want to return to a career in radio somewhere?"

Lexi leaned back to look at him. "Would it bother you if I said yes?"

"No," he answered honestly. "I'd never stand in your way or ask you to give it up. But I'd like to remain in the area, if possible. Do you think we could make a long-distance relationship work if you did?"

She used her finger to ease the frown lines on his forehead. "It's not an issue. I'm perfectly happy being a wife and mother. But if I do decide I want to resume my career, I can take a part-time job with the local station."

He gazed at her for several long moments. "Are you sure?" he asked again. He didn't want her to feel pressured.

"Alexis Madison doesn't exist anymore. All that's left is plain old Lexi Braden, super wife and mother."

Ty laughed. "There never has been, nor will there ever be, anything plain about you, honey." His smile faded as he asked, "But what about the clothes on the bed? When I came home, I thought—"

"There you go again," Lexi said, grinning. "I warned you about thinking too much. I was sorting out some maternity tops for Freddie." She kissed his cheek. "Get used to it, Ty. I'm not going anywhere. You have me for better or for worse, for as long as we both shall live. I want nothing more than to be your wife and the mother of a whole house full of Braden children."

"A house full?"

"Oh, yes." Lexi grinned. "But I'll need help."

Ty grinned back. "What kind of help, Mrs. Braden?"

"Someone is going to have to help me get that house full of children," she reasoned. "Do you think you're up to the task?"

Feeling all the joy and wonder he'd never dreamed would be his to treasure, Ty laughed. "I'll give it my best shot."

"I'd like for Matthew to have a baby brother or sister in a year or two," Lexi said, snuggling close.

"I think that sounds like a good idea." Ty placed his finger close to his son's hand. "What do you think, little man? Would you like to have a little brother or sister?"

Matthew wrapped his hand around Ty's finger, smiled a toothless baby smile and gurgled his agreement.

Epilogue

"**J**eff, if you don't shut off that video camera, I'm gonna have to hurt you," Freddie said through clenched teeth.

"Sweetheart, I thought—"

"Come on, Freddie," Lexi urged. "Forget about him. Take a deep cleansing breath. Now pant, pant, blow. Pant, pant, blow."

Freddie did as she was told, but when the contraction ended, she glared up at Lexi. "I've changed my mind. I don't want to do this anymore."

"Too late now," Lexi said, her smile sympathetic as she gazed down at her red-faced sister-in-law.

Freddie had been in labor for the past eight hours and Lexi knew she had to be exhausted. Sponging the perspiration from Freddie's brow, she offered, "If it's any consolation, you'll forget all about the pain as soon as you see your baby."

"Maybe I will, but I'm gonna make sure Jeff doesn't," Freddie shot back, turning her deep scowl on her husband. She suddenly scrunched her face and gripped Lexi's hand. "Oh, no. Here comes another one."

Lexi coached Freddie through the pain, then glanced up at Ty as he positioned himself at the end of the bed. "It won't be much longer."

Smiling, Ty shook his head. "You can start pushing with the next contraction, Freddie."

"Finally," Freddie groaned. "I didn't think I'd ever get to the end of this."

"You're doin' fine," Martha called from the doorway. She turned her attention to Ty. "I've got everything ready for when the baby pops out, Doc."

"Good. We're almost there," Ty said. "The head is crowning now."

Lexi supported her shoulders as Freddie squeezed her eyes shut and pushed with all her might.

"Oh, Lord," Jeff groaned.

Lexi watched her brother lay the video camera on the bedside table. He looked suspiciously green. "Are you going to be all right, Jeff?"

He nodded a moment before he hit the floor in a dead faint.

"The bigger they are, the harder they fall," Martha said, stepping over Jeff to stand beside Ty.

Lexi felt tears of joy burn the backs of her eyes as she watched Ty place his hands beneath the emerging infant and finish the delivery. "You have a little boy, Freddie," she said, hugging her sister-in-law. She glanced across the bedroom to where her brother lay sprawled on the floor. "I just wish Jeff hadn't missed it."

Freddie laughed as she looked over at her husband. "When he wakes up, tell him *he* had the baby. He'll never know the difference."

Ty watched Miss Eunice's car disappear around the bend of the drive in the predawn light. They'd called on the woman several times recently to baby-sit Matthew. Fortunately, the kindhearted shop owner didn't mind the odd hours he and Lexi were forced to keep.

He smiled. So much had changed in the past few months.

When he made the decision to start the home delivery program, Granny Applegate had given him her heartfelt blessings, retired from midwifery and moved to the warmer climate of southern Florida to be near her daughter's family. Martha had readily agreed to assist him, taking care of the babies once they were born. And Lexi had fallen into the role of paternal counselor and delivery coach when the father was too nervous or, like Jeff, passed out on the floor.

They had formed a very efficient home delivery team. And just in time, too. They'd delivered four babies this week alone; Mary Ann and Jake Sanders's new daughter, Helen McKinney's twins and now Jeff and Freddie's son.

His introspection stopped suddenly when a pair of arms wrapped around his waist from behind.

"What are you thinking about?" Lexi asked, resting her head against his back.

Ty turned to take her into his arms. "I was thinking what a great team we make." He gave her a kiss that left them both breathless. "Is Matthew still asleep?"

Lexi nodded. "I think he'll sleep until it's time to go visit Dempsey."

Luckily Ty had been able to convince Carl that Dempsey would be much happier with the other pigs in Carl's recently expanded hog business. Ty shook his head. He still couldn't believe that he, Lexi and Matthew made a weekly habit of visiting the now full-grown hog.

Ty abandoned all thought of Dempsey when Lexi nuzzled his neck and whispered close to his ear, "I thought we might take a nap before we leave."

"That would be very nice," he agreed, his body responding to the thought of holding his wife, loving her. When Lexi yawned, he kissed the top of her head. "I think you'd better take that nap alone. You've been working too hard."

She shook her head. "Not really. When I first got pregnant with Matthew, I felt this way."

Ty grinned. "Are you trying to tell me you're—"

Lexi nodded, her smile radiant. "I think you're going to be a daddy again, Ty."

"I love you," he said, holding her close.

"And I love you."

They watched the sun rise over the tops of the misty mountains, the light painting the trees with the colors of morning.

"Let's go inside," he whispered. "We have some celebrating to do."

Lexi gave him a look that raised his temperature several degrees. "What kind of celebration did you have in mind, Dr. Braden?"

"Country style, Mrs. Braden." Grinning, he took her hand in his and led her into the cabin. "Country style suits me just fine."

*   *   *   *   *

SILHOUETTE®
DESIRE™

AVAILABLE FROM 20TH SEPTEMBER 2002

EVEN BETTER THAN BEFORE

THE REDEMPTION OF JEFFERSON CADE BJ James
Men of Belle Terre
For Jefferson Cade protecting his only love, Marissa, from danger was easier than living without her had been. But now he was determined to rekindle their passion...and this time he'd never let her go.

A COWBOY'S PROMISE Anne McAllister
Charlie had left Cait Blasingame because settling down wasn't his style. But getting shot had changed his perspective. Now all he had to do was convince Cait they belonged together—forever.

UNDER SUSPICION

THE SECRET LIFE OF CONNOR MONAHAN
Elizabeth Bevarly

Undercover cop Connor Monahan knew he had to bring in suspected madam Winona Thornbury. But it was hard to keep his mind on the case—and his hands off the lady...

ADDICTED TO NICK Bronwyn Jameson
Wealthy, gorgeous Nick Corelli didn't need a new business partner like sexy, spirited Tamara Cole! He thought she must be after his money, but he couldn't resist her...

THE NANNY AND THE BOSS

WYOMING CINDERELLA Cathleen Galitz
Gorgeous multi-millionaire William Hawk was captivated by tantalising nanny Ella McBride. A massive primal desire hammered at his resistance—so for how long could he avoid her bedroom eyes?

TAMING THE BEAST Amy J Fetzer
Loner Richard Blackthorne had hired lovely Laura Cambridge as a nanny for his only child. He certainly didn't want to be attracted to her, but found all he could think about was Laura—as his wife!

0902/51a

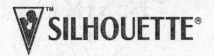

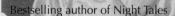

SILHOUETTE®

proudly presents

five wonderful, warm stories from bestselling author

SHERRYL WOODS

The Calamity Janes

Five unique women share a lifetime of friendship!

DO YOU TAKE THIS REBEL?

Silhouette Special Edition
October 2002

COURTING THE ENEMY

Silhouette Special Edition
November 2002

TO CATCH A THIEF

Silhouette Special Edition
December 2002

THE CALAMITY JANES

Silhouette Superromance
January 2003

WRANGLING THE REDHEAD

Silhouette Special Edition
February 2003

1002/SH/LC42

SILHOUETTE® SENSATION™

brings more...much more
from

Suzanne Brockmann

TALL, DARK AND DANGEROUS

These men are who you call to get you
out of a tight spot—or into one!

TAYLOR'S TEMPTATION

August 2002

WILD, WILD WES

March 2003

0802/SH/LC39

SHERRYL WOODS

about that man

It was going to be a long, hot summer...

On sale 18th October 2002

*Available at most branches of WH Smith,
Tesco, Martins, Borders, Eason, Sainsbury's
and most good paperback bookshops.*

1002/136/SH35

SPECIAL EDITION™

SENSATION™

DESIRE™ 2 IN 1

SUPERROMANCE™

INTRIGUE™

*REVEALING OUR FANTASTIC
NEW LOOK SILHOUETTE...*

FROM
18TH OCTOBER 2002

SILHOUETTE®

FREE
1 BOOK
AND A SURPRISE GIFT!

We would like to take this opportunity to thank you for reading this Silhouette® book by offering you the chance to take another specially selected title from the Desire™ series absolutely FREE! We're also making this offer to introduce you to the benefits of the Reader Service™—

- ★ FREE home delivery
- ★ FREE monthly Newsletter
- ★ FREE gifts and competitions
- ★ Exclusive Reader Service discount
- ★ Books available before they're in the shops

Accepting this FREE book and gift places you under no obligation to buy; you may cancel at any time, even after receiving your free shipment. Simply complete your details below and return the entire page to the address below. *You don't even need a stamp!*

YES! Please send me 1 free Desire book and a surprise gift. I understand that unless you hear from me, I will receive 2 superb new titles every month for just £4.99 each, postage and packing free. I am under no obligation to purchase any books and may cancel my subscription at any time. The free book and gift will be mine to keep in any case.

D2ZEC

Ms/Mrs/Miss/Mr ....Initials..................................

BLOCK CAPITALS PLEASE

Surname...

Address..

....

....Postcode ....

Send this whole page to:
UK: FREEPOST CN81, Croydon, CR9 3WZ
EIRE: PO Box 4546, Kilcock, County Kildare (stamp required)

'The Red Lodge' copyright © 1961 by H. R. Wakefield. Extracted from *Strayers from Sheol*; reprinted by permission of Curtis Brown Group Ltd, London

'My Haunted Home' copyright © 1997 by Lawrence Watt Evans

'The Ghost Hunters' copyright © 1997 by Cherry Wilder

'A Place Where a Head Would Rest' copyright © 1997 by Chet Williamson

'The Glowing Hand' copyright © 1997 by F. Paul Wilson

'Finding My Religion' copyright © 1997 by Douglas E. Winter

'Kid Sister' copyright © 1997 by Gene Wolfe

Also available in Vista paperback

Testimony

MARK CHADBOURN

The terrifying *true* story of
Britain's most haunted house

For Liz and Bill Rich, two people trying to rebuild
their lives, the house symbolized a new beginning,
a haven in an enchanted landscape. But within
weeks of their arrival, the enchantment turned to
horror, and their blessed home became a
malevolent prison. Footsteps thundered along
empty landings, apparitions inhabited deserted
rooms; possessions flew, furniture moved. Bill's
business collapsed; his son retreated into a blood-
red hell, uttering demonic curses in a rasping,
guttural, *alien* voice. The house consumed enough
electricity for an office block . . . This is a true
account of what one family, and those around
them, saw and heard and experienced. Read it –
and decide what *you* believe.

ISBN 0 575 60078 0

VISTA paperbacks are available from all good bookshops
or from: Cassell C.S.
          Book Service By Post
          PO Box 29, Douglas I-O-M
          IM99 1BQ
          telephone: 01624 675137, fax: 01624 670923